Suite Charity

A TIMOTHY TROUSDALE MYSTERY

Richard Tyler Jordan

OHB

For Helen Frost and Don MacLeod —
who make the world better simply by being in it.

PROLOGUE

Oh, to be stupid again. I mean *naïve*. To be that fresh-out-of-community-college guy arriving in Manhattan six months ago with big dreams and an unshakable feeling that something amazing was just around the corner.

Greyhound had rolled me into Grand Central Station on a bitter cold February afternoon. I carried one suitcase containing two pairs of jeans, three shirts that could almost pass for "smart casual," a Mighty Mac Barnstormer fur-hood jacket (which made me look like an Arctic fisherman), a battered copy of the classic novel *Valley of the Dolls* (don't judge—that old campy-romantic fantasy is one of the reasons I wanted to move here in the first place), a laptop containing the draft of a novella I wrote in creative writing class in junior college, and a Visa debit card crying out for CPR.

What I didn't have was a job, a place to live, or anything more than a vague plan to become rich and famous. My pockets were stuffed with the three Z's: zero, zip, and zilch. But what I did have a lot of was what my sweet granny—between bouts of smoker's cough—called "gumption," which I'm now pretty sure was her word for "zero self-preservation skills." And back then, I thought *gumption* was all I needed to make a big and amazing life.

But the thing about "big and amazing" is that it's...well, subjective. Winning a Pulitzer? *Big and amazing.* Finding true love? *Big and amazing.* Tripping over a freshly murdered body? Also *big and amazing.* Just not the sort of amazing I'd been meaning to manifest.

So, to whichever divine force, mythical being, or celestial middle manager is in charge of life goals—I say, "We need to talk."

Okay, so I was cash poor. But I was rich in the currency that really mattered: trust. Not "trust" as in "trust fund" (tragically, no), but "trust" in *me.* Trust that one day I'd be a *New York Times* bestselling author. That my face would be smiling from the covers of *Time* and *Publishers Weekly.* That Oprah and Reese would duel over whose book club got to "discover" my novel first. And, naturally, I'd be grinning smugly like Frieda McFadden on her Instagram profile.

New York—loud, frenetic, a bit stinky—was where it would all happen. I knew it!

Call me deluded.

"You're deluded!"

If I'd known in advance all I'd have to go through (and the bodies I'd have to trip over) to reach the top, I might have said, "Actually, no, thank you, Universe. I'll just stay in my small town, flip tots at Sonic, and cultivate an appetite for beer for breakfast."

But instead, I checked into the Rest Assured Motel on 155th Street. Spoiler: it was neither restful nor assuring. That night, in the so-called city that never sleeps, a rat tried to spoon with me. And outside my window, someone was either begging for his life or auditioning for *Law & Order: Cadaver Unit.* Either way, I told myself it was character-building. Fodder for the memoir I'd publish fifty years later, in the waning days of my glorious literary stardom.

The next morning, I logged onto NestQuest and found a studio apartment to share with two other guys in "affordable" Washington Heights.

Then I went to SwellHire Top Temps and applied for literally anything. And *presto-change-o*, within days, I was the assistant to the intern tech copywriter for an industrial waste management company in Jersey City. Yes, nothing says "glamorous Manhattan debut" quite like industrial garbage.

I bought my very first MetroCard. And on Sundays, I haunted the Strand bookstore over on Broadway, pretending to browse the poetry section and trying to look adorably intellectual. My fantasy was that some shy, devastatingly cute nerd would notice me and say, "Hey, wanna come back to my place? I'll show you my first edition of *The Bell Jar*." Which, honestly, could have been hot. Alternatively, he might have offered *FLOTUS Interruptus* by Melania Trump. Not hot.

So, yes. My life was exciting.

Really.

(Okay, not really. But I'm relentlessly optimistic.)

The copywriting gig? Total disaster. In fact, all my subsequent temp jobs started like dreams come true but turned into Netflix true-crime docuseries waiting to happen:

– Barista at Perkatory (turns out I don't steam well under pressure).

– Nail salon helper (what's cuticle oil?).

– Nursing home attendant (sent packing for being "too sensitive," which, frankly, I take as a compliment).

The most recent gig? Working as a PA for my all-time favorite movie star and getting to live in her swanky Tribeca condo penthouse. Smash cut to: murder in her condo. I'm a *person of interest*. Real killer found. I get sacked anyway. Totally unfair. You can read all about that in *Breakfast at Timothy's*, available wherever you get your cheeky murder mysteries.

And then—*boom*—a miracle.

SwellHire Top Temps placed me as a paid intern at the Adele Cummings Foundation for the Arts, Research, and Theater. A multibillion-dollar nonprofit dedicated entirely to giving away money. Buckets of it. Oprah levels of "You get a grant! You get a grant!" Dorothy Parker once said, "I don't know much about being a millionaire, but I'll bet I'd be darling at it."

Me too, Dorothy!

Which brings me, inevitably, to this story. The one with another dead body. It's someone I know—or wanted to know. She was on the verge of becoming famous. A cabaret singer with a voice that sounded like velvet dipped in sin. I instantly became a fanboy the first time I heard her sing.

For me, her murder wasn't just tragic, it was personal.

And as luck would have it, my fingerprints were at the crime scene. You'll see.

1

According to cultural anthropologists, the world is split into two distinct groups: the haves and the have-nots.

Squillionaire Adele Cummings? She lives on Haves Street. She owns the whole flippin' block. The zip code. And probably the moon rights above it.

Adele Cummings is rich. Mackenzie Scott rich. Saudi sheik rich. They say she has mansions all over the world. And a private tropical island in the South Pacific. Also, a fancy-schmancy jet to shuttle her to and from...here to there...and this way and that.

When the Wealth and Prosperity Fairy flipped on Adele's abundance tap, it didn't just flow—it went full-on Old Faithful. It was impossible to put a cork in it. The only thing Adele Cummings could think to do was to give a lot of it away.

This is actually a lot harder than one might imagine, given ambiguous tax laws and the understandable distrust of no-strings-attached freebies. Nothing makes you read the fine print faster than the phrase "just sign here." So, with a deep sense of *noblesse oblige*, she established the Adele Cummings Foundation for the Arts, Research, and Theater with a mandate to find worthy recipients of her billions.

Get the picture?

I'm on the flip side of the affluence coin. Timothy Truman Trousdale here, and unlike super-rich Adele Cummings, I live on Pauper Place. I rent month to month. A relatively recent transplant to NYC from semi-rural Alabama, I work minimum-wage temp admin jobs and share a shoebox with two (present and future) losers. And I fully expect goons from JPMorgan Chase to show up any day now with bolt cutters to pry my perpetually delinquent Visa credit card from my hands.

I'm broke. But it's not that I lack a good work ethic. Far from it. My now-dead daddy drilled into me that early morning start times meant you got stuff done. He'd come into my bedroom all sunshiny before dawn and call out, "Up and at 'em, Timmy boy! You don't want people thinkin' you're useless!" Thanks for the inspiration, Dad.

Trouble is, in New York City, hard work and actually earning enough to live on don't necessarily go hand in hand. One builds character. The other builds credit. And between the two, guess which one my landlord prefers?

Nor do I squander the little I earn. I respect money. Honestly, I'd make a spectacularly generous millionaire—if only the universe would give me an audition. I've already mastered the art of wealth redistribution: lending money to friends who think "repayment" is just a suggestion.

Anyway, in this amazing city, everyone seems to have somewhere important to go and something exciting to do. And for the first time in weeks, I did too!

It was one of those early autumn mornings in Manhattan, with the city air happy it was no longer humid. I practically skipped along the Upper East Side, headed to my new temp assignment at the Adele Cummings Foundation.

Picture me on East Seventy-Second Street—light on my feet,

a bargain-bin *Dancing with the Stars* pro. Wind in my sails, clean jeans, white Oxford cloth button-down shirt, sneakers. I practically tap-glided toward the crosswalk, almost expecting some Broadway chorus boy to burst out of a boutique, grab my hand, and yank me into an eight-count before the light changed.

I arrived at the address provided by the agency: a Beaux Arts Gilded Age house with a fancy front entrance. Two granite Corinthian columns flanked black wrought-iron French doors. The house had a name: *Ravenscroft*. That sounded vaguely spooky. Like a place Edgar Allan Poe might have lived (if the great author hadn't been destitute).

Who goes around giving their house a name? Then I remembered Elvis Presley's Graceland and Thomas Jefferson's Monticello and Michael Jackson's Neverland. Posh people are different from ordinary folk. I guess they'd never settle for a mere number to identify their residences.

Castles and palaces in England have names: Windsor, Buckingham, Highgrove, etc. So why wouldn't American royalty, like Adele Cummings (and Elvis, the King, obviously)?

And, because I am nothing if not a creature of symmetry, I immediately decided my apartment needed a name as well. How about Winterbourne Manor? Otherwise known as 2743-B East Franklin Avenue (above Abu's Kebab Take-Out, entrance via the back alley, try not to trip over the trash cans). I thought a name might make my place sound marginally less like the shit pit it actually is.

I took a deep, nervous breath, walked up two steps, and peeked at my phone screen once again for the name of the person I was supposed to meet: Mrs. Johnston, Corporate Concierge.

Ring, ring! I wasn't sure what to expect. A butler? A maid? In only a moment, as if a hand had been on the doorknob waiting for me, I was greeted by a smiling, stylishly dressed older woman who was probably in her early sixties. She wore a tailored gray tweed blazer over a burgundy blouse and a scarf tied in a careful half-knot just below her collarbone. Her straight silver hair was cut shoulder length and parted dead center. A pearl and sapphire brooch garnished the lapel of her suit jacket. (Nothing like the cheap stuff my stepmother orders online from *Tickytacky.com*.)

"You must be Mr. Trousdale. I'm Mrs. Johnston," she said. "Welcome to Ravenscroft and the Adele Cummings Foundation. We've been eager to receive you. Old Smudgy, here, too."

She patted the head of a docile black Labrador that stood by her side, listlessly wagging his tail.

"Please come in."

Whoa! This reception was the exact polar opposite of how I'd been greeted at my last job! The one where I was living and working in a movie star's chic modern penthouse condo and where I met my first murdered body. There, I'd been savagely mauled by a crusty old paranoid pit bull of a woman who insisted that I'd been sent to spy on her, and she wasn't having any of that! "No siree!"

Still, I stayed on high alert. I'd only been in New York for six months, but that was five months, three weeks, and four days longer than it took to realize that first impressions in this city could pivot faster than a maître d' when a bigger tipper walks in. Smiles turn sinister *fast*. Take that guy panhandling on Forty-Second Street who was all full of sunshine—until my fatal mistake of making eye contact, smiling back, and saying, "Sorry, no change today. Maybe next time."

Cue instant transformation.

He mimicked me in a thundering nah-nah-nah taunt. "*Sorry, no change today. Maybe next time! ASSHOLE!*"

And how about that sweet-looking old lady feeding pigeons in Bryant Park? I asked her—very politely, I assure you —if she could tell me how to get to the Whitney Museum. She stared at me for a long, excruciating moment, then bellowed, *"Do I look like goddamn fucking Google Maps? Jesus fucking Christ!"*

So yeah. Lessons learned. In New York, a smile could just be the protective coating around a grenade.

And yet—there was something about Mrs. Johnston's smile that didn't feel weaponized. She wasn't trying to sell me a Louis Vuitton knockoff, or a bootleg DVD of *Spider-Man 2* filmed from the back row or convert me to an obscure religion. She was just...*lovely*. Like the world's nicest aunt who would bake me cookies for no reason at all.

Stepping into Ravenscroft was like walking straight into a Julian Fellowes period drama—but without costumed servants. The vestibule alone was bigger than my shared shoebox. The parquet floor, probably from the turn of the twentieth century, was in a herringbone pattern. A large orchid dominated a round table in the center of the room. Overhead, a stained-glass Tiffany chandelier cast little rainbow halos through the room.

To my left was a large mahogany-framed mirror (Chippendale?) with an eagle carved on top—wings outstretched like it was about to fly off to defend liberty. On the opposite wall was a marble fireplace with an oil painting of a seriously intimidating woman above the mantel. She held a Cavalier King Charles spaniel in her lap and wore an expression that said, *"Yes, I am better than you."*

The foyer's centerpiece was a sweeping staircase, each step laid with a deep burgundy runner edged with a narrow border of gold, and a glossy dark-wood banister that all but begged me to slide down it. And this was just the entryway! I was stepping into old-world history. I imagined the walls here didn't just have ears—they had stories.

Mrs. Johnston guided me through to what she proudly called "the Grand Drawing Room." Each step felt like a journey into a bygone era. My imagination soared. This was like time-traveling to the glittering decadence of the Roaring Twenties. I could almost hear George Gershwin at the grand piano, the clinking of martini glasses, and the sophisticated banter that must have reverberated through these rooms.

I thought of Jay Gatsby, with his enigmatic charm and doomed dreams. Perhaps F. Scott and Zelda Fitzgerald had been guests at one of Ravenscroft's soirees. Or maybe the sharp-tongued writers from the Algonquin Round Table, with their piercing satire and literary genius, had been here. A place this old—it was all definitely possible.

Mrs. Johnston gestured for me to sit on a plush blue satin settee in the center of the room. "Tea, Mr. Trousdale?" she asked. "Earl Grey? Herbal? Oolong? Which do you require?"

I hesitated. *Tea?* Was this a trick question? The kind posh people ask to test your upbringing and rightful place in society? "Um...anything's fine, thank you," I said, aiming for nonchalance.

Mrs. Johnston paused, giving me a look somewhere between mild amusement and headmistress. "Mr. Trousdale," she said, "if you *prefer* something, then you *require* it." She glanced at the diamond iceberg on her finger. "Just as I require this adornment..." Her gaze slid down to my jeans. "And you require... denim."

Oh. Okay then.

Her comment should have felt like a jab, but she said it with such poise and charm that it didn't sting. It was more like an observation.

"In that case," I said, summoning every scrap of backbone I had, "I *require* Earl Grey, please. And lemon. Thank you."

Mrs. Johnston's mouth curved into a satisfied smile as she poured the tea with the flourish of someone who'd probably done this for royalty. As I took my first sip, she began outlining her own role at the foundation.

"I serve as corporate concierge, and you will report equally to me and our four advisors," she said, her tone landing somewhere between pride and authority.

Corporate concierge sounded glamorous, like she should be booking Broadway theater tickets and limousines for Adele Cummings. But her list of duties—mostly admin—screamed "standard-issue office manager." Then again, this was New York, where job titles were as inflated as real estate prices. I'd already met a telemarketer who insisted he was a *customer outreach specialist*, a librarian reborn as an *information curator*, and a waiter who proudly identified as a *food and beverage consultant*. Even my own temp agency had christened me a *consulting associate*, which, I admitted, sounded far classier than "gofer."

"I've been working for Adele Cummings and her foundation for over twenty-five years," she continued. "I've been here longer than any of the others. I maintain the most sensitive files and keep the whole machine running—while everyone else takes credit for the hum."

She said that lightly, almost cheerfully, but there was a look in her eye that made me think she was exaggerating. "I'm devoted to Ms. Cummings, and she depends on me. For every grant application that comes in, I assign it to the appropriate advisor on our team. If I don't know where something is, it's either misplaced by staff or never existed.

"I've scheduled an informal reception for 9:30," she added. "An opportunity for the others to extend their personal welcome. Following that—presuming we haven't sent you fleeing for New Jersey—we'll migrate to the screening room for a brief orientation presentation. Does that agree?"

Does that agree?

What kind of question was that? Most employers barely noticed the help had heads, let alone thoughts. But I was determined to play it cool. "Awesome," I said, nodding like a bobblehead.

"Awesome?"

"I mean, that's *quite agreeable*. Indeed." *Quite agreeable, indeed? Who am I turning into?*

As the clocks in the house marked the half hour, the foundation's main workforce began to filter into the drawing room. They gravitated towards me like curious relatives visiting a newborn's crib—gently crowding in, peering closely, witness to something brand new. Each introduction brimmed with warmth and camaraderie. Well, except for one noticeably aloof presence. But I'll get to that in a minute. The room otherwise buzzed with a friendliness that enveloped me in a sort of goodwill cocoon.

I couldn't believe it. Somehow, *I* had become the sun in a tiny solar system of delightful, dazzling, attractive human beings —each one orbiting me with a shared mission: to spread Adele Cummings's philanthropic moolah across the arts and humanities universe.

But what really struck me—aside from the fact that they were all well dressed—was how genuine they seemed. Not just about their work, but about *the point* of it. They agreed they weren't just doing a job. It was a *calling*. For life. Like philanthropy meets musical theater.

And OMG, the respect they offered me! After working in offices where I was once referred to as "the neck" (mine's not *that* long), these people made me feel like I was family. They called me *Mister* Trousdale. In fact, everyone at the foundation was Mr. this or Ms. that. It was a rule.

"Ms. Cummings believes that first-name familiarity diminishes the individual," Mrs. Johnston explained. "Here, we elevate each other with formality. It's dignifying. Wouldn't you agree, *Mr. Trousdale*?"

After the many ways I'd been mistreated at other workplaces, this was an amazing novelty. "Absolutely," I managed. Inside, I was thinking, *I've never been dignified at a job before!* I did wonder how they'd address someone who didn't identify as either Mr. or Ms. Maybe *Mx.*? (That's the gender-neutral one, for those of you not fluent in progressive office protocol.)

Honestly, after my last job—where insults were a form of team-building exercise, and my name was mostly shouted in ALL CAPS—this whole thing felt revolutionary. It felt like someone had quietly handed me a fresh start—with a big portion of hope.

I was in a group of kindred spirits united under the umbrella of Adele Cummings's philanthropic vision. And in this moment of welcome, I felt the first threads of belonging weave themselves around my heart.

2

———

The first to greet me was Ms. Neely. She was the sort of person who didn't just *walk* into a room—she *wafted*. Everything about her screamed sophistication—in a quiet, cashmere sort of way. The word "ethereal" fit best.

A brunette bob framed her face. Her cowl-neck sweater draped over her shoulders, and silver earrings caught the light with every subtle tilt of her head.

"Mr. Trousdale, it's a pleasure to become acquainted," she said, offering a handshake. "I'm Ms. Neely. Awards and Allocations." Her voice was warm and polished. "Your surname is deliciously distinguished," she beamed. "It reminds me of my dearest chum, Suzie Schultz, who resides in the Trousdale Estates in Beverly Hills. Perhaps you know her?"

Let's just take a moment to review, dear readers. I grew up in semi-rural Alabama, where "luxury real estate" means a double-wide with a washing machine in the backyard instead of a pool. The odds of my knowing anyone in Beverly Hills are about the same as my popping into Sotheby's to outbid Jeff Bezos on a Monet.

But I suspected Ms. Neely probably didn't mean it literally. It was her way of connecting worlds—her gleaming, curated one and my wrinkled, temp-agency-issued one. And for some reason, it worked. I felt like she was seriously interested in me as a human being.

Sort of.

Ms. Neely radiated wealth. I just knew she was the kind of woman who never dribbled soup on her silk blouses. And yet—she wasn't snooty. Not even close. She had this easy, elegant confidence that probably only comes from living a full, rich life. Despite our backgrounds I felt comfortable around her.

She leaned in. "Mr. Trousdale, once you're comfortably acclimated, I'd be very pleased to show you some of our Adele Cummings Arts Award applications. Your insight may prove invaluable...if you're so inclined." She then explained that I could assist by offering "a fresh perspective" on applicants' backgrounds because I was someone unjaded by years of philanthropy or committee politics. Translation: she thought my small-town, outsider's viewpoint might help spot a hidden gem. Translation of the translation: *You look like you still know what rent costs.*

Honestly, I didn't know what to do with that. At every other job I'd ever had, my opinion had been about as welcome as a swarm of wasps at a picnic. But here? Ms. Neely was treating me like I was already part of the team—like I *mattered.*

Then came Mr. Slater, the foundation's director of Research and Analysis. And let me tell you, he was *adorable.* Tall, broad shoulders, and all the physical features most normal people dream of in a fantasy lover. He had that sort of effortless style that made you immediately think he was interested in you. His hair was a perfect mix of golden waves and premature gray. And don't get me started on his skin. It had that golden, sun-kissed glow that made me certain he used some terrifyingly expensive face cream that only rich people know about—or could afford.

His outfit? A master class in understatement. Perfectly tailored navy blazer, charcoal trousers, crisp white shirt with the collar opened down two buttons. And of course, there was a silk pocket square. Gay? Maybe. Maybe not. I'm often spectacularly wrong about that.

"Mr. Trousdale," he said smoothly, "I happen to have a pair of tickets for the Met's season opener—*orchestra seating,* of course." (Of course.) "But Wagner doesn't speak to me. I'm more of a Puccini purist."

And with that, he reached into the breast pocket of his blazer and withdrew an envelope. "I would consider it a favor if you and a friend would attend on my behalf."

I blinked. Tickets to the Met? Orchestra seating? Did this man just casually hand me a golden ticket to New York culture as if it were a two-for-one coupon at Walgreens? Even I knew they cost a bloody fortune!

Momentarily taken aback by the lavish offer, I stupidly asked, "Why isn't Wagner speaking to you? You two have a bit of a falling-out?"

It must have been an awkward question, because after a moment of confusion, Mr. Slater laughed.

"Well done, you! Almost had me there! You amuse me, sir."

I didn't know what I'd said that could be construed as amusing, but I thought it best to let it drop and hope that Mr. Slater and Mr. Wagner worked things out. The tickets in my hand felt like keys to a new world, one that promised to expand my appreciation of the arts.

On the heels of that introduction, Mrs. Stone floated over to me. She was all radiant, high-voltage charm and *joyful energy.* Around her neck was a lovely string of pearls. As she moved, they caught the light, as if each bead were a tiny moon.

"Ethics and Compliance." She identified her advisory position. "Mr. Trousdale," she said in a melodic, champagne-bubble kind of voice, "my husband will be piloting a clutch of our nearest and dearest to Aspen in his new Gulfstream toy over Thanksgiving. There's room for one more if you haven't made your own *ressies* yet. It would be *marvy* if you would allow us to shuttle you there."

I blinked.

Aspen?

Gulfstream *TOY*?

What even *is* a Gulfstream? A private jet, I think. And what did one wear on a ski holiday to Aspen with people who had names like Remington and wore everyday pearls? But the idea of skiing—*me*, skiing?—was so ludicrous I had a full mental image of myself somersaulting down a mountain and needing to be airlifted home.

And yet...her invitation was so warm, so guileless, so *genuinely nice* that I didn't feel patronized. Mrs. Stone obviously lived in a universe of private jets, snow-covered chalets, and winter vacations. The most fascinating part of it all was that there wasn't an ounce of pretension in her. She was just...naturally magnanimous.

Then a deity strolled into the room. Mrs. Raymond. Everyone seemed to *adjust* to her presence. Like the whole place knew someone fabulous had arrived and wanted to behave accordingly.

She was stunning. Like, movie-star-on-a-press-tour stunning. Her thirty-something skin was a glorious velvety mahogany. Her smile was 100 watts. Her voice was like someone had melted poetry and poured it over ice cream, with a South Pacific garnish. "The Marquesas Islands," she said, when I asked about her accent. "A blend of Polynesian musicality and French rhythm." The words slipped off her tongue like a lullaby.

And before I could properly process how glamorous Mrs. Raymond was, she reached into her clutch and pulled out a gift card. "This is a wee something from my friend Angelica (which she pronounced Ahn-HEL-ee-ka)," she said, holding it out with a conspiratorial laugh. "She means well, but she always forgets I'm devoted to Brunello Cucinelli. Can't imagine why she thought I'd deign to patronize *Valentino*. It's just taking up valuable space in here. Perhaps you'll find something for yourself or a friend. You'll do me a favor by using it."

Wait.

Hold on.

Did this ethereal goddess just hand me a Valentino gift card plucked from her purse like it was a stray Tic Tac?

I stared at it like it might disappear if I blinked. A real, actual Valentino gift card. Like, *fashion week* Valentino. Like, *things I've only seen in magazines next to price tags marked "If You Have to Ask..."* Valentino. And she was *giving it to me* because it didn't match her brand loyalty?

I managed a thank you that sounded only *slightly* strangled while inside I was screaming: *WHAT IS HAPPENING HERE?!*

Because here's the thing. I could tell she wasn't showing off. She was just being generous in the casual way that people who never have to check their bank balances can be. I guessed that in her world, giving away luxury was simply a matter of practicality.

OMG! Who are these amazing people? And how did I land in such a big, deep, fluffy pile of their molted angel feathers? Perhaps their very detachment from need allowed their generosity to flourish. People who don't want something from you can be incredibly magnanimous. It's the envious losers you have to be wary of. Unburdened by the problems that plague most of us, rich people can afford to extend kindnesses and support without ulterior motives. It dawned on me that the real measure of wealth wasn't in the opulence of one's surroundings but in the capacity to offer benevolence without conditions. I filed that away for future contemplation—and practice—when I was rich.

Taking a quick mental step back from the dazzling swirl of welcome smiles and light-reflecting jewelry, I clocked the one person in the room who hadn't offered so much as a nod, a smile, or a single syllable of introduction. I asked Mrs. Johnston who the woman with the antisocial detachment was.

"Ms. Klotz. Policy consultant."

Even her name sounded disturbing, like a spoon grinding in a garbage disposal. *Klotz... Klotz... Klotz...* And of course, I never insult someone's physical appearance—as that's not nice—but I've gotta say, she sorta reminded me in a way of an anteater. That was a wild distortion on my part, but she almost looked as if evolution had momentarily gotten obsessed with eating efficiency and forgotten about symmetry.

Her eyes were smallish and deep-set. And her nose was longer than average and sorta pulled downward. She didn't smile. She didn't even seem to blink. I wasn't entirely sure she even breathed. She just sat in a wingback chair, arms crossed, lips pursed. There was an invisible wall around Ms. Klotz, which made her even more intimidating. She sat ominously like a thundercloud in a beige cashmere sweater, ready to pour disapproval on whatever unsuspecting soul dared to breathe too near her.

Ms. Klotz was probably in her early thirties and every bit as impeccably turned out as the other dazzling creatures flitting around here. She wore a diamond dragonfly hair clip on the side of her sleek bob—though to my eyes, it looked less like it was ornamenting her and more like it was being held captive. Ms. Klotz exuded all the warmth of a full-body airport security scanning machine.

From the moment our eyes met (or rather, the moment my eyes met her judgmental squint), I knew we were not destined to braid friendship bracelets. At least not without a huge amount of effort on my part. It wasn't that she ignored me. Ignoring would've been easier. She assessed me. Like someone silently debating whether I should be erased from her presence using a giant DELETE key.

And it wasn't all that subtle. Her gaze absorbed me from

head to toe. Of course, I smiled at her because that's what you do when you're a nervous new employee and one of the senior staff looks like she'd rather be chewing gravel than sitting anywhere near you. I tried to be cheerful and optimistic as I approached her.

"Ms. Klotz? I'm Timothy, er, *Mr.* Trousdale. It's lovely to meet you."

Her response? A barely perceptible eyebrow twitch. That was it. That was her grand gesture. No "hello." No "welcome." Just the universal facial expression for *I see you. I do not like you. Kindly evaporate.* It was like she was allergic to cheerfulness.

But I was sure I could win her over. Eventually.

My smile—which usually worked like a charm—froze on my face. The corners of my mouth started to twitch. My cheeks went hot. My inner monologue was shrieking, *Abort! Abort! She's immune to charm!* I tried one last lifeline: "Well, I'm sure we'll work well together."

She said nothing.

Nothing.

Not even a passive-aggressive "Mm." I could've been a lamp.

I turned and made a beeline back to Mrs. Johnston, as if she were my emotional support human. She looked at me as if to say, *You've met Cerberus.*

And I had. The three-headed canine that guards the gates to Hades. One woman, one glower, one shattered self-esteem in under thirty seconds. A new record for me.

"She needs a juice box and a nap," Mrs. Johnston murmured sympathetically after witnessing my dismal crash-and-burn.

I wanted to say *she needs an enema*, but I didn't know Mrs. Johnston well enough yet to be crude.

"Don't take it too personally," she added. "Ms. Klotz hardly ever says anything. She barely acknowledges a good morning. She doesn't have to. One of those top-down hires—straight from Ms. Cummings's inner circle."

Mrs. Johnston adjusted her glasses, her tone light but measured. "Comes in two, maybe three days a week—when the mood strikes. Sometimes disappears for weeks. No one questions it." She smiled faintly, as if she'd revealed a state secret and then tucked it neatly back where it belonged.

I nodded in understanding. You don't question a natural disaster. You board the windows and hope you're insured. I didn't know Ms. Klotz, but I really didn't want to either.

"One bit of advice, Mr. Trousdale. When Ms. Klotz gives you an assignment, do exactly as she says. *Never* ask her to repeat herself."

I swallowed hard.

"She will not only remove your head, but she'll detach your manly bits, sauté them with a little shallot and wine reduction, and serve them for lunch like she's appearing on *The Great British Bake Off.*"

Cannibal Edition.

"She found the assistant you replaced quite...tasty."

I had no idea whether Mrs. Johnston was exaggerating, and I didn't want to find out. I made a mental note to bring a voice recorder every time I entered Ms. Klotz's line of fire. If she ever asked me to do anything—no matter how trivial—I would do as I was told, with the quiet terror that one mistake could turn me into a eunuch.

I gulped. "There's got to be a human being in there somewhere," I said, perhaps too brightly. "I'm sure I'll find it eventually." I gave Mrs. Johnston my best little-ray-of-sunshine smile. "She probably just needs time to know me."

As I looked around the room at everyone something shifted in my chest. Maybe a hint of something that felt close to suspicion. I told myself I was being dramatic. That after six months of employment humiliations, I was bound to flinch at kindness.

As the meet-and-greet began to wind down—and these lovely people started murmuring polished regrets about having to return to their offices—Mrs. Johnston turned to me with her soft smile.

"Aren't they all proud of themselves?" she said, watching the advisors glide away. "So well dressed. So well educated." Her smile didn't change, but something in her voice thinned—just slightly. "Not a care in their insulated worlds. Must be nice."

I blinked. It wasn't the words so much as the way she said, *"Must be nice."*

For a moment, something hard flickered behind her eyes. "They haven't a clue."

Then, as quickly as a light flipping on, she brightened again —sweet, composed, grandmotherly. "Well! Perhaps it's time to watch our orientation presentation? If that suits."

3

———

Due to the age of everything else in this office I was expecting Mrs. Johnston to roll out a creaky TV trolley and show an old, grainy VHS tape. Instead, she guided me through to the library, casually nudged open a panel in a bookcase, and led me down a stairway to a *private cinema*. I'm talking red velvet seats, low lighting, and the faint, lingering scent of buttered popcorn.

"Do make yourself comfortable," said Mrs. Johnston, as if we hadn't just descended into the Bat Cave. I settled into a seat, and for the next half hour, I was absorbed in the fascinating Adele Cummings origin story.

An only child from an upper middle-class family in suburban Boston, Adele was a precocious child and had a private education at the prestigious Chalford Academy. Her parents instilled in her the importance of always striving to improve herself and always behaving with dignity and integrity. They taught her the value of gratitude for every aspect of her good life. They insisted, "Those of us with more must do more" —a sentiment worthy of Jesus Christ, Maya Angelou, and Spider-Man.

MIT scouted Adele Cummings, and by the time she earned her degree in biological engineering, she had already made a considerable fortune by licensing her patent for a synthetic bacterium she'd developed in a student research lab. The innovation proved pivotal in improving diagnostic procedures. It was adapted for use in treating a parasitic disease that only people in Southeast Asia were ever affected by.

Before turning thirty, Adele had launched and sold several biotech startups, working across borders and collaborating with researchers from Singapore to Stockholm. She never rested on her laurels, always chasing her next brilliant idea, some frontier no one else had thought to cross.

The general public knew very little about Adele Cummings, and she preferred it that way. While some might have heard about her green energy crusades, she was most proud of her freebie airline, Cummings's Goings—founded, as she once declared in a sharply worded press statement, "expressly to help refugees from so-called 'shithole countries.'" Adele wanted to prove that not all rich Americans were vulgar, narcissistic political grotesques with more money than sense and an alarming allergy to empathy. She liked to say that if wealth really revealed character, then some people should have stayed middle class—where at least their cruelty could be contained to HOA meetings and golf-course tantrums.

The video presentation's voice narration (which sounded like Judi Dench) assured viewers that Ms. Cummings was not, in fact, the "aloof megalomaniac" so memorably described by *The Financial Times of London* but was merely "super self-conscious about her super-huge cup *runnething* over." She just preferred to serve humanity as anonymously as possible.

In fact, Adele Cummings was so secretive that there wasn't a single photo of her as an adult in the entire video. Not even a snapshot of her snipping a ribbon at the grand opening of the water-purification pumping station she built in Senegal—

although there *was* a glossy photo of the ribbon itself. No pictures of her touring the Frank Gehry–designed E. coli treatment center she fully funded in Uganda. None from the time she went to Sweden to accept a humanitarian award.

Naturally, I was dying to know what the squillionaire looked like—just in case she ever popped into the office and I accidentally bumped into her in the hallway. I was told she was "shy" and rarely came to New York. Which sounded suspiciously like code for "Quasimodo's less-attractive sister."

But really—who cares? When you're rich, people pretend not to notice nature's more aggressive vandalism of your appearance. Truthfully, it didn't matter one iota to me what Ms. Cummings looked like. Even if she were a cross between the Elephant Man and Picasso's *Weeping Woman with Handkerchief*, there was so much to admire about her. Most impressive of all was the Adele Cummings Prize—no-strings-attached, tax-free, multimillion-dollar grants awarded for—as the foundation's mission statement proclaimed:

...outstanding contributions to the creative, performing, literary, visual, and media arts.

These were in addition to the garden-variety charities she vigorously supported: cancer research, medical detection dogs, elephant sanctuaries, and environmental protection projects. No individual or group was too insignificant for consideration to win a big chunk of Ms. Cummings's change. Past grant recipients included novelty causes such as Toodle-*Loo*. This nonprofit provided toilets and other sanitation facilities in Bangladesh. And *Barely* Literate, a group of rebellious librarians in Florida who flouted their state's censorship and banned-books laws. (They lured people into what appeared to be brothels but were really "story dens.")

Adele Cummings supposedly studied every grant application and, with guidance from the foundation's advisors, person-ally selected all the recipients of her eponymous prize. Basically, she was an upper-crust fairy godmother with a tax-deductible wand.

Okay, I was in love with Adele Cummings. It was true. If or when I met her, I'd tell her how amazing I thought she was. How much I admired her generosity. I'd thank her for funding orchestras, museums, and scholarships. I'd tell her that what I admired most was that she didn't shout about her good deeds. No photo ops. No YouTube videos of her cradling starving babies in faraway lands. She just gave. Quietly. Decisively. I'd try to sound professional, but even if I tripped over every other word, I'd make sure she knew I thought she was terrific.

After the video presentation, I was given a tour of the rest of the foundation's offices at Ravenscroft. The place was lavishly decorated—but in the way I thought a rich old lady's Manhattan apartment circa late 1990s must have looked. Quite frankly, even though the foundation gave away an obscene amount of dollars, they obviously hadn't used much of it to redecorate their own space since before I was born.

There was a lot of faded mahogany paneling, dusty teardrop crystals on the chandeliers, and threadbare patches on some of the Oriental carpets. Still, the place reeked of old wealth. I could smell it everywhere. It sort of hung in the air, like particles of the lilac-scented talc my granny dusted herself with before church on Sundays—and before talc was deemed the toiletry equivalent of asbestos. Mrs. Johnston even wore a perfume scent like my granny's.

"And this will be your office," Mrs. Johnston announced as she led me to a wood-paneled room larger than my entire shared apartment. My jaw dropped as I took in the furnishings: an antique desk, a plush leather executive chair, an iMac computer, and a widescreen TV mounted on the wall. It even had a chandelier!

Oh, I get it. I'm new. This is an initiation hazing ritual sort of thing. Mrs. Johnston's going to laugh at me for falling for her joke.

But she seemed serious. Then she added, "You'll want to hang something on the walls, so you're welcome to select whatever you like from the gallery upstairs. We understand art is subjective."

Standing there, I, Timothy Trousdale, was simply overwhelmed. Who, I wondered, were the idiot interns before me who let the amazing opportunity to work for Adele Cummings slip through their fingers? I was determined to do everything in my power to make this into a permanent gig.

Almost gone were my thoughts of working on my dumb novella (with the equally dumb title *Suffer Fools*) or even starting another book. Why would anyone with anything better to do endure the grinding, years-long journey it took to cough up eighty-five thousand-plus words—one painful keystroke at a time—only to face the equally Herculean task of finding a literary agent? (A near-impossible feat unless you're related to someone at Curtis Brown.)

And even if, by some miracle, I found an agent, that agent still had to convince an editor to publish the damn book. And even if the editor said yes—which would be another *miracle*—then would come soul-crushing revisions and the near impossible task of finding an actual reading audience in a world that would rather binge reality TV. Nope. Why bother?[1]

I was speechless at the sight of my office and the twinkle in Mrs. Johnston's eyes told me she knew how happy she'd made me. If I could afford to send her flowers, I would. She smiled and said, "There are just a couple of rules we all have to follow."

I was an excellent rule follower. That was my best employee

---

1. If you're writing a novel, please don't let Timothy's negative attitude stop you from pursuing your dreams! He doesn't know anything!

trait because I didn't like to let anyone down—especially anyone who gives me a paycheck.

"One: Unless otherwise instructed, no one outside the advisory team is to access the shared computer folder labeled *Grants*," she said, her tone clipped. "Those files may contain sensitive information—financial disclosures, background checks, or personal matters that are private."

Of course. Crystal clear. No problem-o. I may be nosy, but rules are rules.

"Two: Staff are expected to maintain strict professional conduct regarding all grant applications. Personal opinions, informal commentary, or speculation about applicants or their merits are not to be discussed even in casual conversation, and under no circumstances should such views be communicated via email—internal or external—or any form of social media."

As far as I was concerned, Mrs. Johnston didn't even have to tell me those rules because they were just common sense. Especially when working with potentially sensitive information.

"Finally, rule number three: when you come into the office on Easter, you have to dress as a jelly bean."

I blinked. *I definitely don't want to be a jelly bean—at Easter or any other time!*

"We rotate flavors for our interns. Last year was lemon. This year you'll probably be lime. Very slimming."

I nodded solemnly, already picturing myself waddling through the office in a neon-green candy bean suit, clutching a grant proposal. "Of course. Absolutely. Happy to do whatever."

She let me squirm for a few beats; then the corners of her mouth twitched. "You do know Easter is always on a Sunday, don't you?"

It hit me like a pie in the face. *Right. Sunday. Meaning the office would be closed. No jelly-bean suit required.*

Mrs. Johnston chuckled, a warm, surprising sound. "Rule

number four: maintain a sense of humor. The world's a tough place, but you don't have to let it overwhelm you."

I laughed. Mostly in relief. For the first time, I saw that behind her big diamond ring and rules list, Mrs. Johnston, like me, had a keen sense of the absurd.

4

———

The week flew by, and before I knew it, Friday was here. Sure, there were a few hiccups along the way. I was still getting used to my new job. But other than what I called the "Wednesday incident"—losing a hundred thousand dollars of grant money—I thought I did pretty well.

Oh, about that Wednesday incident. Um, I might have—allegedly—somehow lost a tiny, insignificant transfer of funds to the MacLaine Dance Company. *Oops!*

Now, I still had absolutely no idea *how* that happened. One minute I was just trying to enlarge the spreadsheet so I could actually read it without going cross-eyed, and the next...*poof.*

Gone. The entire account. Vanished.

Of course, *Klotzferatu* was the first to point the finger. "It was Mr. Trousdale," she'd said, cool as a cucumber dipped in nitrogen. "He did something to the file. He was...fiddling."

Fiddling? I wasn't sure I even knew what that meant. But she made it sound like an offense punishable by public execution. Honestly—and I wasn't trying to pass the buck—but I wouldn't be surprised if she'd slipped into my office and "fiddled" just to get me in trouble. I suspected the old "whoever smelled it dealt it" routine. Flipping the blame back onto the accuser by suggesting that the person who first noticed or mentioned the fart is actually the one responsible for it.

I didn't know why, but that woman wanted me gone.

Probably at any other job, I'd have been perp-marched out the door. But here at the Adele Cummings Foundation? I was *praised*. Well, sort of.

I was summoned to Mrs. Johnston's office to discuss the issue. My body reacted like I was about to be booted back to SwellHire Top Temps—dry mouth, damp armpits, and sincere apologies. I sat stiffly in the chair in front of her desk, ready for tears. But she looked at me with a maternal smile and said, "Mr. Trousdale, simple human error should not be punished."

I blinked. *Is this a trap?*

"Experiences that seem terrible in the moment simply teach us not to make that same error again," she continued. "How else are we expected to learn anything? Perfection teaches nothing. But a so-called 'mistake'—especially one that stings a little? That stays with you. That sharpens you. I'd be far more concerned if you *never* erred."

Tears slipped out of my eyes. Not only was I *not* being fired, but I'd also apparently just had a *learning opportunity*. A growth moment. A small detour on the road to professional excellence.

Admittedly, I still had a strong suspicion that *Klotz-o-saurus Rex* had tampered with my computer. But for now, I was safe. Encouraged, even. Only a hundred thousand dollars lighter in the foundation's accounts. If this had been some elaborate scheme to humiliate me, it had spectacularly backfired. Somehow. Against all odds, I'd survived.

Honestly, I'd never felt more supported while being possibly responsible for a financial catastrophe.

Mrs. Johnston then leaned back and, with the calm gravitas of someone who's survived professional trauma herself, shared a personal horror story. "A couple of years ago, I was visiting

MoMA with a friend, and in what can only be described as a moment of historic clumsiness, I lost my balance on my high heels and stumbled into one of Chihuly's priceless glass sculptures. A one-of-a-kind piece. *I—propelled it to the floor.* It shattered into a billion glittering, colorful shards, like some tragic art-world confetti. The entire gallery was aghast. I probably deserved to be taken away in handcuffs." She paused, letting the image land.

I swallowed hard. My little hundred-thousand-dollar mishap suddenly felt no more shocking than knocking over a mattress at IKEA.

"Thankfully, the foundation's insurance covered it," said Mrs. Johnston. "Turns out, 'priceless' does come with a price tag. But I learned something important: when anywhere near fragile masterpieces, wear flat shoes."

She paused for a beat, then added—still smiling, "Or at least make sure you're not the one holding the broken pieces that prove you had anything to do with it. Perhaps, as we rebuild the MacLaine Dance Company's file, we'll discover they're due *more funding*, not less. Right action always prevails."

She smiled warmly. Here was a defender who had personally tangoed with catastrophe and somehow came out intact on the other side, and was able to use that experience to make me feel almost glad to have royally screwed up.

I wanted to cry. Not in a dramatic way, but more like at the end of a feel-good movie when the underdog finally gets their moment, and the swell of music does all the talking. Yes, I was still mortified by the whole hundred-thousand-dollar debacle— but mostly, I was floored by how astonishingly generous everyone (nearly everyone) had been about it. No yelling. No security escort out the door. No public flogging. Just...grace. What sort of parallel universe had I landed in where mistakes weren't punishable by immediate career death? Where being human didn't automatically mean being expendable?

I'd never worked anywhere that insisted on finding silver linings in soul-crushing humiliation, or where people encouraged you to see yourself as a functioning, intelligent human being instead of a two-legged disaster. It turns out, just a *smidge* of positive reinforcement can do wonders for the human psyche.

In fact, I had gone from thinking I was a walking bin fire—*actual rubbish*—to having a confidence so inflated I probably needed a pinprick and a reality check. I was practically strutting down the hallway.

But the universe has unbreakable laws. Like gravity. Thermodynamics. Murphy's. There's the unspoken workplace law that *someone* must always be lurking nearby to gaslight you and make you question your character and values. A human raincloud. The "corporate dementor."

And here at the Adele Cummings Foundation, that role was played—award-worthy, I might add—by Ms. Klotz. Didn't her name even sound like a Disney cartoon villain? Think Scar. Or Monstro. Or Professor Ratigan.

Since the *incident* with the MacLaine Dance Company file, which I still didn't totally understand but apparently was 100% my fault, *Klotztrocity* had gone positively glacial around me. Every time we passed each other in the hallway, she shot me this glance like I'd tracked dog poo across her Persian rug. Once, in a voice barely above a breath, she hissed, "Pity hire."

Charming.

As I said, she never speaks to me. The *Klotztress of Doom* prefers to deliver her wrath through the icy dagger of email. Or the occasional DM that arrived like a digital slap in the face.

Like this little gem:

Subject: Congratulations on Your Latest Triumph
Mr. Trousdale,

I must extend my most heartfelt congratulations on your recent *achievement* with the MacLaine Dance Company project, which I personally spent a good part of the past six months creating. It's not every day that one gets to see such a unique interpretation of responsibility. Your ability to turn a straightforward task into a cautionary tale is truly unparalleled.
I eagerly await your next spectacle, as it promises to be enlightening.
Regards,
Klotz
cc: Staff

Was that not almost eloquent in its viciousness? She practically deserved a Pulitzer for emotional vandalism.

Or this one, which hit my inbox just after I'd made the boo-boo of organizing a spreadsheet alphabetically instead of by grant size (who knew?):

Subject: A Word of Advice
Mr. Trousdale,
I am offering you a small piece of advice, given your recent endeavors. It's quite a simple concept, really, but one that seems to have eluded you thus far: *less is more.* In your case, less initiative could prevent *more* disasters. Consider this a reminder that not all of us are cut out for the groundbreaking work you seem so fond of attempting. Perhaps aim for mediocrity. It suits you.
Regards,
Klotz
cc: Staff

I tried not to take it personally. I told myself we all carry emotional baggage, and maybe she had a tragic past involving a traumatic piano recital when she was a kid.

In an effort to keep my cool, I even tried this thing I once heard about in a TED Talk—imagining your nemesis surrounded by blue light. Supposedly, it was calming and healing. So, in the middle of a staff meeting, I pictured her in a soft, soothing glow, as if I were controlling some kind of celestial dimmer switch. And for a second, I thought it might actually be working. She looked...less ferocious. Then she sneered at my idea for something, and the whole image shattered.

I wondered if she was cc'ing Adele Cummings on those emails, too. I had this recurring nightmare where Ms. Cummings, relaxing on a chaise on the beach of her private island, read every venom-laced email from Ms. Klotz while sipping a piña colada and murmuring, *"Oh dear, not that Mr. Trousdale person again."*

But everyone else in the office adored me. Mrs. Johnston, with her keen eye for style, often lavished praise on my clothing choices. It was obvious that I had no money, and my wardrobe was an eclectic collection from the Goodwill shop over on 101st Street. Yet her compliments felt like a nod to a unique sartorial style I didn't know I had.

Then there was Ms. Raymond, who, every morning, greeted me with an extra bear claw, her maternal instincts on full display. She said she worried I was too skinny. "You're adorable, Mr. Trousdale, but you need more meat on those bones—and maybe a few workouts at the gym."

And Mrs. Stone said I had an "elevated vocabulary," and she believed that if I didn't give up on writing my novella, I was destined for success and might one day even be recognized with an Adele Cummings grant for literature.

Such unwavering backing from those around me wasn't just a morale booster; it was a scaffold around my dreams, a reminder that maybe—just maybe—there was a place for me in the world. I could feel it. Like a whisper of hope wrapped in a warm cardigan. It was almost enough to make me believe I'd finally found my people.

And now, as the sun began to set over Ravenscroft this Friday evening of my first week, I'd not just survived—I'd *soared*. Others in the office noticed too. In a twist so fast, it gave me promotion whiplash, Ms. Neely had tapped me to become a grant application reader, starting Monday. A *reader!* Me! Timothy Trousdale, lowly intern, would be an arbiter of others' artistic dreams. There's no additional pay, but then, unlike my JPMorgan Chase Visa account, I was not defined by money. Not much, anyway.

Ms. Neely said she was impressed with me. *Impressed!* She even said it with a little tilt of her head, which meant I'd made the grade. And come Monday, I wouldn't just be just a gofer, praying Ms. Klotz didn't eat my spleen—I'd actually be reading grant proposals, along with all my other assignments. Judging them. Weighing the merits of people's passion projects like some twenty-first-century Peggy Guggenheim. I'd have influence. I'd have...a say.

Ms. Neely's eyes twinkled with admiration when she told me the good news. "It seems we've unearthed a gem—a mind as sharp as a tack and a work ethic to match!" Her words wrapped around me, signaling my rapid rise to indispensable team member.

Mrs. Stone, who was passing by my office, chimed in, "Better keep that brilliance of yours on a steep learning curve, Mr. Trousdale; otherwise, the Gates Foundation will swoop in and claim our treasure for themselves!"

I'm a treasure!

Not to be outdone, Mr. Slater was nearby and added, "I have it on good authority that Dyonyx Corp is on the lookout for a new cloning source. Let me just scrape a few of your skin cells, and I'll place an order for ten duplicates of Mr. Trousdale. Think of the productivity we could achieve."

As laughter and light-hearted jests filled the air, I allowed myself a moment of whimsy, picturing a brigade of Timothy Trousdales darting through the office and spilling out into the bustling streets of New York City. The thought brought a radiant smile to my face, a smile that spoke of belonging, of being valued, and of the endless possibilities that lay ahead for me.

And now it was the weekend!

5

____

The best thing about Saturdays? No frantic pace. Just glorious, unstructured time. Saturdays are the day the universe hands you the remote control and says, "Here, you pick." It's the reset button. Saturdays are freedom.

Even though I genuinely loved my job—a minor miracle in itself—Saturday was still my spiritual reward for enduring the workweek without being disemboweled by *Klotzenfang*. But most important of all—Saturday belonged to Brad and me. For the three months that we've been together, it was our sacred window of peace and uninterrupted affection.

Sleeping in on Saturday morning with someone you've just fallen in love with is the emotional equivalent of being embraced by a freshly baked cinnamon roll. No agenda. Just the warmth of another human body whose legs have somehow braided themselves with yours, even though the bed is definitely big enough to allow for boundaries. You wake up slowly, sharing bleary smiles and nonsense whispers, feeling like the planet is inhabited by only the two of you. There's magic in that stretch of time—where nothing matters except the fact that you're beside each other.

Who am I waking up with? If you haven't read *Breakfast at Timothy's* (available wherever fine books are sold, downloaded, or narrated by someone far more silver-tongued than this author), let me introduce you to Brad Bradley. Yes, that's his real name. No, I don't call him Brad Squared. Although I was tempted at first. I like that we both have alliterative names. His hair is dark, soft, and just a bit wavy. His eyes are blue like mine and slightly stormy. They have this unfair ability to make me forget what I was saying, doing, or panicking about. He wears wire-rimmed glasses, which shouldn't be hot, yet here we are. Go figure.

Brad's the kind of guy who doesn't try to turn heads—but inevitably does anyway.

He's not short. Not tall. Not lean. Not heavy. Just...proportioned in that way that makes you realize Mother Nature has a favorite child. His T-shirts cling, hinting at a torso that doesn't come from the gym but from some sort of genetic generosity. His cargo pants hang low on his hips, daring you to imagine... He's got an easy confidence: not loud, not flashy, but somehow more magnetic than any peacock strutting nearby. And his hands... Those long fingers and light touch—physical poetry, whether he's playing piano (he trained for the concert stage) or tracing them up and down my bare chest.

I should have better described myself before now, too. I'm ordinary, I think. I've never stopped traffic, that's for sure. I'm skinny in that way people politely call "slender," and I don't have a lot of muscle definition on my longish torso. My T-shirts don't cling so much as hang, and my jeans are as uninterested in showing off as I am. I'm not a head-turner by any stretch, but I've been told I'm a head-tilter—someone you notice gradually, like a melody that keeps circling back until you realize you've been humming it all day.

Back to Brad. There's something sort of Niles Craneish about him, too—if Niles had been less uptight. Brad speaks quietly and laughs a lot. We both laugh a lot! And when he listens—which he always does—it's with his whole head, as though my words are something rare and valuable he's carefully unpacking. He should have come with a warning label. *May cause swooning and spontaneous uncontrollable physical affection in confined spaces.*

I'd love to say Brad isn't perfect. That he leaves socks everywhere or doesn't make his bed each morning or says, "If you know what I mean," too often. But I'd be lying. He *is* perfect. At least perfect for me. He's steady, thoughtful, and never makes me feel unintelligent or ridiculous—even when I know I am absolutely being unintelligent and ridiculous. I've never had an honest-to-goodness boyfriend before. I don't count a couple of guys I casually dated. Yes, I've fooled around a little—but I mean, there's never been anyone *special* special in my life. Until Brad.

I always stay over at his apartment on Friday and Saturday nights, and our Saturday mornings are sacred. Not in a hymn-singing, incense-burning sort of way, but in a "we stay in bed as long as we like" kind of way and lose our minds in insanely deep kisses.

This Saturday a.m., sleep wasn't the only part of the equation—if you know what I mean. When we finally emerged from the duvet and showered (together, of course), we wandered over to the Apollo Diner on Sixty-Seventh for what we've come to call "brunchfast"—where the servers don't judge us for ordering pancakes *and* fries.

Afterward, we strolled hand in hand through Central Park, and I had one of those stupid, embarrassing, full-body epiphanies: *Holy moly, I live in New York, and I'm holding hands with the man of my actual dreams.* I screamed it internally, of course, because external screaming tends to be embarrassing.

And then, because I am a book nerd, we capped things off with a detour to the Strand bookstore, where I heroically limited myself to buying only three books. Which, in my defense, is the equivalent of walking into a patisserie and leaving with just one croissant.

Back at Brad's obscenely grown-up apartment, he put on Lang Lang—because of course he has a proper audio system, complete with vinyls and CDs and knobs you actually twist instead of tap on a phone app.

And by "grown-up," I mean the place had coasters. Matching ones. The couch wasn't bought secondhand off Facebook Marketplace. There were fresh flowers in a vase—*not* from someone's funeral. His glassware had actual stems, his art had actual frames, and don't get me started on the lighting: dimmers, sconces, and lamps that made my own overhead bulb look like an interrogation spotlight.

I melted into his sofa and lay with my head in his lap while he stroked my hair as if I were a spoiled Persian cat.

As the *Goldberg Variations* rippled through the speakers, I basked in the glow of living my perfect life. Sure, there were a few Klotz-shaped wrinkles to iron out. But who doesn't have an office adversary who hates their guts? I think that's universal.

My brain wandered to one of my favorite escapist games: the game of What I'd Do With an Adele Cummings Zillion-Dollar Fortune. You know the one. We all play it. The one where you win the lottery and have to figure out how to spend all that loot. You'll eventually follow in the footsteps of George Soros and fund global health and education projects. But first, you want to splurge and go a bit mad with financial power.

I lazily asked Brad what he'd do if he were a rich philanthropist. I was hoping he'd toss out some brilliant idea that I could casually steal and present at work as another way to distribute Ms. Cummings's loot, as if I'd come up with the idea myself during a particularly altruistic daydream.

Then I remembered...oh, right. *Brad actually is a real-life rich person. Or will be when his mother dies.* Although he's a piano tuner by trade (after his plans for the concert stage were dashed), he's the sole heir to his mother's fortune. She lives in a mansion in Connecticut. It's on *five hundred acres* and called Lynnwood Manor. She won't give him a dime while she's alive because she believes that *unearned money breeds a weak character.* Brad gets it. He's seen friends' children inherit fortunes and become entitled, addicted, or aimless. His mom's convinced that true self-worth comes from struggle and discipline, not comfort. *"A fortune given too soon is a leash, not a gift,"* he's quoted her saying. And he agrees with her.

Which made my whole "what would you do with a fortune?" question hugely stupid.

"What about you?" Brad asked, still gently tracing circles on my forehead like he was trying to hypnotize me. He was succeeding.

I closed my eyes and sighed, going into full daydream mode. I said, "Well, after the year-long, first-class, 'round-the-world cruise... And after I fly my stepmother in on a private jet and video her heart attack when she sees the view from our new penthouse apartment at the very tippy-top of Central Park Tower..." I paused dramatically. *"Then* I'd become a film producer and buy the rights to all my favorite books by authors nobody's ever heard of—like Richard Tyler Jordan—who totally deserve to be on Netflix."

And then I cringed. *Why* did I always blurt out the first ridiculous thoughts that rolled into my brain like rogue marbles? Why couldn't I just say something sophisticated and philosophical, like, *I'd fund a residency program for novelists tackling social justice issues. Or I'd launch a fellowship for young playwrights bringing diverse voices to Broadway.* But no. I was no brighter than that Miss Teen Pageant contestant. You know the one—when asked how she would promote world peace, she blinked earnestly into the camera and said, "I'd hand out scented candles to everyone because people can't be angry when everything smells like lavender." That girl and I should have been besties.

"You're lucky you're cute," Brad said with a chuckle, ruffling my hair.

He was teasing. And yet...as I lay there, all comfy in Brad's lap, Bach tumbling softly through the speakers, I stared up at the ornate brass light fixture hanging from the twelve-foot ceiling, and wondered: *Why don't I have deeper thoughts?*

Brad was only five years older than me, but the kind of five years that came with references to stuff I didn't recognize—like human rights advocates, investigative journalists, obscure Nobel Prize winners. He had taste, too. He even pronounced things properly. Take the Cannes Film Festival, for example. Brad pronounced it correctly: "*Can.*" Not "*Cans*"—like Mrs. Johnston, who I'd come to think wasn't as sophisticated as she wanted everyone to believe. And instead of a macho sports logo or skull-and-crossbones tattoo like other guys, he had a treble clef inked on his forearm. He was what anyone would call "classy."

Brad just had *It*. That *thing*. That elegant, effortless *It thing*. I thought it was more than just that he'd grown up in a mansion in Connecticut. He was the sort everyone instinctively looked to when the waiter presented the wine list. Not because he was flashy about it, but because he just knew about things. Like the difference between a Bordeaux and a Burgundy. Or which Murakami novel to pack for a long flight.

He didn't name-drop or show off or talk like someone who spent Aprils in Paris (even though he *had* spent Aprils in Paris). He just had this sort of worldliness, like his passport was always a little warm from use.

Maybe it was genetic. Or perhaps it was, like, ideas you absorbed from being around fascinating, brilliant people your whole life.

Just being around Brad and the Adele Cummings Foundation and Theater people had *me* evolving at an alarming rate. I was a sponge. For one thing, I now drank tea. Not even regular tea. Loose-leaf oolong. And the other day, I asked my smart speaker in the office to "shuffle music by Gershwin," like I was some old-money gentleman in a silk smoking jacket.

Even better? *I* was the one who suggested to Brad that we watch *Howards End* last week, instead of our usual reruns of *Frasier* and *Downton Abbey*. I'd overheard Ms. Neely and Mr. Slater mention it as a favorite movie of theirs. I actually said to Brad, "It's beautifully shot." Like I was suddenly some refined culture critic instead of just parroting something I'd heard.

So maybe—just maybe—culture *was* rubbing off on me. Perhaps I wasn't just Timothy from Hicksville, the intern-turned-accidental-grant-reader. Maybe I was becoming... enriched. Polished. Like a gemstone that finally gets a chance to sparkle.

Maybe I was too hard on myself, too. After all, it was reasonable to deduce that since I knew Brad valued substance over superficial, he wouldn't spend his time with someone he felt was inferior to him. He liked me the way I was. The same with my colleagues at the foundation. They wouldn't be paying me (albeit minimum wage) and giving me more challenging assignments if they didn't think I had something to offer, would they? I didn't think so, because they could call up SwellHire Top Temps and replace me with another minimum-wage worker if I wasn't measuring up. And they treated me almost as an equal. I decided Brad and others might see me differently from how I see myself.

Then, as if he could read my thoughts—which, to be fair, we'd both been doing with spooky accuracy since we met—Brad gave me a playful cuff on the side of the head. "Right-o, mister! Hop to it. Time to have a different kind of fun," he said, gently

lifting my head from his lap like I was a cat that needed reposi-
tioning.

Oh, goody. Fun. I could *definitely* go for *fun.* My thoughts
instantly flashed to the giggly tickling match we'd had this
morning that ended with me in tears of laughter and Brad
looking smugly victorious. But alas, this wasn't the kind of fun
he had in mind. Not at the moment, anyway.

"All week you've been poring over applications from artists
begging for grant money. You mentioned an installation at the
Quantum Gallery. Something 'squeaky'? Let's go. Incognito. No
one has to know that you're that big, important grant reader
with the authority to make or break creative careers."

I blinked. "You mean *The Squeaky Floor*?"

Brad nodded. "That's the one. Sounds bonkers. Let's check it
out."

I rolled my eyes but couldn't help grinning. "The artist's
name is Astrid Nova," I said, slipping into faux intellectual mode
and recalling what her application said. "It's an interactive
installation. The entire floor is covered in squeaky wooden
planks. Visitors are encouraged to walk around and…'embrace
the noise.' It's meant to be 'a playful disruption of the traditional
art gallery silence and provoke reflection on our discomfort by
drawing attention to ourselves in public spaces.' Whatever that
means."

Brad blinked at me. "Basically, it's an exhibit that forces you
to squeak awkwardly while pretending to understand the
deeper meaning of a noisy floor?"

It sounded interesting. Although not in the same fun way
that involved tickling in bed did. Still, I couldn't help thinking
maybe this *was* what proper, sophisticated New Yorkers did on
Saturdays: attend museum exhibits. Brad clearly thought it
would be fun, and he was—well, he was the worldly one
between us. The one who knew about artists like Edward
Hopper and Al Hirschfeld. If he said squeaky floorboards were

art (and the foundation thought so, too), I was game to check it out.

Besides, it might make me look good in the office if I said I'd dropped by to see Astrid Nova's installation in person. So I grabbed my jacket, checked my hair in Brad's hallway mirror, and told myself: *You are a cultured man of the world, Timothy Trousdale. Now go out and squeak.*

6

S we ubered to the Quantum Gallery in Tribeca, I googled the place and read aloud from their website, "QG is dedicated to exploring the intersection of art and science through immersive installations and experiential exhibitions." There were a couple of pictures, and I turned my phone screen to show Brad. One was of a mirrored room filled with floating orbs, and another was a tangle of neon tubing suspended over a giant sandbox. A third was called *Wolfman's Garden*. The caption read, "Part haunted house, part botanical fever dream."

We entered through the gallery's smoked-glass doors, and I felt the air shift—cooler, quieter, with a hint of pretension. Brad paid the admission fee, and we began our journey. The first room was dominated by a towering sculpture that looked like a combination space alien monolith and a soft-serve ice-cream machine having a meltdown. From a hundred openings, it oozed rivers of neon goo—pink, chartreuse, electric blue—sliding down its surface like an acid-trip lava lamp. The viscous sludge collected at the base in a lumpy mound that glistened under black light. The whole thing pulsed faintly, giving the unnerving impression it might be alive.

Another visitor, a well-dressed older man standing directly to my left, seemed to be playing guide to a woman my age-ish, whom he'd probably euphemistically refer to as his niece or *protégé*—if you get my drift. He was lecturing: "You'll soon learn to identify what contemporary artists are attempting to make us all realize." I think he believed he was Plato conducting a philosophical dialogue with his students. "This piece... It's obviously a meditation on entropy"—(*obviously*)—"or perhaps the tyranny of restrictive form. Notice how the molten medium rejects containment. The artist is inviting us to confront our own discomfort with order." He gave a sage nod, then added, "It's our responsibility to listen to artists and divine their wisdom. Art doesn't answer questions—it renders the questions unanswerable."

"Mm. I see," said niece/protégé. She offered the vacant nod of someone who wasn't about to argue with a man who would probably be paying for an expensive dinner later.

We moved into the next room. There, across every wall, holographic projections of subatomic particles were displayed. Pinpricks of white, flares of violet, blips of gold—they all floated, collided, and ricocheted in endless, hypnotic motion. According to a small plaque on the wall, the installation was titled *Beauty in Chaos*.

I had no idea what the artist was trying to express, but two steps away, someone did. That same pedantic man. "Observe how the artist uses the quantum realm to reveal our own impermanence. Each flicker is obviously a metaphor for human connection—brief, electric, and doomed to dissolve. The randomness is the point; beauty thrives only within entropy."

Entropy again? That was the second time in five minutes (and my entire life) that I'd heard the word and promised myself to look it up ASAP—and *not* use it in a sentence while out in public.

Niece/protégé nodded slowly, squelching a yawn, and with a look that said, *Did I turn the iron off before I left the apartment?*

I snickered, but although I wasn't at all sure what the artist was really saying, there was something oddly captivating about this installation. I couldn't help being drawn in by the sheer uniqueness of it. And maybe that was all he was trying to say.

Then we entered the Quantum Gallery's jewel in the crown. The installation we'd come to see: *The Squeaky Floor*. And yes, it was exactly what it sounded like. A room full of squeaky floorboards.

The moment we stepped into the dimly lit space, it was like being inside a haunted attic. Every footfall triggered a squeak, a groan, or a wheeze—as if the floor had eaten something it shouldn't have and was now loudly regretting it.

All around us, enormous projections of the world's most iconic artworks floated on the walls and ceiling—*Mona Lisa, Girl with a Pearl Earring, Starry Night*. The floor had been transformed into a kind of artisanal funhouse: a grid of wooden panels, each wired with a hidden sound mechanism. The effect? Total cacophony. Like a symphony of rusty nails being pried from planks.

Every step was a surprise. Squeak. Weeze. Squeeeeeeee. Creeeak-pop. It was both deeply silly and oddly profound.

"A commentary on how we literally walk all over art," said the same pompous highbrow. He rolled out the phrase with theatrical gravitas, like he expected applause for uncovering a mystery no one had questioned. I was starting to get super annoyed with his voice.

Despite its seemingly simple concept, *The Squeaky Floor* was actually super fun. And maybe Mr. Intellectual over there was right. For the first time, I began to grasp that art wasn't necessarily confined to mere objects meant to be observed and admired from afar, like a canvas or a sculpture. I thought I started to realize art could be anything that elicits a sensory response. Art is all around us. That was a sudden, eye-opening concept to me.

As I skillfully dodged eye contact with the mentor, to avoid giving away my amusement at his expense, I suddenly caught sight of someone else across the room. In a split second, a wave of recognition and horror washed over me, causing my heart rate to skyrocket. "Whoa!" I said and ducked behind Brad. *Is that Ms. Klotz from the foundation?*

"What's up?" Brad asked, confused about why I was suddenly using him as a human shield.

I did a double take, only to realize… *Nah, it must have been someone who bore a passing resemblance to her.* "That was weird. I thought I saw someone I didn't want to see. From the foundation."

"The Klotz woman?" (He knew who occupied my night-mares.) "We should say hi."

"No way! I don't like running into her in the hallway at work, and I definitely don't want to bump into her on a day off! And certainly not in a semi-dark room."

Even the best Saturdays come with a ticking clock. One minute you're laughing over squeaky floorboards and armchair art critics, and the next you're watching your day vanish. *Poof!* In the morning, Brad would be on an early train to his mother's mansion in Connecticut, but I intended to make the most of the hours we had left. The kind of "goodbye" that leaves you walking funny and grinning at strangers all the next day.

And then…Sunday was for doing my laundry…and Monday was back to work. Damn.

With every other job I'd ever had, Mondays felt like being slowly lowered into a vat of misery. But now? Sure, I'd rather spend every waking moment curled up with Brad, but alas, work was a necessity of life. And my job at the foundation was interesting and (for the most part) fun.

Looking back, that was the last truly perfect weekend... before everything changed. We never know that at the time, do we?

7

———

Fast-forward through a fairly uneventful week to the next Friday. The day was over, and as I was slinging my rucksack over my shoulder, getting ready to leave for my standing date with Brad, Mrs. Stone knocked on my open door. She stood at the threshold, offering an apologetic smile for detaining me.

She said, "One of the many joys of working at the foundation is the liberty we're given to scout for potential recipients of an Adele Cummings grant who might not even know the prize money exists. You see, not all our grantees come to us through applications. Sometimes, guided by our personal passions, we find them ourselves. Ms. Cummings encourages that and even has scouts in piano bars across the country. A singing bartender in Kansas City was awarded a grant that enabled her to record CDs. One of her songs was covered by Taylor Swift."

She said each of the foundation's advisors had their own individual campaign: Ms. Neely, with her love for the grace and fluidity of dance; and Mr. Slater, whose heart lay with the bold strokes of contemporary art. "We have access to discretionary funds that allow us to explore the arts world and recommend creators whom we feel are worthy of support," she said. "We don't need Adele Cummings's express sign-off."

"In fact," said Mrs. Stone, a note of excitement in her voice, "I'm going to see a cabaret performance in the Village tomorrow night. There's a pianist and a singer. He's quite accomplished, and she's becoming well known. They have a unique way of interpreting the American songbook and breathing new life into the music of the early-to-mid-twentieth century. Alas, my darling Remington is away in Zurich for meetings all week. He's always away on business. So I wonder if you'd like to accompany me to the show in his place?"

Mrs. Stone's invitation hung in the air, an offer to step into the heart of what our work at the foundation was all about: finding talent worthy of encouragement and investment.

"The foundation will cover all expenses," she added. "It could be an opportunity for you to see firsthand the kind of passion and potential we seek in the recipients of our awards."

Well, that sounded great to me. But drats! It was the weekend. My long-awaited and valued time with *Brad!* The sudden clash of plans sent a silent groan through my head. When I already had social plans, I wasn't usually very good about changing them at the last minute.

And a small, uncomfortable thought crept in: would Brad think I was becoming one of those people? Career-driven, dazzled by proximity to importance, suddenly too busy for the simple pleasures we'd promised each other.

Mrs. Stone, ever the astute observer, caught the fleeting shadow of disappointment on my face. "Oh, if you've already got a date, don't let me play the villain. Bring him along! Or her," she hastily added. "I apologize for any assumptions."

"It is *him*." I proudly smiled. "And Brad's pretty sophisticated, so I think he'd probably love to see cabaret. And I love Liza."

"Liza?" A beat of confusion raced through her eyes. Then realization dawned. She chuckled. "Oh, no, Mr. Trousdale, cabaret isn't a movie with Liza Minnelli. Well, it *is* a movie with Liza Minnelli...from the 1970s. She won an Oscar. The cabaret I'm referring to is a type of performance in an intimate nightclub setting. It's not about loving Liza. Although I do, of course. I've met her. She's lovely. No, I'm seeing another singer. Lillian Trent."

My cheeks flushed with embarrassment. "Oh...right. Got it," I mumbled sheepishly, realizing I'd just fully revealed myself as an unsophisticated hayseed. A night out on the town in New York with Brad—paid for by the foundation—and there'd be plenty of time afterward for tearing off our shirts and wrecking the sheets. It all sounded terrific. I decided this might be a great opportunity for a different sort of date night with my perfect man. "Let me confirm," I said, and pulled out my phone.

Manhattan Moon was a cabaret club nestled in the basement of a historic brownstone in the Village. The foyer was dim and hushed, a welcome contrast to the chaos outside, and excitement fluttered in my chest. The entryway walls displayed black-and-white pictures of the legends who had performed here— Barbara Cook, Eartha Kitt, Nancy LaMott, and Andrea Marcovicci.

The showroom was stripped to its bones—no proscenium, no scenery, just a small, slightly raised stage and a black grand piano. The lighting was soft. Plate-sized tables contained small votive candles. It was the kind of space that didn't promise glamour so much as it promised proximity to the performer— every sigh, every note, every whispered aside was the audience's for the taking.

The place was packed with at least a hundred people, but Mrs. Stone spotted us from across the room and waved us over.

"I'm so happy we can be together tonight," she said, her eyes sparkling. "I have a strong feeling the performance will be something memorable."

We settled into our seats near the piano. Mrs. Stone was drinking Perrier with a lime wedge, but since the foundation was paying, Brad and I ordered red wine. Then the lights dimmed, and a single spotlight cut through the darkness, illuminating the pianist. His fingers danced over the keys, a familiar melody unfolding and swelling into a crescendo that electrified the room. Then a respectful voice announced, "Ladies and Gentlemen, Manhattan Moon is proud to present—Ms. Lillian Trent."

In that moment, Lillian Trent emerged into the spotlight, and the audience seemed to hold its breath. She stepped onto the stage in a sapphire-blue pantsuit. Her hair was styled in an elegant updo, strands framing her face, a white gardenia tucked behind her left ear. A sparkling brooch was clipped at her lapel, and a pale blue silk scarf woven with silvery threads hung loose at her throat.

Lillian Trent picked up a handheld microphone from the piano top, then sang in a velvet-soft voice:

> *It's a nice day—clear skies...*
> *Autumn's such a lovely season...*
> *But somehow it's lost its reason since...*
> *The new girl's in town...*

Her voice shot through me like a current—warm and electric. It wasn't something I could analyze, but it was something I felt in my soul. I intuitively knew this was *art*. It wasn't the whiny voice of contemporary pop singers I heard on the radio. Lillian was literally touching my heart. It sounded weird to say this, but her voice was truly like an intimate caress. I didn't know how else to describe it. I vaguely recognized the melody. It was sort of old-fashioned and haunting.

As the final notes of the song lingered in the air, the room fell into complete silence—a kind of reverent stillness that felt almost holy. No clinking glasses, no whispered comments, just collective awe. It was as if the entire world had paused to bask in the beauty of a single, lovely voice. I imagined this must've been how people felt the first time they heard Barbra Streisand sing, right here in this very city—stunned that a human being could sound so divine.

She thanked the audience and introduced her piano accompanist: Everett Miles. Everett was exceedingly handsome. His caramel-colored hair caught the stage light in soft glints; his jawline looked like it had been sketched by someone who'd studied symmetry in art. Even from across the room, I could sense a quiet intensity about him—the way he seemed to breathe with the music, his long fingers coaxing it out of the keys rather than merely hitting them.

As a team, Lillian and Everett were hypnotic. Throughout the evening, her voice soared, while his keyboard artistry grounded her. Beauty and restraint, passion and precision—the kind of chemistry that lovers express.

Lillian's set lasted an all-too-short ninety minutes and ended with Noël Coward's reflective "If Love Were All." She left the stage to thunderous applause, and while joining the ovation, my gaze wandered across the sea of faces basking in the glow of the performance. That was when I saw something—*someone*—familiar-ish across the room at the bar. A figure bearing a striking resemblance to Ms. Klotz. What? The office witch? Here at a cabaret club? Surely not.

Shaking my head, I chalked it up to the evening's spell, the dim lighting playing tricks on my eyes. After all, Ms. Klotz's idea of an evening out was probably limited to flapping her wings and searching for an artery to sink her blood-sucking teeth into.

"That was incredible," Brad beamed, an immediate convert to the undeniable talent we'd just witnessed. As an accomplished musician, he knew what he was talking about. "She reminds me of Jane Olivor—a singer from the '70s I crushed on after I discovered one of her albums in a thrift shop."

All I knew was Lillian Trent's singing had transported me—and I was thrilled that Brad and I had both been moved by the experience. The closest I'd ever previously come to being captivated by a singer's voice was when my granny played her old Karen Carpenter records.

Mrs. Stone nodded in complete agreement with what Brad had said and what I was thinking.

"She's brilliant," I said. "This evening is definitely something that will stay with me for a really long time. I'd love to meet her."

Mrs. Stone leaned closer. "She'll be out in a moment. That's part of the fun of cabaret. Performers usually mingle with their audience after their shows. It's a shared world between artist and admirer." She dropped her voice to a conspiratorial whisper. "But we mustn't mention our affiliation with the foundation."

Then she rose from her seat, reached for her clutch, and whispered, "*Salle de bain pour dames.*" I gathered that was French for "I need to wee-wee." By the time she returned, and Lillian Trent still hadn't come to greet her fans, disappointment began to creep in. Maybe my new favorite singer wasn't one for mingling after all.

Still savoring the afterglow of the performance, I leaned closer to Mrs. Stone. "You know, for a moment, when we were all applauding, I could've sworn I saw Ms. Klotz by the bar."

Mrs. Stone raised an eyebrow. "*Our* Ms. Klotz? At a cabaret club?" She let out a chuckle, the idea seeming as plausible as spotting Elvis selling cars at a dealership. "Mr. Trousdale, I think the enchantment of the night might have played tricks on your eyes. I imagine Ms. Klotz's idea of a fun Saturday evening involves less... How shall I put it? Less song and dance and more...cross-referencing her enemies list with the obituaries."

She was right. The idea of *Klotznado* indulging in the world of cabaret seemed improbable.

Shaking her head, Mrs. Stone added, "If Ms. Klotz ever trades her evenings of sharpening her tongue for cocktails and a show, I'll be the first to book a table for her. But until then, I think she will remain the mystery we tolerate...from afar."

By now, I was getting a bit impatient. Why hadn't Lillian come to say hello to her admirers? We had to leave soon because Brad had to be up early to catch the train. So I excused myself, ostensibly to visit the little boys' room.

The show had left me light-headed with melodies, and I was eager to tell Ms. Trent how much her performance meant to me. The two glasses of wine I'd consumed might have helped. I'm one of those people who, after a drink or two, start behaving as if I'm hosting a reunion for my closest friends—most of whom I've only just met.

I found myself navigating the club's back hallway. Dim light bulbs buzzed overhead, their glow a sickly amber. The air smelled faintly of spilled beer and gin, and a vague hint of perfume. An outside door opened, letting in a sharp draft and a rush of city noise—a siren, a car horn—before slamming shut again.

Maybe I'd bump into Lillian Trent in the hallway. That had been my vague, wine-fueled hope. I was a little nervous. I mean why would Lillian Trent care that I thought she was a fantastic singer? Everyone probably told her that, especially after a performance like the one she'd just given. Still, I wanted to add my voice to the chorus.

I wasn't entirely sure what I'd say that wouldn't sound stupid or pretentious. I once saw an old movie with Cary Grant and Deborah Kerr. She played an actress, and I remember when they met, he said, "I'm an ardent admirer." That sounded sophisticated to me. So that was what I planned to say to Lillian Trent.

I was slightly unsteady on my feet as I made my way down

the narrow corridor. The whoosh of a toilet flushing and the hiss of running water echoed nearby. I passed the ladies' restroom and, a few steps farther on, pushed through what I assumed was the door to the men's room.

It wasn't.

The room was softly lit, and for half a second my brain struggled to catch up. I took another step inside, already babbling, "Oh—God, I'm so sorry, wrong door. Terribly sorry!"

It was a dressing room. In movies and TV shows, backstage dressing rooms are hives of activity—fluttering assistants with armfuls of flowers, frantic stage managers waving telegrams, someone touching up the star's lipstick between wisecracks. I'd never actually been backstage anywhere, so I couldn't swear this was how it really was, but if this were a dressing room, I expected at least some activity. In retrospect, I should have just backed away and returned to Brad and Mrs. Stone. So much for hindsight.

Instead, I called out, "Ms. Trent?"

There was no answer. My voice might have been too timid and weak. I didn't want to intrude if she was in her dressing gown or taking off her makeup.

"Ms. Trent? I just want to say..."

Silence.

The air inside was heavy, carrying the faintest trace of perfume. Ah, there she was! Lillian Trent sat before her vanity, her reflection caught in the mirror—makeup flawless, lips parted as if she were about to speak. For half a second, I expected her to turn and talk to me. Then I saw something odd —her gardenia was on the floor. And I noticed there was slackness at the corners of her mouth, an unnatural tilt of her head, her cheek resting against her shoulder. My stomach tightened. There was something terribly wrong with the way her body was positioned.

My heartbeat thudded in my ears as I stepped closer, willing her to stir, to blink, to maybe wake up from a quick nap she'd taken, or make some wry comment about being exhausted after the show and catching her in an unguarded moment.

She didn't.

I stepped a little closer, and as if my movement had stirred the air just right, Lillian moved. Slowly. To the left. Then, like a book giving way under pressure from the ones beside it, she tilted off the chair.

Reality shot through me.

I knew that...

Lillian Trent was...

Dead.

8

As Monday's first light crept through the blinds in my apartment, I opened my eyes, and the memory hit like a stone: Lillian Trent was dead. The cabaret singer with the velvet voice was gone. Murder, the police had said without hesitation. The image of her lifeless body returned to me in full, stark detail, flooding my thoughts until there was no room for anything else. It was the second time this year murder had circled into my orbit, and now it sat heavy on my chest, quiet and suffocating.

I went through my morning pre-work routine like a zombie. But everything felt forced. In the bathroom, I avoided looking in the mirror, afraid of the raw, haunted expression that surely marked my face. Stepping outside into the cool morning air, the world carried on as if nothing tragic had happened.

I arrived at Ravenscroft, patted sweet Smudgy on the head, made myself a mug of tea, ignored the bear claw on my desk, and tried to settle down to work. I busied myself with mundane tasks. Yet I couldn't get rid of the image in my head of Lillian's dead body. It played on a macabre loop. Then I heard a faint knock on my doorframe. Mrs. Stone was standing there, her face a mirror of the turmoil I felt inside.

"Mr. Trousdale," she said, "how are you holding up?" She lowered herself into the chair across from my desk, folding her hands in her lap. "I haven't been able to stop thinking about..."

I swallowed hard, the lump in my throat making it difficult to speak. "Me too. I keep seeing her. Hearing her singing. Clear as day. I didn't know Lillian Trent at all, and yet...I loved her. Does that make any sense?"

Mrs. Stone nodded, tears pooling but not falling.

"The police questioned me again yesterday," I said. "I had to repeat everything—how I'd gone backstage to meet Lillian Trent. How her dressing-room door was slightly open. How I'd called out her name. I'd discovered her sitting in front of the mirror, and I thought she was just resting after the show. I told them it probably wasn't a robbery because her brooch was still pinned to her lapel. Her scarf was missing, but they agreed it was probably the murder weapon and had been taken to remove evidence."

We sat in silence for a while, the air heavy with grief and the unspoken acknowledgment that once you see something like a dead body, it doesn't let you go.

"I want to feel normal again," said Mrs. Stone, her voice small and exposed.

I met her gaze, finding a reflection of my own fears in her words. "I guess we have to find a new normal. We can't let this define us."

Mrs. Stone nodded, wiping away unshed tears. "You're a very wise young man."

We sat for a moment longer, companions in sorrow. Then she stood up to leave. "Thank you for talking, Mr. Trousdale," she said. "It helps."

I forced a smile. "Of course. Any time."

Mrs. Stone walked down the hallway, shoulders tight with

the effort of holding herself upright. And then she stopped to talk to Mr. Slater. He opened his arms, and Mrs. Stone moved into them. They held each other for a moment in shared sorrow.

I looked away, feeling like I'd intruded on something private, and turned back to my computer screen. In the next moment, my email pinged. I'd wanted something to take my mind off the murder of Lillian Trent, and the Universe—ever literal and unhelpfully precise—delivered. It was a message from Ms. Klotz. Not exactly what I had in mind when I prayed for a distraction.

> Mr. Trousdale,
> You'll find many unsorted documents in the *Miscellaneous* folder of the shared drive. Please complete the following tasks:
> Sort all files into the appropriate departmental folders.
> Rename each file according to the foundation's standard naming convention.
> Convert any scanned or image-based documents into searchable PDFs.
> Verify the accuracy, consistency, and usability of each file once processed.
> For this project only, I've given you temporary access to the *Grants* folder. Please use it responsibly.
> Deadline: EOD Friday. 😊
> — Klotz
> cc: Staff

That last bit—verify the accuracy, consistency, and usability of each file once processed—was vague enough to cover anything she might later decide I'd done wrong. It was the kind of instruction that sounded reasonable until you realized it had no actual boundaries, meaning there was no version of this project she couldn't find a flaw to pounce on.

For all I knew, "accurate" could mean anything from "correct folder" to "personally resolving the Middle East peace process." Also, who ended an email assignment with a smirking emoji? That was just downright mean.

Okay. Maybe she didn't have an ulterior motive. Maybe it would be just a quick bit of housekeeping. I tried to convince myself it couldn't be too hard to sort through a few loose records and give them proper file names. Easy-breezy. I pictured myself finishing long before the Friday deadline and thumbing my nose at her.

That is...until I opened the *Miscellaneous* folder.

Mrs. Johnston had made a very big deal my first day about how some files were practically sacred religious scrolls—not to be opened without an advisor's approval. Ms. Klotz wasn't an advisor; she was a policy consultant. But she seemed to wield a lot of power in the office. And she'd told me in writing that I had access to the *Grants* folder. So really, this wasn't breaking a rule; it was following orders. Perfectly safe. Maybe a little gray area.

Besides, I wasn't working on the files. I was just, you know, dragging them into their rightful folders.

And the golden rule—the one I could not forget—was never to question Ms. Klotz. Not even with something innocent like clarification of an assignment. No. My job was to nod, smile, and dive into the shared drive like a digital Indiana Jones, giving searchable names to stray PDFs and praying I didn't unleash some booby trap that would set off alarms in the cave beneath Ravenscroft, where Ms. Klotz lay coiled in the dark, waiting to strike.

But this wasn't a neat little stack of orphans waiting to be adopted. This was the foundation's landfill. Miscellaneous, it turned out, was code for everything no one else ever wanted to deal with. Incomplete grant applications. Folders with names like *Stuff for Later*, *Ask Someone*, and *Fix*. It was a digital junk drawer.

Of course, I knew if I were too slow in completing this project, I'd be branded as lazy by Ms. Klotz. If I moved at my usual fast pace, I'd be accused of sloppy work. There was a ticking clock, and Ms. Klotz had a front-row seat with popcorn, waiting for me to screw up. In my head, she'd even brought some of those old-fashioned theater opera glasses so she wouldn't miss a single bead of my sweat.

The pressure landed. My chest tightened. I'd been pushing down a lot these past few days. Finding Lillian Trent murdered had never left my thoughts, and the police questioned me for hours because I was the one who found her body. And now the sting of Ms. Klotz's smirking emoji.

I started to cry.

Not the full-on sobbing kind—just the quiet, leaky kind that blurs your vision until the screen looks like a piece of modern art. For the first time since coming to the Adele Cummings Foundation, I did not like my job. Not one bit. My own future at the foundation probably rested on doing this project correctly. I could see my immediate future: working late every night, my eyeballs fused with the monitor, eventually disgraced for missing something critical and told to start exploring a career in car washing. I'd wished for a distraction from Lillian Trent, and I sure as heck got one.

Okay. Deep breath. I could hear my daddy's voice—calm and steady, the way it got when something broke at home and we couldn't afford to call anyone. "You just got to fix it, boy. Ain't no Superman flyin' in to save the day." I wiped my eyes, sat up straighter, and put my fingers back on the keyboard. If Ms. Klotz thought she could bury me under a mountain of miscellaneous, fine. Let her try. All I could do was the best I could do.

9

———

First step: don't panic. Second step: panic, but quietly, because everyone around here thought I was brilliant, and I had to keep faking it. I started poking around the files—clicking on things, not really knowing where to begin. And that was when the horror set in. I couldn't tell just by a document's name where it belonged without opening each one and reading the contents. Half the files had tags like *doc_final_FI-NAL_v2*. Or *Use This One Maybe*. Another was labeled in all caps —*DON'T DELETE*. I clicked on another one labeled *PRIORI-TIZE*, only to find it was created in 2007 and last modified in 2019 by someone named TempIntern47. So that file had been floating in *Miscellaneous* for years. A ghost nobody noticed.

I leaned back in my chair, rubbing my eyes as if that would somehow make the madness on the screen make sense. I was digging through layers of past interns' bad decisions, each one preserved like a fossil in a tar pit of neglect. Somewhere in here might be something important, but mostly it seemed like digital lint. Stuff that nobody in a million years would ever need.

Part of me wanted to believe Ms. Klotz had some grand, strategic reason for this project. Or maybe she wanted to see how I handled pressure. Who was I kidding? She'd given me this assignment for one reason only: she wanted me broken by EOD Friday. She wanted to see me buried alive under a digital avalanche, gasping for air while she sipped her latte and told Mrs. Johnston, "Mr. Trousdale isn't quite the right fit."

It was the kind of slow execution only an office veteran could design—death by *Miscellaneous*. My very first job in New York had been at that industrial waste management place, and their unofficial motto might as well have been "crush Timothy and recycle his tears." My boss there had weaponized nitpicking. Misplace a comma in a press release? She'd react as if I'd just rolled a leaking toxic waste barrel into Times Square during the Macy's Thanksgiving Day Parade. Forget to cc her on correspondence? She'd summon me into her office, keep the door open, and deliver a career obituary so grim I should have worn a black veil.

Ms. Klotz had that same evil glint in her eye—the one that said she didn't just dislike me; she wanted to hollow me out from the inside. In my mind's eye, I could see her in the front doorway of Ravenscroft as I left in shame, her arms folded, delivering some faux-sympathetic parting shot like, "It's not you, Timothy... Oh, wait, it absolutely is you." And now she'd handed me this project, her very own booby-trapped maze, designed with no exit and no chance of coming out alive.

The day seeped into evening. My back ached, my eyes burned, and I stopped checking my phone—except when Brad DM'd me. And I didn't want to cry to my boyfriend and risk having him think I was a weakling. But the work never seemed to shrink. If anything, it was multiplying—files within files within files, like Russian nesting dolls. Clicking one opened three more, each containing its own misfit offspring. It felt like I'd been tasked with alphabetizing the ocean while new waves kept rolling in, dumping fresh shipwrecks onto the shore.

It was a small office, so the advisors all knew Ms. Klotz had given me something awful, but they were all obsequious toadies around her. They didn't seem to want to interfere with her plans to destroy me. So their reactions to my plight ranged from quiet sympathy to small acts of kindness.

"You've got this," said Mr. Slater, poking his head into my office and offering a weak smile.

Ms. Neely brought me a protein bar and whispered, "Something to keep your energy up—and your head down."

Mrs. Raymond said, "Hang in there, Mr. Trousdale. She eventually gets bored tearing the wings off flies and freezing goldfish in ice-cube trays."

I knew if I was going to figure this out, I needed a system. So I opened a blank spreadsheet and entered every foundation department name and subfolder I could find: *Grants & Philanthropy, Events & Development, Artist Fellowships & Residencies, Legacy & Heritage Preservation*, and *Emerging Leaders Program*. It was like drawing myself a treasure map, except the treasure was...organization.

Some files were slippery little suckers that could fit in more than one department. I gave them a color code in the file name. Like a digital Marie Kondo, I made three holding folders on my desktop:

Keepers – No-brainers that clearly belonged somewhere specific: invoices, contracts, correspondence.

Floaters – Could go in more than one place: draft press releases, budget spreadsheets, minutes from meetings.

Headaches – Files so mysterious they might as well have been written in cuneiform.

I dragged every folder and file in *Miscellaneous* into one of these folders before trying to figure out where to move them to their final home. Once I'd corralled everything, I renamed each file to the foundation's sacred naming convention—year_month_project_name_version—and converted any scanned images into searchable PDFs.

It actually seemed to be working. The *Miscellaneous* folder was shrinking. I could practically hear the *Rocky* theme music playing in my head.

It was sometime late Thursday evening, and I was running on fumes. My eyes burned from staring at the screen all day, my shoulders ached from hunching over, and I was dying to leave the office, catch the bus, and crash onto my pillow. The deadline was looming—end of day tomorrow—and while I still had a ton of *Miscellaneous* to sort through, I was feeling slightly confident that I could pull this off and be done on time. I was such an optimist!

I was clicking through the digital clutter—one meaningless file after another—when something broke the monotony. A folder named *Restricted_TrentLillian*. It was buried three levels deep inside *Finance_ExpenseReports_Q4_Drafts_Pending*.

TrentLillian. The name stopped me cold. *The* Lillian Trent. The dead singer whose murdered body I'd found at Manhattan Moon less than a week ago? It made sense that I'd find a file for Lillian Trent. She was a cabaret performer, and Mrs. Stone said the foundation scouted for talent. But why was her file stuck in *Miscellaneous*? Didn't it belong in *Grants*? I, Timothy Trousdale, might have saved the day by finding it!

My eyes were already burning from a day of digital spelunking, and my brain felt wrung out, so I should have just dragged it into the *Keepers* folder for later placement into a final folder. I should have ignored the temptation to review it.

Should have...

I clicked on the folder.

There were about a dozen files in there. One was a black-and-white publicity photo of a smiling Lillian, mid-song, her eyes alive with the spark she had onstage. I felt a pang of sadness for the entertainment world's loss. Another file was titled *Grant Proposal*. There I found the standard mix of paperwork an applicant was expected to provide: a cover letter, an artist's statement, and a multi-page proposal outlining her career plan. There was a budget sheet with line items for rehearsal space, accompanist fees, costumes, and publicity by Halcyon Strategies PR, a performer's résumé and bio, letters of support from other singers and musicians, and even a video file titled *Demo*. I then clicked the file labeled *Grant Award Notification*.

There it was! The letter informing Lillian Trent that she was being awarded $500,000. She must have fainted when she received it! There was also a signed NDA and an invoice from Titan Shield International—a private investigation firm.

It was heartbreaking that Lillian hadn't lived to receive her grant money. It could have changed everything for her. She could've recorded a CD, maybe even made a music video. It might have been her big break.

I blinked at the screen, my tired brain trying to reconcile why the Lillian Trent file was buried there in a digital *Miscellaneous* graveyard of things no one wanted to deal with. I could only think it was a slip of the mouse; someone had accidentally dragged it there instead of the *Grants* folder.

The nondisclosure agreement seemed a curious thing too. I knew NDAs were common in the entertainment world—I'd signed one myself when I went to work for Mercedes Ford. Celebrities use them to protect projects, collaborations, and sometimes just contain gossip. But why, I wondered, would a singer getting a prestigious arts grant need an NDA? That seemed weird.

Charities usually like it when the recipients of their largess crow about their generosity. Charitable foundations love press release announcements and photo ops of the happy grant recipient holding a giant novelty check. This NDA seemed like a sort of gag order. It didn't just cover the amount Lillian received in her grant—it covered the very existence of the grant. My stomach did that little cold drop thing it does when a subway car jerks too hard. It seemed the foundation didn't want anyone to know about the award. Not the press. Not other grant recipients.

Confidential Engagement: Adele Cummings Foundation Artist Outreach Special Disbursement

1. The Recipient shall not disclose, directly or indirectly, any information regarding the disbursement amount, payment schedule, source of funds, or any related agreements or communications with the Foundation.
2. The Recipient shall not publicly discuss, publish, or otherwise disseminate the fact of this disbursement, nor the identity of any parties involved, without prior written consent from the Foundation.
3. This Agreement is perpetual and shall survive the Recipient's lifetime.
4. The Recipient acknowledges that any breach will cause irreparable harm to the Foundation and agrees that the Foundation shall be entitled to injunctive relief and all other remedies available under law, without the necessity of proving actual damages.

10

The foundation's offices had long gone quiet and I could almost hear the ghosts checking their watches. Not a soul in sight. Just me, locking up like I was the night janitor. The oil portraits on the walls had that "we know what you're thinking" glare in their eyes. The longer I thought about it, the more the shadows seemed to be alive. My eyes had been sandblasted by PDFs, and my brain was like mud. But there was this tiny smug part of me thinking I just might pull this project off. I'd worked hard the past four days, and I thought, with a little luck, I could actually meet my Friday deadline. That would show *Klotzilla*!

I turned off my computer. Grabbed my rucksack and switched off the lights. At the front door, I set the building's security alarm and stepped outside, where the city was doing its usual restless nightly ritual thing: buses growling by like prehistoric beasts, steam curling from manhole covers in lazy puffs, sirens in the distance. Normally, I found it all exhilarating in a New York–postcard sort of way. But tonight? Oh, man, tonight I was way too exhausted to pay much attention to anything but my desperate need for my pillow and security blanket.

But of course, I was never too tired to talk to Brad. And as I walked to my bus stop, he called. I picked up on the second ring.

"Hey, trouble," he said, his voice doing that warm, melty thing that made the fun part of my anatomy wake up despite the rest of me being practically six feet under.

"Trouble?" I snickered.

"When I see you tomorrow night, you're going to be called a lot of things like that. Some of them...maybe not very polite."

And just like that, four days' worth of stress over Ms. Klotz's booby-trapped project evaporated—like Brad had reached through the phone, plucked the anxiety out of my body, and replaced it with distracting mental images that should come with a *Not Suitable for Minors* warning.

"Promises, promises." I smiled and took a deep breath. "It's been a killer week. My project deadline is the end of the day tomorrow. If I finish on time, we'll celebrate. If I screw it up and get sacked, you'll have to talk me off the roof."

"Either way, I'll be there for you. Lots of comfort."

"What kind of comfort?"

"The kind that lasts twenty-four hours and leaves you physically unable to walk."

I laughed, partly because it was ridiculous, and partly because I was already picturing it. "And what exactly happens during those twenty-four hours?"

"You're the writer. Use your imagination."

I could only titter as we slipped into our nightly song and dance: *What'd you do today? Anything fun? Talk to anyone interesting?* We cooed over each other's activities and circled back to our plans for Friday night. We'd have dinner at our favorite Italian restaurant, and then I'd sleep over at his place. (Well, there wouldn't be much sleeping.) Tonight, there was a little extra heat in our words. I told him I missed him like oxygen. He told me to keep talking like that, and I'd find him waiting at my apartment door by the time I got home.

"Promises, promises," I said again. (I tend to repeat myself. Especially when I'm tired. Or nervous.) In that fraction of a moment before Brad could comment, I said, "Hey, random question? Is there a way to tell who last moved a file in a shared drive?"

There was a beat of silence. "Like a computer network shared drive? Um...yeah...probably. I think you can usually see the file history, like timestamps and even the name of whoever worked on it. Why?"

"No reason. This project I'm working on? There's a file that was maybe accidentally placed in another file, and I wonder who put it there. That's all." I dodged, the words wrapped in a little laugh so he'd think I was just teasing.

"Mm-hm," Brad replied. "Sure it was an accident?"

I blinked, caught off guard. I hadn't even considered it might not be an accident. "Well, I mean...people drag and drop things all the time. Half the folders in that drive look like a game of musical chairs."

And then my bus lumbered up, brakes hissing. Our "goodnights" lingered until I took my seat. After that, the rest of the ride home was a blur—with the scent of diesel and hot brakes, the glow of passing streetlights, and my own stupid love grin reflected to me in the bus window.

I barely remembered getting home. Then bam—it was Friday morning. My deadline breathing down my neck. I boarded the bus again.

By the time I got to my desk, *Klotzergiest* was already in position—coffee mug in one hand and a look of amused malice on her face. She looked up when I passed by her open door, eyes locking on mine just long enough to express, *Oh, look. The condemned man shows up for work.* I could practically hear her thoughts: *There's no way you'll finish by five. You'll flail, you'll drown, and I'll be there to throw you an anchor, applauding as your career-shaped bubbles rise to the surface.*

I gave her my most confident "I've totally got this" thumbs-up. On the outside, I was calm. On the inside, I was a snowman in a sauna.

I was back in front of my screen, facing the *Miscellaneous* folder —my own personal circle of hell. I'd been at this for days—sorting, renaming, dragging, dropping. I optimistically thought I might finish before lunch. Then at 11:45, I opened a subfolder and found something that didn't belong there. How the hell did I miss that the first time around, for crying out loud?! Then, at 2:15, I discovered another folder filled with duplicates of another file. Every time I double-checked my work, I found something else wrong. It was as if Ms. Klotz had designed this structure specifically to test my sanity.

By four o'clock, my computer desktop still had a few files that hadn't found their correct home folders: *Final_Budget_-Draft_v3* or *Q4_Notes* (could belong in *Finance*, *Planning*, or random meeting notes), *Press_Releases_2010s*, *Archive_Comms* or *PR_History* (could go in *Public Relations*, *Media*, or a general *Archive* folder), *Security_FYI_Admin_Memo_ Update* (could fit under *HR*, *Operations*, or *IT*). Each was a fragile tower in my digital Jenga game.

I clicked into one, found something that clearly belonged somewhere else, dragged it out—and the screen froze.

Nothing moved. The cursor blinked. Then stopped blinking.

My heart kicked. I clicked again. Nothing. I stared at the monitor, suddenly certain I'd pressed the wrong key, logged myself out, or somehow triggered a security lockdown that would require three approvals and a conversation about my *competence*. I could already picture it: me explaining, that yes, I'd *almost* finished organizing the files right before the system crashed, and yes, I suppose that did sound suspicious.

In that suspended moment, my mind leapt ahead—again— to life without this job. That I'd been briefly mistaken for someone capable.

Then, mercifully, the screen refreshed.

Everything reappeared exactly where it had been, my files still wobbling in place. I exhaled, clicked more carefully, and reminded myself not to touch *anything* unless I was absolutely sure where it belonged—which, unfortunately, I rarely was.

The clock in the corner of my screen kept blinking like it knew I had to hurry. Every so often, I'd glance up and catch *Klotz Kong* walking past my office doorway, not looking directly at me but definitely thinking (I could tell), *He's cooked.*

My eyes burned. My wrist ached. My mouse hand had gone numb. But the *Miscellaneous* folder was almost empty!

4:52 p.m. One last sweep. I moved the previous stray file into its proper home, then clicked out of *Miscellaneous.*

4:55 p.m. I made a zip file of the whole thing, slapped on a simple name, and uploaded it to a blank email.

Subject: Organized Miscellaneous Folder—Project Completed

Ms. Klotz,

As requested, the *Miscellaneous* folder has been fully reorganized and labeled, and I've uploaded the final version to the shared drive.

The file is named *KlotzProject_Organized_FINAL.*

Please note that this project was completed before the Friday evening deadline, and I trust it meets all your requirements and expectations.

Wishing you a pleasant weekend.

Best regards,

Mr. Trousdale

cc: Office Staff

Done.

Somewhere, in her lair, Ms. Klotz's computer pinged. And

for one glorious second, I hoped the shock would make her choke on a USB stick.

At 5:02 p.m., just as I was slinging my rucksack over my shoulder—deadline nailed, *Klotzarella* temporarily stuffed in my mental spam folder, and my weekend with Brad stretching ahead—my desk phone rang. Mrs. Johnston's extension.

"Mr. Trousdale, before you head out, do you have time to pop by?" Her tone was warm. Not a chilly "We need to talk." So I went without fear.

Mrs. Johnston's office always reminded me of some rich grandmother's sitting room I'd seen in an old movie—if the grandmother had been a corporate concierge with impeccable taste. High ceilings, crown molding, and an Oriental rug hinted at the office's former glory, undoubtedly very posh twenty-five years ago when the foundation was established.

Mrs. Johnston stood as I came in. "You did it!" she said. "I'm quite proud of you, Mr. Trousdale. I knew if anyone could meet that deadline, you could." She lowered her voice a notch, conspiratorial. "Frankly, we all know Ms. Klotz cooked up that assignment just to watch you sweat—and fail. The fact that you not only finished it, but on time too... That's going to ruffle her feathers all weekend."

I gave a modest shrug. "By Monday, she'll have a thirty-point list of my crimes against file folder structure."

Before she could reply, Mr. Slater appeared in the doorway, grinning. "Mr. Trousdale, you're a legend. I don't impress easily, but that was a master class in keeping your cool under pressure. Congrats."

"Seriously," added Mrs. Raymond, leaning in behind him. "I was supposed to leave an hour ago, but I had to stay and watch you win. As I knew you would."

Within seconds, I had a full-blown peanut gallery—handshakes, pats on the back. I knew at least half their enthusiasm came from watching Ms. Klotz's little trap snap shut on nothing.

But that was fine. Victory was victory. I laughed, feeling my cheeks heat, and mumbled something about "enjoying a challenge."

As the little crowd began to drift away, heading out for their weekend, the air still buzzing with their good wishes, Mrs. Johnston said, "I won't keep you, Mr. Trousdale. I just wanted to commend you on a job well done. And it's probably best to leave quickly before Ms. Klotz has a chance to take a look at your work and think up some other torture for you."

We both chuckled in agreement, and I should've just left it at that and gone off to my dinner date. But Lillian Trent was never far from my thoughts these days, and before I could stop myself, I asked—trying to sound casual, "Does it ever happen that someone gets approved for a grant but dies before they can collect it?" I gave a small shrug. "There was a file for a grant for Lillian Trent in the wrong folder. I pulled it aside. There was an NDA in there, too, which seemed...unusual."

Mrs. Johnston's brows lifted, and for the briefest moment, the warmth in her face thinned. Then she smiled—calm, composed, the way a seasoned hostess might smooth a wrinkle in the tablecloth before guests notice.

"An NDA?" she echoed, tilting her head. "That doesn't sound like something we'd issue to a grant recipient. We want our winners to speak publicly, not stay quiet. Ms. Cummings insists on transparency—it's part of our ethos."

She paused, then added more gently, "Are you certain the file was for a confirmed grant? Lillian Trent's name has come through before—inquiries, letters of support—but to my knowledge, she was never formally awarded anything. You may have come across a draft file or internal notes. Sometimes people mistakenly create folders before a grant is even approved."

She gave a soft laugh, polished and warm. "The *Miscellaneous* folder can be a bit of a graveyard, Mr. Trousdale. Full of things that were never meant to go anywhere." Something in her tone was reassuring. But also...final. And for a moment, I found myself wondering if I had misread the file.

A pause—too short to be awkward, but long enough to notice. "In the future, if you see anything with legal instruments, park it in *Legal & Compliance Review* and cc me. I'll handle it."

Then, as if catching herself, she brightened again. "But really, Mr. Trousdale, you've earned a weekend off from thinking about work. Now, go and enjoy. And when you see Ms. Klotz on Monday, give her that happy smile of yours. Nothing will tick her off more than knowing you slept well."

11

Our favorite Italian place was Ragacci's in the West Village. Red-checkered tablecloths, Chianti bottles hanging from the ceiling, a menu longer than the *Old Testament*. Classico Italiano. Brad and I ordered a bottle of red with our entrées (lasagna for me, gnocchi Bolognese for Brad). Yum. But dessert was foremost on our minds. Oh, not the cannoli kind. (Whatever you're imagining is probably about right.) So, obviously, we were eager to dine, dash, and get to it.

Fast-forward to Saturday.

Our morning gymnastics gave way to Brad's kitchen Olympics. Yes, he cooked, too! He made French toast—shirtless. I admired his frame, which came not from the gym but simply from being young. The kind of body time loans you in your twenties, then snatches back with interest. I pinched a piece of egg-battered bread from the skillet, singed my fingertips, and grossly exaggerated the pain like I'd been mortally wounded—just so he'd kiss my fingers, which somehow led to my lips... which led to... Never mind.

By early afternoon, we were out of bed and strolling through Prospect Park. Brad tackled me onto the grass. We wrestled like kids, and he pinned me so fast I flashed back to high school gym class, the time I'd been unfairly pitted against Toby Moran, he of the Neanderthal Moran clan, dripping sweat that smelled disgustingly like boiled hot dog water. This time, with Brad, I didn't mind being humiliatingly overpowered. Even when a passing jogger muttered, "Get a room, guys."

That night, the wine was ample, shirts were forgotten on the floor, and we lounged on the sofa, Brad's laptop on a throw pillow between us, watching videos. One clip led to another until we were binge-watching everything from DIY kitchen hacks to singers butchering Broadway standards.

At some point, I tried to pull up a clip we'd laughed at earlier —a woman taking a vocal swing at "Defying Gravity" and slaughtering it all to hell—but I couldn't find it again. I wasn't all that tech savvy, so I scrolled aimlessly.

"Great. Swallowed into the algorithm's abyss. Now it's lost forever."

Brad leaned closer, squinting at the screen. "Maybe not. Everything leaves a trail if you know where to look."

"A trail?"

He shrugged. "Files don't really disappear. Every time one's opened or moved, it leaves a footprint in wet cement. You just need to know where the cement is."

Brad traced his fingers over the trackpad with the casual flair of a Gen Z-er who'd been born knowing keyboard shortcuts. "Every click leaves a receipt: time, title, the digital equivalent of a paper trail." He tapped a few keys. "Command plus Space opens Spotlight. Type Safari. Boom—browser history." He scrolled with muscle-memory efficiency; the list popped up. "And if it's a file, you just hit Get Info. Mac keeps timestamps on everything —when it was created, when it was last accessed. Basically, your computer is an elephant that never forgets."

And there it was—the overly enthusiastic woman still hilariously murdering "Defying Gravity."

"Receipts," Brad said.

I squinted at the screen. "Wait—you're telling me this was just...sitting there the whole time? I just had to know a few keystrokes?"

"Everything leaves a trace. Calls on your phone. Your Spotify playlist. Even your toothpaste splatter on my mirror. Systems track more than you think. What you open. What you search. Which files you moved. All of it leaves metadata breadcrumbs."

Then Brad snapped the laptop shut like he was slamming a gavel. "Speaking of breadcrumbs, I've got a whole loaf defying gravity."

We both smirked, and my excitement was deep, insistent, and very much not OSHA-compliant. And just like that, our bingeing tipped into something hungrier—that delirious rush of wanting and being wanted.

12

───────

Sunday morning, that cruel and unrepentant beast, arrived far too early. Brad kissed me goodbye at the door, off to catch the train to Connecticut for Sunday with his mother—a ritual born not of duty, but genuine affection. They were best buds. He promised to text from the train, and we agreed to see each other on Friday—though, honestly, my odds of surviving five Brad-less days were about the same as a house-plant under my care.

When the door clicked shut, the air in the apartment felt especially heavy. I lasted all of twelve seconds before climbing back into bed. The sheets still breathed Brad's scent. And as I lay there, thinking of his warmth, it hit me that I hadn't thought about work once all weekend. No Ms. Klotz and her insufferable assignment. Not even my odd interaction with Mrs. Johnston, or her strangely smooth dismissal when I asked about Lillian Trent's grant file.

She'd also flat-out said the foundation didn't use NDAs, and her reasoning made sense. The foundation wanted publicity. It was part of the whole image. But the way she said it felt like a pat on the head. *Move along, kid. Nothing to see here.* That stuck with me, because this was the same woman who told me on day one: "If I don't know where something is, it's either been misplaced or never existed."

Except—there *was* something to see. I'd seen it with my own baby blues. A grant file for Lillian Trent. An NDA on foundation letterhead. With Lillian Trent's autograph. Why would Mrs. Johnston have lied to me about that?

Or maybe Mrs. Johnston hadn't lied. After all, the foundation was a three-ring circus, and she couldn't possibly keep track of every trapeze act. Or maybe I'd misread the documents in my rush to get the project completed on time. Curiosity was rattling the lids and scattering the trash in my brain.

As I lay there thinking, inhaling Brad's pillow like it was scent-marking from a bear—I started to recall the computer tutorial he'd given me last night. Right-click. Activity log. Time-stamps. Usernames.

I remembered he'd said, "Every file leaves receipts."

I sat up. "Holy mother of metadata, Batman!" The foundation's shared drive maybe wasn't just a filing cabinet. It might be a diary. A tattletale. A gossip columnist in server form. Which meant I could probably find who the careless person was who dropped Lillian Trent's file in the wrong folder and maybe prove the NDA wasn't just my imagination. I just had to tap a few keystrokes on the computer, and...

Voila! Easy-breezy. I could even do it today. Sunday. And Ravenscroft would be as quiet as a crypt. I preferred sleuthing over my usual weekend chores anyway. Laundry would always be there.

If anyone discovered I'd been in the office, I had the perfect alibi, too. I was double-checking a couple of details in the report I'd given Ms. Klotz. That was the kind of thing any honorable, highly neurotic intern would do. And if I were caught, they'd clap me on the back and say, "Way to go, Mr. Diligent!"

I glanced at the clock. Hopped in the shower and reluctantly washed Brad's "receipts" off my body. I dressed. Made the bed. Brushed my teeth, cleaning the mirror of any toothpaste splatter, as I was now paranoid about that, too! Then I grabbed the crosstown bus.

Ravenscroft's Beaux Arts façade didn't need medieval gargoyles to ward off evil. It had the modern equivalent: high-tech security cameras jutting from the facade like cyclopean eyeballs. Somewhere, in a fluorescent bunker with TV monitors, a bored pseudo-cop was probably sipping burnt coffee and watching me loiter like a nervous date who'd shown up too early.

I'd learned a thing or two about building surveillance back when I worked for Mercedes Ford and lived in her ultra-secure penthouse. That place had more hidden lenses than a casino in Vegas. If you picked your teeth in the lobby, you'd end up on someone's screen and being recorded in a ledger as *Dental Floss Guest #47: Lobby Cam 3*. Which was why, standing in front of Ravenscroft's wrought-iron doors, I did what any self-respecting, law-abiding intern would do before going into the office on a weekend when you weren't really supposed to be there: I smiled at the camera and gave a friendly little wave. Because nothing says "not breaking and entering" like a dorky Sunday-morning pageant wave, right?

I held my key card up to the camera as if to prove my honorable intentions, then tapped it on the security badge reader. For a breathless second, nothing happened. Then—beep—a tiny green light winked at me, and the lock clicked. I eased the door open, slipped inside, and froze, waiting for alarms to scream or red lights to flash. Nothing. Just silence. *Phew.*

The hush in the vestibule was heavy and a bit eerie, like the place had been holding its breath since I left Friday evening. As I made my way toward my office, my footsteps echoed on the parquet like I was in a museum after hours. Except there were no dinosaur bones or *Mona Lisa* here—just stormy landscapes and the foundation's "modern" acquisitions: canvases splattered with paint that looked, to me, less like high art and more like ketchup flung on a wall during an Oval Office tantrum. *Still Life with Big Mac and Impeachment.* Several bronze busts kept silent guard from their pedestals.

I stepped into my office and even though I was the only heartbeat in the building, I closed the door for privacy. I plopped into my chair and turned on my iMac. It blinked to life with its cheerful little chime. In the silence, it sounded about as subtle as a trumpet in a meditation class.

I logged in. Clicked on the shared drive. And scrolled to the *Grants* folder. I opened it, and there it was: *Restricted_ TrentLillian.* Just where I'd parked it. Yippee! I opened the folder and scrolled down. Yep, Lillian's publicity photos, bio, recommendation letters. They were all there. But something was missing.

I scrolled through it again. Um, where was Lillian's NDA? And what about the invoice for the private investigation services? That was weird. I'd absolutely, positively, definitely seen them in this folder. Or at least I was 90–99.9% sure I had! Or, damn, did I maybe accidentally drag them somewhere else? After all, I'd been wiped out by the end of the day on Friday, and what if *Klotz-o-Matic* discovered that I'd lost or misplaced those documents? She'd use my carelessness to prove her point about my ineptitude!

I sat there a moment longer, my iMac glowing in the dark like a smug little robot, stubbornly refusing to cough up the files I knew were supposed to be there. Brad's tutorial floated back to me in random fragments. But what exactly were his instructions for finding buried files? I didn't want to call him and interrupt his time with his mom on Sunday. But I also really needed to find those files. If only to prove to myself they actually existed. And if there were ever a perfect time to dig around where I shouldn't be digging, it was right now, on a Sunday, in an empty office.

Finally, I cracked. I texted Brad: *Have a minute?*

Brad's almost-instant reply was a thumbs-up emoji.

When I called, he seemed genuinely happy to hear my voice. I was definitely excited to hear his—partly because he had the kind of voice that made me feel everything was going to be okay, partly because it was just so damn seductive, and partly because I knew he'd have ideas to help me find those documents. I explained my problem, and he went right into tech-guru mode.

"First step—have you checked Trash? Sometimes files slip in there without you realizing."

I dragged the cursor toward the bottom right corner. "Okay. Wastebasket. Opening... Oh God. There's, like...thousands of things in here."

"Good sign," Brad said. "Look for anything that resembles what you're missing. The Trash is like a kitchen drawer full of batteries and rubber bands—you'd be amazed at what you'll find in there."

I scrolled. My eyes blurred. "I feel like I'm a ghost hunter. I don't see anything that looks right."

"Just take it slow. Look for anything familiar—a folder name, a file icon you recognize."

My eyes darted over dozens of random PDFs, screenshots, and docx files. "Nope. Hopeless."

"Not hopeless, just messy," he said. "Okay, if it's not in the Trash, we'll try..." Five minutes later, after a couple of other pointless actions, he was about to give up. Then he had a last-minute thought. "Do you have Time Machine running?"

"Time Machine running?"

"Apple's backup system," he explained. "It basically rewinds your computer, lets you see what a folder looked like days ago. You scroll back in time, watch your documents reappear."

Wow! Is that even possible? I sat up straighter. "Okay, Time Machine. But how do I—I've never—"

"Relax," he said, patient as a saint. I could practically hear the smile in his voice. "Open System Settings. There's an icon that looks like a clock with an arrow wrapped around it. That's Time Machine. Click on it."

"Clock with an arrow...clock with an arrow... Got it."

"If backups are running, you'll get this star-field screen, with your folders stretching back into infinity. Very *Doctor Who*. From there, you can move back day by day, see what was in your Documents or Desktop."

I clicked on Time Machine as carefully as if it were a detonator. There was silence on the phone as I squinted at the screen. Then I nearly shouted, "I think it is running. There's a green icon. A little clock with an arrow around it. It says, 'Backups available.'"

Brad's laugh was warm. "Well, look at you, Mr. Keyboard Cowboy."

On my screen, files stretched away into infinity like a hall of mirrors. "Oh my God. It's like being abducted by aliens."

"Okay, on the right-hand side of the screen, you'll see arrows and a timeline. That's your control panel. Use the arrows to step backward day by day."

I fumbled with the mouse, the windows sliding backward in a dizzying cascade. "It's...whoa. It's like rewinding reality."

"Exactly," Brad said. "Now, navigate to the folder where your files should be. Don't worry about what's there now—look for what was there yesterday or the day before. Every time you go back a step, the computer shows you what that folder looked like then."

I clicked, heart hammering. Folders opened and closed as though I were leafing through the pages of my own past. "Brad... wait. I think... I think I see them."

"That's the idea," he said. "When you spot the missing files, select them and hit Restore. The computer will drop them back into place, right where they were the other day."

I held my breath, moved the cursor, and clicked. The files shimmered into existence on my desktop, as if they'd only been playing a long, elaborate game of hide-and-seek.

"Oh my God. They're back. Brad, they're actually back."

"You did it! Now breathe," he said. "Time travel is real."

I grinned at the phone, slipped into that crime-scene-investigator voice I'd heard Ted Danson use on *CSI: Cyber*. I parroted my boyfriend, repeating that files don't just pack their bags and shuffle off to Buffalo on their own; someone has to move them.

"Computers look innocent," I reiterated, sounding like the know-it-all I was becoming, "but they're terrible at keeping secrets. They leave digital fingerprints—time stamps and user logs—all over the place. A few clicks here, a bit of scrolling there, and I'm the Sherlock Holmes of cyberspace. *Elementary*."

I could hear a chuckle in Brad's voice. "You're a smart guy, Timothy. You can do this. I believe in you."

If only I could match his confidence! Brad was going into lunch with his mother, so we hung up, and I set to work on my own.

I clicked on the NDA file I'd rediscovered. Now came the tricky part—remembering Brad's instructions for getting the metadata. I right-clicked, and a menu bloomed onto the screen. *Aren't I smart?*

Next step: Get Info. A new window sprang up, spooling out a

column of details. I squinted at the fine print until my eyes landed on those magical words: Last Modified By.

Woo-hoo! In this case, Last Modified By was followed by a name that wasn't mine: RMorris. That was a relief! Sort of. It meant I hadn't accidentally dragged the NDA from Lillian Trent's file to this folder. But who the heck was RMorris? It didn't ring a bell.

I grimaced. The name sat on the screen, daring me to make sense of it. It wasn't someone from the foundation staff—at least not anyone I'd met or heard of. And I didn't think the Adele Cummings Foundation had a satellite office somewhere with other employees.

I leaned back in my chair, my facial muscles morphing into something wary. Whoever this RMorris person was, they'd had their hands in the foundation's digital cookie jar on August 28. Yesterday. Saturday. When the offices were *closed*. Which meant maybe they were with IT. The tech wizards behind the company's computers. But IT wouldn't mess with the foundation's files. So now, instead of just one mystery, I had two: who the heck was RMorris? And why did they move Lillian Trent's grant folder?

To find the who, I pulled up the foundation's staff directory. Maybe I hadn't met RMorris because they worked remotely. If they were an employee, they'd be listed somewhere in the alphabet soup of the foundation's staff or vendors. I was momentarily hopeful when I came across the name Robert Morrison. Right initials, but a reference note said he was the contact at *Oops-a-Daisy!*, a floral shop in New Jersey. And I was a million percent sure *Oops-a-Daisy!* wouldn't have access to the foundation's computer files.

I tore through the staff directory, consultants' index, and even RSVP spreadsheets from past galas. Nothing. No RMorris. Until...finally, I dropped the name into the email contacts search bar.

Bam! *Rachel.Morris@mymail.com!* I drummed my fingers on

the desk. "All right, Rachel Morris at My mail dot com, who the hell are you?"

I went back to the staff directory, then to the community outreach mailing list, even the past events sign-in sheets—click after click, like turning over stones and not even finding any worms. I was about to give up when my eyes caught a folder I hadn't noticed before because I hadn't had to drag anything into it: *Grants Denied*. I clicked on it. Therein was a subfolder labeled *Performers_Jazz_Cabaret*. My pulse quickened. I clicked again and...buried deep in that list was a file labeled *Morris_Rachel_X*.

Bingo!

But *Grants Denied*? Rachel Morris apparently was one of the thousands of people aiming to get their mitts on some of Adele Cummings's fortune but failing to do so. And I wondered why, with all Adele's billions, she couldn't just throw a little scratch to every artist who applied for a grant. I mean, what was the big deal for someone so rich? And wasn't art supposed to be subjective? Maybe not. Maybe what they really meant was that *taste* is subjective. Jerry Herman versus Stephen Sondheim. Picasso versus Norman Rockwell. Doris Day versus Dua Lipa. You can argue all day over taste preferences—you won't get anywhere.

I opened the file expecting... I didn't know what I was expecting exactly. Rachel Morris's grant application was there. She was a singer. There was one glowing testimonial letter that read like a love sonnet. That in itself seemed odd, because from my limited experience at the foundation, I knew that most applications were accompanied by multiple letters of commendation, usually from prominent people in the category in which the applicant qualified.

Oddly—and I'd never seen this before—there was a rebuttal letter to that one testimonial:

Ms. Morris has cultivated a reputation as a cabaret performer, but her capacities are overstated. While not

untalented, her abilities do not match the scale of her ambition. I have witnessed performances in which her range faltered, her timing slipped, and her interpretations leaned more on bravado than subtext. Perhaps the committee should distinguish between self-aggrandizement and true artistry before advancing her grant candidacy.
—Anonymous

Anonymous? Yikes. Who takes the time to trash someone in writing but doesn't sign their name? Maybe another singer with too much envy and not enough gigs. Or perhaps it was an ex, a roommate, or someone she'd double-crossed. The sort of troll who wanted to stick the knife in but not get caught holding the handle. Or perhaps someone playing puppet-master, trying to nudge the advisory board into a decision without leaving fingerprints.

There was another file in Rachel's folder titled *Committee Notes*. It contained a letter addressed to the foundation and signed by Rachel Morris herself. If you asked me, the language was pretty unsportsmanlike. But what stopped me cold was this: the letter wasn't just about Rachel herself. It was almost as much about my new favorite but now murdered singer, Lillian Trent.

To the Adele Cummings Foundation Grants Committee,
By not awarding a grant to me, you prove, once again,
that the Adele Cummings Foundation rewards the showy
over those who've suffered for their art. Or is it retaliation
because I earn my bread and butter at an office desk? I
have spent years of sacrifice and humiliation, while you
hand a half-million bucks to Lillian Trent just because
she bats her lashes and belts out a tune. Spare me.
Don't delude yourselves. You mistake Lillian Trent's
attractive appearance for star quality and her voice for

talent. I can no longer stand by quietly while you reward mediocrity at my expense. You'll regret giving a grant to her rather than to me. You won't be able to parade her around like a prize pony. Don't forget, I know things.

—Rachel Morris

Talk about sour grapes! (Although, to her credit, at least it wasn't anonymous.) Rachel Morris's letter was filled with so much bitterness along with what sounded pretty much like a thinly veiled threat. I wondered if blame and resentment were a common thread among those in the arts who didn't get what they thought was rightfully theirs.

And how did Rachel Morris even know that Lillian Trent was getting a grant—and the amount? As far as I knew, there was never an official announcement. At least not while I'd worked here. And per her NDA, Lillian was forbidden from talking about it.

I was eager to see for myself what Rachel Morris's own talent was like. So I clicked the file labeled *Performance Sample*, which was part of the supporting material required for all applications.

I could tell right away that an amateur recorded the video. Probably someone with an iPhone. The picture wobbled, the colors were flat, and the audio had the tinny echo of a high school auditorium. The scene opened in a dreary nightclub, where the so-called "stage" was little more than a space cleared of chairs. A black baby grand piano hogged most of the area, leaving little room for the performer. A handful of tables were scattered through the shadows, most of them empty, their few occupants slouched in silence. Then, through muffled speakers, a monotone voice that sounded bored and indifferent said, "The Purple Parrot welcomes Rachel Morris."

The pianist, bless him, gamely hammered away at "A Cock-Eyed Optimist" as a young couple at one table leaned over their drinks, clearly not ready to abandon the conversation they were having.

What made the performance especially heartbreaking was that Rachel obviously thought she was terrific.

She wasn't.

I wondered what made people like Rachel keep chasing a dream, even when talent just wasn't there. Maybe it was about a needy space inside, carved out by years of wanting to prove to the world that they're special. Perhaps it was also the myth we all buy into—that persistence beats talent, that if you believe in yourself and grind away long enough, the fairy godmother of show business will finally tap you with her magic wand. Or maybe it was the applause itself—however small the crowd, a little clapping can feel like oxygen, proof you exist. And of course, giving up meant admitting it would never happen, which was harder than dragging yourself back onstage one more time.

I actually knew that feeling. No one in my family ever told me I was special or encouraged my ambition to be a writer. Their indifference had trained me to keep my dreams folded up, like scraps of paper hidden in a drawer—safe, but unseen.

Watching Rachel now, her arms outstretched, practically begging the room to love her, a chill crept over me. What if I weren't any different? What if I were just as deluded, believing in a talent I didn't have? Oh, God—what if I were the literary equivalent of Rachel Morris? The thought petrified me.

At the end of a dozen songs and a handful of silly anecdotes and attempted jokes about her life and career—one involving a disastrous audition where she claimed she'd been so nervous she'd spilled her *cawfee*, forgotten her lines, and asked the casting director for *waw-duh* while trying to *tawk* her way out of it, all before ordering an "expresso" she swore she didn't even want—the polite applause sounded more like *Thank heavens it's over* rather than *Encore!*

And that sorta broke my heart a little more for her. Because actually, Rachel Morris wasn't really all that bad. She was adequate. She could definitely carry a tune. Heck, I had to admire her courage, standing there doing what most of us wouldn't dare in a million years. I absolutely couldn't do what she did. But then I'm not a singer. Sadly, Rachel wasn't either. But she didn't know it.

And that, I realized, was why the Adele Cummings Foundation had turned down her grant request. They didn't hand out tens of thousands of dollars to unremarkable people.

The video ended, and I couldn't help comparing Rachel Morris to Lillian Trent. I'd never heard a voice like Lillian's. It wasn't just the music—lots of people could hit those notes—it was the way she poured herself into every lyric, like the song had been waiting all its life for her to sing it.

Rachel, on the other hand, for all her enthusiasm, was—colorless.

She was an enigma, too, because I still didn't really know who she was or how and why her login credentials were on the grant file. The question gnawed at me, a dull ache that wouldn't let go. And maybe that was why I suddenly wanted to do something mindless, something mechanical—just to quiet the noise in my head. I left the office, telling myself I really had to do a load of laundry.

14

Laundromats are like purgatory with fluorescent lighting. I sat in a cracked plastic chair, watching my socks tumble in slow motion and trying not to expire from tedium. A guy in a grease-stained hoodie paced between machines, muttering to himself. A cement-mixer-built woman with stringy, lime-green neon hair and clumpy eyeliner folded a pile of muumuus, her eyes darting toward me every now and again as if she suspected I was trying to steal her dryer heat. A teenager slumped against the wall, scrolling his phone, giving off a faint, undefined sense of menace. The washers hummed, the dryers clanged, and the air smelled of detergent mixed with these people's misery. I made a mental note to remember this scene for one of my future novels.

My head kept circling back to two things: Rachel Morris with her grudge against the foundation. And Lillian Trent, the songbird who, until her murder last week, had been ascending the showbiz ladder. What was their common denominator? Their connection? Other than being performers. I kept chasing that question until the obvious finally glared at me like a neon OPEN sign in the window of a closed diner. Their parallel was the foundation, of course. It touched both women's lives—Rachel, on the outside, clawing to get her hands on some grant dough, and Lillian, on the inside, apparently reaping the benefits of the foundation's generosity.

The buzzer on the dryer snapped me back to reality and forced another question: Why was I even wasting my already more than half-eaten-up Sunday thinking about anything that had to do with work—or murder? Nobody was paying me overtime, for crying out loud. My daddy had a saying about that: "Don't be mendin' fences that ain't broke just 'cause you like to use the hammer." He was usually right about philosophical things. I hadn't been asked to go poking around in the foundation's business, and Lord knows it wasn't part of my job description. Maybe it was time to start thinking of something else.

Like—my novella. The one I'd recently said I'd be stupid to waste my energy on because finding an agent, publisher, and readers was nearly impossible. But Rachel Morris's cabaret video had wormed its way into my brain. Watching her performance didn't just make me sad; it made me want to avoid her fate. To prove I wasn't like her. That I wasn't going to be the novelist equivalent of a third-rate cabaret singer. That famous quote from Samuel Goldman popped into my head: "The harder I work, the luckier I get." With that in mind, I shoved my laundry into my gym bag and headed home, determined to get to work and edit a few chapters.

Monday morning came with a knot in my stomach the size of a watermelon. I was a hundred percent sure the *Klotzinator3000* had already found a million errors in the project I'd slaved over. Surely, she'd been sharpening her fangs all weekend and rehearsing the exact tone of withering contempt she'd use to destroy me—in an email, of course, because as you know, she never spoke directly to me. I'd started rehearsing my apologies, excuses, a humble plea for mercy.

I arrived at Ravenscroft and stopped in the break room for tea. Mrs. Johnston was also there. She looked over her readers and said, "You may be interested to know Ms. Klotz won't be in today. For two weeks."

Praise the Universe! Relief surged through me. I wanted to shout hallelujah and throw my arms around Mrs. Johnston, but I settled for a dignified, "Oh, that's good to know." Inside though? Fireworks. A marching band with majorettes twirling flaming batons and confetti raining down like New Year's Eve. Two weeks without *Klotztrocity!* Two weeks to breathe.

Two weeks to maybe even sneak back into the shared file and dig for more answers to my increasingly curious/nosy questions about Lillian Trent and Rachel Morris. It was glorious. It was liberating. It was—well, I should have known the feeling was too good to last long.

"Mr. Trousdale...?"

I looked over my shoulder to find Ms. Neely. "May I have a word, please? In my office."

She seemed a bit more distant than usual, and when we reached her office, she closed the door behind her.

"Mr. Trousdale, you know the rules. No one outside the grants advisory board team is to access files that may contain sensitive information about applicants."

Oh, damn! How the hell did she even find out I'd been in the *Grants* folder yesterday? Maybe security told her. Damn cameras! Or maybe Mrs. Johnston mentioned I'd seen a *Grants* folder and ratted on me. My brain went into a full panic spiral, and my mouth tried to keep up.

"I-I only...! I mean, Ms. Ms.-Klotz had me doing... I-I wasn't —I didn't mean—!" I sounded like some malfunctioning wind-up toy.

Ms. Neely squinted at me and made a face that said, *What*

the hell is this guy yammering about? "But you've proved yourself competent and discreet, so I'd like you to do a job that requires some confidentiality."

What? This wasn't about me rummaging through the *Grants* file? She was giving me a job that required someone dependable around sensitive materials?

Ms. Neely continued, "Mr. Trousdale, the foundation is producing a commemorative book to mark our upcoming thirtieth anniversary. It will highlight past grant recipients, major milestones, and our many successes in the arts community, world culture, and research. I need you to spend some time in our off-site storage facility, collecting old files and documentation."

A book? She wanted me to work on a book? My heart did a little somersault. Maybe all that grunt work I did for *Klotzquake* had paid off, making others see me as a dedicated employee who worked hard to get a tough job done. Here I was, being handed a project that would turn into an actual book. True, it wasn't exactly my own novel sitting on a Barnes & Noble "Staff's Picks" table. It would be more like a glossy brag-sheet for the foundation—but still. Ink on paper, pages bound together, something I could point to and say, *I helped make that.*

I could've kissed Ms. Neely for tossing me this assignment. She clearly considered it busywork, the sort of thing you delegate when you've got better things to do. But where she saw drudgery, I saw destiny.

"All of our files should have been digitized by now," she went on, "but we haven't gotten to the oldest ones yet. Here's a list of what I need you to find: original documents, photographs, and handwritten letters. Of course, we'll provide an expense account for transportation and lunch. Mrs. Johnston will arrange all that for you."

15

———

Buckled into the backseat of an Uber, I stared out the window at the city skyline, thinking how insanely lucky I was. Just six months earlier, I'd been stocking shelves at the Piggly Wiggly in Claberville, Alabama, saving every paycheck for my big move to New York City. And now I was livin' the dream—temping at the Adele Cummings Foundation. Sure, it was meager wages. Sure, my bank account had the life expectancy of a fruit fly. But this was a big opportunity—one I knew plenty of people in this city would kill for. I was on my way. *Life was sweet.*

The car joined a traffic jam through the Lincoln Tunnel, and an hour later we were on the main drag of Hoboken, New Jersey's less glamorous side. We arrived at Secure Storage—a run-down, windowless, five-story concrete structure behind a tall, barbed-wire fence. It screamed Soviet-Era tenement block.

Inside, the man at the desk ordered me to prove who I said I was. My Alabama driver's license alone didn't cut it. I tried to joke about offering a cavity search, but he blinked at me like he'd never heard of sarcasm. I finally gave him Ms. Neely's phone number, and she vouched for me with some security password she hadn't shared with me.

A clanky, slow-moving freight elevator drew me up to the third floor. The six-digit PIN Ms. Neely provided enabled access to the storage room, which stretched out like an industrial cathedral—high ceilings crisscrossed with exposed pipes and vents, concrete floors echoing with my every step, fluorescent lights buzzing faintly overhead. The air smelled of dust, paper, and something mildewy. Long rows of gray metal shelving four tiers high, stacked with identical bankers' boxes, marched away into the distance. It was quiet enough that I could hear the tick of the fluorescent ballast and the faint rasp of my own breathing. I felt like a visitor to a morgue.

Each box had a code stenciled on the side. *GP-01-05. BM-99. PR-CLP-03.* Luckily, Ms. Neely had given me a printout of which boxes contained the required documents. After a few hours of hauling boxes on and off the shelves and rooting inside for specific papers, I could feel the dust working its way into my skin. My hands were turning dry; the cardboard edges of the boxes left faint red scratches across my knuckles. My eyes itched, and my back ached. This, I decided, was why historians often looked so cranky in documentaries—chronic dust irritation.

I probably could have completed the assignment a lot faster, but the problem was that every time I opened a box, I ended up reading old memos, press releases, even thank-you notes Adele Cummings had received from the likes of Michelle Obama, Melinda Gates, and even Queen Elizabeth. (Pat on the back to Mr. Confidentiality here; I completely resisted taking pictures of anything.) I kept telling myself I'd just skim a page or two. But then I'd find some juicy line about an advisory board committee member storming out of a meeting or someone suggesting the foundation hire Barry Manilow to sing at a gala. Suddenly twenty minutes here and thirty minutes there had sucked away a lot of the day. It wasn't my fault I was constantly being interrupted by these fascinating footnotes to the foundation's history. It was thrilling to realize that I, Timothy Trousdale, was the only one on the planet who had access to this material at this very moment! I even found the foundation's original mission statement, written in Adele Cummings's very own handwriting. I was mesmerized. I loved her even more.

I sat on the squeaky metal folding chair, staring at her words. Here was a rich lady who didn't have to do anything more than sit on her can eating bonbons all day if that was what she wanted, but instead she'd used her wealth to improve the quality of life around the world. And God knows this dumpster fire of a planet definitely needed to hit the Refresh button.

After hours of digging through dozens of boxes, the afternoon was winding down, and I'd collected most of the items on Ms. Neely's list. I'd been so absorbed in my work (and several DMs from Brad) that I'd even forgotten to go out for lunch. So I figured I deserved to leave early. After all, I had to cross state lines to get home. And really, there were only a couple of items left to retrieve. I could stretch those out tomorrow and make it look like I was still chipping away at the assignment.

I shoved the files back into their boxes and wiped dust from my hands onto my jeans, already envisioning the long crawl back to Manhattan. I opened the Uber app on my phone and tapped in my destination. "No drivers in your area. Wait time approximately 1 hour 15 minutes." *One hour? Is my driver coming from Mongolia?*

Panic set in. I supposed I could take a bus. But that would take forever. And a taxi would cost a bloody fortune. I wasn't sure my Visa card could take the strain until I could be reimbursed by Mrs. Johnston. I was stranded. Marooned in the middle of New Jersey, inside a cavernous warehouse that seemed to grow colder and more unnerving by the minute. I was hungry. I hadn't even clocked a McDonald's in the area when we drove through this morning. An hour-plus to kill? What was I supposed to do? Gnaw on a file folder?

I slumped into the chair, phone limp in my hand. I guessed I could play sudoku. Or Wordle. With a groan, I turned back to Ms. Neely's list. I might as well dig up a few more documents while I waited. That would make me finish earlier tomorrow and give me a bit of downtime afterward.

The next item on the list was the minutes from the inaugural advisory board committee meeting on January 23, 2002. The very first meeting. My eyes searched the shelves for *AC-01-02*. I found it and lugged the box from the shelf onto the chair. I pulled off the lid and dug through a neatly stacked and labeled pile of manila folders until I found the one marked *Adele Cummings Foundation Minutes.*

Bingo!

I wondered what a charitable foundation advisory board committee talked about in its very first-ever meeting. Were they all high-fiving and toasting with champagne to the future of planet Earth and the human race? Did they sketch out grand visions? Scholarship funds for poor kids? Endowments for theaters and libraries, so Adele's name would shine on bronze plaques across the world?

I flipped the page and scanned the text. There was a lot of dry language that included words like "agenda" and "quorum," and "budgets." Someone with the initials L. J. proposed something. And someone else with the initials J. R. "seconded."

Yawn!

I was just about to close the folder and set it aside with the other collected materials when my eyes snagged on three words: *Suspected foul play.* It was attributed to someone in the meeting identified as G. S.

"The foundation will serve primarily to mitigate lingering negative perceptions associated with the unresolved investigation into the disappearance and perceived *death* of Mr. Charles Brandt."

What the heck? And who's Charles Brandt?

Of course, I had to read further. Someone with the initials D. K. said, *"PR experts at Halcyon Strategies will reframe Adele Cummings not as a subject of controversy, but as a patron of enduring cultural value."*

Controversy? My chest tightened, and the words blurred in front of me for a moment.

Someone else added, *"While the foundation's works will stand on its own merit, its greater purpose is to ensure that Ms. Cummings's public identity is no longer defined by the suspicious disappearance of her husband."*

My pulse quickened. And then, like static clearing on a radio, I sort of remembered something from ages ago. Vague news reports from throughout my childhood. Something about a very rich lady—married to a man who disappeared into thin air. It had all happened before I was born. But every so often when I was a kid, the story would reappear when someone thought they had new information about the case. I sort of recalled TV news anchors with grim baritones talking about the "years-long, on-going investigation," "unanswered questions," and "body never recovered…presumed dead." I'd never really paid much attention to the story and had filed it away in my head as tabloid myth.

I scanned the rest of the minutes from that meeting. They offered no more gossipy information and were pretty boring. I closed the folder and rooted further in the box. I withdrew a thick accordion file labeled *Press Archive—Charles Brandt Disappearance.* It was stuffed with newspaper clippings. I reached in and withdrew a handful.

The headline on the first one, dated April 1, 2000, screamed:

BILLIONAIRE'S HUSBAND VANISHES

The article recounted how Charles Brandt, husband of Adele Cummings, had failed to return to their cliffside villa on the Amalfi Coast in Italy after a walk one summer evening. Police, the reporter noted, had immediately turned their attention to Adele, who "could offer no satisfactory account of his whereabouts."

Beneath the headline was a grainy black-and-white photo of a twenty-something woman. It was captioned, "Adele Cummings —suspect." It was the first picture I'd ever seen of her. She wore a long, sleeveless summer dress and an oversized sun hat, her smile bright and untroubled, as though she were the most care-free woman in the world.

Beside her stood a model-handsome man about the same age. The caption read: "Husband missing since Sunday." Between them, each holding one of her small hands, was a child: "Five-year-old Helena Brandt." The little girl looked nothing like the radiant parents flanking her. While they beamed with effortless charm, Helena stared at the camera with a sullen, distrustful expression, her mouth drawn tight, her features oddly severe. She wasn't cute in the way newspapers like to portray missing persons' children. Unsmiling. Unposed. As if she already knew something neither of her parents wanted printed beneath a headline.

I had no idea that Adele Cummings had had a child. Of course, I could think of a dozen good reasons why an insanely rich person would want to keep their child's identity private: the possibilities of kidnapping, blackmail, stalkers, exploitative media, etc. Yes, it was best to hide her name. Protect her from the kind of attention that turns children into headlines.

Another clipping:

POLICE SEARCH CHATEAU — NO BODY FOUND

This one described a full-scale sweep of Adele Cummings's

sprawling estate in Burgundy, France. I wondered why, if the guy went missing in Italy, did they think he'd be in France. I supposed beyond-rich people could find ways of secretly transporting dead bodies from one country to another. Helicopters, cadaver dogs, and divers in their private lake had all come up empty. Detectives, the article said, had carted away boxes of financial records and personal papers, but "no evidence of foul play" was made public.

And another headline really shocked me:

ADELE CUMMINGS: PERSON OF INTEREST

In clipped language, the piece laid out a bunch of theories for Charles Brandt's disappearance. The most lurid of which was the "hidden body" theory. Investigators had found a sealed-off room in Adele Cummings's estate on Lake Como. The space had been walled over during a renovation. But that turned out to be prior to Adele owning the property. No human remains were recovered, and Adele was never officially charged with a crime. Yet sources admitted she remained "the sole person of interest."

I sifted through other clippings, all with similar headlines. One dismissed the investigation as a "witch hunt." Another accused the police of targeting Adele simply because she was one of the richest people in the world. One announced Adele's plans to fully sponsor a new performing arts center in London, which her critics derided as being a distraction from the scandal. This wasn't a tabloid fever dream from my childhood. This was real. A shocking story my generation had pretty much forgotten.

16

———

The Uber dropped me at my building, and I ducked into Abu's for a chicken shawarma wrap before trudging upstairs, bone-tired. Weirdly, when I finally hit the sack, I couldn't sleep. My eyes were closed, but I was still staring at images of what I'd seen in the foundation's old files. The headlines about Adele's husband vanishing. The photo of them looking so happy together with their daughter. The advisory board committee minutes that all but admitted the foundation had been dreamed up as a public relations effort for Adele's reputation-laundering. And of course, the speculation that Adele's husband might have been murdered—maybe by her hand.

I hated that there was any suspicion hanging over the great woman! Innocence—and surely, she was innocent—shouldn't need spin doctors. Innocence shouldn't need a foundation built like a marble shield against skeptics. Shouldn't the truth be enough?

Maybe not. Perhaps the headlines had poisoned the well, so to speak. Maybe once people suspect you of something, you can't simply stand there with empty hands and say *trust me.*

Maybe you need professionals to shout louder than the press. Maybe forming a charitable foundation was Adele's way of pushing back against a narrative she couldn't control.

I was sad. Sad that Adele had lost her husband in such a mysterious way, and when she was so young. I was still clinging to my devotion to her. But the press clippings rattled me. Phrases like *person of interest, unresolved investigation, no body found.* My sadness bled into doubt, then into fear. What if her husband hadn't vanished without help? What if the public speculation was right? What if Adele Cummings, my hero, the woman whose name was on all those generous grants, had had a hand in her husband's disappearance? Nope! Not possible.

Or was it?

I turned over and punched the pillow. Then another thought crept in. Even if she hadn't had anything to do with her husband's disappearance—even if she'd just been dragged through the scandal and bruised by suspicion—the foundation still wasn't born from pure generosity. It was strategy. A PR scheme to reframe Adele Cummings's public image. Who did that? Rich people, obviously. People who decided the answer to whispered accusations was to buy back their good name with malaria vaccines and water-purification plants.

And if the whole foundation thing had been conceived just to polish Adele's image—did that cheapen everything it did? The childhood immunization programs? Polio eradication campaigns? All the international humanitarian projects? I told myself the good stuff was still good stuff. Did the motive behind it matter? I hated that my faith in Adele, my starry-eyed belief that she was simply a wonderful human because she gave and gave, was cracking.

I was beginning to understand what people meant when they said *never meet your heroes.* I hadn't personally met Adele Cummings, but my work at the foundation put us at one degree of separation from each other. Heroes were supposed to inspire, not leave you wondering if they'd disappeared their husbands and bought their way back into society with scholarships and symphonies. I guessed maybe all philanthropy was a little self-serving. Maybe every hospital wing named after a billionaire was just another way of rewriting history.

Alas, the pedestal I'd set Adele Cummings on was tilting.

And even if she did have something to do with her husband's fate? Desperate people do desperate things in desperate marriages. I'd read enough true-crime novels to know that. Maybe she'd felt trapped (even though she had private jets and could escape to literally anywhere). Maybe he was cruel (even though she'd surely have security protection). Or maybe he turned out to be a fortune hunter. After all, he was merely a high school algebra teacher before they met. Maybe she just did what she felt she had to do to survive.

It wasn't fun to realize I'd been worshipping a woman who, for all her fortune and appearance of magnanimity, might not just be flawed, but—guilty. But guilty of what? Who knew? But I felt my adoration begin to curdle into something sour.

I got to the office early the next morning, set the files I'd collected on my desk, and fetched my tea. Killing time before Ms. Neely's arrival, I reread those early-days advisory board committee minutes again. Motions proposed and carried. Budgets debated and approved. The kind of administrative filler that could put an insomniac to sleep. But then my eyes snagged again on "Suspected foul play." And another word I hadn't been able to forget: *Halcyon.* Halcyon Strategies, as in the PR firm. *"Engage Halcyon Strategies to reframe public perception of Adele Cummings."*

Halcyon. I knew a lot of words, and for some reason that was one of my favorites. But it was one I'd never use in public. Not out loud anyway. Too pretentious, they'd say. Like I was trying to impress somebody. *I keep waiting for my* halcyon *days to arrive—the calm, golden ones I know are out there somewhere.* I had a whole lot of words like that in my head. Words I treasured but kept to myself. Words like *ephemeral. Resplendent. Ineffable.* All of them felt wonderful to write, but I'd be embarrassed if I ever let them slip past my lips in public. In Alabama, using words like those would've been head-scratchers and gotten me teased. In New York, they would just make me sound like a poseur (that was another word I kept to myself).

Which was why, staring at *Halcyon* now, slapped onto the name of a PR firm, it felt sort of weird. *Halcyon Strategies* sounded like a shadowy conglomerate in a soap opera, run by a dynasty of backstabbing heirs. A company that swallowed smaller companies whole while its CEO schemed over champagne and caviar in their mansion.

It wasn't a word I saw every day, but I knew I'd recently come across it a couple of times lately. Then it clicked—Lillian Trent's folder! I'd seen it when I was sorting through Ms. Klotz's project. *Halcyon Strategies.* Now, paired with these foundation minutes, it felt like a thread that needed tugging. I'd check it out. But first, I was excited to deliver to Ms. Neely the fruits of my labor in Hoboken.

At a bit past nine, I walked into Ms. Neely's office with my haul cradled in my arms. She looked up from her screen and smiled. "Excellent, Mr. Trousdale. This will help us keep momentum on the book project. It's going to be quite special."

I couldn't help grinning and feeling all useful and productive. I loved being part of a team and being seen as a valuable contributor. "I'm really excited to be part of this project, Ms. Neely. To think I'll have even a tiny role in helping tell the amazing story of the Adele Cummings Foundation... That's the kind of thing I'll brag about for years. Anything else you need, let me know."

I hesitated for a second, then pressed on. "Will there be much about Adele Cummings herself in the book? I mean, I know she's so private and all? And with good reason, I guess. Yesterday, while I was sorting through the boxes, I came across some old clippings. About...well, about Ms. Cummings's husband. The, uh, unsolved mystery of his disappearance...and her being a person of interest."

For the first time since I'd met Ms. Neely, I felt a chill radiate from her. She looked at me in such a way—her eyes weighing the words I'd just said.

There was a beat just long enough for me to realize I should have kept my big, fat trap shut. I hurried on. "It just—I mean it made me wonder... I mean, it must have been such a difficult time for her. I hope she's okay now. I know you can't get *over* those things, but maybe you get *through*..."

Then Ms. Neely said, lightly but with an unmistakable edge, "Mr. Trousdale, the foundation's rules—of which you've been made aware—apply as much to paper as to pixels. I guess you decided for yourself what else might be worth a peek. Some files are meant for particular eyes only."

She wasn't at all mean about it. But nevertheless, heat crept up my neck. She hadn't been unkind, but she'd said enough for me to realize I'd let her down. I mumbled something about being really and truly and awfully sorry for unintentionally crossing a line. Her eyes returned to her computer screen, and she tapped on her keyboard—my cue to leave.

Before I reached the door, she added, almost casually, "Mr. Trousdale—curiosity can be a fine trait in a writer. But you must be careful crossing boundaries set for you."

I managed a nod, my throat dry, and slinked out. Back at my desk, I replayed her words: *careful crossing boundaries set for you.* In other words: *You're nobody. Just a dumb intern. Fetch files. Don't ask questions. Be grateful we even let you through the door.* Even if that wasn't what she said—or even meant—that was what I heard.

I wanted to kick myself. Why had I even mentioned the newspaper clippings? Why couldn't I just hand over the documents, smile, and go on to the next task? I loved this job. I didn't want to jeopardize everything because of my stupid nosiness. I was here to be of service. Nothing more. If I wanted to stay in this job—and I did—I couldn't afford another slip.

What Ms. Neely had said kept circling in my head. But honestly—what was so wrong with me reading a few old newspaper clippings? I could've found the exact same stories in a Google search. It wasn't like I'd set out to dig up dirt on Adele Cummings.

But now...

It was a fact that Adele's husband had vanished. It was true that Adele had been considered a person of interest. And the advisory board committee minutes confirmed the foundation's plans for "reimagining her legacy" with the help of Halcyon Strategies.

It was sort of starting to feel very mysterious. Like the foundation wanted something hidden and buried. I totally understood wanting to put that whole unpleasant part of Adele's private life behind her, but was that the simple reason for Ms. Neely's reaction? Because from personal experience, it often seemed the harder someone tried to bury a thing, the bigger that thing probably was. Just look to the White House for examples.

Okay. From now on, I'd just blindly follow the rules and do as I was told.

As if I could!

17

———

I didn't have time to think about it much longer because in the next moment, Mr. Slater was in my doorway, holding his ubiquitous mug of coffee and being all tanned and avuncular. He was the sort of man who could talk you into doing just about anything without you realizing it. Not because he was manipulative—he was just incredibly sexy. And with me, apparently, that was sometimes enough to override common sense. "Mr. Trousdale," he said, voice calm and pleasant, "could I trouble you with a task—if you have the time?"

Wouldn't you love to work someplace where your boss made it sound like you had a choice in assignments? That was the thing about this office—it often felt like I was being *invited* rather than *directed*. And with Mr. Slater, it didn't seem passive-aggressive. Still, I was paid to do whatever I was told, and honestly, I was thrilled to help each of these extraordinary people. (Well, everyone except you-know-who.)

I sat up straighter. "Your wish is my command."

"We're pulling together outcome summaries for past grantees," he explained. "It all ties in to our upcoming thirtieth anniversary. I'm also doing a series of lectures. I need to present a *record of impact*. Proof that the foundation's grants have actually done worthwhile things. The kinds of things we can point to and say *this is the difference we make*."

He handed me a printout with the names of a dozen past grant recipients. "I need you to find press coverage—newspaper articles, reviews, mentions in journals, photographs for these people. We need to show the practical as well as the personal side of our foundation. You can start by Googling their names. But don't stop there." He handed me a paper. "This will get you into the library databases we subscribe to: ProQuest, LexisNexis, Newspapers.com, etc."

I looked down at the login credentials like they were top-secret launch codes. This wasn't scutwork—he was asking me to do real research.

"Obviously, check the foundation's *Grants* folder too."

"Um...the *Grants* folder?" I looked at Mr. Slater and hesitated. "It's just—Mrs. Johnston told me that was off-limits. Ms. Neely was especially adamant it's only for the senior advisory team."

Mr. Slater chuckled, as though I were being adorably dim. "Mr. Trousdale, I *am* the senior advisory team—or at least part of it. If I'm the one handing you the keys, you're not sneaking in through the window. You're walking through the front door."

Easy for him to say—he wasn't the one who'd nearly been vaporized by Ms. Neely's glare a moment ago.

"Right. Of course," I said, cheeks burning a little. Mr. Slater *wanted* me poking around, but Ms. Neely had been disappointed in me for even *glancing* at newspaper clippings she said were for VIP eyes only. So which was it? Faithful team member or nosy intern who didn't know his place? Clearly the advisors needed to coordinate their messaging—preferably before I developed a stress ulcer.

I straightened in my chair, trying to sound professional and not secretly thrilled that he thought highly enough of me to give me this important assignment. "Got it. What's my deadline?"

"Would it be possible to have the material in, say, a week? But no pressure. I'm not Ms. Klotz. I don't believe in firing off three reminder emails every hour or standing over someone's desk until the work is done. Just get it to me when you can—I'd rather it be completed properly than yesterday."

After my brush with Ms. Klotz's management style, Mr. Slater's approach felt like a spa day.

For the rest of the week and into the next, I combed through Google, ProQuest, and LexisNexis. *The Daily Nation* in Nairobi boasted about the foundation's sponsored mobile health vans bringing medical services to remote villages. *El Espectador* in Bogotá reported on microloans helping women launch cottage industries. And *The Globe and Mail* in Toronto covered a financial literacy program. I found photos too, including one of a woman standing proudly in front of a village bakery she'd established in the mountains of Peru. And schoolkids in Malawi, wearing identical uniforms, smiling for the camera from their brand-new foundation-paid-for desks.

And just when I thought the foundation was all world-saving, globe-trotting heavyweights, there'd be something small and quirky: the Ozark River Theater Guild, which used their grant to buy a rickety old barn and turn it into a community playhouse. Or the Frost-MacLeod Collective, a group of sheep farmers in the Scottish Highlands who received a grant to restore a centuries-old stone footbridge across a stream. Each file was its own little world, and I couldn't stop diving in with awe and admiration for what had been accomplished with Ms. Cummings's money.

It took a week, but my project was complete. It dawned on

me that for all the hours I'd spent in the shared folder, no alarms had gone off. It was as if no one noticed—or cared—that I'd been rummaging through the foundation's digital equivalent of a locked vault.

And that was when a thought crept in. If no one was keeping an eye on the *Grants* folder, maybe while I was there, I could just quickly, almost accidentally, take a teensy-weensy *glance* at other non-assignment files. Like maybe do a global search for Rachel Morris? Or Titan Shield International. Maybe Halcyon Strategies. Or even Charles Brandt—Adele Cummings's long-lost husband? Those were the names that had been swirling around in my head. I knew I was supposed to "be careful crossing boundaries set for you." But my curiosity was like a popcorn kernel lodged in a molar. And it was tormenting me.

Honestly, I did try to talk myself down. *Just do your job, Timothy. Don't go peeking.* But I reminded myself that peeking isn't snooping. (Even if I just invented that to justify what I was about to do.)

My fingers hovered over the mouse as if clicking might set off alarms, complete with red lights and a trapdoor under my chair. I took a breath. Then another. My pulse spiked. I kept one eye on the monitor, the other flicking nervously toward the doorway. Then, with a silent apology to my better judgment—I glanced up at the door again, palms sweating—and clicked.

I quickly typed *Rachel Morris* into the search bar. A folder instantly popped up: *Temp_Placement.*

What the heck? This was, like, the foundation's Human Resources folder, and Rachel Morris had her own file. *Did she work at the foundation? As a temp?* Within the file was a subfile labeled *Incident Report_RachelMorris_SKlotz_20August.*

I clicked. The foundation letterhead appeared. Below it, in clipped prose:

Incident Report
Prepared by: Stephanie Klotz
Subject: Rachel Morris (Temporary Administrative Assistant)

Summary of Incident:
On August 20, at 10:47 p.m., subject Rachel Morris was discovered in the Foundation offices, actively reviewing the Foundation's internal computer files. When confronted by myself to explain her presence after office hours, subject claimed she had entered the premises to "retrieve personal belongings."
Per Foundation policy, NYPD officers were contacted. Subject was escorted from the building without incident.

Prior History:
This incident follows a previous infraction in which subject, Rachel Morris, was found, after being expressly forbidden to do so, accessing files relevant to potential grant awardees, specifically Lillian Trent.

Disposition:
No charges will be filed by the Adele Cummings Foundation at this time.
Placement agency contacted. Rachel Morris will cease to be in their employ.
Internal recommendation: do not disclose particulars of incident outside Foundation leadership.

I stared at the screen, pulse drumming. Not only had Rachel Morris worked as an assistant at the foundation, but she'd also been caught red-handed rifling through sensitive grant information—information tied directly to Lillian Trent. This was in addition to the sour-grapes letter from her I'd already seen. So

Rachel was an untalented singer moonlighting at a desk job—and had been a hair's breadth away from being arrested for criminal activities.

And now, by opening this report, *I* was essentially doing what Rachel had done. Prying where I had no right. Staring at things expressly forbidden. One wrong click and I'd be escorted out, my future hauled away with the same cold efficiency.

The irony dug its nails in. The only thing separating me from Rachel was that Ms. Klotz had caught her. I still had a chance to step away—immediately—and redeem myself.

"Mr. Trousdale?"

Holy moly! I nearly shot out of my chair. My heart was thudding so hard I half-expected it to echo off the office walls. Ms. Raymond was in the doorway, perfectly composed, holding a manila folder against her chest. How long had she been standing there? Probably long enough to see that I'd been totally absorbed in something on my computer screen. And now, she surely saw the panic written across my face. Damn!

"Oh! Hi!" I said too brightly, voice cracking like I'd just hit puberty again.

Ms. Raymond seemed to be studying me. Or maybe I only imagined it.

"Apologies for interrupting you," she said. Her tone was warm, pleasant, the same as it always was.

I forced myself to nod, my hand still hovering near the mouse, the Rachel Morris file still open. Could she see the reflection in my glasses? She crossed the room and approached my desk. I was in a panic. I wondered how I could unobtrusively exit the shared file.

"You're obviously very busy, but when you have the opportunity, may I please ask you to take a look at these press summaries and proof them for typos? Of course, as a writer, if you see anything you think could be improved, by all means make suggestions. Any chance you might find time to complete this by the end of the day? I'd really appreciate it." Her smile was professional as she handed me the file. Nothing threatening. Nothing unusual.

"Absolutely," I said quickly, snapping the folder open as though I couldn't wait to get started. My voice was too eager. Too fake. My skin prickled. Did she know what I'd been doing? Surely not. Was this just another routine task—or an investigation?

"Much appreciated, Mr. Trousdale," she said softly. Then she left. No fuss. No accusations.

But the moment she was gone, my chest was tight with the feeling that maybe she'd seen more than she let on.

18

Proofreading is one of the things I do best. It demands a sharp eye, relentless focus, and, in my case, a slightly unhinged obsession with spotting misplaced commas. I often carry a red pen to restaurants, which means no menu is safe from my scrutiny. It's less a hobby, more a compulsion—and yes, okay, I get pretty smug about it. But being smug is a proofreader's reward. It's the only area where I feel superior to nearly everyone else on the planet.

My all-time favorite misprint? When I worked for the movie star Mercedes Ford, I saw a press release my odious boss Jarred Evans had written. It proudly announced Mercedes's signing on to star as the voice of a new Disney cartoon *heroin*. Yep, without the *E*. As in Schedule I Narcotics!

Did I tell Jarred I'd spotted his boo-boo? Hell no! First, he never wanted my input on anything. Plus, I wasn't about to rob myself of the joy of watching that typo waltz into the world like Snow White on meth. I imagined somewhere in Burbank, a strung-out Mickey Mouse slurring, "Heh-heh! Happiness is a lie, kids!" And then lighting a cigarette with a FastPass.

Over the next couple of hours of reviewing Ms. Raymond's

press summaries, I waged war against dangling modifiers and apostrophe abuse. One praised the foundation's programs as "a win-win for all *intensive* purposes." Another declared that students were "reaping what we *sewed*," which was surely news to the fashion and agriculture communities. And then there was the name "Dr. Kendra Shite," celebrated space-habitat designer. Her last name, I discovered, was—*White.*

What struck me most wasn't the errors themselves, but the fact that this place was crawling with highly educated rich people who apparently couldn't spell their way out of a mono-grammed Gucci bag. Money and academic degrees don't neces-sarily make you smart. Maybe they just buy the right to be sloppy. Like why bother getting it right when you have *people* to mop up after you? People like me, armed with eagle eyes and the perverse thrill of catching subject-verb disagreements and their/there/they're train wrecks.

Honestly, it wasn't a tough assignment at all. I enjoyed it. And I finished with lots of time to spare. No one needed to know I was Speedy Gonzales with a proofreader's scalpel. So I spent a while afterward volleying lascivious DMs with Brad—part shameless flirting, part proposals that would've made a porn star blush. Every line was laced with enough anatomical innu-endo to qualify as a biology lesson.

After that, with at least a half hour more on my hands, my thoughts drifted back to the enigmatic Rachel Morris.

I was intrigued by her because, apparently, she wasn't only a not-very-good singer, a poor sport about not getting her mitts on grant money, and the writer of a letter that practically screamed *threat* in twelve-point Times New Roman...but she'd also once actually worked right here in this very office. Had she even maybe sat at my desk? Or used this very keyboard to type her angry little manifesto?

And that was when I remembered Rachel and Lillian had something else in common besides career goals—they both had ties to the foundation. Lillian had been a prize recipient (who never got her prize), and Rachel was one of its discarded temps. Two women orbiting the same star—one basking in the glow, the other burned by it.

If that wasn't worth a closer look, what was? Obviously, I had to sneak a peek at Rachel's employment file. For journalistic integrity, of course.

Alas, her file was basically a ghost town. Other than Ms. Klotz's incident report, it was empty. That didn't quite add up. At the very least, there should have been correspondence between the foundation and SwellHire Top Temps—a contract, billing forms, and that end-date notification that was mentioned in Ms. Klotz's incident report explaining why Rachel's placement was cut short. Shouldn't there have been some paperwork from Mrs. Johnston, too? She maintained the employee files. A copy of the NYPD report? None of that was here. The absence didn't seem logical. Or professional.

Which made me wonder...because if there was one thing I'd learned by cleaning up the *Miscellaneous* file mess, it was that this place documented *everything*—grant recipient thank-you letters, vendor invoices, press clippings, audit reports, legal correspondence. And yet, for Rachel Morris—caught red-handed raiding the cookie jar and escorted out by the police? Nothing. Weird.

I played around with a few ideas for finding out more about Rachel. I could stalk her social media. That was all public information. Sure, poking at someone's socials is voyeurism with a search bar, but an Instagram or Facebook page might tell me a lot. It could reveal people she knew, connections she had, gigs she'd played, dates and venue locations. Little breadcrumbs.

Of course, there was another option. The simplest but scariest for me because I was pretty introverted. I could stop sleuthing like a creep and just...meet her. In person. Near the surface of my brain, I knew the idea was probably insane. So of course…

I chewed my lip for a moment. Then the foundation's contact list obligingly coughed up Rachel's email address. Obviously, I couldn't risk using the office computer to reach out to her. That would be like sending Ms. Klotz an engraved invitation to sack me. So I picked up my phone.

I loathed typing on that thing. My thoughts flowed so much more freely when I could use all ten fingers at once rather than relying on two thumbs that could barely coordinate well enough to button a shirt. And don't get me started on predictive text—it never had the faintest idea what I was really trying to say. Recording a voice message was even worse. It seldom understood me. I couldn't risk "Interview subject" becoming "Invertebrate sandwich." She'd think I was high and ordering jellyfish on rye at a deli.

I opened a new message window and typed:

Subject: Cabaret Feature Article
Dear Ms. Morris,
I'm working on a feature about New York's cabaret scene for *Stage Left* magazine, and your name came up as someone who might have valuable insights. I'd love to hear your perspective on the state of cabaret today—the challenges, the opportunities, and what it's really like for singers in this fading art form.
If you'd be open to a short interview—maybe over coffee —I'd be grateful.
Best regards,
Timothy Truman

I'd hovered over the sign-off. Using my full name suddenly felt…unwise. I went with my middle name instead. Close enough to the truth to sleep at night.

19

Rachel Morris agreed to meet me the next morning at the Cobalt Cantina on West Seventy-Third. To her credit, she didn't flinch when I suggested the slightly cruel hour of 7:00 a.m. I got there ten minutes early, claimed a corner table, and practiced not sounding like a fake journalist for a fake online theater magazine.

I knew it was Rachel as soon as she walked in. She was smaller in person than she'd appeared on the video, and her outfit—neat but uninspired—didn't do her any favors. The houndstooth blazer-and-skirt set had the look of a thrift-shop find. (No shade. I proudly frequented *Le Château du Good-will* myself.) Her hair was pinned back with a plastic faux-tortoiseshell clip, more for containment than style.

Rachel spotted me waving, and her whole demeanor brightened in an instant, like a lamp just plugged in. She offered a smile that wanted to dazzle. She was probably thrilled at the idea of being interviewed for my story. As though this small moment might deliver much-needed publicity. From the doorway, she cocked her head toward the barista counter and mimed lifting a cup to her lips.

"So," she said when she finally arrived at the table and sat down with a to-go cup, "you're Timothy Truman, the writer who wants to know about the cabaret scene. How can I help?"

I blinked. *Of course. Truman. I'd already forgotten my own alias.*

"Thanks for meeting me," I said brightly.

"No worries. It's not every day someone wants to talk about cabaret singers who aren't headlining at the Carlyle."

I asked permission to record our conversation and tapped my phone screen. "It's hard to read my own notes," I explained, and started with an easy question: "So, how did you find your way into the world of cabaret?"

Rachel smiled. "I was auditioning for Broadway and off-Broadway musicals—you know, cattle calls, with a thousand other girls all belting the same sixteen bars of anything from *Les Miz*. One night, a friend took me to a cabaret open mic in the Village. I sang my audition number and got better comments than I did from casting directors. I realized...oh, maybe this is where I belong. Intimate room, live piano, people actually paying attention."

"What do you love most about cabaret?" I continued.

"The audience connection, I guess. You're not an insignificant nobody on a stage with a big cast. You're right there. Fans are only a couple of feet away. You can see their faces, feel whether they're with you or not. When it works, it's electric. When it doesn't"—she shrugged—"well, you drink your complimentary glass of house wine, then go home and cry. Welcome to my world."

I jotted something meaningless in my notebook and tried to look deeply interested. "So, who are the cabaret biggies today? The ones shaping the scene? And where do they perform?"

"Well, you've got your regular heavy hitters: Maxine Dela-Croix is still packing 'em in at Don't Tell Mama. Eddie Salazar does this wicked Cole Porter set over at Birdland. And there's always someone new coming up at the Duplex." She leaned in, lowering her voice as if confiding a secret. "Just don't bother with the Purple Parrot. A dive! If you play there, it's basically over."

I nodded, remembering the video *she'd* made at the Purple Parrot. The spotlight was barely working, the microphone was squealing, and she was doing her damnedest to score with the sparse audience.

"Right. And I've heard sometimes the toughest crowd in cabaret is other cabaret singers. Too often they're scoping out the competition in the guise of support."

She snort-laughed. "You're pretty smart for such a young guy. What are you, just out of college? How do you even know about cabaret? Probably helps that you're gay—you get the whole performing-for-an-audience-that's-also-secretly-judging-you thing. Oh, no offense if you're straight."

She was onto me. I really didn't know much about cabaret, but I thought I was improvising pretty well. And yeah, the age thing. I was trying to look older. I'd been cultivating a five-o'clock shadow since a week ago Tuesday. It was still sort of a whisper, but I thought it suggested maturity.

And she'd put her finger on something else. Being gay *had* given me a certain way of seeing the world. A lifetime of learning to read a room, to sense the undercurrents, to perform a version of myself while calculating who was safe and whom to keep my distance from. It had sharpened me. Made me observant. Maybe even insightful.

Rachel continued. "Yeah, it's brutal out there in the club world," she said. "You're pouring your heart out, and half the room's measuring their own material against yours."

"And the hardest part of working in cabaret?" I asked.

Her smile soured. "Staying afloat, of course. Cabaret's like the stray cat of show business—it survives, but no one really feeds it. If you're not already a famous cat, you've got to drag your family and friends in to see you—and there's a cover charge and a two-drink minimum. It gets expensive. And you're lucky if you get paid in cash, not just applause. You have to hustle. Pick up gigs wherever you can. I work office temp jobs just to get by."

I shifted in my chair because I realized yet again that Rachel and I were in exactly the same financial/career boat. Two struggling wannabe artists. I bobbed my head and pretended to jot something down again, trying to sound casual while nudging her. "I've been researching the cabaret scene, and I think there actually *are* some places that offer support for performers." I quickly rattled off the names of a couple of just-made-up, off-the-cuff charities. "The Manhattan Arts Initiative. The New Horizons Fund. Maybe you should look into them. In theory, they're supposed to help out and give artists a chance to breathe a little." I paused, then added, as if it had just occurred to me, "And there's the Adele Cummings Foundation. They make a lot of noise about supporting the arts."

Rachel gave a sharp, cynical snort-laugh. "Oh, please! The Adele Cummings Foundation? They may be good at eradicating mosquitoes in some Third World swamp country and rescuing elephants in Malaysia—but don't ask them to save an artist. They're good with slogans—'supporting diverse voices'—but the reality? It's not about art. It's about optics."

Her voice hardened. "They hand out checks to people who already have a foot in the door. People like Lillian Trent. She's dead now, but she was on the verge, and they were giving her one of their big awards this year. She didn't even need their help. But prestigious philanthropic foundations want to be associated with rising stars rather than unknowns. Adele Cummings attaching a grant to someone who's already shimmering makes them look discerning and influential. So the rest of us keep hustling and hoping we might be next on their list. It's all bullshit."

I sat there, pen hovering above my notebook. Part of me

wanted to nod in agreement because I wasn't supposed to know that Rachel had been rejected for grant funds by Adele Cummings. But another part of me bristled because I was pretty loyal to the foundation. I'd seen enough during my short time there to know they were doing amazing things all over the world. Important life-saving programs were being fully funded. Just because Rachel hadn't gotten what she apparently perceived as her fair slice of the nonprofit pie didn't make the whole enterprise an unworthy pretense.

She added, "I know firsthand 'cause I used to work there."

It was hard to keep my face neutral. *She was opening up and moving precisely in the direction I wanted her to go.*

"I mean—I did about six months temping at the foundation. Nothing glamorous. Admin stuff. Filing, making copies, answering phones. I was really excited at first. They seemed really nice. Except for one bitch. For a while, they pretended that I was a valuable member of their team. That I was a godsend from Heaven's holy temp pool. I thought I might even have a future there."

"Why'd you leave? A singing gig? Wanted to explore other opportunities?"

She toyed with her coffee cup, passing it between her hands as she decided how much to reveal.

"To be honest, they ended my assignment. Abruptly. Someone there had it in for me."

Someone had it in for me. We've all heard that line before. It usually translates to "*I slugged the boss*" or "*I forgot to come to work a few times.*" It's the universal anthem of the aggrieved employee who could never quite admit they might've been part of the problem.

Rachel continued, "The Adele Cummings Foundation claims they're all about helping artists in need—until they find one of them is answering their phones. Then suddenly it's awkward. It didn't seem relevant when I started working there to tell them that I was a singer. It's nobody's business how I spend my free time."

As I watched Rachel playing with her cup, eyes dark and wounded, my cynicism wobbled. Maybe she wasn't dodging personal responsibility; maybe she really had been ambushed. Because if there were anyone at the foundation capable of "having it in" for someone, it was Ms. Klotz. I was eager to hear her side of the termination story. Because remember the MacLaine Dance Company fiasco? I still thought Ms. Klotz had had a hand in that!

Rachel must've read the next question in my eyes, because she quickly moved on, like she didn't want to get into the specifics of why she left. "I'm actually glad I'm not still there. I poked around a little, and there's stuff going on that I don't want to be associated with. I got a look behind the curtain, so to speak."

A look behind the curtain? Did she mean she'd witnessed favoritism, politics, quiet back-room deals? There was something in her tone—less gossip, more residue. Like whatever she'd seen had left a stain she couldn't scrub off.

I tilted my pen against my notebook as if I were about to write something. I wanted to nudge her toward the thing I couldn't stop thinking about—Lillian Trent. I cleared my throat, trying to sound casual. "You mentioned the foundation was giving Lillian Trent one of their big awards this year. Such a tragedy about what happened to her."

Rachel made a face. "Tragedy?" Then she immediately backpedaled, as if she realized how naked that sounded. "Sure, it's always tragic when someone dies like that. But..." Her eyes seemed to avoid mine. "Well, let's just say not everyone thought she deserved what she was about to get—except maybe her murder."

Whoa! Did I hear that right? Was she saying Lillian Trent didn't deserve a grant, but she *did* deserve strangulation? Who even said something like that out loud? About a person barely cold in their grave. Even if they were showbiz rivals. My face twitched; then I heard myself, thin and strained, say, "That's... pretty harsh."

"Yeah, well. Life's harsh. Cabaret's harsher."

She took a long sip of coffee, like she was trying to wash the taste of her own words out of her mouth. "Sorry. That sounded weird. Forget I said it. Don't print any of that. It's just—I admit I'm envious that the foundation practically gift-wrapped a career for Lillian. She was about to be launched as the next Marilyn Maye. Hell, she even copied Julie Wilson's gardenia behind her ear. Of course, I think Julie copied Billie Holiday. There was a lot of fuss about Lillian. She had a 'look.' She knew how to schmooze with club owners.

"Meanwhile, I'm hustling temp jobs, praying my Visa doesn't get declined at the grocery store. She gets a golden ticket. Some people just fall upward, you know?"

Her words could've been lifted straight from that indignant letter I knew she'd written to the foundation. The same acid, the same bruised resentment, and not a syllable about Lillian's genuine talent. Only animosity. I was hearing it raw, unfiltered.

"Lillian Trent was a prop," she continued. "A safe bet. Someone they could hold up as proof of their commitment to the arts. What about the rest of us? But I don't think she was actually going to get any money. Just a hunch."

I let her words hang in the air, scribbling a meaningless squiggle in my notebook just to keep up appearances. Then I leaned in a little and lowered my voice like I was sharing a secret. "I'm learning the world of cabaret is a small one. Everybody knows everybody else—or at least they know the other players. Have you heard anyone say anything about Lillian's murder? Like why they think it happened? Who might've... Maybe a motive...?"

"Well, according to the police, it *wasn't* a robbery gone

wrong. If you knew her, you'd draw your own conclusions. Lillian had sharp elbows. Was quick to grab the spotlight—even when it wasn't hers. You've heard about the piano stunt? Yeah, she was trying out a new accompanist last year—a talented guy but just starting out in the scene. They'd rehearsed for a new show. Everything nice and tidy. Midway through their opening night set, right in the middle of a number, Lillian shifted into another key. The poor pianist scrambled like mad to keep up— he couldn't. She held her money note, without his backing, and the audience went wild. Standing ovation for her, polite coughs for him. Guess who never worked at that club again? Not Lillian.

"Oh, and her open run at the Blue Note? It was only supposed to be a weeklong double bill with Jessica Larkin, a singer everyone likes. But Jessica got food poisoning opening night and couldn't go on. Lillian could. She took the whole show like it had been her plan from the start. Maybe it was. Audiences raved about her. When Jessica came back a couple of days later, the owner told her not to bother. And he extended Lillian's run as a solo. That was Lillian."

Rachel's anecdotes were like so many showbiz war stories we've all heard—the ones where a performer's ambition came with casualties. Streisand eclipsing the star in her first Broadway show. Garland turning a concert rehearsal into a blood sport. LuPone equally revered and feared by creative teams. I'd always heard show business was a kick-boxing match with sequins. And Lillian... Apparently, if she were onstage, someone else was out in the cold. That might breed the kind of resentment that festers. And things that fester sometimes get infected.

I tilted my head, feigning casual curiosity. "But Lillian's talent was undeniable. That's why the Adele Cummings Foundation was giving her a grant. Right? I mean, why else?"

Rachel leaned in, lowering her voice. "There was talk about Lillian when I worked there. I heard it firsthand—up close and personal. Two camps, you know? People lobbying for and against her. One side said she wasn't the right choice for a big cash prize. For one thing, she was already working—critics were buzzing, club owners were booking her. She didn't need the boost.

"The whole point of the grant, they said, was to help artists who *can't* catch a break. Like me. Not someone who already had a spotlight. And let's be honest—Lillian Trent wasn't exactly Miss Congeniality. Ask anyone. Total diva. Nice voice, yeah, but backstage? She burned bridges. Some people at the foundation were worried her reputation might tarnish the award. Like, if she flamed out in public, it could reflect badly on the whole prize. On Adele Cummings herself."

Her words stuck to me like burrs. The arithmetic wasn't hard to add up. On one side were the detractors—people for whom Lillian's death meant they wouldn't have to watch her skyrocket on the foundation's dime and possibly drag its reputation down with her. On the other were the boosters, who could still brag that they'd won Adele Cummings's approval, that their influence had secured the grant. Even if the money never left the account, they still got their victory lap.

But maybe there was also a third category. Someone outside the foundation entirely. A jealous or vengeance-seeking singer —Rachel came immediately to mind. Or maybe that humiliated piano accompanist. Or the girl who'd gotten sick with botulism or whatever it was. I was confused. I tried to keep my pen scratching, though my head was spinning. I wondered who at the foundation had been rooting for Lillian's rise—and who had been arguing against it. And why.

"Sounds like a lot of dissension at the foundation," I said lightly. "Is that normal for grant decisions?"

Rachel tilted her head, considering my question. "Normal? I mean, disagreements didn't seem to happen all that often. But once in a while...you put four smart people on a committee, and they found four different ways to argue about 'artistic merit.' But with Lillian?" She hesitated. "It felt...territorial."

I nodded as if I were cool and analytical, but inside my head, gears were grinding. *Territorial? Over Lillian? Why? Who?* I forced out a breath, pretending I was merely digesting harmless background information and not the potential ingredients for murder.

"Okay," I said lightly, "got it. Maybe I should talk to someone at Adele Cummings—for background, for context. Anyone you'd recommend?"

Rachel's mouth curved into a smirk. "Nice try. I signed an NDA. Can't name names. I've already said way too much anyway." She glanced at my phone, which was doing its voice-recording thing.

I kept my face neutral, pen hovering over my notebook like I wasn't all that invested. *Play dumb.* "Maybe just off the record—between the two of us, you can *imply*—nonverbally—who has the most clout at the Adele Cummings Foundation. The one who has the great woman's ear when it comes to awarding grants? Mrs. Stone? Ms. Neely? Mr. Slater? Ms...." *Oh fuck! I shouldn't know the names of the foundation's advisors, should I! Duh!*

Rachel's eyes met mine—appraising. "You've done your homework. Smart guy. But I guarantee none of them will talk to you. The Adele Cummings Foundation's a clam. Honestly, I'm not even sure Adele Cummings actually exists—not in any currently *living, breathing* sense at least. Never saw her. Not once. She's like Garbo...or J. D. Salinger. I got the impression no one's laid eyes on her in years. They told me she's shy. Reclusive. But after a while, you start to wonder if she's even real. People talk about her like she's a saint or a ghost, depending on the day. Everyone knows *of* her—but who actually knows the *real* her?"

Adele Cummings, a myth? Until this moment, I'd have laughed off such an absurd theory. What was next—she was holed up on some private island with Santa Claus, the Easter

Bunny, and the Pillsbury Doughboy? But the way Rachel said it, it didn't sound like a joke. It sounded like a possibility. And I had to admit, sometimes the atmosphere at the foundation felt empty, like Adele Cummings was only a name. The way people talked about a famous ancestor.

Rachel glanced down at her cup, then back up at me with an almost apologetic look. "Wish I could be more helpful. There are things about the Adele Cummings Foundation you're better off not knowing, Timothy."

Better off not knowing? As I absorbed Rachel's words, my brain started pitching conspiracy theories. Maybe the advisors were laundering donations through famine-relief ships. Maybe Adele Cummings was cryogenically preserved beneath Ravenscroft. Maybe the grant decisions were made by horoscope. Or—more plausibly—someone was sleeping with someone they shouldn't, and everyone else was pretending not to notice. I lingered on that one, picturing sexy Mr. Slater with his shirt off in the office.

Curiosity's a chronic condition with me, and I couldn't help circling back to Lillian Trent's five-hundred-thousand-dollar prize. "Just hypothetically, if someone were approved for a grant from the foundation but couldn't collect it for one reason or another...does the foundation have a contingency plan? Like a runner-up in a beauty pageant?"

What I was really wondering—what I dared not say—was whether someone next in line for Lillian's grant might have helped her take her final bow. Just as she, in her own ambitious way, had "helped" other singers exit the stage.

Rachel smirked and drained the rest of her coffee. "Like I said, you're smart. You can probably figure it out. Money doesn't stay in limbo for long—it just finds another pocket. There's always someone ready to collect the pennies when they fall between the cushions."

She hesitated, as if she realized she'd already said too much.

Then she pushed her chair back, slinging her purse strap over her shoulder. "We got off track. We were supposed to be talking about the world of cabaret. But I've gotta get to work. Hope I helped a little. You seem nice. Good luck with the article. Spell my name right."

Again, Rachel hesitated. Then she added, "I'd be careful about asking too many questions about Lillian Trent, if I were you. The cabaret scene has a lot of cobras in the grass. Same with the Adele Cummings Foundation. Better not go anywhere near those posh people. They cap their teeth to hide their fangs."

She started to leave but suddenly stopped and studied me for a beat with a sort of smirk. "There's a singer I know... If you ever want to get laid, I know he'd eat you with a spoon. He has a type. Be sure to send me a link when the piece comes out."

Eat me with a spoon? What the hell? What happened to #MeToo? Was it canceled? How was this not a microdose of sexual harassment?

Rachel left her empty coffee cup on the table—along with me, blushing. Had she really just offered to pimp me out for someone's extracurricular activities? I mean, I guessed I was flattered, but...

Frankly, I'd taken her measure, and she was... How to put it? Not low-class, exactly. A perfectly lovely person. Just cut from a different bolt of fabric. Any friend of hers was probably similar. And besides, I didn't multitask well—emotionally or sexually.

Her invitation rattled around in my head, along with everything else she'd said—especially that bit about being careful how deep I dug into the cabaret scene. And her warning about my colleagues at the foundation. There was only one person there whom I knew had fangs. And I knew they were sharp.

I suddenly felt like my nosiness had maybe cracked open a door to a secret room—and something darker than I'd imagined was lurking inside.

20

I was never late for work—well, hardly ever. I prided myself on punctuality the way some people pat themselves on the back for flossing daily. Don't forget, I had been raised where punctuality was next to godliness. Show up late to church, and the preacher would make you the sermon illustration ("The *Devil* pushes the snooze button!"). And my work-ethic-obsessed daddy believed "on time" meant you were already late. So when I arrived at Ravenscroft a whole seven minutes past my usual start time, I was harried and practically on my knees before Mrs. Johnston.

She pursed her lips and dramatically tapped the crystal on her Lady Rolex. (FYI, I sort of suspected Mrs. Johnston's Rolex was fake because Brad has a Rolex, and his second hand sweeps smoothly over the face of the dial. Hers sort of hiccups forward. I'm just saying.) "I thought perhaps you'd been abducted by ICE agents," said Mrs. Johnston. "Then I remembered they only terrorize the brown people in America."

I couldn't exactly say, *Sorry I'm late, but I was interrogating a possibly homicidal ex-employee about Lillian Trent's murder and foundation corruption.* So I went with a classic combo: a delayed *bus* and an *insane* line at the *coffee place.* To which she raised an eyebrow and said, "Perhaps Mr. Starbuck should provide your next performance review."

I was mortified. Until I realized Mrs. Johnston was toying with me. Like her crack about the jellybean costume for Easter. There it was again, her dry wit lightening the mood. I hated that I sometimes couldn't tell if she was acting. And I couldn't help wondering if that old saying *in humor, there is truth* meant she actually did take exception to my tardiness...or wanted me deported.

I filled my tea mug and settled down to work. An email from Ms. Neely requested that I please use my creative writing skills to come up with some "inspirational quotes" to attribute to Adele Cummings in the foundation's thirtieth-anniversary book. The example she used was "With great power comes great responsibility." Hmm. I didn't take Ms. Neely for the Spider-Man Fan Club type. But it was still a good illustration. A place for me to start.

Oh boy—this sounded like a dream assignment. Me, Timothy Trousdale, ghost-writing for the grande dame of philanthropy! This job just kept getting better! And maybe my words would be published in the book! Maybe I'd even be mentioned in the acknowledgments: *Adele Cummings wishes to thank her talented collaborator, Timothy Trousdale.* But really, just contributing to the book in some small way was all the thanks I needed.

Inspirational quotes. In other words, she probably wanted Oprah's soul wrapped in Atticus Finch's moral backbone. I could do that. God knows I'd memorized plenty of Maya Angelou. And Bruce Springsteen's entire discography was basically a master class in working-class redemption. I was ready to summon all that gravitas for Adele Cummings. I just had to sort of get into her mindset.

I figured her words would have lots of humility. Those

always looked good in quotation marks. She needed to sound worldly, wise, and selfless. But the longer I stared at my screen, trying to sift wisdom from the ether, the more my excitement began to twist itself into panic. I realized I hadn't lived enough to have any really deep thoughts. I'd had disappointments, sure— rent I could barely afford, a few promising jobs that went nowhere—but nothing that felt sufficiently instructive. What did I know about existentialism?

And what if Adele Cummings hated the words I wrote for her? What if she thought they were dumb? What if she felt they didn't sound anything like her? Of course, that wouldn't be my fault. I'd never even heard her voice. She might have the flat, synthesized calm of a GPS giving directions, for all I knew.

And why *outsource* her eloquence in the first place? Why not just have Adele jot down a few of her own *real* thoughts or dictate them to Ms. Neely? Surely, after thirty years of serving humanity, she'd said or thought something profound and quotable. Then again, maybe she was too busy saving the world.

So I got down to work. I tried to imagine what rich and famous people might say to offer hope to the simple folks. I'd read a lot of aphorisms on Instagram—like the ones floating across religious memes that had sunsets or misty lakes in the background: *"Do what you love, and the money will follow," "Do what you love, and you'll never work a day,"* and *"Do what you love, and if it's not right for you, let it go, and the universe will send you what you're meant to receive."* I knew from personal experience that the last one was total bullshit. I let go of my health insurance once, and the Universe sent me appendicitis.

But I eventually came up with some absolute gems! They'd look swell engraved on the base of a statue of Adele Cummings. I was already picturing them in *Bartlett's Familiar Quotations.*

What do you think? Too James Baldwin? Mother Teresa?

*Art is not a luxury of the privileged. It is the language
through which humanity remembers itself.
*True giving is not measured by what we part with, but by
what we make possible.
*To support creation is to participate in evolution.
Philanthropy is love translated into action.

Damn! Am I good or what? Move over, Yoda!

I pasted my faux-wise, pseudo-spiritual pearls into an email
to Ms. Neely, and she responded almost right away. She liked
them!

"They're quite good, Mr. Trousdale. You've managed to
balance moral conviction and gentle insight. I may tweak a
couple, but otherwise...well done, you!"

I was ecstatic. Maybe I was actually enlightened and didn't
know it! "Please let me know what Ms. Cummings says about
them," I wrote back, certain she'd tell me we'd soon find out
because she was emailing them right away to the boss for
approval.

"Ms. Cummings won't be reading them," Ms. Neely
responded. "She trusts her team to communicate her vision.
Again, well done."

I was deflated. It made me wonder how many famous
sayings in history had been borrowed, massaged, or flat-out
invented by someone other than the sage to whom they were
attributed. Maybe Mrs. Shakespeare punched up her husband's
soliloquies. Maybe Winston Churchill had a copywriter in the
War Rooms. And who's to say Jesus Christ didn't have some
disciple draft the Sermon on the Mount, then stole all the
credit?

I was confused. It sounded less like Adele Cummings
empowering her staff to vouch for her and more like
ventriloquism.

That was when I remembered what Rachel Morris had said

earlier over coffee: *"I'm not even sure Adele Cummings actually exists."*

That was starting to make a little sense, sorta. Maybe Adele *didn't* exist. Or maybe no longer existed. At least not in her original form. A counterfeit philanthropic deity conjured up by Halcyon Strategies PR—just like her eponymous foundation itself.

But I didn't have time to think about it further because just then Mr. Slater emailed to say he needed *this...* Then Mrs. Stone called asking me for *that...* After which Mrs. Raymond had heard I'd done well writing fictional quotes and asked me to draft a letter to her dentist—something polite but firm about a new implant "not feeling grand enough for the price of $2,500."

After eight hours of slogans and uplifting verses, I left the office, exhausted. The M72 bus sighed to a stop. I climbed aboard and fed it my MetroCard. I grabbed a window seat and tried to decompress as we lurched past dog walkers, taxies, and Door-Dash delivery e-bikes cutting through traffic.

I popped in my earbuds and hit play on the voice memo from my morning interview with Rachel. Her voice filled my head, low and conspiratorial: *Not everyone thought she deserved what she was about to get—except maybe her murder.*

I flinched at the words all over again. She'd told me to forget she said it. How could I forget? And now, it didn't sound like a slip of the tongue. It sounded like a truth that had escaped before she could stuff it back in her mouth.

Lillian had sharp elbows. She was quick to grab the spotlight— even when it wasn't hers. Honestly, I'm not even sure Adele Cummings herself actually exists—not in any currently living, breathing sense at least... Like Garbo...

I didn't have time to analyze those words because the bus arrived at my stop. I paused the recording and got off.

As I walked the two blocks to Winterbourne Manor (my shitty apartment above Abu's?), it hit me: maybe, over the years, Adele Cummings had just become a "brand." Like Betty Crocker. Or Sara Lee. Aunt Jemima isn't real. Neither is Chef Boyardee or Mr. Clean. But people still buy into *their* stories. Maybe Adele Cummings started out real but was now merely a mascot. My head was exploding! Then...

Brad—beautiful, thought-absorbing Brad—called. He said he missed me like crazy, and I said it right back, because I did. Hearing his voice made the part of my anatomy along the treasure trail below my navel hum. He asked about my day, and I told him it had its highs and lows. (I didn't mention that someone wanted to "eat me with a spoon.") I said I might be published sooner than later and proudly recited one of the wise sayings I'd written for Adele Cummings—the one about *philanthropy being love translated into action*. He said he thought it was amazing and called me a "deep thinker" and said he could tell I wrote it because it sounded like something I'd say. I was floating away on his admiration.

Then he told me about his day, and being called to tune the piano at Kelly Ripa and Mark Consuelos's penthouse, and meeting Robert Downey Jr., who was visiting there.

Our lives were absurdly glamorous. Here we were, two young guys in love, lucky to be living and working in exciting and thrilling New York City, chasing our dreams and passions, and brushing up against other fabulous creative people.

Once we hung up, my brain went to my tummy, and I realized I was craving a chicken shawarma wrap from Abu's. My hunger collided with thoughts about poor, murdered Lillian Trent. Pill or not, no one deserved the kind of final curtain call she got. Then my memory revived what Rachel Morris had said about "cabaret cobras." And Ms. Neely's suggestion that Adele

Cummings was maybe too lofty—or too lazy—(or non-existent) to bother offering her life-affirming thoughts for the anniversary book. Sometimes I just couldn't turn off my thinking! I needed a distraction.

And I got one! The Universe usually does that for me. *Ask, and ye shall receive* sort of thing. I was in line at Abu's, ordering my wrap, when a text message pinged on my phone. I looked at my screen, expecting Brad's usual flirty emojis: 🔥💋😈👅.

Instead, I saw a WhatsApp DM:

07:17 — No Caller ID (delivered)
I'm on to you. Rules are rules for a reason. Consider this your only warning.

I froze. For a second, I couldn't tell whether the sound I was hearing was my heart pounding or a bus rumbling by. My brain tried to make sense of what I'd read. First denial ("spam message?"). Then logic ("wrong number?"). Then skin-prickling panic. The phone suddenly felt radioactive in my hand. I glanced around Abu's, convinced someone was watching me. A guy in a hoodie stirred his coffee. A lovely woman in a hijab scrolled her screen. Normal life continued while mine had just tilted sideways.

My mouth went dry, my appetite gone. The smell of garlic and toasted pita now made my stomach twist.

Still, I'd arrived at the head of the line, so I placed my order. I looked at my phone again. The screen's reflection showed a face —mine—pale and troubled. It took too long to get my wrap, and when it was finally handed to me, I quickly left the restaurant, desperate for fresh air.

Outside, the city noise pressed in on me. Another thought that occurred to me was that Rachel maybe wasn't the only one who'd noticed my curiosity about Lillian Trent's murder. Maybe someone at the foundation had seen the files I'd opened on the sly. My surreptitious Sunday login. Maybe Ms. Klotz, who seemed to monitor all my activities, had decided to send me a warning. Maybe one of them was "on to me."

I stood there, the paper wrap growing warm and greasy in my hand, the garlic scent suddenly sickening. My pulse thudded in my ears so hard it drowned out the traffic. I told myself to move—walk, breathe—but my body wasn't listening. A horn blared somewhere close by, sharp as a gunshot, and I flinched hard enough to drop the shawarma. It hit the pavement with a soft, pathetic splat.

When I bent to pick it up, a black sedan slowed beside me. It didn't stop—just slowed—the way a car does when the driver's looking for an address—or someone. My breath caught. The window was tinted, the driver invisible. For three terrible seconds, the car idled, engine humming. Then it rolled away, merging into the swarm of city traffic.

I stood alone on the sidewalk, my dinner ruined, my thoughts louder than the street noise. Maybe it was nothing. Maybe it was everything. Either way, I thought maybe I'd crossed some invisible line I wasn't aware of—and whoever sent that message was *on to me*.

21

B y the next morning, I'd read the message at least a hundred more times. The words didn't change, but their meaning seemed to: *I'm on to you. Rules are rules for a reason.* Maybe it wasn't an actual threat after all. Maybe *someone* just cared about my safety and wanted to offer advice. I'm looking for a best-case scenario. Like when I was six, and my mother caught me about to stick a fork in the toaster. Loving concern, with just a whiff of doom.

A few more reads after that, and it felt biblical. Not like locusts or rivers of blood—those were old-fashioned plagues. This was more like an eleventh plague, custom-designed for me. A plague where humanity survived, but I very much did not.

After all those rereads, I never once took it as a joke.

It was definitely a threat.

So you can imagine the state Mrs. Johnston found me in when I arrived at Ravenscroft the next morning. I was dazed, hollow-eyed from a sleepless night, and running entirely on dread. She intuitively knew something had burrowed under my skin.

"Mr. Trousdale," she said in that ever-genteel voice, "forgive me for prying, but you look a little...rattled."

I was such an open book. I gave Mrs. Johnston a shrug. "Just stuff. Like, I can't stop thinking about Lillian Trent. Her murder. I wish I knew who killed her. And maybe I'm a little stressed about Ms. Klotz coming back next week."

"I think about those things, too. We can't do anything about them. But I'm always here if you want to talk. I may not have answers, but I'm a good listener if you need to confide in me."

I wanted to hug Mrs. Johnston and tell her everything—about the files I'd read, about meeting Rachel Morris and what she'd said about stuff going on "behind the scenes" here at the foundation, about the threatening message some anonymous tormentor had sent to me.

But of course, I couldn't. She was the foundation's corporate concierge, for crying out loud. If she knew what I'd been up to, I'd be out the door before lunch. My SwellHire Top Temps status would be DNR (*Do Not Reassign*). Every other employment agency in Manhattan would be warned about me. I'd never work again and be forced to move home to Alabama. (That'll never happen! No matter what!)

And I couldn't go to Brad for solace either. For one thing, he wouldn't understand because he'd never get himself tangled up in anything this level of stupid. Brad had what I called *grown-up sense*. I also didn't want him to see me as weak and pathetic, someone who needed rescuing. I'd hate for him to look down the road to our future and see me as someone he had to worry over and protect. He'd just told me how proud he was of my "deep thinking," and I wanted to stay that version of myself in his eyes: the clever, capable guy with the artsy mystique and the emerging career. Not the nervous office temp who might've accidentally poked a bear—the cabaret kind, with a pianist and a microphone and claws sharp enough to draw blood.

So I did what any self-respecting neurotic would do: I

smiled, poured myself a tea, and pretended everything was absolutely A-okay. Until another message pinged. And it wasn't a WhatsApp DM from Brad.

09:36 — No Caller ID (delivered)
Keep your head down. I'm watching.

Oh, great! Not at all what I wanted this morning. I'd almost trade that message for one from Ms. Klotz. Almost.

I let the message sit in my head for a beat, then decided to take Mrs. Johnston up on her offer to talk. As I walked to her office, I made up a hypothetical scenario. One that would hopefully obfuscate the truth behind my desire to see her.

I sat before her desk and stuttered like an idiot, "Mrs. Johnston...if someone—say, a friend—found some information about something they maybe shouldn't have and then realized an anonymous someone else knew about what the friend found...and that anonymous someone else started sending weird or threatening messages warning the friend to back off and keep quiet and that they were watching their friend... What would you do?"

Mrs. Johnston took a deep breath, folded her hands on her desk, and made the exact face people make when a pun or the punchline of a joke flies over their head. Baffled. "Is that a question or a riddle, Mr. Trousdale? I left my decoder ring at home. You'll have to speak plainer."

"Okay," I said, trying to sound casual but hearing the wobble in my own voice. "Let's say a friend of mine—or someone's friend—just found out something not great about someone else or maybe some*thing* else. Doesn't matter. The point is, it's maybe a bad kind of thing my friend—someone's friend—wasn't supposed to know about, and nobody should know about it because there could be someone important involved. And then —somehow—an anonymous somebody else found out that the friend knew about the bad situation. And that anonymous somebody sent my friend a cryptic message. Not exactly a threat. But maybe a threat. Close enough to a threat. Now the friend's freaked out. They think they're being watched. Doesn't know whom to trust. Can't talk to anyone about it. What would you tell this person to do?"

Mrs. Johnston grimaced—a diplomatic, half-puzzled smile that said, *I have no fucking clue what you're talking about.* "That's not any clearer," she said. "But it sounds like—a *friend* seems to have stumbled on to something that a mysterious somebody else knows that they know about. And this mysterious someone has warned that your friend should step back and forget the whole thing—or else. Have I got that right? More or less?"

Yes! Mrs. Johnston just proved again that she was a pretty smart cookie. I nodded. "That's basically it, and why I'm not myself today," I said. "I'm sort of concerned for this, um, friend. They're pretty upset. Any advice? For my *friend*?"

Mrs. Johnston tilted her head, weighing her words. Then she steepled her fingers and twisted her mouth as if she were giving serious consideration to her thoughts and forthcoming words.

"Well," she said, "it sounds as though your friend's in a tricky spot. Maybe even a dangerous one. This is New York, dear— people play by different rules than they do in smaller towns like where you were raised. Everyone's got an angle, and not all of them are harmless. If your friend has discovered something that someone else doesn't want him to know—and is firing a warning shot across the bow, your friend ought to take it seriously. Maybe it's just me because I'm practical, but I didn't get to my age by ignoring caution signs."

Mrs. Johnston's voice softened. "My wise mother used to say, 'Don't stir the pot if you don't have to. It only brings back to the surface what's settled.' If there's even a chance your friend could be hurt, he ought to walk away—quickly. Curiosity killed the cat —and in this town, there are bigger and more dangerous predators. Whatever your friend has stumbled on to, if it doesn't directly concern him, best to leave it where he found it. Move on and forget the whole thing. That's my advice."

Her words made perfect sense. I nodded, grateful. Mrs. Johnston was right. So I'd just do my job, keep my head down, and live a peaceful, un-murdered life with Brad. That was the plan. In theory.

In practice? Well, I'd never been good at leaving pots unstirred. And my curiosity didn't just kill cats; it bought them chewy snack treats and play toys.

22

For the next six hours, Mrs. Johnston's advice played like a broken motivational tape on loop in my head. I tried to follow her advice. I really did. I kept my head down, nose to the grindstone. I drafted email responses to inquiries about grant funding—one for an app that promised to translate barnyard moos, oinks, and cock-a-doodle-doos into human English. Another proposed researching how ghosts influence Alexa smart speakers. I summarized a report for Mrs. Raymond's next advisory board meeting and proofed the introduction Ms. Neely had written for the anniversary book. But my thoughts refused to stay leashed. They kept slipping the collar and circling back to those freaky anonymous messages.

Then, somewhere along the way, I started to reason—*Wait a minute! Someone's sending me threatening messages because they're afraid of me.* Which was frankly hilarious because I was basically a wimp. But someone out there clearly thought I knew something—about something. Or wanted me to *not* know about something.

Threats were a power play, right? The schoolyard bully demanded your lunch money. The teacher said, "Your attitude will go on your permanent record." Even my stepmother threatened to "turn this goddamned car around" when ten-year-old me sang "It's Raining Men" from the backseat. (She said it was the noise level. But I was sure it was the forecast: "Expect rising body parts, occasional moaning winds, and long, sticky summers projected to last throughout Timothy's life.")

I thought browbeaters all wanted the same thing: obedience. They got off on proving they could make you flinch. But underneath, it was about them trying to wrestle back control of their own impotent lives. Threats, tantrums, ultimatums—it was really just panic.

There was that famous quote: "Knowledge is power." I used to think it meant academic knowledge—people with lofty degrees. But now I was thinking that knowledge could be leverage. It was a quiet kind of power. The kind that made some people nervous.

That thought gave me an almost electric rush. Power wasn't always about money or titles; sometimes, information was currency. Just ask blackmailers. Or hackers who sold people's personal data. Or even Ronan Farrow, whose exposé about Harvey Weinstein brought down the notorious Hollywood mogul and changed acceptable behavior in the film industry. Maybe I had my own currency now. And if someone was worried about what I might do with my knowledge, maybe I could be the one in control.

At least, that was what I told myself. In reality, the thought of someone keeping their eyes on me made my stomach twist into a sailor's knot. But another part of me—the part trying to be adult—kind of liked it. Someone thought I was dangerous. Even though I was not some sort of Norman Bates monster. The most dangerous thing about me was my writer's pen.

But maybe that was it! Writers had started revolutions. Thomas Paine had pamphlets. The English barons had the Magna Carta. People today had Substacks and viral Twitter threads. A blogger could tank a brand in twenty-four hours. A memoir, like Prince Harry's, could peel back the curtain of the powerful. Maybe I was more dangerous than I realized.

But also, maybe—the author of those messages didn't know I was really a wuss.

I was thinking about that last message and the way it had been phrased: Keep quiet...and your head down... I'm watching. It was starting to sound less like a promise of violence against me and more like they simply didn't want a public scene. They only wanted me silent.

But the thing is, once you start believing you've got cards to play, you can't help looking for your next move. And I began to circle back to what Rachel Morris had said about Lillian Trent and her rivals in the cabaret world. Lillian had sharp-elbowed singers and humiliated her pianist, and maybe one of them hadn't moved on from their grievances. It was possible someone was still nursing an old wound. Maybe someone wanted revenge —so they killed her. I needed to find out.

By the time my bus lurched to the stop nearest my apartment, I'd talked myself into following leads Rachel Morris had inadvertently given me. I hoped they might provide more information about why Lillian had ended up strangled to death. Maybe they'd even have information about who was sending me cryptic text threats. So, killing two birds with one stone (my dinner meal and reliable Wi-Fi), I popped into Abu's and grabbed a seat at the counter by the window. I went to Lillian's Facebook page. It was like reading her diary.

Lillian's timeline was filled with selfies, champagne toasts to herself, boasts about celebrity fans, and audiences who "wept during my last note." She wasn't shy about her own magnificence. In one photo, she was wrapped in sequins, clutching a flute of champagne. The caption read, "Another standing ovation! I swear, audiences just keep getting more emotional— or maybe I keep getting better." Another photo showed her onstage, drenched in a pink spotlight, the caption read, "I'm not a diva—I just break out in hives around mediocrity."

Lordy, she'd seemed so down-to-earth the night I saw her perform. Maybe she was a great actress, too! After about ten minutes of going through her posts, even I was starting to feel slightly murderous—and I was someone who liked her (at least onstage).

I found a long thread of eulogies written by admirers. I was touched by their sincerity:

You were magic, Lillian. Heaven just got its headline act.

Can't believe you're gone, Lillian. The stage lights will never shine quite as bright again.

No encore could ever be enough. Rest in peace, Lillian.

But not all the posts were tributes. Some looked like sympathy on the surface, but on closer examination, they seemed to ooze something darker underneath.

Hannah_J: Funny how some folks suddenly turn into saints when they die. Such hypocrisy.

23 Comments · 68 Likes · 8d ago

SoniaVee: Boo-hoo! Crocodile tears for you today.

17 Comments · 54 Reactions · 12h ago

Miles92: I used to think revenge was ugly. Then I learned how satisfying it sounds in C minor.

31 Comments · 71 Reactions · 6d ago

They were all a bit puzzling. Especially that last one. I wondered what "revenge" Miles 92 was talking about. The thread of replies to that last one caught my attention:

Hannah_J: Wow. Bitter much?

Miles92: Not bitter. Just honest. Some people forget what she put others through.

SoniaVee: Everett, don't. Not here. It's not the time.

Miles92: New rule: don't help someone find their spotlight unless you're okay standing in the dark.

Hannah_J: That's in the past. Let it go.

Miles92: Hard to "let it go." Some singers don't just hit high notes—they hit below the belt.

SoniaVee: This isn't helping.

Miles92: Maybe not. They say karma takes requests. I hope it's in the mood for jazz.

I clicked on Miles92. A profile picture showed an exceptionally good-looking thirty-something guy smiling like all was right in his world. His cover photo was a wider shot of him seated at a grand piano. A neon sign mounted on the exposed-brick wall behind him read Manhattan Moon. That was Lillian's last club gig! And now I recognized Miles92. He was Everett Miles— Lillian's accompanist!

I hadn't really paid much attention to Everett Miles that night at the club. For one thing, I was with Brad, and I had complete tunnel vision around him. And for another, I was so absorbed in the magic of Lillian Trent, I'd pretty much blocked out everything else around her.

And now, a memory of Everett surfaced. Onstage, he and Lillian had amazing chemistry. A mix of affection, exasperation, and effortless timing. She was the cool, glamorous wit with the perfect comeback line, and he was the earnest foil, forever a step behind but impossible not to love. Together, they had that rare spark that made teasing feel like foreplay.

They'd bantered between songs, trading stories about the "joys" of rehearsing together. At one point, as Lillian introduced her next song—Sondheim's "Getting Married Today"—she told the audience that when she'd first suggested doing the number in her act, Everett had tried to talk her out of it. "'It's way too hard,' he told me. 'It demands superhuman focus and superb breath control from the singer.'"

Lillian had turned toward him, hand on hip, the picture of mock offense, and said, "Sweetheart, the thing is, I don't breathe—I project."

The audience roared. Everett rolled his eyes, hammering a few dramatic chords like exclamation points. He shot back, "Because of you, I now swear in rhythm."

"Swear all you like, my love. The audience only hears me." Lillian threw the audience a wink that encouraged them to laugh and applaud in agreement. In that moment, they were an electric duo. Two pros sparring for laughs and applause. Their banter had felt effortless, even affectionate.

And now I found myself staring at Everett's Facebook comments, trying to reconcile those with the man I remembered. That post certainly didn't sound like a man mourning a partner or colleague. It sounded like someone still picking at an old scab.

I couldn't square the two versions of him—the easy-going accompanist and the bitter voice behind, "They say karma takes requests..." Which was the real Everett Miles? Maybe Lillian and Everett were only best buds when they were performing together. Like Sonny and Cher.

I scrolled deep into Everett's Facebook page, which was filled with gig announcements and selfies at the piano. There were dozens like that—posts from a man who'd spent most of his life in piano bars. I scrolled down to a picture of a piano keyboard, a single red rose lying across middle C. The caption read: " 🌹 🎹 Is she gone yet?"

Is she gone yet? I looked at the date/timestamp, and my finger froze on the screen. It was posted the afternoon of Lillian's murder.

For a moment, I just stared at it, waiting for my brain to come up with an innocent explanation. Maybe "Is she gone yet?" was part of a song lyric or a line from a Broadway musical. I was especially curious because I remembered Lillian and Everett seeming to have as much fun onstage as we in the audience were having. Teasing each other like old friends. She'd even called him her "other half in B-flat." But here he was posting something that now felt...ominous. "Is she gone yet?"

And speaking of someone being "gone," if I was remembering correctly, that night at Manhattan Moon, Everett had followed Lillian offstage immediately after their set. Maybe he'd seen someone backstage who wasn't supposed to be there. The someone who killed Lillian Trent.

Without giving it much thought, I tapped Miles92 on my screen and sent him a message.

Everett,
My name's Timothy Truman. I'm a writer working on a feature for *Stage Left* magazine about the creative dynamics between cabaret singers and their accompanists. Your name's come up as someone with great insight into that world, and I'd love to include your perspective. Would you be open to a quick chat or a coffee sometime soon? Nothing formal—just a relaxed conversation about collaboration, chemistry, and what really happens behind the scenes. I sort of have a tight deadline, so if you could message me back soon, that would be great. Thanks so much for considering.
—Timothy

23

———

I t was Friday! I was seeing Brad tonight! Dinner at our usual Italian place—Ragacci's—then we'd get all snuggly. We'd have all day Saturday and Saturday night. If it weren't for his non-negotiable Sunday visits with his damned mother in Connecticut, we'd have the entire weekend together. *Sorry, Mrs. Bradford, I don't even know you, and I hear you're actually very nice. I'd love to be your son-in-law.*

Alas, Friday also meant...I was only two days away from Monday. That was when Ms. Klotz returned to the office. *Bugger all!* No doubt she'd spent her away-time poring over that awful project she had me do. If she'd found even one thing to criticize (which, of course, she had), I'd get one of her "development chat" emails. That was her euphemism for emotional dismemberment.

I couldn't imagine why that woman disliked me so much. Unless she'd mistaken me for Timothée Chalamet, in which case...fair enough. It was soul-crushing knowing someone hated your guts—especially when you knew you were a nice person and couldn't pinpoint what terrible crime against humanity you'd committed. Or maybe it was my clothes. I once overheard her telling Mr. Slater, "Mr. Trousdale dresses like a substitute teacher," which I didn't think was an insult until she added, "in a struggling district." Maybe she resented that everybody else in the office seemed to have taken me under their wings. Or maybe it was the fact that I was alive.

Sometimes I wondered if I really was doing something wrong—if there was a smugness in my attitude I wasn't aware of. But then I remembered that some people simply woke up searching for a scapegoat to blame for their miserable lives.

I had the same helpless feeling I had when my daddy remarried, and I suddenly inherited monster stepsiblings who treated me like dog poo. Colt, my stepbrother, was an Olympic-caliber narcissist. His name might conjure rugged appeal, but the guy wouldn't even appeal to his own reflection. He had a gift for turning arguments inside out until you wondered if you really were the thick-headed dum-dum he made you feel you were.

My dad—sweet, gentle, trusting—was a long-haul trucker who spent weeks on the road. Colt knew exactly how to manipulate him.

"That's a stupid job," Colt had said during one of Dad's rare weekends off. "You're a shitty stepfather with a shitty job. If you don't quit and find something less embarrassing, I'll make sure Mom leaves you. I can make that happen. Your life will be hell."

And just like that, my daddy folded. By the end of the week, he'd handed in his notice, claiming it was "for family reasons." He took a job at the nearby Tyson poultry plant—long hours, the smell of disinfectant baked into his skin. He hated every minute of it. His life became the hell Colt had promised.

Then there was my stepsister, Catrine. A real piece of work, that one. She mistakenly thought I was competition for her mother's attention and affection. Hardly. I couldn't stand my stepmother (though I was always pleasant to her face).

Even now, when I journaled and wrote an anecdote about Catrine, I disguised all my mean references behind the nickname I'd given her: Dump Truck. Not my kindest label, I admit —but it fit, and as far as I was concerned, she earned it. Once Catrine set her sights on someone, she backed them into a corner slowly and methodically, flattening anything in her path without ever breaking a sweat.

Much like Ms. Klotz, Colt and Catrine didn't hate me quietly. They spread their disapproval like sneeze germs. I once overheard Catrine tell one of her friends she was "protecting" them from my "pretensions" and "delicate sensitivities." What a load. What she was really doing was making sure everyone saw me the way she wanted them to see me: small and insignificant.

So yes, I'd had my fair share of being despised. I'd escaped Colt, Catrine, and my stepmother when I went to junior college, then moved here to New York. But I couldn't escape Ms. Klotz.

One thing I'd learned—the hard way—was that you can't control other people's misery, only how much of it you let splash onto you. Some people carry storms around; if you stand too close, you're going to get drenched. So I decided not to waste the weekend dreading Monday or Ms. Klotz. She could stew in her own unhappiness juices. I, on the other hand, had time with Brad to look forward to—and two full days to know what utter happiness felt like. Philosophically speaking, that was enough for me. Practically speaking, I was just hoping to satisfy my hormonal fantasies.

Brad and I were eager to get our clothes off and destroy each other. So we ordered our meals from Ragacci's to-go and raced back to his apartment. Of course, the only food we were actually starving for was each other's skin and bones. We put the to-go boxes in the fridge, opened a bottle of Chianti, tore off our shirts, and wrestled into bed.

It had been five days since we'd been together, and our starving bodies clashed with the storm and chaos of a Beethoven symphony—*Number Five*, to be precise—with its fierce *da-da-da-DAAAH!* Fate hammering at the door and demanding to be let in. Every touch was an intense collision of heat and breath. Time and the world disappeared. We were volcano and lava—hot, messy, and alive.

The night had the weight of an Alabama summer—thick and shimmering with heat. That was how it felt to me. We moved in sync, toward something we didn't want to end. But some things were inevitable. They eventually demanded surrender.

When it was over, I couldn't speak. I wanted to. There was so much to say. But language wasn't really even necessary. Brad and I were communicating telepathically. Even the part of me that usually overthinks everything had gone utterly quiet. I was in another world.

Then, after a relatively short time, without planning it, my fingers found their way back to Brad's chest, tracing the dark, silky hairs with the rise and fall of his breathing.

And it started all over again. This time was different. It was like the slow and steady swell of Ravel's *Boléro* instead of fiery Beethoven. Our rhythm began to rebuild—gentler but still desperate. Each movement, each breath, drew us closer to a finale. The tempo climbed until our bodies crescendoed with heat and wounded-animal sounds.

When we finally woke Saturday morning, sunlight was spilling through the shutters, cutting the room into bands of gold and shadow. The air smelled faintly of gym clothes and sweat from all the energy we'd burned through the night before. Brad stretched naked beside me—his muscles lengthening beneath his skin like something sculpted and alive. I watched the way the light touched him, the way it caressed his shoulders, the hair that covered his chest and trailed down his stomach. He caught me looking and grinned, that lazy, knowing grin that always made me forget how to breathe.

"Breakfast?" he said.

Breakfast, indeed! After showering (together), we sat at his kitchen table and devoured the meals saved from the night before. I thought I now preferred my lasagna to be a day old and eaten for breakfast! Maybe it tasted better because it marinated overnight.

Finally, with meat sauce staining his lips, Brad said, "I didn't have a chance to ask how your week was. Guess I had other things on my mind." He said this with a lascivious grin.

For a split second, I thought about spilling everything about the week: the threatening text messages, my interview with Rachel Morris, her suggestion that a jealous cabaret singer could have murdered Lillian Trent, my excavation through Lillian's Facebook pages. Instead, I pivoted. After my tall story to Everett Miles—that I was writing an article for *Stage Left* magazine—I sort of actually believed that and said to Brad, "I'm thinking of trying to write some articles on spec. Something to supplement my temp job income." That wasn't *not* true. I was "thinking" about doing some freelance stuff.

"That's a brilliant idea!" Brad agreed. "What'll you write about?"

Damn! I really hadn't thought that far ahead. But since I'd told Everett the interview was for a piece about pianists and their singers, I hedged and said, "Maybe something about cabaret culture in New York. Behind-the-scenes stuff. You know, what makes a singer and accompanist really click. I've been thinking about it since we saw Lillian Trent."

"Excellent topic," Brad said. "Most people don't realize the pianist is the singer's safety net."

I smiled, playing it cool. "Right. I'm trying to set up an interview with a pianist who was suggested to me. What sorts of questions should I ask? Like maybe, how much does the accompanist shape a singer's performance?"

"You've got really good instincts," Brad said. "A bad accompanist can sink singers before they end their first song. A good one knows how to breathe with the singer." He looked at me with that gentle, teacherly expression that always made me want to learn everything he knew. "Why the sudden interest?"

I shrugged. "Curiosity, mainly. Especially since we saw Lillian Trent's act. I'm sorta fascinated with cabaret now. And I figured that could be a good angle for an article." What I wished I could say, but didn't want Brad to think I was an idiot, was that I was keen on finding out who killed Lillian.

"That's a great place to start," Brad agreed. "Accompanists have the best gossip in the business too, but they guard it like state secrets. But if you get one talking, they'll tell you who forgot their lyrics, who drank too much, and who slept with whom between sets."

He gave me a playful grin. "You'll make a great journalist, Timothy. You've got that nosy instinct."

If only he knew.

24

───────────

The temperature in Ravenscroft dropped twenty degrees when the *Klotz Reaper* swept in at 9:03 on Monday morning. Her eyes searched the offices like a hawk surveying a field of unsuspecting mice. I thought if I stayed perfectly still, maybe she'd mistake me for furniture. I braced myself for her forensic dissection of that blasted project. I expected the ceremonial burning of my self-esteem.

It didn't happen. Not a word. Sometimes waiting for judgment is far crueler than receiving it. It's the anticipation that gets you.

By ten thirty, I started to think maybe the coast was clear. Maybe she'd found new prey. I let myself start to believe I'd worried unnecessarily. So I surrendered to foundation busywork: I alphabetized expense reports, cross-referenced application grant categories, and pretended to look "engaged" every time someone walked by my doorway. It was too quiet, too calm, like just before the shark fin breaks the surface.

Then a message pinged on my phone. But it wasn't Ms. Klotz. It was from Everett Miles:

Hi Timothy. Happy to help if I can. We can meet tonight at the Purple Parrot before the show, if that works for you. I'm playing for Monica Marks. How 'bout 6:30? Let me know.

My heart did a triple axel. The pianist who had backed up Lillian Trent—and whose Facebook posts practically bled resentment toward her—had agreed to talk to me. Apparently I was getting good at inventing imaginary writing projects, because so far I was batting a thousand when it came to suspects saying yes.

Then again, I thought maybe people like to be interviewed. It gave their lives a narrative arc. They thought they were the protagonist in a story and worth quoting. You could see it in their eyes when you pulled out a notebook: *Finally,* they thought, *I'm important.* The promise of being remembered—or even just recorded—did strange things to people. It was like church confession but without the guilt, and with the chance to sound profound. Maybe that was why Everett agreed to meet. Not because I'd convinced him I was writing some incisive piece about cabaret culture—but because, deep down, I think everyone wanted their lives to be printable.

For about five full seconds, I was elated. Then reality sank its teeth in. What exactly was I going to ask him? I'd told him I was writing an article about cabaret singers and their accompanists, which sounded intellectual in theory. Except that I'd made it up on the fly. I hadn't the foggiest idea what info such an article should actually contain. Other than the brief ideas Brad had given me.

All I really wanted to ask was, I saw you follow Lillian Trent offstage after your show, and then she turned up murdered. Explain *that* to me, *buster!* But I needed a road map to get there. Something that would sound journalistic enough to pass as legitimate but not so probing that he'd smell the ulterior motive wafting off me.

No, I needed to ease into it. Warm him up with the kind of questions that sounded thoughtful and flattering, the way George Stephanopoulos did when he was circling a headline for *Good Morning America*. Something simple like, "Tell me about your job as an accompanist"—which made me sound like I understood cabaret. Or maybe, "What's it like working with strong personalities onstage?" (Translation: what's it like working with divas who would eat their young if it meant they'd get the spotlight?)

If I could get him talking about the work—the grind of rehearsals, the politics, the egos—maybe he'd loosen up and start talking about Lillian Trent. I just had to act casual. Charming, even. Still, underneath the panic was a flutter of excitement. This was maybe my chance to get closer to the truth of Lillian's murder. Certainly, closer to someone who'd actually been there moments before she was killed.

Panic crept in. What if I didn't ask the right questions? What if I didn't dig deep enough? Or what if I dug too deep, too quickly, and he realized I wasn't really writing an article about cabaret singers' accompanists? I remembered what Rachel had said about "cabaret cobras." My questions had to feel organic.

That was the thing about me—I was always thinking I'd be found out. It wasn't *impostor syndrome* so much as *impostor certainty*. I'd never quite shaken the feeling that I was one mistake away from being laughed at, corrected, or replaced. It was a leftover reflex from growing up with people who treated my curious nature like an illness. I had to act like I knew what I was doing.

I tapped my phone screen and dashed off a quick message: *Excellent! Meet at PP tonight 6:30. Thanks!*

For a few blessed milliseconds, life was positively radiant. I leaned back, basking in my own brilliance. Timothy Trousdale: fake feature article writer, fake office prodigy, fake administrative savant. The gods of good fortune were shining down on me.

Right. Not so fast. Another ping changed everything. This time it came from my desktop computer. My eyes darted to the screen. My stomach lurched. My smile dissolved. And my blood pressure vaulted like a gymnast. There it was: an email from *Dr. Klotzenstein's Monster* herself. The princess of darkness risen once more from whatever managerial pit she nested in.

My optimism that life was good immediately died. My hands were shaking as I clicked the email.

From: Ms. Klotz
Subject: Assignment
Mr. Trousdale —
I've observed there are thousands of old emails in the
foundation's general message center. Some date back
nearly twenty years. Please review each and categorize
them appropriately. Confirm that each message has been
answered. Flag anything you consider noteworthy. This
is an excellent opportunity to demonstrate attention to
detail. Please send a comprehensive progress report by
Friday at 5 p.m.

I stared at the screen, trying to decide which was more likely: that Ms. Klotz actually believed this was an "excellent opportunity" (and for whom?) or that she wanted to see how long it would take before I jumped off the roof. After a moment of anxiety-filled silence and tears welling in my eyes, I typed my reply with professionalism:

I will begin reviewing the general emails immediately.

Then I sat back and let the full horror sink in. The assignment was sadistic. Twenty years of emails. WTF?

The foundation clearly operated on a "better safe than subpoenaed" philosophy, so every email since the George W. Bush administration was still on file. And what exactly was she even asking me to do? And what did "noteworthy" even mean in Ms. Klotz's world?

Inbox archaeology, that was what it was. I'd be excavating thousands of ancient messages from the dawn of dial-up. I could already see my future as my soul drifted toward the recycle bin. "When I'm dead and gone, tell Brad I love him."

I sighed and opened the foundation's Message Center. Unlike my approach to the *Miscellaneous* folder assignment—with the color-coding and obsessive cross-referencing I'd developed—this time I decided just to dive right in and see where the current took me.

The current took me straight to hell.

Hours vanished. My posture dissolved into a question mark. By five o'clock, I'd managed to process maybe thirty emails—and generate a dull, throbbing headache. I couldn't stay late because I had to get to my interview with Everett Miles. I shut down the computer, grabbed my jacket and rucksack, and raced for the bus. If I hurried, I could get to Times Square and the Purple Parrot on time.

25

———

I arrived at the Purple Parrot a little before six thirty, winded from my half-jog up Eighth Avenue. The entrance was a black steel door with a faded caricature drawing of a bird. No other signage identifying the club. I tugged on the handle once, twice—locked.

There had to be another way in; fire laws required that. I peeked into the scary, dark alley beside the building and started to walk toward a red light in the distance. The alley reeked of urine and garbage. But there was a door at the end. I hesitated, then pulled the handle. It opened!

A stale smell hit me the moment I stepped inside—beer, damp carpet. The door swung shut behind me, carrying a draft that stirred the single overhead bulb hanging from a cord. Its weak light revealed a narrow corridor lined with cardboard boxes stamped with liquor logos: Bacardi, Smirnoff, Jack Daniel's. I followed down the dim hallway until it opened into the main room. I recognized it immediately from Rachel Morris's video: dime-sized tables, a beat-up baby grand piano, and what I'd previously described as a suggestion of a stage—a space beside the piano with a microphone stand leaning to one side.

The Purple Parrot was not purple. And if there had ever been a parrot, it had probably flown into a wall during an especially tragic rendition of "You Light Up My Life."

"Hey!" A voice startled me.

I turned to find a bear in a leather jacket, with a shaved head and a neck thick as a tree trunk.

"We open at seven."

"Sorry," I sputtered. "Everett Miles. I'm meeting him. An interview. He's expecting me."

The bear looked me up and down, then growled, "Wait." He disappeared back into the shadows, leaving me alone with the faint, insect-like buzz of a flickering neon sign that said LIVE MUSIC TO-NITE. (The spelling alone told me everything I needed to know about the venue.)

Somewhere behind the bar, an older woman emptied ice into a sink. She glanced at me suspiciously—probably wondering what sort of idiot had come in early to get a good seat for a nobody-singer's cabaret act.

A moment later, Everett Miles appeared—handsome, tallish, perfect nose, dark bushy eyebrows. Hot! He wore the musician's uniform: black shirt opened down four buttons, revealing a crop of hair rambling over his chest, sleeves rolled up past his wrists, black jeans, black shoes. He gave me a polite but skeptical nod.

"Timothy?" he asked.

My hand shot out to shake his as I tried to act more confident than I felt. "Thanks for meeting me. I really appreciate it."

"No worries. I'm having a G&T—fortification before *la diva* arrives. Want one?" Everett called out to the woman behind the bar and ordered his drink. I asked for an iced tea, please.

We settled at a sticky table near the piano. And, as I had with Rachel Morris, I asked permission to record our conversation. "I just don't want to get anything wrong."

"So, you're writing an article about piano accompanists? That's cool. Most people are only interested in the singers."

I felt myself beginning to relax a bit. He had that kind of easy confidence that made me feel like he could become a friend. I tried to hold his gaze, doing my best not to get distracted by the dark hair visible in the V of his open collar. "I mean, you're half of every performance, but the spotlight always lands on someone else," I said, hoping my voice didn't sound as shaky as I felt. "I think that's fascinating. And worth writing about. How'd you get into it? Being an accompanist, I mean?"

Everett chuckled, swirling his drink. "Necessity. I came to New York to be the next Sondheim. But the rent came due. So I learned to smile and nod and pretend the applause was all for me."

I laughed, encouraged. "Have you worked with a lot of talented singers?"

"Well, I've worked with a lot of so-called *singers*." He lifted his glass, swirling the gin. "Talent's optional in this line of work. Let's just say I'm musically non-discriminatory. I've played for angels and foghorns." He leaned back, looking amused. "But I smile and pretend I'm livin' the dream."

"Must be challenging though," I said. "Especially if the singer isn't really a singer. I've seen a few of those while doing my research."

He leaned in a little, conspiratorial. "That's when you smile the brightest. Rule number one: never let the audience see you panic. Rule number two: never tell the singer they were flat—unless you enjoy unemployment."

I found myself genuinely laughing this time. For someone whose Facebook posts dripped venom, he was disarmingly easy to like in person—sharp, funny, magnetic. I jotted a few words: Smile. Panic. Rules. "What do you think makes a great partnership between singer and accompanist?"

"Trust," Everett said, without hesitation. "You can't fake that.

Singers have to know you'll catch them if they fall—figuratively or otherwise. And you have to know when to follow and when to lead. It's like dancing with someone who thinks they're Fred Astaire but might actually be Elaine Benes."

I thought that was hilarious. Elaine was my favorite *Seinfeld* character—the queen of awkward confidence. She had rhythm in theory, but chaos in execution, which, if I was honest, felt like a metaphor for my entire life.

"You sound like you've had experience with both," I said.

"More Elaines than Freds, I'm afraid. But every once in a while, you get a Lillian Trent."

My pen paused in midair. I thought it would take a lot longer for us to get here, but he'd gone straight to the real reason for my visit.

Everett didn't notice my surprise, but he was gazing toward the piano now, thoughtful. "That woman had timing in her bones. A total bitch a lot of the time, but she was something to see onstage."

I hesitated, letting the silence stretch. I'd learned to let others speak and not interrupt their train of thought because they often revealed much more than expected. Everett stared at the piano stool as if he were watching a ghost sit down.

But the silence stretched too long, and I was concerned about getting us back on track.

"Lillian was special," I said. "I didn't know her personally, but I've checked her out on YouTube. And of course—her death was...shattering." My throat tightened unexpectedly. Was I getting to the crux of the interrogation too quickly? I didn't know the logical next question to ask, so I just said, "It's just awful. Her murder, I mean. Such a loss."

"Yeah. A loss," Everett quietly agreed. "Although some don't see it that way."

"Meaning?"

He drained half his drink before answering. "Meaning

Lillian Trent was the kind of diva who demanded loyalty from everyone around her but couldn't be bothered to return the favor. She also demanded perfection from others but not from herself. When things went wrong onstage—which is bound to happen—it was never her fault. And she treated other singers like unpaid backup vocalists—competition to be crushed rather than colleagues to be respected. And yet somehow, she floated through it all, utterly convinced she was destined for greatness simply because she deserved it. And guess what? It was happening."

I wasn't all that surprised by Everett's ill regard for Lillian. He'd been pretty up front in his comments on her Facebook page.

"Why'd you keep working with her?" I asked. "I know it was a payday, but you're an amazing accompanist. I bet singers are lining up to work with you. You didn't need her."

He pulled a face. "Actually, our time together was over. Unexpectedly, as it turns out," Everett said as he set the glass down. "A week before that last show, she basically told me to get lost. Said she was getting a huge grant from the Adele Cummings Foundation and wouldn't require my services anymore. Her exact words were: 'I'll finally be able to afford someone who plays music, not just notes.'"

My God, that was cold! I was mortified for Everett. Totally dumbfounded. How could anyone say something like that to their creative collaborator? I would have killed her. Well, not literally, but I thought I would have gone onstage and totally ruined her show. Or refused to play at all. But then I supposed Everett was the one who would have suffered the most. Lillian was the star and could put the word out that he was unprofessional or some such lie. Sometimes life's indignities need to be sucked up.

Everett found his voice again. "That totally crushed me. I'm pretty great at what I do. I didn't know she saw things differently.

And just to twist the knife, she added, 'You're okay for some singers. But I'm moving into a whole different league now. I can't keep you around out of pity.' Those words are seared into my memory."

Everett shook his head, jaw clenched tight. There was real heat in his eyes now—anger, yes, but pain too, raw and close to the surface. "I wanted to kill her," he said flatly. Then, almost too fast: "Of course, I didn't." His gaze drifted past me, fixing on something that wasn't there. "But I could've made trouble. Real trouble. She was getting this big fat grant from the Adele Cummings Foundation—six figures—and it was supposed to be confidential until their official announcement."

He let out a bitter laugh, low and sharp. "And yet there she was, running her mouth. Bragging to me. To everyone. Rubbing it in like it was some kind of victory. Five hundred thousand dollars. Like it was nothing. Like I was nothing. Would she reward me for all my support? All the hard work I'd put in? I don't mean like giving me a slice of the grant pie or anything. But maybe take me along with her. Nope. The irony was, I'm the idiot who contacted a friend at the Adele Cummings Foundation and suggested Lillian should be considered for a grant."

That stopped me in my tracks! Everett had a friend at the foundation? A memory flashed into my head: Mrs. Stone inviting me to join her to see Lillian Trent's cabaret show. She'd told me how the foundation's advisors were encouraged to scout for promising artists who might qualify for some of Adele Cummings's money, and there was a singer that a friend of hers thought she'd like.

I couldn't come right out and ask if Everett and Mrs. Stone were chummy because why would I even know Mrs. Stone's name? I was masquerading as a freelance writer, not a lackey in a charity foundation's office. I wanted to circle back to Everett's confession that he wanted to kill Lillian, and I said the first stupid thing that came to mind: "Who do you think killed her?"

The bartender, prepping for the "crowd" that would soon be descending on the club, came around and dropped small bowls of peanuts on each table. Everett took out one and rolled it between his fingers. "Funny thing, everyone talks about how much they miss Lillian now. But plenty of others, not just me, aren't really sorry she's gone. Sure, we've lost a terrific singer but..."

He hadn't answered my question, but I couldn't push further. I hesitated, tracing a finger along the rim of my glass and said, "Yeah, others I've talked to act like she's frozen in amber—preserving the talent, but none of the chaos."

Everett huffed a quiet laugh. "Death by murder does wonders for one's reputation. Lillian's become a saint postmortem."

I pretended to jot something down on my pad. "Still, the way it happened... I mean, to die like that...right after a successful show. You guys had just finished your set that night, right?" I was trying to sound more curious than sniffing around for dirt.

He studied me, the faintest narrowing of his eyes. "We're not talking much about me or other accompanists."

I flushed. "So sorry, Everett. I just think maybe I'll do a piece about Lillian after this one. Might as well get your memories while they're fresh. Is that okay? Can you tell me what happened at the end of the show that night...after you guys left the stage?"

Everett looked past me, toward the piano again. "Like I told the police, it was an uneventful night. Other than...you know... how it ended. The audience's energy was great. She lit up the room. After the show, we went our separate ways. But the more I've thought about it, she did seem a bit distracted during the set. No one would've noticed but me, and I thought maybe she was feeling bad about how she'd treated me. Although I should have known better.

"She wasn't exactly nervous—just maybe more preoccupied than usual. I remember she said she was meeting someone after the show. Wouldn't say who, just told me she wasn't going to bother with an encore. No after-show champagne with friends and fans either. That was unusual because she lived for the attention and adulation."

He paused, swirling the ice in his glass. "I figured maybe it was a date. There was always somebody new. They never lasted more than a few weeks. It was always just about sex. Except she'd hinted the latest one was a better catch than most. 'A good career move,' she'd said. But we never really got into our respective love lives. She had no interest in mine, and I had no interest in hers."

Just as I was about to ask Everett to offer an alibi for where he was immediately after leaving the stage, a woman's voice called out, "Everett! Sound check!"

"Oh, fuck," Everett said. "The diva du jour. She's early." He turned in his chair to face her.

Monica Marks arrived in a frilly, teal-colored chiffon dress that bulged in all the wrong places. "Let's get to it, babe!"

"Give me five," Everett called back, looking at his watch.

"You got two." Monica swept toward the makeshift stage.

Everett sighed, set down his glass, and stood. "Sorry, Timothy. Duty calls. The glamorous life of the underpaid accompanist-slash-life coach. The house'll be empty as usual tonight. Nobody comes out on a Monday."

I absolutely couldn't let Everett go without nailing down his answer to my most important questions. Standing, I said, "Thanks for meeting me. But before I go—since you've probably thought a lot about it—if you had to hazard a guess, completely off the record, who do you think murdered Lillian Trent? The police ruled out robbery."

Everett's jaw tightened. He paused for a long moment, thinking carefully before speaking. He looked over his shoulder and scanned the room. "Okay, you didn't hear it from me, but Lenny Barron comes to mind. The manager at Manhattan

Moon. Lillian signed a contract to appear there on weekends over the next six months. The afternoon before she died, she called him and said he could 'go suck an egg' because once the Cummings grant money poured in, she wouldn't play anywhere less prestigious than the Carlyle. She laughed when he said he'd sue her because he'd spent a ton on advertising and fixing up the room just for her."

God, I didn't want this interview to end. I suspected Everett had so much more he could reveal. But I could tell he was eager to get to the piano—if only to placate his singer. I flipped open my notebook and tried to sound casual. "Just one *last* last question. One thing stood out when I was looking into Lillian's socials. You commented on her last Facebook post with… *'Is she gone yet?'*"

He exhaled hard through his nose. "Oh God. That." Everett ran a hand through his hair. "It was an inside joke between us. Every night, halfway through the set, Lillian would step off the stage, and I'd get five minutes for a solo number. Just me and the mic. I'd say, *Is she gone yet?* It always got a big laugh."

His voice softened a bit. "It was part of the bit. I'd bask in the spotlight for a short time, and then she'd come back and blow the roof off with her next number. We did that at every show. It was…our rhythm."

He looked me in the eyes, then added, "You really should be careful asking these types of questions, Timothy. The cabaret world is a small one. Sometimes a mean one. I'm just saying…'cause you're cute and I wouldn't like to see anything bad happen to you."

I blinked. Was that a threat wrapped in flirtation? Or flirtation wrapped in a threat? Either way, it gave me a weird little shiver—and not the sexy kind. I thanked him again for his time and hustled off to the bathroom. My iced-tea-filled bladder was grateful for the release, and my curious mind was reeling from everything Everett had just said.

By the time I returned a few minutes later, Everett was at the piano, coaxing a few warm-up chords from the battered keys. Monica was testing the mic, her voice echoing against the low ceiling: "Check, check...one, two, three. God, this place stinks of beer and piss."

I grabbed my phone and rucksack, mouthed a quick "thank you" to Everett, and slipped out the back door into the night—carrying with me more questions than I'd come in with.

I caught the bus on Eighth Avenue and found a seat. Earbuds in, I hit play on my phone's voice memo app—to make sure I'd captured the interview and clearly got the name of the manager at Manhattan Moon. Everett's voice filled my ears—calm, resonant—talking about "trust between performer and accompanist." I wanted to get to the last bit and scrolled through the recording, thumb dragging the scrubber bar. I heard the piano and knew that I'd gone too far. I dragged the scrubber back a little, the tinny sound of music dissolving into silence.

Then—a woman's voice—had to be Monica Marks. "Who's the skinny dude you were talking to?" she said.

"A writer. Doing a piece for *Stage Left* magazine."

"*Stage Left*?" Monica's voice was filled with question marks. "Never heard of it. Except when Snagglepuss in the cartoons says, 'Heavens to Murgatroyd! Exit, *stage left!*'" She used the Southern drawl of the flamboyant animated mountain lion's voice and laughed at her own joke. "I'll Google." A moment later: "Huh. Nothing. No website. You sure that's what he said?"

"I think. He's writing about piano accompanists. And Lillian Trent."

"What'd you tell him?"

"Take it easy. I was careful." A pause stretched—then, with a faint, smug curl to his words, Everett said, "I tossed him a bone."

A bone? He'd said it so casually—but the words carried a chill. A prickle ran down my spine. Until this moment, I thought I'd been playing writer/detective pretty convincingly. No one noticed my quiet interrogations. Not the advisors at the foundation. Not Rachel Morris. But the words "I tossed him a bone" meant maybe Everett suspected me of being other than what I'd presented myself as.

But if Everett wanted me distracted, he'd just made sure I couldn't think about anything else.

26

Have you heard the word *wanker*? Or *tosser*? In British English, they mean idiot, jerk, loser. I used to have a pen pal over there who used those words in practically every email: "Some *tosser* nicked my skateboard!" Or "My ex is a total *wanker*." I thought both common nouns applied to *me*, because I'd somehow managed to get myself into something potentially dangerous.

What I didn't get was...well, a lot. I couldn't make out why poking around a murdered woman's legacy suddenly felt like my life's calling and moral duty. Or why I couldn't just leave well enough alone. And I didn't understand why people like Lillian Trent seemed to attract both worship and disdain in equal measure. I heard Diana Ross was like that. And Madonna, too. How was it that the same charisma that drew people in could also make people eager to see them fall?

I also couldn't understand how the Adele Cummings Foundation mistook Ms. Klotz's cruelty for leadership. It was the same kind of hypocrisy you found in organizations with gleaming reputations and miserable employees—wholesome branding, toxic workplace. Perhaps there was a corporate handbook somewhere that stated, "Make the intern cry twice daily, and advancement is assured."

And if I was being honest, I didn't understand myself either. At a time when I should be thinking only about Brad—his seductive voice, his maddeningly sexy body, the way he looked like some exhausted Greek god when he was sleeping—I was instead spiraling about a dead diva, her bitter, long-suffering accompanist, and the singer-not-singer Rachel Morris. Oh, and you could throw in my obsession with Adele Cummings and her missing or dead husband, too. I just couldn't stop wandering into chaos. I must crave drama. Or maybe—simplest of all answers—I was just a *wanker* who could turn a cryptic text notification into a scene from a Hitchcock film.

But I didn't have a lot of time to think about any of that right now because it was Tuesday, and Ms. Klotz had me slogging through her bloody awful email excavation scheme. Curiously, during the night, I thought I'd come up with an idea for sorting through the mess. I was putting the idea into practice, picking one email at random, then doing a global search for every message from the same sender. I'd group them together, then separate them into whatever subject they had in common: grants, gala invites, unpaid invoices, whatever. Once I'd done that, I could tie them together and move on to the next cache. It felt almost scientific.

My system actually seemed to be working! It was efficient, and every time I dropped an email into a designated folder, endorphins kicked in. By noon, I'd built a whole digital filing cabinet of emails and their follow-up responses. Only twenty-five million-billion to go!

I returned from lunch early and was feeling a little bit cocky about my rate of progress. So, with the extra few minutes of my own time, I decided to fool around a bit. I sent a quick DM to Brad to check in (I interrupted him while he was tuning a piano in the presidential suite at the Ritz-Carlton). Then I had a quirky idea and typed my *own* name into the email search bar. I honestly wasn't too surprised when there was a match. An email from SwellHire Top Temps popped up. It was confirmation that they were sending Timothy Trousdale to the Adele Cummings Foundation to begin a trial, open-ended assignment. The correspondence was directed to Mrs. Johnston.

Employees never get to see their personnel files—they're like the Dead Sea Scrolls of HR. So, since the message was about *me*, I was obviously curious. It was a rare opportunity to play email eavesdropper. And honestly, it wasn't like I was prying into payroll data or performance reviews. This was just a letter. Harmless digital chatter. Practically public record. If people were going to write about me, shouldn't I have the right to read what they say? It wasn't snooping—it was *fact-checking.*

I clicked on the email and soon had a wide smile splayed across my lips. Mrs. Johnston had queried about my background and experience, and the response was very satisfying:

From the Desk of H. Lister/SwellHire Top Temps, Inc.
"Your future starts today...and could end on Friday."

Regarding your query, Timothy Trousdale has been a valued member of the SwellHire Top Temps team for six months. Throughout several placements, Timothy has demonstrated professionalism, adaptability, and a cheerful disposition in even the most demanding environments. His organizational and interpersonal skills make him a standout among our *consulting associate*s. His composure during challenging times is exemplary. We would gladly recommend Timothy for any role requiring integrity, discretion, and the ability to remain calm when all around him are losing their heads.

Aww, that was a terrific recommendation! I thought. *Thank you,*

198   RICHARD TYLER JORDAN

H. Lister (have we met?)! And every word of it was true—although they conveniently left out that little matter of how I could've sued them for millions for placing me in a dangerous work environment where my odious boss got murdered, and the homicidal boy-toy husband of a movie star nearly forced me to jump from the forty-fifth floor of a Manhattan penthouse. (Check out *Breakfast at Timothy's* for all the juicy details.) But of course, no one ever volunteers information that makes *them* look bad. People edit their history the same way publicists edit celebrity bios. Still, yes—a terrific commendation.

In my stupor of self-satisfaction, I almost missed the postscript at the bottom:

> P.S. We also wish to extend our appreciation to the Adele Cummings Foundation for their continued partnership with SwellHire Top Temps, Inc., following the unfortunate incident involving one of our former placements, Ms. Rachel Morris, who was terminated following an interpersonal conflict with foundation staff. Again, we regret that situation and appreciate the foundation's willingness to give us another opportunity to demonstrate the high caliber of our associates, such as Timothy Trousdale.

I blinked at the screen. *Terminated after an interpersonal conflict?* Was that what had happened to Rachel? And what exactly qualified as an "interpersonal conflict"? A heated argument? A murder-suicide pact? Ms. Klotz's official incident report said Rachel was fired after being caught rummaging through the foundation's grant files. She'd made it sound like Rachel was committing espionage. So, which was it? A professional disagreement or a break-in?

And I remembered Rachel telling me that someone at the foundation *had it in for her.* I suspected you-know-who. She'd also said something else I'd clocked, about the foundation being all about helping artists in need—*until they discover one of them is answering their phones*. I took that to mean they don't like dual identities. You're either a gofer or a dreamer, but not both.

I pondered for a moment. What exactly had Rachel done to deserve termination? Why the contradictions between Klotz's incident report, SwellHire's apology, and what Rachel herself had told me? I knew people made up reasons about why they'd lost a job. *I was misunderstood... It wasn't a good fit.* Or *my boss was crazy.* Nobody in a million years has ever said, *I sucked at the job.*

But here was what bothered me: the foundation's version wasn't just different from Rachel's—it seemed *strategically different.* As if someone had decided what would look worse for the employee and what would look best for the foundation.

I decided I needed a break—and maybe I could surreptitiously query Mrs. Johnston about why Rachel Morris had been let go. So I grabbed my tea mug and strolled down the hallway to what we euphemistically called the *Hydration Station*—the glorified breakroom. It was absurdly posh. A gleaming Keurig sat beside a tower of flavor pods arranged by roast intensity. There were jars of different loose-leaf teas, bottles of spring water, baskets of organic oat biscuits, dehydrated fruit crisps, and a bowl of lemons.

Mrs. Johnston was just putting away her reusable lunch bag when I appeared in her doorway. She never went out for lunch. "Why pay twelve dollars for a sandwich when you can make it at home for pennies—and a pinch of love?" she liked to say.

"Good lunch?" I asked, adopting my most casual just-passing-by-and-thought-I'd-pop-in tone.

"Mm. Quite," she said. "Tuna salad on whole wheat. How's the new project coming along? Ms. Klotz must believe you're capable of completing her *extra-special assignments.* I think she secretly likes you."

I nearly spilled my tea. "Ms. Klotz hates my guts! That's so obvious! I can feel it radiating through the walls."

"I was being facetious, Mr. Trousdale. Remember office rule number four: maintain a sense of humor?" Mrs. Johnston chuckled. "She doesn't have to like you. We're not in the business of matchmaking. But if you weren't performing well enough, she'd have had me replace you by now."

Her logic was infuriatingly sound. People didn't have to like you to keep you around—they just had to find you useful. It was a bleak sort of comfort.

"But what'd I ever do to her?" I challenged. "I'm probably the most recent in a long line of temps who were either fired by her or who quit. How many were there before me anyway? Ten? A hundred?"

"We do have somewhat of a revolving door when it comes to maintaining temporary staff," Mrs. Johnston admitted. "But of course, I can't discuss personnel issues."

I nodded but hoped I might still glean a bit of specific information about Rachel Morris. "I wouldn't dream of asking for specifics, but if I only knew a bit more about the intern I replaced, maybe I could find a way to survive. Because I know for sure Ms. Klotz is looking for reasons to find me disposable."

I paused, lowering my voice just enough to sound wounded. "I'm hanging on by a thread, Mrs. Johnston. I just... I worry that I'm walking through a minefield, and I'd hate to accidentally step where someone else already exploded. Plus, if I had to leave here, I'd miss working with you."

That earned me points. She folded her arms, considering. "Well...let's just say your predecessor had...differences of opinion with an advisor."

I grimaced. "The usual suspect?"

"Personally, I found her hardworking and enthusiastic—if occasionally irritating. Her vowels were aggressively flattened. She deployed *you guys* with alarming frequency. That said, someone—I don't have to say who—felt there might be an issue brewing."

An issue *brewing*? Like something coming in the future? Like Ms. Klotz was psychic and knew that, down the line, Rachel was going to do something inappropriate and decided to take pre-emptive action? We all have imminent issues, for crying out loud. With enough pressure, any one of us can have a full-on meltdown at any time. But you can't forecast that with any certainty.

Mrs. Johnston gave a little shrug—the kind that said she'd already reached her daily quota for sharing confidential information. "I was just told she had to be replaced. And then you came along. So...happy end-of-story for everyone, I'd say."

Not for Rachel Morris.

I knew HR protocols and professional discretion boxed Mrs. Johnston in, but her bland finality only made me more suspicious. I left the break room and headed back to my office to continue wading through quicksand, sinking deeper with every email.

27

When the skies are gray, and your mood's gone poof!
Listen to the rain on your old leaky roof!

Those were the lamebrain lyrics to a dumb advertising jingle for Silver Lining Assurance—a discount home-owners' insurance company that sponsored every radio weather report in my part of Alabama when I was a kid. I used to think it was the most moronic piece of doggerel I'd ever heard. Almost as bad as "Meow, meow, meow, meow," for a barely feedable brand of cat food. So naturally, I had to write my own parody version:

If your ceiling's crying—boo-hoo-hoo!
Our stupid insurance covers that too!

Back then, I thought I was clever. And now, all these years later, I was humming that damn tune again while riding the bus, and rain slapped against the windows. It didn't help that I couldn't decide if my despair was merely nostalgia resurfacing or a reflection of how depressed I felt. Surely the latter. Thanks to everything going on in my life, my mood had definitely gone *poof—like the leaky roof!*

As I stared at the fogged-up window, my mind replayed Mrs. Johnston's earlier comment about the "imminent issues" Ms. Klotz felt certain would appear out of nowhere from the intern I replaced (who definitely had to be Rachel Morris). *Issues about what?* I wondered. Because the more I thought about the way Ms. Klotz had treated *me*, the more certain I was she'd probably projected her own "issues" onto Rachel, too. I could understand Rachel not quitting because she needed a job. But I wanted to know the actual circumstances that led to her being replaced by me.

But what excuse could I use to coax Rachel into another interview? Maybe I'd say I'd spoken to Everett Miles—which was true—and needed to fact-check a few things. But what if she pressed for specifics before agreeing to meet? I guessed I could mention Lenny Barron, the manager at Manhattan Moon—the guy Everett claimed was angry with Lillian for dumping their contract. Still, I doubted Rachel had ever graduated beyond singing at the Purple Parrot, so her insight into Lenny's management style at a swanky upmarket venue would probably be limited. Just a hunch.

The truth was I wanted to know what Rachel meant by her crack about getting "a look behind the curtain" when she worked at the foundation. I almost didn't care what the pretext was for us meeting again. I just needed to find out more about the connection between the foundation and Lillian Trent— other than Lillian having been on track to receive a large grant. Rachel Morris was the only link I could think of. Which was why I was now doing the stupidest thing ever. And I actually hated myself for it.

I texted Rachel. But not a normal "Hey, can we arrange a follow-up interview?" No. I wrote, *Hey, about that friend you said would "eat me with a spoon"? Let's discuss.*

The moment I hit send, my stomach dropped into my shoes. What had I just done? I wasn't even remotely interested in meeting anyone. I'm in love with Brad. This was just a ploy.

And yet, here I was—bartering away my dignity for intel like some spy in a John Le Carré novel. I could practically hear the ominous background music as I stared at my phone, waiting for her reply. A typing bubble appeared. Then disappeared. Then reappeared. What was she doing—agonizing over her wording, deciding whether to trust me?

Then my phone *pinged* with a WhatsApp DM. But it wasn't Rachel. And not Brad. I recognized it instantly.

6:43 — No Caller ID (delivered)
Rules, Timothy. I thought you understood the rules.

Oh, Christ! I stared at the message, the bus humming beneath me, the city blurring past outside. Someone was still watching me. Still close enough to know what I was up to. I was already feeling morose, and when I was this blue, I sometimes lashed out because I almost didn't care about the consequences. I typed fast, thumbs trembling.

I don't know what your damn rules are! Stop hiding and tell me who the hell you are and what you want from me!

I hit send before I could second-guess myself. Three dots appeared. Then vanished. The silence that followed felt like someone holding their breath on the other end—waiting for me to make the next wrong move.

The bus lurched over a pothole, and a cold shiver snapped through me. I wanted to call Brad. He was the calm one, the brainy one; he'd know what to say and tell me what I should do. But this wasn't something we could talk about over the phone while I was riding the bus. Plus, he'd probably insist I call the police. And if I said I wouldn't, then he would because he loved me and wanted to protect me.

As for "rules," Everett Miles had talked about rules. Number one: "Never let an audience see you panic." Number two: "Never tell a singer they sang flat." But I doubted that was what my phantom was talking about. Then I also remembered his warning just before I left the Purple Parrot. "You really should be careful asking questions... The cabaret world is a small one... Sometimes a mean one." At least his voice in my head had replaced the damn insurance company jingle.

Then I was startled by another *ping!*

Finally! Rachel: *Awesome. Tomorrow? 7:00? Delancy Rooftop?*

At least one thing was going my way. I hunched over my phone, shielding the screen as if someone on the bus might see what I was doing and rat me out to Brad. I tapped a thumbs-up emoji and pressed Send.

28

─────────

The Delancy Rooftop was an upscale lounge with a killer view of Manhattan's skyline and the Williamsburg Bridge. Rachel was already there when I arrived —leaning in close to a guy. A *very* good-looking guy, I might add. They were laughing—the laugh people share when they were either flirting or plotting something.

My stomach did a slow, sinking roll because—oh, damn—it had to be *him*. She'd brought the guy. *The one with the spoon.* I thought I'd be able to meet her on her own to squeeze her for intel about the foundation. Then I'd agree to a blind date to keep her happy and later cancel it with some invented deadline for the fictional article I *wasn't* writing. Once, maybe twice— three times, tops—until the poor guy got the message.

Before I could retreat, Rachel spotted me and waved like she was flagging down a rescue boat. The guy looked at me too, and —of course—he had the kind of face that made you reconsider your moral principles. Ruddy complexion. Strong jawline. Wide shoulders. An Ultrabright® toothpaste smile that could've sold life insurance to a corpse.

He was polite too. As I walked toward them, he stood and offered his hand to shake.

Rachel said, "Thane, Timothy. Timothy, Thane."

Thane. Of course his name is *Thane.* Like his parents knew he'd grow up handsome, they gave him a name that suited a Marvel superhero.

Rachel beamed like she'd just orchestrated a royal engagement. "See? I told you he was sort of adorable." She giggled at Thane.

I could feel the blood blossoming in my cheeks. Like the time my gym teacher cornered me in the locker room and said I had "excellent form." Which was odd, since I was no athlete. I couldn't even sprint away from gym teachers.

Thane laughed softly. "You didn't oversell." He said this in a clearly audible aside to Rachel, as if I weren't there.

I was pretty sure my face was now the same shade as the maraschino cherries in the garnish tray on the bar.

Rachel gave my arm a friendly squeeze. "Relax, Timothy. You look like you're about to be interrogated by the police for a crime you didn't commit."

If she only knew.

Thane leaned in a little, his smile easy. "So, Rachel tells me you're a writer."

"Well, kind of. Sort of. I'm trying," I said, too quickly.

Rachel rolled her eyes. "He's modest. He's probably brilliant. Nerds usually are."

On my bar stool, as Thane's knee accidentally-on-purpose brushed mine, I realized with sinking dread that my fear had come true: he liked me. Even worse, I had to admit there was a sort of instant vibe between us. I ordered something from the bartender that I didn't really want—an artisanal beer—just to have something to hold, preferably between me and my growing sense of doom.

Thane was warm and friendly, told me his last name was

Granville, and asked the kind of first-date questions that make normal people feel valued and people like me break out in a rash. "How long have you lived in the city? What kind of music are you into? How is it that someone as cute as you is single?"

I laughed too nervously and took a swig of beer. *He just assumed I'm single.* I didn't want to lead him on, but I also didn't want to be rude. Or *honest,* which was the more dangerous option because, I admit it, I was maybe, sort of, actually, slightly attracted to him. Not enough to do anything about it, of course. *I'm definitely not looking!*

"And you?" I asked to be polite. But I substituted "line of work" for the "cute and single" part of the query.

"Five years. A singer, like Rachel. The American songbook—Ella Fitzgerald–type stuff."

Of course he was a singer. I vaguely remembered Rachel telling me that. Cabaret was their common denominator. Even though I didn't know him well enough to pass judgment, I could tell he was definitely above her social class and probably a better singer, too. Just guessing.

Meanwhile, the bar was getting really noisy, and I was terrified I wouldn't be able to have a meaningful conversation with Rachel. So I pounced. "When we met the other day, you predicted I wouldn't be able to get anyone from the Adele Cummings Foundation to talk to me for the article."

I looked at Thane and explained, "I'm doing a piece about the cabaret scene. That's how Rachel and I know each other." I turned to Rachel. "I got an interview," I lied. "They were very helpful. And I think I know who the difficult one is that you told me about. The one who 'had it in for you.' Ms. Klotz?"

"Bingo!" Rachel grimaced. "You journalists are so good at wheedling information from people. I would have sworn that bitch—and everyone else there—would never speak to you. They're so tight-lipped when it comes to press."

Of course, I lied. Ms. Klotz hadn't spoken to me. Ever! About anything! But Rachel didn't need to know that. Let her think what she wanted.

"Okay, Mr. Writer. Off the record. I told you my assignment at the foundation ended abruptly. That part's true. But maybe I brought the end on myself. I came across some stuff that I think nobody's supposed to know about. Maybe not even a certain billionaire—if you get my drift."

Now we were getting somewhere. Rachel was about to reveal the deepest, darkest secrets of the Adele Cummings Foundation. Maybe the charity was a sham? Like the Trump Foundation? Or Ms. Klotz was doing something nefarious, and she didn't want it discovered. All wishful thinking on my part.

"That woman pulled some other serious shit on me," Rachel went on. "When the agency dropped me, the recruiter told me, confidentially, that SwellHire got this detailed report claiming I'd been caught going through grant files. It said policy consultant Stephanie Klotz and a whole battalion from the NYPD escorted me out of the building. That was total baloney. Mostly. Yes, I *did* snoop around Lillian Trent's confidential file a little. I confessed to that. I just wanted to see how much money she was getting. The world was going to know soon anyway. And I wanted to maybe understand why I was turned down.

"You're not going to believe this!" Rachel continued with so much resentment in her voice that I thought she might explode. "Lillian *effing* Trent was getting *five hundred effin' thou* from Adele *effing* Cummings! I said, *No effing way, Jose!* How? Why? I would have killed for that!"

Rachel's wine buzz had turned to a wobble, and her words were sliding around each other, saying things she probably otherwise would have kept to herself. And she'd just casually said she'd *kill* for Lillian's grant money. My brain snagged that. A turn of phrase, sure. People say that all the time. But still, it stuck to me like lint.

Rachel hailed the bartender for a top-up of her Chardonnay,

then continued to spout off. "Ms. Klotz somehow knew I'd seen those files. She monitored all my computer time. Like she had nothing better to do. I'm sure she was sabotaging me. Setting me up so I'd have no defense when she decided it was time to pull the plug. For instance, I think she swiped my computer access card and logged in to my account. Afterward, she turned my card in to Mrs. Johnston and said she found it on the street outside Ravenscroft, and I was obviously negligent. That was bull. And she could have returned it to *me* instead of nosey Mrs. Johnston."

What Rachel said about Ms. Klotz using her credentials to access files actually made some sense. I remembered that, early in my job placement, I'd stumbled across Lillian's NDA and the Titan Shield International investigators' invoice in the *Miscellaneous* folder—and then, suddenly, they vanished. When they reappeared, they were buried in an entirely different, and completely inappropriate, directory. The audit tag read "RMorris—last modified by."

So if Rachel hadn't moved them, maybe Ms. Klotz had—using Rachel's login credentials. But why would she do that? I asked Rachel if she still had her access card.

"That was the first thing I had to surrender when Mrs. Johnston off-boarded me," Rachel explained. "Said she felt bad about me leaving and insisted she didn't have a clue why I was being let go. Come on. The woman prides herself on knowing everything that goes on in that hellhole of an office. She had to know it was Ms. Klotz. Those rich bitches all stick together. I never trusted her. Such a faker."

I didn't appreciate Rachel—an obviously disgruntled employee—saying anything disparaging about the elegant Mrs. Johnston, my personal Mother Hen. And Ravenscroft was the furthest thing imaginable from a "hellhole." But of course, I didn't say anything. I didn't want to risk alienating her. I still had to squeeze her for more info. Disagreeing with her wouldn't help. I needed her chatty—and maybe drunk—not defensive. I finished off what was left in my bottle, ordered another, and deftly changed the subject.

"I talked to Lillian Trent's accompanist, Everett Miles, for my article. Seems like a nice guy. Had some interesting things to say about the cabaret world in general...and Lillian's murder specifically." Of course, he hadn't really, but it was worth fibbing about to see how Rachel would react.

Rachel nodded, cautious. "He would know. He played for me a few times before he got busy with all of Lillian's gigs. She said he wasn't to waste time with me. Typical diva."

I blinked. "She actually *said* that? Out loud? Not to 'waste time with you'?"

"Well, not only me directly," Rachel said. "She meant all the other second and third-tier singers, too. Someone told me she overheard Lillian say that at the Duplex one night after a set. She was bragging that she was rising so fast, and Everett didn't need to waste his time on 'girls who were still learning their keys,' or something equally nasty."

I let out a low whistle. "Wow. Charming. I mean, I heard she had a reputation for arrogance, but that's next level." A shiver went down my spine. I'd heard enough about Lillian by now to know that she didn't just burn bridges—she blew the ashes in peoples' eyes. "I sort of got the impression their partnership— she and Everett—wasn't exactly a love match," I added, trying to bait her.

But before Rachel could respond, Thane leaned forward. "Small world. I actually know Everett. A little. Well, I *knew* him. Past tense. Tangentially. We dated a couple of times. Nice enough, I guess. Seriously talented. Maybe a little Jekyll and Hyde. A bit of a temper when things didn't go his way. Didn't seem to cope well with all the stress of working with Lillian. Frankly, I think he's sort of an unhappy guy. He sometimes talked about playing for her and said he was tired of it...or her.

I'm not sure which. Or both. I got the impression she treated him like the help rather than as a collaborator. He said one of them would probably end up killing the other."

My jaw dropped.

"As a joke, of course," Thane quickly added when he saw my reaction. "Cabaret people live on melodrama." He toyed with his beer bottle, rolling it between his palms. "But I admit I did think of that when I'd heard Lillian was murdered."

I could feel my pulse soaring. Everett Miles: Bitter. Jealous. Maybe even homicidal?

Thane looked at Rachel and chuckled. "You also mentioned the Adele Cummings Foundation a minute ago. I remember Everett saying something about an advisor there. A woman named, um, Stone, I think. I wonder if she ever got over her crush on him."

Something inside me snapped to attention.

Rachel barked out a laugh, nearly spat out her wine, and doubled over on her barstool. "Ha! Mrs. Stone! That one crushed on a lot of hot guys. Like the UPS driver. Attractive woman—polished, elegant—but seriously repressed. Her husband's some corporate bigwig who's never home, so I guess she finds her own extracurriculars.

"The day Everett came by to drop off Lillian's grant application? I remember she practically melted when she saw him," Rachel said. "Hanging on his every word, plying him with tea and compliments, giving him this whole breathless tutorial about how the foundation chooses its recipients carefully, but she was sure Lillian Trent was an excellent candidate for a big award, and she'd personally review the application. And she wouldn't let him leave until he played the piano for her. They say, 'money can't buy class.' Turns out, when a sexy and talented man's in the room, Mrs. Stone's just like everyone else with eyeballs."

Thane snorted. "That's funny because Everett joked that she

was ready to adopt him—or do something a lot less maternal. Was she blind to the fact he's gay? Or maybe she likes a challenge."

"Mrs. *Stone*?" A laugh caught in my throat. "*The* Mrs. *Remington* Stone? The one who jets off to Aspen skiing holidays in her husband's *private* Gulfstream?"

Oh, damn. Big mistake! I wasn't supposed to know any-thing about Mrs. Stone or who she even was—beyond what anyone might pick up during a brief visit to the Adele Cummings Foundation for an interview or a passing introduc-tion. Yet here I was, sounding like someone with inside informa-tion. Thankfully, neither of them seemed to notice my gaffe. Even so, I gripped the bar to steady myself. Because if Rachel and Thane were right, that meant the very same Mrs. Stone who'd taken me to see Lillian Trent at Manhattan Moon that fateful night hadn't been swooning over the cabaret singer at all. She'd been ogling Lillian's accompanist.

I flashed back to that night at Manhattan Moon. Just after Everett and Lillian finished their set, Mrs. Stone had excused herself to find the ladies' room. At the time, I hadn't thought twice about it—she just needed to pee. But now...I wasn't so sure. Maybe she'd gone looking for Everett.

The Delancy Rooftop was suddenly spinning a little, and I couldn't tell if it was from the beers I'd polished off, or the sudden memory of the night Lillian Trent was murdered. I must have gone quiet and distant because, suddenly, Rachel was snapping her fingers. "Earth to Timothy." She laughed. Her voice yanked me out of the loop playing in my head.

Then Thane glanced at his watch. "Righty. I should get going. We're cutting the first track of the new album early in the morning. I need to be fresh."

We all stood, and for a second, no one seemed to know how to end the night. Thane smiled, expectant, and held out his phone. "Can I get your number, Timothy? Maybe we could grab a coffee...or something...sometime when you're not in deadline mode?"

My heart did a little tug-of-war with my brain. "Absolutely," I said, tapping my number on his screen. "FYI, I'm pretty swamped for the next couple of weeks. My editor's already sharpening his guillotine."

Thane chuckled softly. "I like your sense of humor. I look forward to when you're not working under the gun. I think you're nice."

He pocketed his phone, then hesitated. "Mind if I...?" Then he leaned in and kissed me! A polite brush of lips, light as breath, but warm enough to make my navel ache.

Instantly, guilt detonated—hot, blinding, ridiculous. I hadn't asked for the kiss. I hadn't wanted it. But I admit I liked it. And now I was the worst person alive. I could almost feel Brad's moral radar pinging. I forced a smile.

As I watched him leave, I couldn't help thinking that if I didn't have perfect Brad—if life had rolled the dice just a little differently (I was glad it didn't)—Thane would've been the sort of guy I would definitely be interested in.

Thane was barely two feet away when Rachel, with a lasciv-ious smirk, said, "What'd you think? I hear his spoon's in his pants...and it's more of a ladle."

I nearly choked.

29

As soon as I left the bar, I called Brad. It was still drizzling—like the weather itself was guilt-tripping me—so I ducked under the awning of a discount clothing store that proudly advertised *Two Hoodies for Ten Bucks!* Brad picked up on the second ring, sweet as ever, his voice the sound of home. I said I'd been at the Delancey Rooftop to interview a couple of cabaret people. Technically true. And that I'd had a couple of brews. Also accurate.

What I didn't mention—what I *couldn't* mention—was the kiss. Because how did you explain a kiss that wasn't exactly a kiss? And how did you confess to something that wasn't your fault, and you didn't fully engage in, but that, for one split second, made your stomach flutter? The psychology of omission is that by withholding information, you're not deceiving anyone (except possibly yourself), you're protecting them from unnecessary concerns. So I wasn't lying. I was just—selectively disseminating facts. *I know—semantics.*

I told Brad I'd had a good evening but missed him and couldn't wait for our standing Friday-night-through-early-Sunday-morning date. Every syllable of that was absolutely true.

But when he said he was proud of me for "pursuing my free-lance writing dreams," I felt a thousand times more guilty. Because somehow, in trying to sound casual about my little side project, I'd let him believe I was actually writing an article—when in reality, I was sleuthing.

Just as we were about to hang up, Brad asked, "Everything okay? You sound...off somehow."

Well, of course I did. I was juggling guilt, fear, and mild arousal. "Exhausted," I said, which was true enough.

"That's what you get for staying out late with all your other boyfriends." He laughed.

Brad was teasing, of course, but the words hit me like a pinprick straight to the heart. I fake-laughed, tried to sound affectionately indignant, but inside I felt like a fraud. It made me even sadder than I'd been all day. Because the thought of "other boyfriends" wasn't funny to me. It was unfathomable and unbearable. I couldn't imagine a world or a time where there was anyone other than Brad.

Because I was absolutely certain there wasn't a better man on the planet. The mere idea that someone could ever come between us—or that I might do something to make him not love me anymore—made my eyes well up. Brad was the first thing that had ever felt solid, safe, and right in my entire life, and I would do anything to protect that. Love is selfish, okay?

By the time we hung up, I was a mass of guilt, confusion, and rainwater. I stood under the awning, watching the drizzle turn sideways, and thought: *There's only so much chaos one brain can handle before it explodes.*

Between my phantom stalker sliding into my DMs about *rules*, Ms. Klotz waging psychological warfare at work, Rachel half-joking that she'd *kill* for Lillian Trent's foundation grant money, and Thane's reminiscence about Everett Miles, saying he and Lillian were destined to kill one or the other, my neurons were tap-dancing on thin ice. Add Everett on my voice app telling Monica Marks that he'd "tossed me a bone," maybe to deflect from something darker he was hiding, plus the Adele Cummings enigma (Dead? Alive? Cryogenically preserved?) and her missing husband from twenty-five years ago—I felt like a human stress ball someone was squeezing.

And now, somehow, I'd managed to add to the list the unwanted kiss from a handsome stranger with delusions of romance—and a euphemism in his pants.

By the time I made it back to my apartment, I was only half a Blanche DuBois away from being collected by men in white coats.

I carried my anxiety into the next morning, and I prayed I wouldn't be around if the UPS man came to deliver a package to Mrs. Stone. The day moved along. I was keeping up with Ms. Klotz's sadistic assignment, playing the dutiful temp, and pretending I wasn't being emotionally waterboarded. But even as I clicked through the foundation's ancient emails (I was finally into the 2010s), my mind was drifting back to last night's "interview" and the ideas Rachel and Thane had planted in my head.

I remembered Rachel complaining that Ms. Klotz had swiped her computer access card and used her credentials to monitor her cyber footprints—and maybe even fabricate grounds for firing her. It had sounded paranoid at first, except... now, as I thought about it, it sort of didn't.

Then there was Thane, with his aside about dating Everett Miles and remembering Everett said he'd *kill* Lillian Trent or she'd *kill* him. People say things like that all the time—"I could *kill* my boss" or "My ex is *murdering* my soul"—but this sounded...*plausible.*

And finally, what they'd both said about Mrs. Stone—

elegant, *married* Mrs. Stone—apparently a honeybee in search of a stamen and Love Potion No. 9. They'd painted a version of her I'd never imagined, even though I did sometimes imagine others' intimate relations. My imagination sometimes bordered on voyeurism. It wasn't like I *wanted* to picture other people's sex lives—it just happened. I saw an attractive couple, and suddenly my brain was staging a scene where they were undressing each other—complete with camera angles and theme music by James Horner.

"Stop it!" I suddenly said to myself aloud—just as Mrs. Stone was walking by my office door.

She peeked in. "Stop what, Mr. Trousdale? Are you having a heated debate with the devil on your shoulder or am I interrupting a bad daydream?"

"Sorry. There's a riot going on in my head," I said, forcing a weak smile. "I've got Ms. Klotz's impossible project. My roommates' usual feud over the rent money. And...I'm still having a hard time getting a grip over finding Lillian Trent's dead body. I know it's been, like, three weeks, but the images hit me at all hours, at all sorts of unexpected times. Maybe this is what PTSD is like."

Mrs. Stone's expression softened. "It's probably normal. That was a horrible night. You'd think our brains would have evolved to file away unpleasantness and move on. But sometimes...I still see Everett at the piano—beautiful and talented. And Lillian standing there beside him."

There was something in her voice—warm and wistful. And that caught me. Maybe it was nothing except the fact that Everett's name slipped past her lips before the dead singer Lillian's. And she said *Everett* was beautiful and talented— not *Lillian.* Something about that landed oddly. Probably because I'd just heard the gossip about her alleged crush on Mr. Piano Fingers.

I told myself I was reading way too much into Mrs. Stone's

tone. She was far too elegant, too composed, too *married*, to be mixed up in anything as messy as an affair. As if desire only belonged to the lower classes. People could admire musicians without it being scandalous—I practically melted when Brad played. So what she'd said was probably harmless. Or maybe... Freudian. Because if there was one thing I'd learned, it was this: the order in which people said other people's names often revealed who was most important in their thoughts.

I managed a nod, but my brain had already time-traveled to that fateful night at Manhattan Moon: Lillian Trent and Everett Miles leaving the stage. Mrs. Stone excused herself to find the ladies' room. Until this moment, I hadn't thought much about that. People have to pee. But now...it occurred to me that maybe she'd gone to congratulate Everett on a terrific show—and bat a few of her seductive Bambi-like eyelashes. Maybe she'd even knocked off Lillian Trent.

"Maybe it's a good thing I found Lillian's body and not, say, a fan or a friend. Or even you..." I mused. "You went through the back hallway shortly before I did, remember? What if you'd seen something—or someone? You could have been hurt."

Mrs. Stone slowly nodded as she seemed to be recalling the events of that night. "I hadn't considered that. I even forgot that I'd left our table. And Lillian must have been killed right around the same time. I'm horrified to think that I might have been only a few feet away when it happened. And maybe the killer was still around. Oh, this is freaking me out, Mr. Trousdale."

I'd watched enough episodes of *Homicide Hunters* on TV to know that after a traumatic event, some people's brains temporarily block out or blur details. It's a totally normal form of self-preservation. *Stress-related amnesia*, they call it. The brain's focus narrows, and it might record only fragments of an experience. It had happened to me.

"Lately, bits I'd forgotten about that night have started coming back to me," I said. "Maybe our brains *have* evolved but hide stuff until we're emotionally equipped to handle it. The makeup vanity in Lillian's dressing room, for instance. I sort of now remember cosmetics were scattered all over the place. She probably struggled with her killer. Has anything like that come back to you?"

"No," said Mrs. Stone, almost adamantly. Then, as if her thoughts were reaching back and scanning a scene in a movie, she said, "I sort of remember someone came out of the ladies' room and they held the door for me. And the kitchen was nearby, too. I could hear the clatter of pots and pans. But otherwise..." She paused, her nose wrinkling in delicate disapproval. "Oh, and a perfume. I smelled something ghastly. Like what I imagine that Sarah Jessica Parker fragrance I've seen advertised might smell like. I think it's called *Lovely*. Although anything marketed as 'Manhattan sophistication'—isn't."

This was the first time I'd ever heard even a subtle hint of snobbery in Mrs. Stone's voice. She always gave the impression of wealth without condescension, a natural grace that made pretension seem ungracious. But that little jab about cheap celebrity-endorsed perfume carried a trace of disdain—like she'd caught a whiff of the wrong crowd.

And now that she'd mentioned perfume, another memory tugged at me, too. A scent in the back hallway at Manhattan Moon—something old-fashioned. I remembered while I was looking for the men's room, a fragrance had taken me by surprise and straight back to my grandmother's wake, where the funeral director had rouged her cheeks, teased her hair into obedient curls, and—worst of all—spritzed her body with something sickly sweet that clung to the air around her coffin. A similar type of cloying perfume had floated through the back hallway of the nightclub that night.

"Did you see Everett Miles when you were back there?" I asked as casually as I could, aiming for curious rather than investigative.

Mrs. Stone gave a quick shake of her head. "Why would I?"

I wanted to say, *Why wouldn't you? It wasn't exactly Times Square. You couldn't miss him if he were there.* Instead, I said, "Just that he and Lillian went that way a few minutes before you. I thought maybe you'd crossed paths."

She looked deep in thought, as if replaying the timeline, then shrugged. "No. I didn't see either of them."

30

I can't really figure out what species of alien reptile Ms. Klotz is, but my money was on Zyloth dragon (from the outer rim of the Lizz'ar Galaxy). She wasn't cold-blooded in the literal sense, but if anyone could drop a room's temperature by sheer presence, it was her. I couldn't help wondering what made her this way. Power? Privilege? Poor potty training?

Mrs. Johnston once told me that Ms. Klotz had arrived at the foundation without any of the advisors being consulted. One of those "this is happening, so deal with it" appointments, she'd said. But who the hell was Stephanie Klotz?

Ms. Klotz worked when she felt like it. There didn't seem to be any accountability. No oversight. Must be nice. You'd think that kind of setup would make a person *pleasant*—grateful, even. Instead, she walked around as if we'd all been handpicked to disappoint her. I'd never seen anyone in the office be unfriendly to Ms. Klotz; that wasn't their style. But I could tell they were careful around her. She was a lone wolf in a pack of golden retrievers. People lowered their voices when she passed or suddenly developed a passionate interest in the copier.

And what exactly did she do as the foundation's *policy consul-*

tant? I'd never seen her consult with anyone. But maybe those things were done over cocktails, after office hours at a posh bar with waiters in tuxedos. Her professional background? She was barely in her thirties, which didn't seem like enough time to have accumulated much actual experience in anything—unless it was in the dark arts. And where had she gone to school? Probably one of those snooty Whitmore Academy for Young Women-type places where instruction included fencing, French, and the fine art of weaponizing raised eyebrows. Of course, it was none of my business—but you know curiosity was my best skill.

I'd once asked Mrs. Johnston what, exactly, Ms. Klotz did around here. She'd lowered her readers, gave me the look people reserve for children, and people who are slow to get a point.

"She reviews documents...drafts statements...and occasionally terrifies lawyers. She's the person they bring in when the other advisors don't want to get their hands dirty. If something goes wrong with a grant or a staff member, Ms. Klotz reviews the policy." I thought that was polite foundation-speak for *making the problem disappear.*

That explained a lot. Especially why everyone in the office went a little rigid whenever her heels clicked down the parquet floors.

But where did she come *from*—originally, I mean? Nobody just materializes without leaving a digital footprint. I decided to see what I could find out.

I started with the obvious: Facebook. Stephanie Klotz appeared several times. One was a dental hygienist in Tulsa. Another, a party planner in Boca Raton. Stephanie Klotz, the travel agent, posted endless photos of her Labradoodle, Muffin. All these Stephanies were smiling, and all definitely not *my* Ms. Klotz. Absent from every photo were the small, deep-set eyes and long nose.

Then I tried Instagram—same result. There was a Stephanie Klotz who crocheted baby bonnets, another who taught hot yoga in Portland, and one who seemed to be a professional dispenser of motivational quotes. None of them bore the faintest resemblance to the woman who'd called me a "pity hire."

So I moved on to LinkedIn. Surely, I'd find her there. Everyone with a résumé had a LinkedIn profile. But Ms. Klotz? Nothing. No photo, no job history, no trace of her existence. It occurred to me that I still had the LexisNexis login credentials that Mr. Slater had given me, so I typed her name into the search bar. The page came up blank. No public records, no property deeds, no litigation, no alum notes. Nothing. I tried variations— S. Klotz, Steph Klotz, Klotz-Stephanie—with the same result. It was like searching for a fictional character in a census database. I started to think maybe she was in the witness protection program.

I'd hit a wall—a corporate, soundproof wall. Google, Facebook, Instagram, LinkedIn, LexisNexis... Nothing. If Stephanie Klotz had a past, it had been dry-cleaned.

Curiosity might not have killed the cat, but it had definitely lured me into the foundation's intranet—specifically the Staff Resources drive, a place I technically had access to because I'd been assigned to help reorganize twenty million-trillion light-years' worth of digital clutter.

Inside was a folder labeled *Advisors Directory*. Not HR files— nothing sensitive like salaries or Social Security numbers—just the internal roster used for whom to contact in case of emergency. I clicked it open. The usual suspects appeared. The five people I knew and saw around Ravenscroft every day. But no Stephanie Klotz.

Then it hit me. Right. Ms. Klotz wasn't technically an employee. Maybe she wasn't listed because she was a *consultant*. That kind of role sometimes bypassed HR entirely.

So I backed out one level and opened the folder

marked *Contract Personnel*—where external consultants, vendors, and short-term specialists were listed. Surely, she'd be in there. And she was!

Sort of.

A folder labeled *Klotz, S.* sat between a communications consultant who'd left in 2019 and a fundraising strategist whose contract had expired two years before I was born. I clicked it open. Inside was almost nothing—one meager page. No home address. No date of hire. No contract. No HR notes. No onboarding forms. Not even a phone number.

Just a single entry:

Emergency Contact:

Jason R. Pritchert, Esq.

(Private number — restricted)

That was it. Her entire presence in the system. No résumé. No background check. No references. No "Welcome to the Foundation!" email. Nothing except a lawyer whose phone number was too sensitive even for the directory. It was like she'd been air-dropped into Ravenscroft, and the team had simply shrugged and accepted the parachute as valid identification. Even for this place, that seemed weird.

I stared at the screen, baffled. Because what if Ms. Klotz had a brain aneurysm (although she was more likely to give one to someone else) and died in the office, and we had to call someone to identify her body? What if she tripped down the mahogany staircase and went full ragdoll? What if that big oil painting in the vestibule fell off the wall and beaned her on the head, and she got amnesia and forgot her name, and someone in her family had to nurse her back to health? Who exactly were we supposed to call?

None of it made sense. Normal people left digital breadcrumbs. Normal people didn't list their emergency contact as a lawyer—and only a lawyer. Inside, I was spiraling about Ms. Klotz's near-total lack of a past, and I was halfway through imagining a scenario in which she shed her human skin in the bath-room. Then my computer chimed. I looked at the screen, and my stomach dropped. Speak of the devil (or Zyloth dragon). A new email. From *her*.

I clicked it open and read Ms. Klotz's icy declaration:

Mr. Trousdale, why is this *simple* project taking so long to complete? I expected it to be done ages ago. I've never encoun-tered an intern with quite your level of...struggle.

Three words: Iceberg. *Titanic*. Me.

Inside, I was screaming. My shaking fingers found the keyboard. I typed the kind of reply you write when you're trying to appease a creature who might eat you alive.

Ms. Klotz,
Thank you for your email. I've completed 90% of my review of the general email communications, including internal memos and correspondence with external part-ners. I'm currently cross-referencing a handful of flagged exchanges (mainly from the early 2000s) where the metadata appears incomplete or corrupted—possibly due to system migrations. I expect to have those recon-ciled within the next few days. At this point, the majority of the archive has been catalogued, annotated, and orga-nized according to your specifications. If there are any particular categories you'd like me to prioritize in my final summary, please let me know.
Best regards,
Mr. Trousdale

Polite. Efficient. Civilized. Not a single passive-aggressive adverb in sight. What I wanted to write—but wouldn't dare:

P.S. I hope you're aware that the intimidation you deploy so efficiently doesn't inspire respect—only caution.

People don't admire you, Ms. Klotz. They simply learn
how not to trigger you.

But of course, I was the best little boy in the world, so I kept
my thoughts to myself and pressed Send. If there were awards
for professional office restraint, I'd be shortlisted for sure. That
was my revenge: impeccable professional manners. I'd funneled
my frustration into punctuation—every comma a clenched jaw,
every period a full stop on the urge to tell her where she could
file her two decades of emails. My sign-off—*Best regards*—was
my diplomatic code for *I hope you step on a Lego in your bare feet!*

What I hated most was that Ms. Klotz suggested I was a
terrible intern. And the worst part wasn't her saying it—it was
how cleanly it slid into place with what I already thought about
myself. I could practically picture Adele Cummings standing
behind her, nodding in grim agreement: *Yes, yes, this tracks.* The
thought hollowed me out. She saw me as *less than.*

For a moment, I wondered if I should even bother trying to
redeem myself in her eyes. What was the point? What would it
change? But because I had this deeply stupid, self-destructive
work ethic, I leaned in, blinked back the humiliating sting in my
eyes, and forced myself to continue the endless scroll of subject
lines. I wasn't driven by pride or ambition, but by a miserable
cocktail of stubbornness, shame, and (yes) a slow-burning
hatred for Ms. Klotz.

And then—only a moment later—I jolted upright. A subject
heading blinked at me from the screen: Grant Consideration—
Lillian Trent. Now, this was interesting! I clicked on the envelope
icon. It seemed to be a chain of messages between Lillian Grant
and Mrs. Johnston. *Mrs. Johnston?* Not an advisor? Oh, right, of
course. Mrs. Johnston was the foundation's point person
between grantees and the advisors.

I eagerly read the first message, the most recent. My jaw
dropped, and my anxiety level shot to stroke level.

31

———

There are moments in life when exhaustion outruns itself and flips into clarity—sharp, sudden, almost violent. The kind of clarity you get when your phone rings at 4 a.m. or when a shadow in the night moves. This was one of those moments.

The email subject line instantly dragged me in. My pulse kicked hard—an instinctive warning I chose to ignore. I clicked open the message, hoping for something ordinary and forgettable.

It was absolutely *not* ordinary. And the moment the thread expanded, I felt an instinctive tightening in my chest—alarm, maybe. As if some part of me already knew that whatever lay inside that chain of messages was about to change something I thought or understood.

The message at the top of the chain seemed to be an unanswered plea from Lillian Trent. I looked at the sent date. It was just a few days before she was murdered.

August 25, 1:05 p.m.
From: Lillian Trent

Mrs. Johnston,
This will be my final message unless I hear from you
right away. As advised by the New York Attorney General's
Charities Bureau, I am now formally requesting
written and *notarized* confirmation of the status of my
grant application—specifically, whether it has been withdrawn,
misplaced, or rejected.
I want to be clear: I would not be pursuing outside guidance
if I believed your lack of communication was
normal. I have tried repeatedly to resolve this directly
and privately with you. But the silence has now created
severe professional consequences for me. Based on my
understanding of a forthcoming grant from the foundation,
I declined multiple performance commitments for
the upcoming months—engagements I cannot now
recover.
At this point, I am simply asking for transparency. If
there has been an internal error, a delay, or any issue
with my application, I would appreciate knowing before
I am forced to take further formal steps.
I am still hoping this is all a misunderstanding.
Please let me know.
Thank you,
Lillian

Lillian's message hung there at the top of the email chain—
tight, polite, and clearly written by someone starting to panic. I
stared at it for a long while, feeling that familiar pinch in my
chest, the one that whispers *something's wrong here*.

There was a tremor beneath Lillian's sentences. And
suddenly I felt this odd prickle at the back of my neck—because
I knew that tone. I used it myself whenever I was afraid of being
told I'd overstepped. Or misunderstood.

But this wasn't about me. Not yet. If I wanted to understand how Lillian had reached this final, brittle attempt at being heard, I needed context. I needed the beginning, not the end. So I scrolled all the way down to the very first email, bracing myself without quite knowing why, and began reading in chronological order.

May 23, 10:04 a.m.
From: Mrs. Eleanor Johnston
To: Ms. Lillian Trent
Subject: Grant Consideration – Artist Development Program
Dear Ms. Trent,
On behalf of the Adele Cummings Foundation, I am pleased to inform you that your grant application has been advanced for further consideration in this year's Artist Development Grant program. Our advisory board was impressed by your artistic achievements. You will be contacted when the Advisory Board makes its final determination.
With best regards,
Eleanor Johnston

It was the usual template. I'd seen identical wording in a dozen other files. But this one felt different—maybe because I knew how the story ended. I knew Lillian wouldn't live long enough to receive her grant money. I scrolled up.

May 23, 10:17 a.m.
From: Lillian Trent
Dear Mrs. Johnston,
Thank you so much for this wonderful news! I am truly honored to be considered for one of Adele Cummings's grants. Would you be able to provide information about the amount I can expect to receive and a general time-

frame for the Advisory Board's final decision? I
completely understand this process takes time—I'm
simply thrilled to be considered.
Warmly,
Lillian

I could practically see her smiling while typing that message!
I kept going.

May 28, 2:49 p.m.
From: Mrs. Johnston
Ms. Trent,
At this stage, the Foundation cannot provide a specific
amount or timeline. Please review and sign the attached
NDA and return it at your earliest convenience.
Regards,
E. J.

Curt. Efficient. Slightly frosty. A little unusual, I thought, for
Mrs. Johnston—the woman who branded herself as the
welcoming face of the Adele Cummings Foundation. She
usually signed emails with enough warmth to heat a small
cabin. Still...I'd seen how busy she was. The phone glued to her
ear, the parade of grant applications and recipients who always
seemed to require her hand-holding. People like Lillian probably blurred together for her—another artist, another set of
questions she'd answered a hundred times.

May 28, 8:02 p.m.
From: Lillian Trent
Dear Mrs. Johnston,
As requested, here is my signed NDA. Please let me know
if you need anything else from me.
Thank you again for this opportunity.

All the best,
Lillian

Still bright. Still grateful. Still ready to believe.

June 13, 1:15 p.m.
From: Lillian Trent
Dear Mrs. Johnston,
I hope you are well. I've left a voicemail and wanted to
follow up here.
May I ask whether the board has reached a decision
about my grant? I'm beginning to finalize my cabaret
club schedule for the fall, and any estimate of the grant
amount would be enormously helpful.
Thank you so much,
Lillian

The tone hadn't changed much, but there was a faint tight-
ness now. A thread of nerves.

July 14, 9:31 a.m.
From: Mrs. Johnston
Ms. Trent,
Your inquiry has been noted. As previously stated, you
will be contacted when there is news.
E. J.

Not rude. Just...weirdly closed. I swallowed.

July 28, 9:42 a.m.
From: Lillian Trent
Subject: Re: Follow-Up on Grant Status
Dear Mrs. Johnston,
I apologize for the continued messages. It has now been

two months since I returned the NDA you asked me to
sign.
A friend mentioned she received a decision on her grant
within two weeks last year, which makes me worried that
something has gone wrong with my application.
Please confirm that my file is still active and under
consideration. If helpful, I'm happy to come by the foundation in person to discuss it.
Thank you,
Lillian

There it was. The first real crack. Confusion mixed with
embarrassment. Her hope was eroding.

July 28, 10:10 a.m.
From: Mrs. Johnston
Ms. Trent,
Further inquiries will not accelerate the board's delibera-
tion process.
E. J.

Cold. I kept going.

August 1, 4:26 p.m.
From: Lillian Trent
Subject: Concerns About My Application
Mrs. Johnston,
I understand you must be extremely busy, but I am
becoming concerned that something is wrong. I recently
learned that other applicants' grants were announced
publicly, yet I have received no information—positive or
negative—despite my repeated attempts to inquire.
Could you please confirm whether decisions have been

made? If my application has been withdrawn or rejected,
I would appreciate knowing so I can move forward.
Thank you,
Lillian

Now Lillian's tone had changed. No more nervous politeness.

August 1, 4:27 p.m.
From: Mrs. Johnston
Out of Office Auto-Reply: Returning Aug 12.

August 8, 9:14 a.m.
From: Lillian Trent
Mrs. Johnston,
I've reviewed the Foundation's publicly available tax
filings, including the 990-PF. According to those docu-
ments, several Artist Development Grants were
distributed in July.
I'm worried I may have misunderstood the process.
Could you let me know whether a decision has been
made on my grant?
Thank you,
Lillian

Still polite. Still giving them the benefit of the doubt. Still
hoping there was an innocent reason for the radio silence. There
wasn't one.

August 16, 8:06 a.m.
From: Lillian Trent
Mrs. Johnston,
I plan to contact the New York Attorney General's Chari-
ties Bureau. I don't want to take that step unnecessarily,

so I'm writing once more to confirm that my application
is still active.
Thank you,
Lillian

My breath caught. There it was. She'd begun investigating.
Pulling threads.

August 20, 3:44 p.m.
From: Lillian Trent
Mrs. Johnston,
The Charities Bureau advised me to request written
confirmation of my grant status. They mentioned that
delays are unusual. Please confirm whether my applica-
tion is still being reviewed or whether the Advisory
Board has already reached a decision.
Thank you,
Lillian

Her tone was steady. Measured. Professional. But this was
someone who knew something was wrong. And then...nothing.
That was the last email she ever sent. Silence. And a few days
later...she'd be dead.

My fingers drifted off the keyboard. The room felt smaller.
Tighter. For some reason, this didn't seem like miscommunica-
tion or an admin oversight. It seemed like Lillian Trent had been
shut down, shut out—or maybe even—silenced. But why? I
closed the chain. The cursor blinked on the now-empty screen,
like a heartbeat fading. Something wasn't right. Not at all.

32

I sat there, my eyes not really seeing anything on the screen, but the entire email thread replayed itself in my mind like a documentary I wished I hadn't watched. Every message. Every unanswered question. Every quiet plea from a woman who was now dead.

I genuinely couldn't believe what I had just read. Why had Mrs. Johnston stopped answering Lillian's messages? She wasn't a careless woman. She took pride in representing the foundation. Hell, I thought she was defined by her job. And she wasn't the kind of person who ignored someone in distress. At least...I didn't think she was. And why hadn't she just *told* Lillian something—anything? Even telling her the grant had been withdrawn would be better than all the uncertainty. Why the lack of transparency?

I thought the foundation prided itself on integrity, accountability, "ethical stewardship of philanthropic resources." I'd heard Mrs. Johnston use that phrase a couple of times. And yet here was a grantee begging for answers, warning that she'd contacted the attorney general's office for support, and still the silence continued.

The attorney general. OMG! My stomach clenched. If Lillian had really gone that far—if she'd started raising red flags—Mrs. Johnston could be in serious trouble. The foundation could be in jeopardy, too. And by extension, Adele Cummings herself—someone who probably didn't know what was going on in her eponymous offices.

Adele Cummings, who'd already endured so much personal tragedy and loss. It wasn't fair. Adele, whose name meant something—meant everything—to the people who worked here.

If the AG found negligence, mismanagement, or even the *appearance* of impropriety, the foundation could be audited, sanctioned, or fined. Programs could be shut down. Confidence in the charity could collapse. Hell, the Adele Cummings Foundation might not survive. And the idea of that...and all the good this place did around the world...

The idea of this beautiful, hopeful place collapsing under scandal—it made something tighten painfully under my ribs. I adored Mrs. Johnston and the other advisors. Plus, I genuinely loved working for the foundation. For all its quirks, its chaos—and Ms. Klotz—it had become a home for me, a place where I felt...useful and somewhat important. Even valued.

So yes, I had a vested interest in figuring out what had happened to Lillian Trent's grant. Not because I was convinced anything criminal had occurred—I wasn't even sure yet what I believed—but because understanding felt safer than jumping to conclusions. I wasn't delusional enough to think I could fix anything—but I wanted to help, if I could. To keep things from spiraling into something that could destroy the foundation.

But the truth was—I had no idea what to do. Or where to go. Or how to even begin. Not remotely. I was drowning, and I knew it. This wasn't sloppy filing or misnamed folders anymore. This was a dead woman's email. This was legal exposure.

I couldn't sit with it another second. I pressed my palms hard into my eyes, as if I could physically shove the panic back where it came from. My chest felt tight, shallow, like the room was depriving me of oxygen. I couldn't handle this alone. That was the truth. I *needed* help.

And God, I hated that. Especially because Brad thought I was a very capable man. He thought I had my life stitched together. That I was steady. Reliable. Someone with an actual backbone—not this soft, quivering worm masquerading as a spine. If he saw me now, unraveling over emails from a murdered woman, he'd realize the truth: I wasn't brave. I wasn't even very good at pretending that I wasn't scared.

But this was bigger than my pride. Bigger than my need to seem grown-up. Bigger than my job as an intern. For the first time since I'd arrived at the foundation, I felt real fear. Not the fear of Ms. Klotz and her carnivorous intern-eating appetite. Real existential fear. Something was wrong here. Deeply wrong. Wrong in a way that made the air in the office feel colder, heavier, like Lillian's unanswered emails were still vibrating somewhere in the walls.

I needed Brad's help. Even though it meant letting him see how far out of my depth I truly was. Even if it meant disappointing him—or worse, proving him right to worry about me. I trembled, but not because of embarrassment. I had a scary premonition that I might have found the reason why Lillian Trent was murdered. And I might be the one person on the planet—other than her killer—who knew.

33

B rad opened the door before I'd even finished knocking. He had one shoe on, one in his hand, his coat hanging off one shoulder like I'd caught him mid-decision. His face lit up for half a second—wide-eyed, delighted—until recognition caught up with logic and the expression snapped into startled alarm. "Timothy. What's wrong?"

It was Wednesday. Two full nights before our next planned date. I wasn't supposed to be on his doorstep, rumpled and breathless, like someone who'd run out of places to go. "I'm sorry," I said automatically. "I know I'm interrupting."

Brad dropped the shoe by the door and reached for me. "Hey. Stop. Nothing else matters." He stepped forward and wrapped me in his arms—exactly where I needed to be.

I was aware of how I must've looked: pale face, wrinkled shirt, anxiety leaking from every pore. Not exactly the fantasy version of myself I liked to present to him.

Brad closed the door behind us and turned toward me with the quiet precision of someone approaching a frightened animal —slow movements, soft eyes, no sudden noises. Without asking a single question, he crossed the room to his wine cabinet, selected a bottle of red, and uncorked it with a practiced pull. He poured two glasses, mine a little fuller than his. He always did that, but tonight it felt less like a courtesy and more like triage.

With his arm warm and steady around my shoulders, he guided me toward the couch. "Drink," he insisted.

I obeyed, the wine slipping down in a warm rush that steadied my hands but not quite my breathing. Brad watched me with that unwavering, perceptive gaze of his—like he was reading the fine print in my expression, waiting for the exact moment I was ready to meet his eyes.

When I finally did, he was prepared.

"Okay," he said. "Tell me."

I set the glass down and took a deep breath. I began, my voice weak, "Ever since Lillian Trent died, I've been...casually looking into it. I mean, I didn't even know I was doing it at first. Until weird things started piling up. I guess I want to know who took her away from the world."

"I know," Brad said, one eyebrow rising.

"You know?"

He shrugged, and his hand came to rest lightly on my back. "Go on."

Everything came rushing out of me all at once. "My life's unraveling," I said. "I haven't really been doing interviews. Well, I have, but not for any magazine article. I've been talking to cabaret people, yes. But to find out more information about Lillian. I met with a singer. And Lillian's piano accompanist. Some others. And I found old articles about Adele Cummings by accident. About her husband disappearing years ago, and she might have had something to do with that. And the real reason her foundation was created in the first place—to prop her back up in society. I tried to make sense of things, but nothing fits, Brad. Nothing."

He nodded slowly, letting me spill.

"And then there's work. I haven't told you how terrible one of my bosses treats me. Ms. Klotz—the office dragon. She hates my guts and has been trying to find every conceivable way to get rid of me. She's awful. Totally awful. I'm miserable. She picks apart everything I do. And she's one of the reasons I can't ask questions about what's going on behind the scenes there because I was told on my first day that she'll literally eviscerate me. And Mrs. Johnston..." I swallowed hard. "She's nice, but I can't talk to her either. Not after what I found."

Brad frowned. "What have you found?"

I took out my phone. I'd done the unthinkable. I'd forwarded the entire chain of emails between Lillian and Mrs. Johnston to my own personal inbox—something every employee handbook on earth would tell you *never to do*. If anyone at the foundation found out, I could be written up or possibly fired on the spot for mishandling private correspondence. The thought made my stomach pitch, but I opened the thread anyway and handed the phone to Brad. The weight of the discovery felt heavier now; showing it to someone else made the risk—and the truth— impossible to ignore.

Brad's jaw set and he stayed silent as he read the messages. When he finished, he looked up at me, questioning.

I continued, "Something weird's going on at the foundation."

Brad leaned back, exhaling slowly—an alarmed but measured breath. "Timothy," he said softly, "this looks serious."

"I know. And I don't know what to do. Mrs. Johnston could get in trouble. The foundation could get sanctioned. Adele— God, Adele Cummings could be in the headlines again, and I know how much she values her privacy. And I love the foundation. I love my job. I don't want to hurt anyone, but I can't ignore this either."

There was a long silence. Then Brad reached over, took my hand, and laced our fingers together in a way that made something break open in my chest.

"You're not alone in this," he said, quietly but firmly. "You don't have to figure it out by yourself. And you shouldn't. This isn't a scavenger hunt. Someone's been murdered."

I let out a shaky breath. "I didn't want you to think I was… incapable."

"Timothy," he said gently, brushing his thumb over my knuckles, "you came to me because you *are* capable. You knew this was something you shouldn't shoulder alone. That takes maturity. Not weakness."

A tear—just one traitor—slipped down my cheek. Brad caught it with his thumb.

"Let's take this one step at a time," he said. "Together, we'll figure it out." His voice dropped, softer and steadier, into something that felt like protection. "I've got you."

And for the first time since opening that email thread, I felt the ground stop tilting beneath me. I looked into Brad's eyes and felt as though I were wrapped in a warm security blanket. I said, "Just now, when I told you I was investigating Lillian Trent's murder, what did you mean when you said, 'I know'?"

"I just know. I can read you. I think maybe it's a soulmate thing. I figured you'd tell me what was going on when you were ready. I never want to push you or coerce you. I just want to love you."

34

Over the course of the next hour, everything that had been rattling around in my skull like loose metal fell out. I told Brad about Rachel Morris. Her envy of Lillian's grant, her threatening letter to the foundation. Her statement to me that Lillian had enemies and "Not everyone thought she deserved what she was about to get—except maybe her murder."

I told him about Lillian's accompanist, Everett, and the insane remark Thane had quoted back to me—that either Everett or Lillian would probably end up killing the other. I told him about Mrs. Stone and her alleged obsession with Everett and her apparent jealousy of Lillian's association with him. And I mentioned that, according to Rachel, from when she'd worked there, one faction at the foundation wanted to deny Lillian getting a grant.

And I told him about the newspaper articles—the ones detailing Adele Cummings's missing husband, the police suspicions, the decades-old shadow that still hung over her life. I told him about Ms. Klotz, with her razor-sharp disdain and unexplained authority. And I told him what I'd found in the archive: that Lillian's files had been moved, not just misplaced, and that whoever did it had used Rachel Morris's old login credentials. Presumably, that someone was Ms. Klotz.

And then—because apparently the dam was fully broken—I finally told him about the threatening DMs I'd received. The creepy anonymous ones. The ones that told me to follow the rules or they'd do something we'd both regret. I hadn't planned to say any of that out loud. But once I did, I couldn't stop talking.

Brad looked at me. Deeply focused. Like he was assembling the pieces of a puzzle only he could see. "Okay," he finally said, leaning forward, elbows on his knees. "So what you've just described is a situation where basically a few people may have had a motive to kill Lillian Trent."

I sucked in a breath. "I..."

Brad's eyes narrowed. "Those DMs you got? Whoever sent them knows you're digging around. Which means they've met you. You know them."

I shivered so hard I almost spilled my wine. I stared at my hands, feeling sick. "I don't know what to do with all of this. I can't go to the police. The last time I found a murdered body and thought I had a good suspect, you told me I didn't have enough evidence."

"No police. Not yet," Brad agreed. "Right now, you only have impressions and *possible* motives. If you go to the police now, they'll either dismiss you outright or drag the foundation into a full investigation. And you'll probably lose your job. We need more intel. Actual solid information."

"How?" My voice cracked embarrassingly. "I can't ask around the office. Ms. Klotz will have my head on a pike. And the whole foundation feels like one of those locked-room mysteries—and I'm trapped inside."

Brad threaded his fingers through mine and gave a reassuring squeeze. "We'll figure something out," he said, his voice low and warm, the kind of steady tone that made me believe him even when the world felt like quicksand. "But for now, you need a moment that isn't swallowed by all this." He shifted closer, guiding me gently back into the sofa cushions. His movements were slow, careful—an invitation, not an assumption—giving me every chance to pull away if I wanted to.

I didn't.

His thumb brushed along my cheekbone, feather-light, and then he leaned in, pressing his forehead softly to mine. The warmth of him, the nearness, the scent of his aftershave and red wine—it all folded around me, stealing the breath from my chest in the most welcome way.

"Timothy," he murmured, "you've been carrying the weight of the world. Let me hold some of it for you." His fingers moved to my shirt buttons and began unfastening them with a gentleness that felt almost reverent. Not rushed. Not hungry. Just... caring. As if he were peeling away the day and all my anxiety.

"Breathe," he whispered. "Breathe with me." His hands roamed up and down my chest, steadying me as he pressed a soft kiss to my lips—slow, lingering, electric in a way that made the world shift. Another kiss, then another, each one saying *You're safe. You're not alone. I'm right here.*

I reached for his T-shirt and lifted it over his shoulders and head. His skin against my face was alive and sent a current of excitement through me.

"You don't have to figure anything out," he murmured. "We're here to take care of each other."

The universe outside Brad's embrace disappeared. His closeness, his warmth, his scent, the softness in his eyes...were all I could focus on. He cupped the back of my neck and kissed me—deeply and passionately, like we owned each other's bodies and souls. I let myself fall into something deeper than I'd ever imagined.

Into Brad.

Into us.

I let everything else go.

35

Late for work the next morning, I had to make a frantic search for my underwear, which had somehow migrated halfway down the hallway. As I scooped up my shirt and jeans, Brad appeared at my side, holding a steaming mug of Earl Grey. Looking me up and down, he said, "Sorry you have to go to work in the same clothes you wore yesterday. You should stash a few things here for an emergency."

The word *here* landed softly but decisively. Not *my place*. Not *sometime*. Just here—as though it were already understood. I felt an unexpected swell of something warm and steady. But was he talking about convenience or continuity? I like to think of a future that included spare socks and an extra toothbrush.

I took the mug from him, our fingers brushing, and smiled. "That does sound dangerously domestic," I said. I checked myself in the mirror above the dresser and took a grateful gulp from the mug—hot and fragrant. "I think I look well loved."

"God, don't say things like that standing here with your shirt unbuttoned," he smirked. "All I have to do is look at that dark hair on your pale chest and—well, never mind. I need to stay upright today; I'm tuning three pianos at the Waldorf."

He gave a soft laugh, then added, "By the way, you never said if you followed up on that piano accompanist's suggestion about talking to the manager at Manhattan Moon. Lenny somebody... Barron? The one Lillian kicked to the curb when she thought she was getting a big windfall."

I hesitated, fastening the last button on the shirt. "Everett was just tossing me a bone. I heard him use that very phrase on my voice memo. I'd forgotten to turn it off when I left to go to the bathroom after our interview. It recorded him telling the singer he was working with that he was only pretending to be helpful to me. Just a distraction. He was giving me something meaning-less to chew on, so I'd stop asking real questions. I figured Lenny wasn't important. Just misdirection."

Brad straightened the waistband of my trousers, giving me that calm look of his. "Breakups create motives. This Lenny guy might have held a grudge against Lillian for dumping him and his club."

I took another sip of tea, considering my reflection in the mirror: rumpled shirt, eyes still intoxicated by last night's close-ness. "If you think I should..."

"I'm just saying...New York is full of people who'd murder for less than a bad split-up. You've already convinced a bunch of others to talk to you about Lillian. Maybe explain to Lenny that you're with the Adele Cummings Foundation—which is completely honest—and explain that Adele is always looking for worthy recipients of a grant. Also true."

He gave me a mischievous smile. "You may as well play your ace card, Timothy—that sweet face that apparently makes people love to confess things."

Manhattan Moon felt different during the day. It was my lunch hour, and the moment I stepped inside, the place felt far different than the last time I was here. The amber wall sconces still glowed along the walls, but instead of sultry warmth, they cast long, exhausted shadows across the room. Chairs rested upside down on the round tabletops, the stage area sat dark, and the microphone stood straight and still—a thin black silhouette waiting for someone to coax it back to life.

Then I saw Lillian Trent—smiling at me from a poster that was still hanging by the bar. Maybe it was now sort of a memorial to her.

SIX-MONTH EXCLUSIVE RESIDENCY – FRIDAY & SATURDAY NIGHTS

The gloss on her photo caught the light, making her look alive for a split second—like she might blink or laugh or toss off one of her perfectly timed jokes. My stomach clenched hard. She'd promised to perform for six months at this place. Instead, she'd ended up dead on the floor of her dressing room just down the hall.

An older woman in a black T-shirt and apron was crouched near the bar, working at a darkened patch of carpet with a spray bottle and cloth, her movements slow and methodical. I recognized her—the hostess who'd checked our names off the reservation list the night I was here with Brad and Mrs. Stone. She seemed to be one of those jack-of-all-trades employees every cabaret club relies on: greeter, bouncer, cleaner, crisis manager —whatever the job demanded.

She moved with the weary patience of someone who'd spent decades cleaning up after other people's nights out: spilled cocktails, shattered glasses, the occasional drunk who mistook a candleholder for a microphone. When she noticed me, she paused—not hostile, just curious; the attitude New Yorkers reserved for people who appeared somewhere unexpected. Before I could say hello, a door behind the bar swung open, and a man stepped through, letting a square of bright backroom light flare behind him.

"You the guy?" he asked and squinted at his watch.

I blinked. "Probably. Timothy. Adele Cummings Foundation. Are you Lenny?"

He didn't smile but jerked his chin toward a table by the piano. "Make it quick. I got deliveries coming."

I sat, and he slid onto the chair opposite me, folding his arms. "So," he said, "what does Adele Cummings want from me now? Another songbird you're gonna yank away with the promise of a fortune?" His tone wasn't loud, but it had weight.

"Never," I insisted. "Trust me, the foundation had nothing to do with Lillian Trent abandoning her commitments to you. Honestly. No, I'm here because we're always searching for talent to support. I thought maybe you'd have some ideas. Is there anyone as good as Lillian Trent you can endorse?"

"There's no one as good as Lillian Trent," Lenny said firmly. "One of a kind. She may have been a bitch, but some of the best ones are."

"I noticed the poster," I continued. "Is a six-month residency a typical thing at Manhattan Moon?"

His mouth tightened. "Only for her. But she screwed me, and I'll never let that happen again. We had a contract. I sank a ton of money into that girl—advertisements, fixing up the bar—and then she goes all, 'You're small potatoes. I'm destined for bigger things,' and leaves me holding the bag."

I swallowed. This seemed like the right moment for commiseration and to bring up Lillian's other backstabbing. "I've heard she wasn't exactly Miss Congeniality, even to the guy who played piano for her. He even pushed for her grant from the foundation," I said. "Maybe if the foundation had done a better job of screening her, she might not have been offered a grant in the first place. Character's important to us. We're conscious of optics."

"I know I'm not the only one she shafted," Lenny said. "She burned through people. Didn't care who she stepped on if something better was about to land in her lap. Lillian always thought she was on the edge of being a big success. And I guess it was about to happen."

He paused, and when he spoke again, his voice had a brittle edge. "Middle of the day. I'm in my office arguing with a keg distributor, and my cell rings. Lillian. I pick up, smiling—by then she'd been packing the place. I figured she was calling to talk about new vocal arrangements, or maybe some diva-ask about the comps list. Instead, she says a big fat grant from Cummings was due any day, and she'd be quitting me after Saturday's show. Greener pastures and all that. She salted the wound and said she'd never have to step foot in this 'flea-bitten joint' again. She actually said that. We're not exactly the Purple Parrot, for Christ's sake. Said she was about to have her pick—Birdland, 54 Below, the Carlyle. Then she says—and I quote—'go suck an egg, Lenny.' That girl had a potty mouth, so I guess she coulda said a lot worse."

I winced. It sounded harsher coming from Lenny than it had when Everett told that story. "I'm sorry," I said softly.

He gave a small shrug and a humorless laugh of resignation. "Yeah, well, I'm no saint either. I lost it. Said I'd get even with her big time, and she'd regret everything. Said I'd sue, too. Which is hilarious, because what lawyer can I afford to hire?"

His eyes were almost sad in the low light. "That was the last time we ever talked. Her gloating in my ear. Me threatening to sue when we both knew I wouldn't. I didn't even see her last performance 'cause I was too angry. Hell, I might have done something to her. And then boom...someone did the job for me. Well, not 'for me.' I didn't want her dead."

He looked away, blinking hard. "Talk about irony—her career's finally blasting off, she dumps Everett—the guy who literally knew her keys better than she did—and right after that, the big fancy check she was counting on just...evaporates. Poof." He turned back to me, confusion and accusation tangled in his voice. "Why'd you pull her grant? Was it the affair she was having with the guy over at the foundation? Bad optics, right?"

What the hell did Lenny just say? My heart lurched so hard it felt like it smacked against my ribs. There were two big points: Lenny saying that Lillian's grant had been withdrawn—and something about an affair with someone at the foundation. For a second, I genuinely wondered if I'd misheard him.

And then the other thought hit me, colder and sharper: how did *he* know about the grant at all? It hadn't been finalized. Which meant someone had talked. I stared at Lenny. My brain did a full series of cartwheels—then set itself on fire. *An affair?* There was only one other man at the foundation. Mr. Slater. Although Lillian didn't have to have an affair with a man, of course. That thought alone nearly gave me a stroke, because Mr. Slater had set off my gaydar the moment I met him.

He didn't interest me personally, of course. But the opera tickets he'd slipped me? The fact that he was, undeniably, the best-dressed man in Manhattan—monogrammed shirts, cuff-links, cologne, the Louis Vuitton over-the-shoulder bag he treated like a beloved pet. His mysterious personal life, with absolutely zero mention of a wife, girlfriend, or lover. The clean emotional slate of a man whose private world was either a fortress or a void.

God, stop it, I told myself. *Not every impeccably groomed man who offers you Wagner and moisturizes is gay, for crying out loud! It's a cliché.*

And yet, the thought was already circling, slow and silent— like a shark that smells blood.

What if it was him?

Mr. Slater? Having an affair? With Lillian Trent? My gaydar just short-circuited on the spot. A secret relationship might be tied to her grant money? It was too much to take in. Way too much. And yet—my gut told me Lenny wasn't lying. This wasn't a rumor. And he didn't realize he'd spilled a whole pot of tea.

I sat there, absorbing what Lenny had said. "Did she ever brag to anyone other than you—and maybe Everett—about being a grant recipient, or mention the Adele Cummings Foundation by name? She wasn't supposed to," I said.

"I know. The NDA. She told me. But Lillien loved to brag—especially about her career and how much luckier she was than any of her friends. Her Facebook page is a love letter—to herself. She didn't care about rules. Even though she'd been warned."

"By whom?" I asked.

"Probably that woman. The fan. From the foundation."

My spine straightened.

"Woman? Fan?" I asked, though I had a suspicion.

"Sharp looking," he said. "Always dressed like she was going to a fancy country-club tea or something. Shoulder-length hair, pearls. Came in most nights when Lillian was on. Always sat at a table close to the piano. Usually alone. Ordered Perrier with lime for herself and a G&T for Everett at the piano. Watched the show. Then left as soon as it was over."

My mouth went dry. "Did you catch her name? The woman? The fan from the foundation?"

"Suzie can check the reservation books," he said and cocked his head toward the woman cleaning the room. He leaned back, eyes on me. "Why are you really here, kid? Because I got a gut feeling this ain't some nostalgia tour you're on. You don't look old enough—or sophisticated enough—to even know what cabaret is. Except maybe you think it's an old movie with Liza Minnelli that your grandparents watched on TCM."

I swallowed, and my silence probably spoke volumes about the true nature of my visit.

"Look," Lenny said, "I'll tell you this much. The last few months, Lillian acted like someone standing right on the edge of a big break. You know the drill—walked a little taller, was maybe more demanding and condescending than usual, like she was about to make the world apologize for every hardship it ever threw at her."

He rubbed a hand over his jaw. "She kept gloating about that grant the Adele Cummings Foundation was giving her. 'Once the money hits, everything will be different,' she said. As if she could already feel it in her hands. But then...something shifted. The spark went out of her. She didn't seem excited about the money anymore."

A chill rippled down my neck. "Why?"

Lenny shrugged. "She started evading the subject when I brought it up, saying things like, 'I have to play this right.' That's not the stuff you say when you're on solid ground."

"What do you think she meant?" I asked.

Lenny lowered his voice to match mine. "I think she knew the deal wasn't as definite as she originally thought—and had bragged about to everyone. Maybe the foundation got cold feet about supporting her. Like I said, maybe the affair had something to do with it. Maybe she pissed off the wrong person."

He leaned in, elbows on the table. "Whatever it was, kid... She seemed nervous. And Lillian Trent was made of titanium. But let me tell you something. I loved Lillian. With a great big capital *L*. She was the real deal, talent-wise. Maybe the twenty-first century's Garland or Streisand. She didn't deserve what she got. I'll go to my own grave sorry that things got bad between us."

36

I returned from my lunchtime meeting with Lenny Barron, and somehow Ravenscroft felt...off. The polished floors in the vestibule still reflected the chandelier's warm, buttery glow. The same orchid sat perfectly posed on the entryway table. The familiar hum of money doing noble things drifted through the air like always. But Lenny's comments clung to me. Especially the blockbuster theory about Lillian having an affair with someone at the foundation. And what he'd said about Lillian growing anxious that her grant might vanish. And Mrs. Stone showing up at Manhattan Moon night after night—maybe to support Lillian, maybe to flirt with Everett Miles.

Speak of the devil: As I made my way toward my office, Mrs. Stone was descending the grand staircase. Graceful as royalty, her hand glided along the banister, and her pearls snagged the chandelier's light, bouncing back cool flashes. Her gaze met mine, and she paused and offered her usual elegant nod.

But...had her smile always been that tightly calibrated? Had her eyes always flicked away that quickly, as if my face were too bright to look at for long? Or was I now seeing her through the warped lens of Lenny's puzzling remarks and finding potential menace where there was none?

Lenny's voice wouldn't leave my head: what he'd said about Mrs. Stone being at nearly every one of Lillian's shows; how she always slipped the hostess a tip to sit as close to the piano as possible; how she sent Everett Miles a gin and tonic before each performance.

And then came the memory again—her excusing herself after Lillian's final show to find the ladies' room. The bathroom that was conveniently located right next to Lillian's dressing room. My pulse spiked. Why had she gone to see Lillian perform so often? Was anyone that devoted a fan? Or maybe it was Everett she'd gone to see and support.

Before I could chase any of those thoughts to their terrifying conclusions, my phone buzzed in my pocket. Unknown number. I slipped into my office, shut the door, and answered on the third ring.

"Timothy Trousdale?" a woman's gravelly voice asked. "The kid who came to Manhattan Moon today?"

"Um...kid?" My pulse leapt. "Yes, that's me."

"Suzie here. From the club. Lenny told me to call and say the name's *Stone*. The woman who came to see Lillian Trent a lot. Marguerita Stone. It's in the reservations book a bunch of times."

Every muscle in my body tightened. I'd forgotten that Lenny said he'd confirm the name I'd suspected.

"One more thing," Suzie said casually. "You work at Adele Cummings, right? Tell your co-worker, the woman who came in that night Lillian Trent died, we've got her hair clip. If she can describe the dragonfly, she can have it back."

My brain suddenly snagged. "Dragonfly...?"

"Found it by the bar after the show. Pretty sure it's hers. I remember because she pulled that old 'Don't you know who I am?' stunt when I told her the show was sold out. She flashed an employee ID from the Adele Cummings Foundation. Zero seats available, but she insisted she wasn't leaving. We got fire laws about occupancy in a room, but I let her stand at the bar. Clip must've fallen off during the show. Almost vacuumed it up. I thought she'd call to ask if anyone had found it, but I haven't heard a peep."

Something inside me stopped. Not slowed—stopped, like my bloodstream had frozen solid. A sharp stillness went through me. I knew that hair clip. Of course I did. Every staff meeting, every briefing, every budget review—Ms. Klotz wore it perched in her hair on the side of her head. Her signature accessory, equal parts whimsical and terrifying. A dragonfly hair clip attached to a human pterodactyl.

And I realized I hadn't seen Ms. Klotz wearing it lately. Not in days. Maybe not in weeks. Not that I was looking. Then a weird memory flashed—a quick flicker—the night of Lillian's final show. I thought I saw Ms. Klotz in the audience that night. Someone at the bar who reminded me of her. I'd told Mrs. Stone, but she'd laughed and said my eyes were playing tricks. Because why would Ms. Klotz be there? She didn't seem the type to haunt a late-night cabaret. Except now...maybe she was the type.

Suzie's voice cut through my spiraling thoughts. "Tell her she can pick it up from the office whenever."

Click. The line went silent.

In a daze, I slowly lowered the phone. My hands were ice cold. The room felt small, the walls inching closer. Ms. Klotz had been at Manhattan Moon the night Lillian Trent was murdered? Using her foundation credentials to get into a sold-out show? And losing her signature hair clip? Had she maybe met with Lillian backstage? Confronted her about the grant? About the affair? Killed her?

My breath snagged painfully in my throat. And then—

A movement.

I looked up—

—and jerked back so hard my chair wheels almost skidded.

Ms. Klotz was standing in my doorway. Hands folded neatly over an immaculate suit, hair pinned with a clip of diamond daisies on the side. Her expression was carved from stone, eyes fixed on mine—cool, assessing, as if she'd somehow overheard every treasonous thought I'd just had about her.

"Check your email," she said, her voice so cold it made my spine cinch.

Then she turned on a razor-sharp heel and walked away, leaving the air in the doorway vibrating behind her.

For a full five seconds, I couldn't move. I wasn't sure if I'd even breathed at all.

I opened Ms. Klotz's email. Short, but vicious—like she was carving the words into me with a scalpel.

Mr. Trousdale,

I have reviewed the project in which you were to sort the *Miscellaneous* shared drive into the correct departmental folders. You were to relabel files according to the foundation's naming convention and convert all scans into searchable PDFs. I stated this explicitly. You confirmed that you understood. You obviously did not.

What you delivered is disorganized, mislabeled, and in several cases completely unusable. This is the second time you've disappointed me. I gave you an opportunity to improve after the MacLaine Dance Company grant debacle. We need to discuss your future.

Klotz.

cc: staff

I stared at the email, numb—hollowed out—like someone had reached through the screen and punched me square in the solar plexus. Weeks had passed since I'd turned in that project.

Weeks. I'd let myself believe the silence meant I'd done well. I should've known better. In Ms. Klotz's universe, silence wasn't approval—it was incubation. A clinical waiting period while she sharpened her claws to surgical points.

She waited all this time? My brain whirred. She waited until I was finally sleeping better, finally feeling like I was succeeding. And then—bam—she emerges from her swamp lair to lob a grenade at my self-esteem? And the way she wrote "We need to discuss your future." Who does that?

God, I'd had demonic bosses before. Jarred Evans at my last job was the classic example. He was just plain mean and ended up murdered. (Not by me. Obviously.) With Ms. Klotz's icy hatred, she might actually be worse—if less physically bombastic. Maybe not deserving to be murdered, though at this point, I wasn't so sure. She was definitely off her rocker.

But my misery wasn't just about the project she'd deemed incompetently done. It was everything else—an avalanche of revelations that hadn't stopped rolling since lunch. Lenny's words still ricocheted inside my skull: Lillian growing terrified that the grant she'd counted on was slipping through her fingers. Mrs. Stone haunting her performances—night after night—less like a supporter and more like a stalker. Ms. Klotz's dragonfly hair clip turning up at Manhattan Moon, the same night Lillian died—proof she'd been there, slipping through the crowd, unnoticed. And then another shocker: Mr. Slater— impenetrable, immaculate Mr. Slater—maybe sleeping with Lillian Trent.

Each revelation felt like a floorboard giving way beneath me. My pulse climbed into my throat, hammering so hard it felt like it was trying to escape—trying to warn me something terrible was gathering just beyond the edge of what I understood.

37

I shoved back from my desk and bolted down the hallway—flying past Mrs. Johnston's office. She looked up as I streaked by. But I didn't stop. I pushed open the bathroom door, dashed inside, and locked it. Then I pressed my back against the wall and let gravity take over—sliding down the cold tile until I was on the floor, knees pulled tight to my chest.

And then I broke. Not a manly sniffle or a slight dampening of the lashes. I cried. Hard. The kind of crying that rips through your chest and leaves you shaking. Hot tears blurred everything. My breath came in pitiful gasps that echoed off the tile. I pressed my sleeve to my face, trying to stifle the sound, but there was no stopping it.

The tile was cold beneath me, but my body felt feverish, trembling. For a long while, I just sat there and let my emotions hit me like waves crashing hard and fast against the small, fragile island of me. Each one heavier than the last. Each one harder to survive.

I stayed long enough for the sobs to shrink into ragged, shaky breaths. Finally, when I could stand, I washed my face at the sink, splashing cold water over my blotchy cheeks until I thought I could pass as *almost fine*. I avoided my reflection. I didn't need visual confirmation of how wrecked I probably looked.

For a moment, I considered the simplest solution of all: leaving. Just slipping out before anyone officially told me I was finished. I could pack up my bag, avoid the awkward meeting, spare myself the humiliation of being *managed out*. It would be easier. Quieter. No one would stop me.

As I reached into my pocket for my phone, my fingers felt a folded scrap of paper. I knew it was the sweet note Brad had given me recently. I pulled it out slowly. Brad's handwriting—slanted, a little too neat—jumped out at me: *Whatever happens, remember you're not alone.*

My throat tightened all over again, but this time it wasn't despair. It was resolve.

I stood there holding the note, feeling something settle into place. Beneath the emotional wreckage, something shifted. The crying had wrung me out, stripped me down to essentials—something leaner, sharper. Truer. My nerves felt pared back to steel wire.

Then came defiance. Small at first. Then gathering strength.

I wasn't invincible, but I wasn't helpless either. The Adele Cummings Foundation and the cabaret world were nests of intrigue, and I'd wandered into them with the innocence of a lamb. But I wasn't so innocent anymore.

And this internship? It was never meant to be my destiny. It was a placeholder. A pit stop. A plot point. I was a writer. I wrote novels. Or I would. Someday.

If Ms. Klotz decided to go full-on termination mode and hurl me into unemployment? Fine. Bring it on, sister.

I smoothed the note, folded it carefully, and put it back in my pocket. I wasn't done. I wasn't shrinking. And I sure as hell wasn't leaving before the story was finished.

I finally pulled myself together and walked back down the

hall to my office. But the moment I sat down at my desk, I knew something was wrong. My computer was an obedient, well-trained pet that went to sleep after five minutes of inactivity. I'd been gone at least fifteen minutes. But the screen was awake and fully alert. Like someone had been sitting in my chair two seconds ago.

Displayed on the screen was a document on foundation letterhead titled *Grant Recipients — Quarter Three.*

It was a list, and Lillian Trent's name was there—bold and highlighted in red. And her five-hundred-thousand-dollar grant figure sat next to it. My stomach flipped. I didn't open this. I checked the time stamp. It had been opened four minutes ago. My pulse went ballistic.

There was an asterisk next to Lillian's name, and my eyes drifted down the page. I scrolled to a footnote at the bottom: *FOLLOW THE RULES.

I froze. Someone had been at my desk. Someone had accessed my computer. It had been timed perfectly. A shiver slid through me, but then something that wasn't terror bubbled up.

I remembered the anonymous DMs I'd been getting for weeks. Cryptic. Unsettling. Impossible to categorize as a threat or a warning. And now this? It probably should have frightened me, but it didn't. I was almost indifferent. With my brand-new transformation from snowflake to...well, maybe hailstone, I suddenly had the feeling the message maybe wasn't meant to scare me off. Maybe—just maybe—someone was trying to tell me something they couldn't say directly. Someone who was watching me. Someone who was steering me.

That message could be a breadcrumb someone hoped I'd recognize. My heart hammered—not with fear, because I wasn't afraid anymore—but with the feeling I was staring at a message written in a language I almost understood. Like seeing a road sign in a foreign alphabet and guessing its meaning. I lifted my eyes from the monitor and looked out into the hallway.

Smudgy was wandering lazily down the corridor, and Mr. Slater and Ms. Raymond were in a huddle beside a potted fern. They both looked up at the same time and gazed in the direction of my office, as if they'd been talking about me. When they realized I was looking at them too, they quickly averted their eyes. Had Ms. Klotz already told them of her plans for me? Was I now the walking dead?

Let them whisper. Let them think I'm the wrong hire in the wrong job. At this point, I didn't have much left to lose. And that freedom—however reckless—made something sharpen inside me. I was more determined than ever to find out why Lillian Trent's grant was withdrawn. And why she ended up a strangled dead body. When you're convinced you're getting fired, the rules stop feeling sacred. They start feeling optional.

38

———

I knew I wasn't long for the charity world of Adele Cummings. Not after Ms. Klotz's excoriating rebuke of my work. And why did she even have to bring up that old MacLaine Dance Company mess again? Ancient history. Get over it, girl. I even found myself waiting—ridiculously—for Mrs. Johnston to ride in to my defense. She didn't. Perhaps I'd overestimated my standing. That realization alone felt like a reprimand.

So I made a decision—one completely at odds with my usual diligence and sense of responsibility: Going forward, I was "quiet quitting." In other words, doing exactly the bare minimum.

I wouldn't clean up the break room like Cinderella—we had a "surface maintenance coordinator" (custodian) for that. I wouldn't water the plants just because I thought they looked "sad." That "extra mile" I used to go was now closed due to construction. Because let's face it, I wasn't paid much, and I was stuck in an abusive environment. And I was obviously not valued by the person who seemed to wield the most power here. I wouldn't let Ms. Klotz emotionally dismember me anymore. It was the twenty-first century, for crying out loud. Nobody sacrificed their dignity for a job.

"You cannot oppress the people who are not afraid anymore"—thank you, César Chávez!

I sat back in my chair, strangely proud of myself. Quiet quitting wasn't laziness. It was self-respect. And bizarrely liberating. I pulled up my inbox and saw several unread messages flagged "urgent." In the old days (two minutes ago), that would have spiked my cortisol to medically concerning levels. Now? I sipped my tepid tea and daydreamed about Brad's armpits.

The Adele Cummings Foundation was about to discover I was no longer their panicked little intern. I was Timothy Trousdale—quiet quitter and soon-to-be-great American novelist!

It was finally Friday evening, praise be, and Brad suggested we eat in at Ragacci's and "download the highlights of our week" over a bottle of Chianti. Personally, I would've preferred going straight to his place and making Brad my meal. But he was convincing—as always.

"You've had a horrible week," he said. "You need a proper date night. With linen napkins. And menus. And people to wait on you."

I was already genuinely feeling better about my lot in life. All it took was Brad's smile, the kiss he gave me when we met outside the restaurant, and my newly adopted work philosophy.

It was weird how my feelings about the Adele Cummings Foundation had done a complete one-eighty. Four weeks ago, I couldn't wait to arrive at Ravenscroft every morning. I'd pet Smudgy, make a mug of Earl Grey, and dive into whatever assignment I was given. I felt honored to be part of the foundation's mission. And I adored the advisors. I'd even thought of shelving my lifelong dream of becoming a world-famous novelist because it seemed like I'd been chosen for this higher purpose of serving humanity.

"Okay," Brad coaxed. "I know the week's been a bear. Tell all."

I took a giant sip of Chianti—more like a gulp—because this conversation required emotional lubrication.

"Well," I said, setting my glass down carefully, "I told you I had a meeting with the manager of Manhattan Moon. It made me more stressed. Remember that list I had of cabaret people who I thought might've had it in for Lillian Trent—singers and even her accompanist? Well...I've added a few others who had sketchy relationships with her."

Brad looked at me, mid-sip from his glass.

"The amended list contains some zany speculations," I said. "Maybe even half the people at the foundation. I've penciled in Mrs. Stone, Ms. Klotz, and Mr. Slater."

Brad grimaced. "Ms. Klotz, maybe. But not Mrs. Stone! She's way too lovely. Elegant. She probably sends handwritten thank-you notes and remembers birthdays. She's not the...*murdery* type."

"I also think I'm probably getting fired."

Brad set down his fork. "Fired? Timothy, they love you. Mrs. Stone said so while you were busy finding dead bodies at Manhattan Moon. You're not getting fired."

"Maybe it's not up to her," I said, and explained I'd come to terms with the whole idea. "And anyway, office temps are always needed somewhere. SwellHire could place me somewhere with less drama. Somewhere I can just do a job, get paid, and have time to write best-selling novels."

I also told him I'd decided to spend whatever time I had left before being sacked digging into why Lillian Trent was killed—and whether it had anything to do with her grant being withdrawn.

"That has to connect somehow," I said. "There's too much

weirdness at the foundation for it to be random. I've spent the past two days poking around places I'm probably not authorized to go—but, well, here we are."

Concern flickered over Brad's face, and I hurried to alleviate his fears.

"No, I didn't hack anything," I added quickly. "I barely know how to update my phone. I still have login credentials from a past project assignment. Someone should've revoked them, but...didn't."

"Promise me you won't do anything illegal," Brad said, pointing at me with his fork. "I know you think tattoos are sexy, but I don't want you finding a new boyfriend in cellblock D at Rikers."

I laughed. "I said *your* tattoo is sexy. Not one attached to a guy named Two-Toes Henderson or Spider-Face Delgado. I am not prison-flirt material."

He grinned. "Good to know."

"So here's the deal." I leaned in. "I found something strange —really strange—about Lillian Trent's grant. You know, the five-hundred-thousand-dollar award? The foundation canceled it."

Brad froze. A noodle dangled from his fork like a worm. "Why would they cancel her grant?"

"I'll get to my theory. But here's the part that made my brain melt." I lowered my voice. "In the grant system—the software where all payments are tracked—the cancellation is logged the day before Lillian died. But where it's supposed to show the money going back into the foundation's accounts or being redirected...there's nothing. Blank."

Brad frowned. "The money has to be somewhere. Maybe they moved it to a general fund? Saved it for another program? Or...I don't know...granted it to someone else?"

"I thought so too. So I cross-referenced every other grant from this quarter. Every dollar—every penny—is accounted for. Nothing matches the missing amount. It's like the foundation snatched five hundred thousand dollars off the table and then pretended it never existed."

Brad leaned back, blinking hard. "Surely there's a reasonable explanation. The Adele Cummings Foundation isn't some shady back-alley nonprofit. They have auditors, accountants, compliance officers—oversight. Even billionaire-funded charities have legal guardrails. My mom's foundation does."

I took a long sip of Chianti. "Whenever my daddy misplaced his keys, he'd say, 'Nothin's ever lost—just out of hand.' And he was right. The keys always turned up where he left them. So if Lillian's grant money is missing...it's sitting somewhere. In someone's hand."

I leaned closer. "But it gets weirder. I checked the foundation's last Form 990-PF—the IRS report they have to file. There's a line for reversed grants: 'Recoveries of prior-year grants.' Lillian's missing money isn't listed there."

Brad stared at me with the expression parents reserve for toddlers juggling knives.

"Timothy...if you're onto something real, this could be dangerous. When large sums of money disappear, and disappear on purpose, people do crazy things." He squeezed my hand. "The kind of crazy where they hurt people to keep it quiet."

A cold ripple crawled up my spine. "Yeah," I whispered. "Maybe the money and the murder are connected."

"Sweetheart," Brad said softly, reaching across the table and taking my hand, "you need to be careful. Honestly? I don't think you should go back to that office."

"Trust me, I don't want to go back," I said. "Klotz is making my life a nightmare. She wants me to quit. I'm not giving her that satisfaction. If she fires me, she's going to have to explain why to everyone else who thinks I'm a star."

"I get it," Brad said. "But don't try to figure this out alone. You need someone who actually understands this stuff. Like my mom's foundation attorney—he's brilliant with compliance issues."

I said, "I can't drag a lawyer into this! I can't afford one, and I don't want anyone thinking I'm trying to bring down Adele Cummings. She's amazing. The staff is amazing. It's just...somebody is doing something rotten."

Brad leveled me with a look. "Timothy, you wouldn't be betraying Adele. You're protecting her. She doesn't manage the books personally—she has people to do that. And if one of those people is stealing or manipulating funds? You're not equipped to safely expose that all alone."

Brad could be annoyingly logical—in a sexy, take-me-by-the-hand-and-shelter-me way. "If you make one wrong move, you could tip off the guilty party," he said. "They could fire you—or worse. And Adele stays in the dark while someone drains her foundation from the inside."

"Okay." I sighed. "Fine. And wouldn't it be fun if Ms. Klotz were doing something illegal and I got to expose her? I mean, can you imagine? Watching her perp-marched in handcuffs? I'd frame her mugshot. Maybe get my own tattoo of her prisoner number."

Brad smirked but pushed on. "My mom's attorney is discreet. You don't even need to mention the foundation by name. He'll tell you what's normal and what's not—and whether what you found is harmless or...not."

He smiled that soft, achy, dangerous smile—the one that made me want to devour him whole. "You're not in this alone. It's me and you. All the way."

Then we went back to his place and wrecked the sheets.

Again.

39

Ach! I hate finances. I mean the language of finances. Not numbers in general—those I can handle. I can add, subtract, and even calculate a tip without using my phone. But don't ask me to reduce fractions or figure out what x is doing in an equation. And if anyone ever asked me to count backward from a hundred by sevens, I'd flunk—spectacularly. So naturally, when I met Layton Prescott, the financial guy for Brad's mother's foundation—a man who spoke fluent IRS-*ese*, the deadliest of all romance languages—I was bored stiff.

The atmosphere in Brad's apartment was solemn as we sat in the living room, sipping chamomile tea—Mr. Prescott's preference—and I endured phrases like "restricted asset reallocation" and "unreported prior-year adjustments." All my deep-sleep trigger phrases. When he uttered "capital expenditure anomaly," I was pretty sure I developed spontaneous narcolepsy.

"So," said Mr. Prescott, in a serious tone, "Brad tells me you're writing a novel. You have questions about the financial aspects of a hypothetical charitable foundation for your story?"

I didn't think he believed a word of my "fiction," but he was polite enough to play along. I took a breath. "Right. Hypothetical. So, my story takes place at a charitable institution here in New York. And the main character is a temp office intern there. Like me. But not me, of course. The charity gives away oodles of money, and one of the recipients—a cabaret singer—gets murdered before she can collect her award. Then the money she was supposed to get…vanishes. The main character smells a rat."

"Interesting plot," Mr. Prescott said. "Disturbingly realistic, actually. When grant money disappears, someone has made it disappear. And whoever that someone is… They don't appreciate being investigated."

I continued, "I should also say the missing grant money doesn't show up in the foundation's accounts anywhere."

"Fascinating," said Mr. Prescott as he leaned forward. "Let's unpack this. First: if a foundation promises a grant but doesn't pay it out—for any reason—it has to be formally canceled. The cancellation appears in the internal ledger. It might be labeled 'Grant Payable — Canceled,' or 'Grant Reversal,' or 'Adjustment to Prior Grants.' The wording varies from foundation to foundation, but the record itself has to exist."

He continued, "If the grant money was already set aside—budgeted, announced, prepared for disbursement—and then reversed by the foundation? That money must go back into the foundation's accounts. Either back into another program's budget, back into the general fund, or back into whatever pool it originally came from. But it goes somewhere. It doesn't just… evaporate."

"Okay," I said. "But—in my story—the money isn't recorded as being returned or redirected."

"Every single dollar has to have a destination," Mr. Prescott said. "A canceled grant isn't allowed to just…float away."

"And what if the system doesn't show the reversal?" I asked. "Even though it was definitely marked for distribution?"

That made Mr. Prescott sit up straighter. "The IRS wouldn't like that. A reversed grant must appear under 'Recoveries of prior-year grants.' It's required. If it's not there, someone either accidentally—or intentionally—prevented it from being reported."

Brad looked at me. "Timothy...it doesn't sound as though your fictional foundation is following the rules. That's good for your story, but not for real life."

Prescott agreed. "Even private billionaire-funded foundations can't hide money. Not legally," he said. "They have to track every penny. They have to report every transaction every year. Foundations are one of the most heavily regulated financial structures."

I countered, "Maybe, in a place where literally millions of dollars are handed out left and right, a measly five-hundred-grand drop-in-the-bucket might not be missed. Could someone hide that much?"

Prescott gave me a level look. "You'd be surprised by the level of creativity some people achieve with altering financial records," he said. "They can rename transactions. Bury them under vague labels like 'technical correction' or 'miscellaneous adjustment.' They can move the money around internally and hope no one examines the details."

I said, "What if someone does look closely?"

Prescott's expression shifted—calm but edged. "Then you—er, your story's character needs to tread very carefully. People who tamper with financial records tend to be...jumpy, to put it mildly. Missing money, especially if a grant was quietly reversed with no proper documentation, puts them in a very precarious position. And people in such positions often do menacing things."

Then Mr. Prescott launched into a long, unsettling example. "You've no doubt heard of Bernie Madoff," he said. "But there's another case I always think about—a woman named Marla Grintley. Most people have never heard of her, but in nonprofit and municipal accounting circles? She's a classic cautionary tale.

"For nearly twenty years, the people in the town of Redfield Crossing, Ohio thought Marla was the backbone of their little town. She worked in the town hall and handled budget allocations, vendor payments—all the boring financial guts that keep a small town running. She had a big smile, knew everyone's name, hosted the annual winter coat drive, etc. Everyone liked and trusted her.

"No one asked why a civil servant with a modest salary drove a brand-new Lexus every other year, or how she managed to buy a sprawling horse property outside of town. Folks just said she was 'smart with money.' Turns out she was smart with *their* money.

"You know where this is going, right? Behind the façade of civic goodness, Marla Grintley had built one of the most outrageous embezzlement schemes in small-town history. She created a 'temporary holding account'—her words—meant for processing outgoing funds. In reality, it was a private account she controlled exclusively. She siphoned money into it bit by bit, then buried the transfers in vague line items labeled 'community enrichment' or 'regional partnerships.' By the time anyone caught on, she'd taken almost seven million dollars."

"Seven million bucks?" I choked. "From a tiny town in Ohio?"

"And she might've gotten away with it for another twenty years if she hadn't taken a month off to oversee some renovation work in her home," Mr. Prescott explained. "A temp—like the character in your story—was filling in for her, stumbled across a statement from a bank the town didn't do business with. The temp took it to the city manager. The city manager called the state auditor. And the auditor called the FBI.

"Federal agents finally arrested Marla right at her desk. No one could believe the woman who organized the holiday food drive had been bleeding them dry for two decades."

Mr. Prescott spread his hands in that way usually reserved

for a preacher warning his flock about the wages of sin. "So yes —people do unnerving things when big money is involved."

"So, in my story, someone at the foundation probably played around with Lillian Trent's—I mean, the fictional singer's grant?"

Prescott's eyes were sharp and perceptive. "That's more than possible. It's plausible."

The air in the room shifted—an almost physical drop in temperature. Brad set his tea down, eyes narrowing with a seriousness I'd only expect if his piano caught fire. "Timothy," he said, "I'm getting really worried. If someone at the foundation is smart enough to manipulate the financial books, they're probably smart enough to pin it on someone else. On you."

A pulse of dread went through me.

"Think about it," he continued. "Lillian's grant money vanished. And the dance company's money before that, too. Remember? And you've touched both grant files. You've been accessing what should be protected files. It would probably be relatively easy to throw you under the bus. They can prove—with login receipts—that you've been snooping. Those systems are supposed to be locked down. Password protected. No organization would ever give that info to a temp employee they hardly know. And yet—they did." He paused and leaned forward. "That might be the plan. Make you look like the one who tampered with the grants."

My chest tightened. I nearly forgot how to breathe. Because Brad was right. How many times had I been rifling through the foundation's secure folders, and nobody stopped me? No warnings. No raised eyebrows. No "Hey, intern, what are you doing in the restricted database?" And Ms. Klotz—of all people—hadn't said a word. Not even a passive-aggressive DM. She absolutely would have accused me of misconduct.

But she didn't.

Which meant: Maybe she wanted me to access those files.

Mr. Prescott stared at me. "Look," he said, "if canceled grant money is not reallocated and not properly logged, it's not an accident. It's not incompetence. It is a crime. And people who hide corporate money do not want to be found out."

He folded his hands, his tone taking on a grave, almost clinical edge. "In my experience, embezzlers will do anything to protect themselves. And they protect themselves aggressively. So if your character is planning to keep looking for clues at the foundation—and you strike me as someone persistent—there's something else you need to check."

He paused, letting the warning sink in. Then he said, "Any time a foundation takes back a grant, there should be two notes in the system. First: 'We canceled it.' Second: 'Here's where the money went instead.' If that second note is missing...?"

Brad's arm tightened around me. "You're right," he said to Prescott. "I'm dating an extremely persistent intern."

But when he turned back to me, the pride in his smile faltered. I could see fear.

And suddenly, I understood. If I'd discovered a secret that someone risked their career to hide—what else might they be willing to risk to keep me quiet?

40

Sunday morning arrived rude and gray. As Brad slipped into his jacket and prepared to head to the train for his day in Connecticut, he hesitated in the doorway, clearly weighing something. Finally, he gave me a soft, reluctant smile.

"I hate leaving you like this," he said quietly. "But stay here awhile. It's yucky out there. Go back to bed where it's warm. Your laundry can wait a few hours."

As a matter of fact, I was planning to sleep in. My body was wrecked from our weekend gymnastics, and my brain felt like a snow globe someone had shaken, and a flurry of murder suspects whirled past. All their motives, all their grudges, all their possible motives for killing Lillian Trent and stealing her grant money swirled around inside my skull.

Frankly, I could imagine any one of them doing the deed. Everett Miles, the accompanist, had a piano technique that made the keyboard sound like a full orchestra, but Lillian had cut him loose days before her death. He was angry and maybe bitter enough to strangle the life out of her. Rage can turn even gentle artistic souls into lunatics.

Rachel Morris? Unremarkable as a singer. Not very interesting as a person either. In the shadow of Lillian, who had real talent, she'd convinced herself she deserved the Adele Cummings grant. Knowing that Lillian was getting a large sum must've burned like battery acid inside. Jealousy ferments. People have committed terrible acts over smaller perceived injustices.

Then there was that other singer—Jessica Larkin—the one who was supposed to double-bill with Lillian at the Blue Note. The one who got food poisoning hours before showtime. In New York cabaret circles, food poisoning was maybe shorthand for "someone wanted you nowhere near that microphone." If Jessica Larkin believed Lillian had sabotaged her big night, she'd definitely have a motive: revenge. The kind that burns a lot longer than an upset stomach.

And what about that newbie accompanist Lillian had humiliated? Halfway through their opening number, she'd blindsided him by modulating into a completely different key without warning. The audience had laughed at him. In the cabaret world, onstage humiliation has a half-life longer than uranium. Your reputation is your currency. One bad night, and suddenly no one wants you back. If Lillian had made him look incompetent, that could mean lost gigs, lost income, and maybe a violin-string-tight grudge. Some people forgive. Some people nurse wounds. And some people wait for the moment to return the favor.

Mrs. Stone obviously lingered in my thoughts, too. Elegant. Polished. Married to money. And apparently a fixture at every venue where Lillian and Everett performed—always requesting a table closest to the piano and always sending Everett a gin and tonic. She'd gone backstage the night Lillian was killed—ostensibly to use the bathroom. The ladies' room sat right next to Lillian's dressing room. Convenient? Maybe she knew that Lillian had dropped Everett from her act. Did Mrs. Stone retaliate out of loyalty? Had her refined manners cracked just enough to confront and murder Lillian?

And then there was Mr. Slater. I liked him. He was always nice to me. And I wanted to emulate his level of stylishness when I became rich and famous. But if he—as an advisor at the Adele Cummings Foundation—was having a secret affair with Lillian Trent while she was a grant applicant? Even I knew that was a massive professional no-no! Staff shouldn't sleep with grant recipients. Ever. It was the nonprofit equivalent of sleeping with a student or a client. It could undermine the entire institution's integrity. A clean-cut, elegant man with a secret? That really had me wondering.

Which left the final suspect—the one I was least surprised by: Ms. Klotz. The shrew whose jewel-encrusted dragonfly hair clip had ended up on the bar floor at Manhattan Moon the very night Lillian Trent was killed. Why had she even been there? She'd flashed her Adele Cummings Foundation employee ID to get into a sold-out show as if she were Homeland Security. Was she there to discuss why Lillian's grant had been reversed? Maybe she wanted to confront Lillian about her relationship with Mr. Slater? I seriously didn't think she was there because she liked cabaret. I couldn't picture her enjoying anything that didn't involve inflicting human suffering. Of course, even villains need hobbies.

And then, of course, there was the small matter of the missing grant money. The money that should have been Lillian's. The foundation deliberately canceled it. And it appeared someone with organizational skills erased its trail. And if Ms. Klotz had known Lillian was about to expose something—money, misconduct, misappropriation—well, even dragonflies bite.

Any one of them could have killed Lillian. And somehow—through bad luck or bad karma—I'd become the little intern who knew too much.

As I stared at that snarl of motives and secrets—money gone missing, sabotaged performances, backstage tantrums, jealous crushes, illicit affairs, and one dead singer—a realization slid down my spine: sometimes guilty people slip up. In novels and movies, that's how they're caught. They overestimate themselves. They forget one detail. They grow sloppy, arrogant, careless. They leave one tiny thread from their crime dangling—and the whole cover-up unravels. Sometimes.

So maybe all I had to do was watch and pretend to be harmless. Let them believe the intern was just a naïve young guy who wore thrift store clothing. Except—small problem—I didn't have the luxury of time or patience. Ms. Klotz was ready to fire my ass at any moment.

I lay in Brad's bed, staring at the ceiling, trying to figure it all out—and how I was going to survive long enough to expose whoever had killed Lillian and absconded with her grant money. I wasn't bold. I wasn't heroic. Mostly, I was terrified. But I had to think of *something*. Before I got fired. Or worse.

I turned the possibilities over and over in my head, rejecting most of them almost as soon as they formed. And then, eureka! Somewhere between panic and exhaustion, an idea surfaced.

41

The idea arrived the way good plot twists in my favorite mystery novels sometimes do—quietly, like a cat slipping into a room through a slightly open door. I was still lying in Brad's bed, replaying all the suspects in my mind like a gruesome casting call, when a snippet from some old Agatha Christie book—or maybe it was *Only Murders in the Building*—floated up: a gathering of all the suspects in one place, everyone watching everyone else, tension simmering like a pot about to boil over. They did this all the time in mystery stories. Gather all the suspects in one place, let the tension rise, and wait for the guilty party to crack. If it worked for Hercule Poirot, Jessica Fletcher, and three New Yorkers with a podcast, maybe it could work for me.

But I didn't have a drawing room in a country manor. This was Manhattan. And then—bam—the idea hit me so hard I actually bolted upright. *Cabaret! A tribute to Lillian Trent!* A sort of memorial night at Manhattan Moon! It could be billed as a celebration of talent and the performing arts. All donations would go to lesser-known artists who needed funding to promote their shows. It was a brilliant idea!

Everyone in the cabaret community would have to be there. Other charities, too. Every single person with a reason to love Lillian, hate Lillian, or envy Lillian. A tribute night was one event none of them could refuse without looking guilty, heartless, or suspicious. Even better? It gave me a built-in stage. A literal one. And a captive audience. And...opportunities for them to make mistakes. Because guilt makes people twitchy. And murderers, according to every mystery novel I'd ever inhaled, cannot resist hovering near the scene of their crime.

If I could get Lenny Barron on board, he'd pack Manhattan Moon with cabaret insiders and charity organizations that purported to help artists. The suspects would be boxed in. Their reactions would be monitored. And I'd be watching.

I grabbed my phone and started typing a message to Lenny, my fingers shaking with adrenaline. My pulse thudded hard. Because this wasn't just a tribute. It was an emotionally charged mousetrap.

And I hoped—no, needed—the murderer to walk straight into it.

Monday arrived with all the enthusiasm of a cat dragging in a dead mouse—technically a gift, but no one wanted it. Least of all me. After the disaster that was last week—Ms. Klotz's evisceration by email, her dragonfly hair clip turning up near a murder scene—I expected to step into the foundation trembling like a Chihuahua at a fireworks show. But oddly...I didn't.

I was tired, sure. Nervous, yes. But beneath the anxiety sat my newly minted screw-it-all-to-hell energy. Maybe thanks to that cathartic crying jag I'd had in the bathroom. Maybe thanks to the quiet-quitting resolve pulsing through me. Either way, I felt...lighter. Maybe that was what resignation felt like. I was ready to be fired if that was where this ship was sailing.

Physically, Ravenscroft looked status quo. But something was definitely different. My workload had evaporated. Usually, the advisors tossed assignments at me like I was a golden retriever. Research this. Proofread that. Dive into the digital archives and find every email Adele Cummings sent in 2007. But today? Nothing. No urgent messages. It felt like the whole staff knew that I shouldn't be given any job that required follow-through beyond lunchtime. Which suited me just fine. If they didn't need me, I could focus on what mattered: the tribute for Lillian.

I'd spent half of Sunday convincing Lenny Barron to host the event at Manhattan Moon. It took some finesse, but I knew exactly which pressure points to press. I reminded him how the cabaret community practically ran on grief solidarity. How singers showed up for one another in the way theater kids showed up for a castmate's performance. A memorial show would pack the room—sold out, guaranteed. And because I wasn't above light emotional blackmail, I suggested turning it into a fundraiser for struggling cabaret artists. A win-win: Lenny got a full house and a halo. The cabaret world got to play glamorous martyr. And the foundation? They'd be compelled to attend or risk looking like soulless oligarchs who didn't care about a grantee dying on their watch.

Lenny, to his credit, saw the brilliance immediately. "A tribute show?" he'd said, practically vibrating. "Kid, that'll get press. That'll get every diva from Midtown to Queens lining up with a ballad and a cocktail dress." He did a quick calculation in his head—I could practically see it happening. "A full house. Might finally make back some of what I sank into her. Let's do it."

It had that *Pitch Perfect* optimism—scrappy, musical, and wildly unconcerned with whether this was a good idea.

And now, on Monday morning, with Ravenscroft giving me the silent treatment and my to-do list containing exactly zero actual responsibilities, I had an opportunity to write the press release I'd promised Lenny, announcing the tribute event. Of course, I had to write it on my phone so it couldn't be traced back to my work computer.

FOR IMMEDIATE RELEASE
Contact: Lenny Barron, General Manager
Manhattan Moon Cabaret
Email: Lenny@manhattanmoonnyc.com
Phone: (212) 555-0194

MANHATTAN MOON PRESENTS
A FUNDRAISING TRIBUTE TO LILLIAN TRENT

New York, NY — Popular cabaret club Manhattan Moon will host a heartfelt fundraising tribute to the late Lillian Trent, whose unforgettable voice and luminous stage presence made her a cherished figure in New York's cabaret community. The memorial performance will take place on Monday evening, September 12, at 7:30 p.m.

The evening will feature performances by some of the city's most celebrated cabaret artists, including Vera LaRue, Cameron DuMont, Josie Everhart, and the Silvertone Trio, with additional guest performers to be announced.

All proceeds from ticket sales will go toward the newly created Lillian Trent Artist Support Fund, a GoFundMe initiative dedicated to providing emergency financial assistance to cabaret performers facing hardship.

Manhattan Moon general manager Lenny Barron said, "Lillian devoted her life to this community. This tribute honors her spirit the only way we know how—through music, generosity, and coming together."

Seating is limited. Tickets and donation information are available through Manhattan Moon's website.

I reread the press release for the tenth time, making sure

every line sounded respectful and polished. I attached it to an email and sent it off to Lenny.

Lenny's mailing list was legendary. It contained absolutely everyone in New York—performers, agents, and theater critics. If a person had ever clapped in the vicinity of a stage, Lenny had their email. I'd asked him to expand the blast to ensure that every advisor at the foundation's email addresses were included. And Adele Cummings, too. I'd stumbled upon her personal email address weeks ago in the depths of the foundation's shared drive. Which, in fairness, I probably wasn't supposed to give out.

But I did. So sue me. A tribute to Lillian Trent deserved every possible body in the audience—including the woman who'd built the institution that employed half the people on my suspects list.

I sat back, a little breathless and a tiny bit proud. It wasn't every day that a press release written by me—Timothy Trousdale, former innocuous host at the Chili Exchange and aspiring bestselling author—would land in the inbox of Adele Cummings herself. Whether she read it was another matter entirely. (Had she ever read my inspirational quotes?) But the advisors on her foundation team surely would. And the best part was, they wouldn't know I'd written it—much less that I'd done it on foundation time. I mean, what else did I have to do?

42

———

Against all known laws of probability, I was still employed when Lillian Trent's tribute day arrived. I was convinced Ms. Klotz kept me around for sport. The woman seemed to draw spiritual nourishment from seeing me flinch whenever we accidentally met in the hallway. I thought maybe she didn't want me fired. She wanted me available for batting practice.

Throughout the week, I pestered poor Lenny for updates on the RSVP list. I kept pretending to be calm while, inside, I was a tangle of nerves. What if my suspects didn't show? Brad assured me I had nothing to worry about. He said the tribute wasn't all about loyalty and grief. It was also about optics. And sure enough, Mrs. Johnston booked three tables to accommodate the foundation's advisors and herself.

What struck me most was how blissfully unaware they all seemed. They had no idea the tribute was my idea, or that the press release they'd read had been written by me. And they certainly didn't know I'd be attending. As the day drew to a close, they gathered their things and drifted out of the office in little knots of well-tailored philanthropy, gliding off toward Manhattan Moon.

Monday night had been chosen for the tribute for one simple reason: it was the only night New York's performers were actually free from their own gigs. Cabaret rooms were dark, Broadway was shuttered, and the city's singers and musicians were available to support one another. It was the one night Manhattan Moon didn't have to compete with a dozen other rooms full of torch songs.

I slipped out of the office shortly after the others and caught the M2 bus uptown. By the time I reached Manhattan Moon, Brad was waiting outside, looking maddeningly handsome in a charcoal-gray blazer and a maroon turtleneck. Cue my swoon.

"Ready?" he asked, fully aware I was a package of raw nerves.

I was absolutely *not* ready.

Manhattan Moon was vibrating with energy. This tribute to Lillian Trent was packed and turning into the cabaret equivalent of the Met Gala—with everyone who had ever worked a night-club room for tips and applause. I scanned the tables and spotted Everett Miles seated with Thane Granville. (Were they dating again? They certainly made an unreasonably adorable couple.)

And then I spotted several of the foundation's advisors clustered at two side-by-side tables. Mrs. Stone noticed me and nudged Ms. Neely, who nudged Mr. Slater, and the three of them turned in perfect choreographed surprise. They waved with the kind of enthusiasm people deploy when pretending they're thrilled to see you.

So much for my slipping in unnoticed. A small numbness washed over me. I genuinely liked these people. I didn't want any of them to be a cold-blooded killer. That particular distinction was reserved for one person.

Mrs. Stone wore her ubiquitous pearls and carried a black clutch. Ms. Neely looked classy in the Gabriela Hearst suit she'd worn all day. Mr. Slater, in a Tom Ford blazer, was impeccable without being flashy.

Then I noticed Mrs. Johnston arrive with Ms. Raymond, their office attire embellished with little accents that transformed their work clothes for the evening. A gray cashmere shawl for Ms. Raymond, and a lovely pale blue silk scarf with tiny silver threads for Mrs. Johnston. Perfectly theatrical for this festive evening, I thought with approval.

But where was Ms. Klotz? I scanned the room. Oh, there she was. Seated away from the other advisors (naturally). She was with an older woman whom I didn't recognize, but who looked like she was rolling in dough like all the foundation peeps. I could usually tell.

Then the event formally began. Lenny swept onto the tiny stage in a tuxedo, tapped the microphone, and offered a smile. "Good evening, friends," he purred, prompting a warm ripple of applause. "Tonight we gather in sadness...but also in gratitude—for the luminous, occasionally maddening, always unforgettable force of nature that was our beloved Lillian Trent." He pressed a hand to his heart, letting the room fall quiet.

"We'll share songs and stories—because we're cabaret people and physically cannot stop ourselves. And we'll celebrate Lillian Trent—a talent none of us will ever forget. As if she'd let us!"

The room answered with a ripple of knowing laughter.

"Lillian had a way of making an impression," Lenny went on. "On audiences...on accompanists...and on anyone who dared change her lighting cues." A wave of chuckles rolled through the room again, punctuated by a few sympathetic groans.

"Love her or fear her—and let's be honest, for many of us, it was a rotating schedule—we all understood one thing: when Lillian Trent walked onstage, the air changed. Something electric was about to happen."

Lenny let the silence bloom just long enough for the sentiment to land; then his face brightened. "First up tonight, someone who knew Lillian—and her high voltage—almost intimately. Please welcome Lillian's accompanist...Everett Miles."

Everett made his way to the piano wearing his all-black uniform. He sat at the keyboard and offered a small, sheepish smile, then leaned into the microphone. "I owe Lillian Trent a lot," he began. "More than most people know. We worked together for about a year. And if you ever worked with Lillian, you know she had two modes: inspirational...and 'run for your life.'"

The room exploded with laughter and a smattering of applause, the audience appreciating the humor—and truth.

"She wasn't just a diva," he continued. "She was, at times, almost a kid-sister figure to me—if your kid sister is the type who can compliment you and insult you in the same breath and make it sound like both are from a place of love. She was a blend of charm and madness. But my God—her artistry. Worth every emotional bruise."

The room appreciated Everett's irreverence. It was exactly the kind of honesty the crowd understood. Lillian had been brilliant and impossible in equal measure, and pretending otherwise would've felt more disrespectful than telling the truth. His candor landed like a release valve.

Everett smiled warmly, then looked down and rested his fingers lightly on the keyboard. "But Lillian was a total pro. A week before we went on that last night...on this very stage...she told me she was moving on and wouldn't require my services. The audience never knew we'd fought only minutes before. Whatever her flaws—and there were a few—Lillian respected the stage. She never let personal drama bleed onto it."

Everett's voice softened. "But I want to be clear: Lillian was extraordinary. Working with her made me better. She demanded excellence because she believed songs deserved nothing less—every phrase polished, every emotion honest, every note treated like it was as important as all the others. To Lillian, a song wasn't just something you performed. It was something you shaped until it finally revealed its soul."

He looked over the audience, his expression open in a way that felt almost naked—like he was offering up something fragile and hoping we'd hold it carefully. "I was lucky to be part of her journey," he said softly. "Even the difficult parts." Then he turned back to the piano. "I wrote this the day after she died... just trying to capture what she meant to me. This is *Lillian's Theme.*"

The first notes slipped into the air, and the melody unfurled —elegant, aching, threaded with grief and love. It hit everyone. It was the truest kind of tribute. Music written by someone who'd loved her. No one who hated Lillian Trent could have composed something that raw and tender about her.

Right then and there, I crossed Everett Miles off my list of suspects.

The evening progressed, and Lenny introduced singer after singer. Each spoke reverently of Lillian and performed a song they felt captured her spirit: "But the World Goes 'Round," "You Must Believe in Spring," "Goodbye for Now," "My Love Is a Wanderer," and "Send in the Clowns." Some anecdotes were amusing on the surface but carried...shading. The kind of stories that sounded affectionate unless you actually knew Lillian—at which point they were beautifully wrapped insults. Anyone who had known Lillian caught every pointed layer.

The final singer—a soft-spoken alto—ended the program with Lillian's signature song, "New Girl." The last note hung in the air like a plea. People around me dabbed at their eyes. Even Rachel Morris, who I imagine normally cried only when someone else booked a gig she thought should be hers, was sniffling into a tissue.

Lenny returned to the microphone and, in a solemn voice, said, "My friends, I know Lillian would have appreciated that you took the time to be here tonight. But before we let the spell break—please stay for a champagne toast to her life and legacy. On the house—of course. Raise a glass, share a memory—or gossip. Lillian would have loved that."

The room exhaled. Chairs scraped back, voices swelled, and servers threaded through the crowd, balancing trays of champagne like precious cargo. Soon, the place was breaking into clusters—pockets of whispered memories, and the faintest shimmer of professional rivalry. People smiled warmly as they measured one another's careers.

Brad and I joined the tide, slipping into the currents. But my nerves snapped to attention. This was it. My suspects were all here, all confined to the same room. It was time to work. And Rachel Morris was the nearest target.

43

"The lineup was...okay, I guess," Rachel said as we mingled after the performances. "But I can't believe they didn't ask me to sing. I would have killed 'em with 'Midnight Comes for Us All.'"

"I'm sure it wasn't personal," I said—though I was fairly certain the program had been vastly improved by Rachel remaining seated in the audience. Some performers shine onstage; others shine by staying firmly off it.

"It *was* personal," Rachel snapped. "Lenny put it together. He's never liked me. Never booked me. Ever. But I'm not complaining." She said this in the universal tone of someone with a lot of resentment. "At least I got to scope out the room," she added. "My first time here, actually. I had no idea it was so small. And the acoustics? They desperately need a new sound system. And did you see those cocktail prices? I could never afford to perform here—not if they expect my friends and family to drink."

I gave her a questioning look, and she barreled on. "And the forty-five-dollar cover charge? Gimme a break! I wouldn't pay that if Patti LuPone sang with her tits hanging out. Forty-five bucks? For a stool and a spotlight! Forget it!"

Her bitterness was obvious—but so was her penny-pinching, her self-interest, and the fact that the only thing she seemed capable of killing was the evening's vibe. I was pretty sure Rachel Morris hadn't paid money to buy a ticket to Lillian Trent's last show, then killed her. She was dramatic, not very talented, and financially strapped. But probably not homicidal.

So I basically crossed her off my list.

"Well, that sort of rules out Rachel," I whispered to Brad. He nodded and gently guided us back into the flow of the room, letting the crowd carry us along. We drifted toward a lively little knot that gave off unmistakable performer energy—big gestures, big voices that carried even while whispering.

Which was how we ended up with Jessica Larkin—one of my less-than-prime murder suspects. Her smile was warm and, of course, I already knew about her digestive history—thanks to Rachel's almost operatic retelling of the time Jessica got food poisoning before a show at the Blue Note that she was meant to share with Lillian.

Jessica sipped from her glass and said, "Lillian would've loved tonight. She always said the show must go on, no matter what. Even when I was sick as a dog the night we were supposed to double-bill. She thought I was a wuss for not getting my fanny on stage."

She laughed—self-deprecating and affectionate. "Everyone whispered that Lillian poisoned me, which is ridiculous. If she'd wanted me silenced, she wouldn't have used food. Besides, I know exactly what did it. I had a Caesar salad for lunch. The anchovies were the color of old pennies. I even said, 'These look suspicious.' And then, like an idiot—I ate them anyway."

"But the rumors—" I tried to interject before she talked over me.

"I'm in the bathroom for, like, two days—green as Elphaba,"

Jessica continued. "I had to miss the show. Then I got fired. And suddenly the rumor mill decides Lillian masterminded the whole thing." She rolled her eyes and laughed. "It maybe sounds like something she'd do. But just this once, I can vouch."

And just like that, I mentally crossed another name off my suspect list. Jessica had never been high on the leaderboard anyway. You can't be a cold-blooded killer if you refuse to hold even a lukewarm grudge.

Then a shift in the room's energy made me look to my left. A shadow drifted into our little circle, and suddenly Mr. Slater was beside us—his gaze lingering on Brad with unmistakable appreciation. He held his champagne flute in both hands, as if guarding it from potential thieves—or flying away.

"Mr. Trousdale," he said, "I'm happy you came tonight. And this must be the famous Brad I've heard you talk about. You both got a small glimpse tonight of how extraordinary Lillian was—and how special she was to the cabaret world."

Jessica Larkin arched an eyebrow. "Some of us know exactly how special she was—to *you*."

Color rose almost instantly in Mr. Slater's cheeks. He opened his mouth, closed it, then opened it again, not sure how to respond. "Despite rumors, we were never any more than friends," he said. "I'm on the Adele Cummings advisory committee. I was merely a convenient stepping stone for her. Or so she thought."

He glanced down at his champagne flute. "I just wish I'd seen her last show. I was supposed to be here. And take her out afterward. But I got stuck in Connecticut. The police actually questioned me because they found text messages on her phone between us about the date. I had to prove I wasn't in town."

Someone came prepared with an alibi.

But it was when he said, "I still can't listen to her last voicemail," that something in his voice cracked. Not for effect. It was an unguarded expression of grief. It stopped me. His sorrow wasn't theatrical or performative; it was the kind that genuinely lodges in a person and doesn't let go.

Yeah, there are plenty of good actors out there, but I found myself taking a small mental step back and studying him more closely. And in that moment, I believed—whatever secrets Mr. Slater was carrying—we all had them—they weren't about guilt. Not the murderous kind, anyway. So I crossed him off my list. Not a killer. Or at least...not *my* killer.

I scanned the room again, this time looking for one specific face. Ms. Klotz. If I were ever going to confront her on semi-neutral ground, it was here, in a public setting—where she was unlikely to snip off my family jewels while witnesses were present.

It took a moment, but I spotted her a few tables away. And I began to quiver like a leaf. There she was: posture rigid, arms welded across her chest, expression carved from solid New Hampshire granite. She was talking with another woman, the one who radiated similar patrician energy—silvery coiffure, the unmistakable aura of someone with oodles of dough.

I didn't want to interrupt, but I also knew opportunities like this were rarer than smiles from Ms. Klotz herself. And besides —speaking of jewels—I felt my pocket for the dragonfly hair clip I'd convinced Lenny to let me return to her. If nothing else, it provided a diplomatic excuse to speak with her.

"Back in a sec," I said to Brad. Though even I wasn't entirely sure I'd return in one piece. I approached Ms. Klotz the way one approaches a reptile whose bite requires antivenom and a heli-copter evacuation. When I was close enough, I reached into my pocket.

"Ms. Klotz?" I stammered. "I-I'm sorry to interrupt. I just... I have something of yours." My voice cracked, which was abso-lutely not the effect I wanted. "Lenny—the club manager—asked me to return this to you."

I opened my hand. The dragonfly hair clip glittered in my

palm, its diamond-encrusted wings catching the lights. "He said it probably fell out of your hair the last time you were here."

Ms. Klotz's eyes narrowed. First with curiosity. Then with an indignation that sent a cold crack straight down my spine.

"Why the hell do you have this?" she said, her voice low and accusatory.

The hair on my arms stood up. I didn't know why I expected gratitude from her—after all, this was the *Klotzinator*. But the blade in her tone sliced clean through whatever courage I'd brought to her table. "Maybe you dropped it... It was at the bar here. The cleaner found it." I swallowed, painfully aware my voice had shrunk two sizes.

Her stare sharpened into something metallic and carnivorous. "I left it in the bathroom—at Ravenscroft," she said. "Again, why do you have it?"

My mouth dropped open. I'd already explained myself. Did she think my story would change?

"And what do you mean, 'the last time I was here'?" she continued, leaning in so close I could smell the sharp piney aroma of gin on her breath. "I've never been here." The chill in her voice could've flash-frozen champagne. "Another one of your creative interpretations, Mr. Trousdale? Your attention to detail remains...deeply disappointing."

That did it. My stomach folded in on itself like origami. Before I could process the humiliation, the woman at Ms. Klotz's table leaned in for a closer look at the hair clip.

She immediately lit up. "Oh my goodness!" she breathed, her whole face brightening with astonishment. "This is marvelous!" She reached toward the dragonfly clip as if it were a newly discovered Fabergé egg. "I've been heartsick over its disappearance! It belonged to my grandmother." Her delight was so genuine, it startled me. "Thank you for returning it," she said, clasping my hand with gratitude. "My daughter means to say thank you too—"

And just like that, I was the Good Samaritan. The hero of the heirloom.

But wait a gol-darn minute! What did she just say? Not the "thank you" part. Not even the bit about the hair clip belonging to her grandmother. No—the D-word. "Daughter."

Daughter?

My brain stalled like a bad engine in an old car. Ms. Klotz had a mother? A human mother? Because honestly, up until this exact moment, I'd assumed Ms. Klotz had been spawned in a bog somewhere—possibly the love child of a swamp witch and Bigfoot.

"Helena, say a proper thank you," the woman instructed.

Who the hell is Helena?

Ms. Klotz looked like she'd been asked to swallow a live scorpion.

I opened my mouth to tease her with a sarcastic "You're welcome," but I knew better. And anyway, she had already turned away, slipping the dragonfly hair clip into her clutch.

I stood there, buzzing with adrenaline. Perfect. Absolutely perfect. I tried to do a good deed—return what might very well be evidence in a murder investigation to the prime suspect— and she repaid me by insinuating that I stole it? Lenny Barron said it, so I guessed I would, too: *Bitch.*

And of course, she was lying about never having been to Manhattan Moon before. Suzie, the hostess-slash-cleaner, could identify her in a lineup. But I wasn't suicidal enough to challenge Ms. Klotz to her face. Not here. Not with witnesses who might need trauma counselling after seeing whatever unanesthetized surgery she'd perform on me.

Instead, I turned around—and collided straight-on with Mrs. Johnston, who had materialized at my elbow with the stealth of a cougar. My savior! She'd seen the whole thing with Ms. Klotz. Every syllable, every glare, every icy drip of venom.

"You know she'll interrogate you under hot lights first thing in the morning," Mrs. Johnston said almost smugly. "She'll probably slide bamboo under your nails just for added fun." She gave me a pitying look. "If you thought you'd score points by returning that hair clip... You've only reminded her that it went missing in the first place."

Brad appeared at my side just in the nick of time. My well-tailored guardian angel sensing, uncannily, that I was seconds away from spiraling into a full-blown panic attack. He slipped an arm lightly around my back—not possessive, just grounding—and turned to Mrs. Johnston to help change the subject. With an easy, polished smile, he said, "I've been admiring your scarf. Hermès, right?"

Mrs. Johnston turned, pleasantly surprised. "Why, yes, it is." The effect was immediate. Mrs. Johnston's eyes softened; the hard edge that had flashed across her features a moment earlier dissolved. She lifted a hand to her scarf with almost girlish pride. "Thank you," she beamed. "One of my favorites."

Brad nodded. "Teatro series. I recognize it. I got my mom the same one last Christmas. She loved the little stage curtain detail in the corner. Very subtle." He leaned in, pointing. "Right there."

Brad was like that—instinctively kind, reflexively polite. Even to people I was quietly sizing up as suspects.

Mrs. Johnston followed his finger, then gave a vague smile. "Yes. Lovely detail."

Brad grinned. "They only made a few in that colorway. Wild to see another just like my mom's."

Mrs. Johnston's smile held too long. Too still. She didn't know what the heck he was talking about. There was no flicker of understanding in her eyes. Even I knew Hermès often produced scarves that told miniature visual stories, and in the Teatro—or theater-themed designs—there was a pulled-back velvet-drape motif. Other than the brand name, Mrs. Johnston didn't realize what she was wearing. She probably hadn't purchased the scarf. Too expensive.

"It's a classic look," Brad said warmly, his charm working at full diplomatic capacity. But the room had begun to feel too small, and I desperately needed space away from Mrs. Johnston. I let my eyes wander, searching for an escape hatch, a distraction. Maybe someone I suddenly needed to say hello to. Any reason to move away.

As my gaze drifted over the thinning crowd, the tables littered with empty champagne flutes, my eyes landed on the framed poster of Lillian Trent hanging near the bar. She looked exactly as she had the night I saw her perform here. Frozen mid-glamour: the shimmering dress, the sparkly brooch, the smile that could hypnotize a room, the lovely scarf with the tiny silver threads that glittered under the lights.

The scarf...

...Much like the one wrapped around Mrs. Johnston's neck.

My breath suddenly snagged—sharp, involuntary. A thought occurred to me. *No. That's ridiculous. Not possible.*

Except...Lillian's scarf was missing when I found her body.

My pulse began to thunder in my ears.

Mrs. Johnston's gaze followed mine—first to my face, then to the poster, then back again. Her smile—which had turned almost girlish when Brad admired her scarf—stiffened at the edges. A tiny tremor, barely there, but unmistakable.

And then a horrifying thought cracked open inside my skull —sudden, blinding, violent. What if Mrs. Johnston's scarf wasn't just similar to Lillian's? *What if it was Lillian's?*

A shock ripped through me so hard I nearly lost my balance. The room tilted. My breath seized. My vision tunneled. Because if that were true, something else logical would follow. Maybe Ms. Klotz wasn't lying about never setting foot in Manhattan Moon before. Maybe the woman whom Suzie, the hostess, described wasn't Ms. Klotz at all. Maybe...it was the woman standing before me wearing a scarf.

Oh God. Maybe...

The thought landed like a blow to the chest, and for a second, the only sound I could hear was my own heart roaring in my ears. My brain raced. I'd noticed before that all the women in the foundation's office were roughly the same Pilates-toned build. Even Mrs. Johnston, who was thirty years older than the others, had once laughed that they could all "swap wardrobes like sorority sisters," and joked she'd "kill for one of their Chanel hand-me-downs."

At the time, I thought it was just office banter. But now? Now, standing here in Manhattan Moon under dim lighting, shifting shadows, and in a crowd that ebbed and flowed like a restless tide, a memory hit from the night Lillian was murdered...right here.

My gaze crept back to the scarf around Mrs. Johnston's neck. The room felt suddenly airless, the walls drawing in. And now she stood beside me—calm, composed.

A tremor ran down my spine. A cold shiver as fast as lightning. My God. Mrs. Johnston could have worn Ms. Klotz like a mask. I even thought I'd seen Ms. Klotz here that night.

I looked at Mrs. Johnston. And she looked at me. The sweetness she wore at the office—the lilac lotions, the soft eyes—fell away. What remained was something alert and assessing. A flicker crossed her face. It was the flicker of someone running silent arithmetic at high speed. Someone determining exactly what I'd realized, what conclusion I'd reached, and exactly how fast she needed to act.

The air between us tightened—thin and ready to snap. My heart slammed against my ribs, like a primitive drumbeat of *Danger! Danger! Danger!* I reached blindly for Brad's coat sleeve, needing something solid to hold on to. "I—um—I need to—find the little boys' room," I babbled, my voice pitched an octave too high. "I'll be right back."

Except I couldn't turn my back on Mrs. Johnston. My instinct screamed, *Don't.* I edged away, step by careful step, the way one retreats from a predator in the wild—never breaking eye contact, never exposing the soft parts. Because in that moment, with Lillian's scarf around her throat and that expression on her face, Mrs. Johnston wasn't the warm Mother Hen of the foundation. She was something else. Maybe something dangerous. And she had her eyes on me.

44

Inside the men's room, I leaned over the sink, gripping the porcelain until my knuckles went white. "Not possible," I whispered. "She didn't do it...couldn't... Ms. Klotz is the killer! She has to be."

I let cold water run in the basin as my mind careened through every possible angle, every alibi, every scenario that might make Mrs. Johnston not the killer. But nothing made sense.

How could sweet Mrs. Johnston physically strangle someone thirty or so years younger? Why would she even try—unless... My thoughts spiraled, looping tighter and tighter until I felt faint. Nothing connected. Nothing aligned. Nothing allowed me to breathe. I splashed water on my face—hard enough to sting. I needed air. I needed the world to stop making life so hard. I needed Brad.

I pulled open the men's room door and staggered into the hallway, pressing my back against the wall as I tried to slow the pounding in my chest. The muffled buzz of the club down the corridor felt miles away.

Then I smelled perfume.

A familiar scent—sharp, elegant, unmistakable. And suddenly I knew why. It was the same fragrance I'd caught a month ago in this very hallway as I'd been making my way toward Lillian Trent's dressing room on that terrible night.

The realization landed hard.

It was Mrs. Johnston's scent.

I'd been with her only minutes ago, which was why I hadn't questioned it then. But here—in this hallway, with my nerves raw—it finally connected. Why hadn't I recognized her scent before?

Then—a soft voice in the shadows. "Mr. Trousdale."

My blood iced over.

Mrs. Johnston stepped forward. The weak hallway light caught her face. Her expression was grandmotherly, concerned. "Are you all right, dear?" she asked gently. "You rushed off so quickly..."

I instinctively took a step backward.

She took a step forward. "Oh, my dear," she murmured, "you really shouldn't run around frightening yourself with insane ideas." Another step closer.

The air grew heavy as she moved into my space. Her perfume wasn't soft anymore; it smelled cloying, suffocating.

"Rules, Timothy. How many times did we talk about rules? You're otherwise pretty clever," she said, her voice thinning into a colder register. "Clever young men can get themselves into all sorts of trouble." The hallway lights flickered—pulsing like a warning. "Mr. Trousdale...may I call you Timothy? You can call me Eleanor." She moved closer, and her next words were not a question. They were a verdict. "You won't say anything, will you?"

My throat constricted. I tried to speak, but no sound came out.

Mrs. Johnston—Eleanor—opened her clutch and withdrew a small gun. A pearl-handled revolver. I was horrified. It almost looked like a toy—but the way she held it, steady and precise, told me it was real. She'd probably practiced using it, too.

Help was only a few feet away. Literally just down this hallway, which reeked of booze and old-lady perfume. A hundred people. Laughing, toasting, clinking glasses—utterly unaware I was about to die a ridiculous death.

"I hoped I wouldn't need it," she said, glancing at the gun. "But hope is for people with nothing to lose."

I opened my mouth to yell, but what came out was a pathetic scrape of breath. My throat locked. My brain kept screaming *shout*, but my body wouldn't obey. I couldn't risk her firing the gun. Not with the barrel so close. One move, one sound too loud —and she'd reflexively pull the trigger.

I was frozen. Not just with fear, but with the awful, sudden certainty that she'd thought this through. That she wasn't bluffing. Yes, she was an older woman. But the gun made her something else entirely.

"Don't panic, dear," Mrs. Johnston said. "Panic makes things messy. Why don't we step outside?"

Talk about a cliché straight out of some old Warner Bros. film-noir B movie. But clichés become clichés because they work. And Mrs. Johnston didn't need to raise her voice. The gun in her hand was all the volume required.

My legs obeyed her command before my brain could object. My vision tunneled; every beat of my heart felt like it might burst through my ribs. I pushed the crash bar on the metal exit door, and it gave way into the cold night air. I stumbled into the back alley. The only light came from a cracked fixture above the door—a bulkhead sconce with a rusted cage around a dim bulb. The light carved everything into harsh angles: bottles and crushed cans, the rain-slick asphalt, a hulking overstuffed dumpster exhaling its stinking rot. The door shut behind me with a metallic thud—too final.

For a split second, instinct howled: *Run. Bolt. Get away.* But could I? Was there even time? Or would turning my back simply get me killed faster?

"Much better," said Mrs. Johnston. "Private. No interruptions."

My breath smoked in the cold night air. I swallowed hard. "You don't have to do this, Mrs. Johnston. Please. Whatever you think I know—I don't..."

"Oh, Timothy." She gave a soft, pitying sigh. "You *know* what you *know*. Pretending otherwise doesn't change anything."

She adjusted her scarf—Lillian's scarf—and the silver threads glinted in the weak alley light. "You know why I wore this tonight?" she said softly. "Because it was symbolic of how clever I am. I was congratulating myself for pulling the wool over everyone's eyes." A small, satisfied smile curved her mouth. "You're too observant for your own good," she said. "Sharp eyes. Quick mind. All excellent qualities in a novelist..."

She took a step closer. "But those are unfortunate attributes in a witness."

Another cold wave rolled through me. I blindly backed up until my spine crushed against the metal side of the dumpster. I hadn't even realized I'd been retreating. From within the club, muffled laughter floated through the walls. Someone had started to sing—someone who had no idea I was moments away from being murdered.

"Why?" The word scraped out of me, thin and frayed. "Why do you have to do this?"

"Because...nothing is going to ruin my plans. Remember when you came to me with that pathetic story about a 'friend' who'd 'maybe' stumbled onto something they shouldn't have, and I quoted my mother saying, 'Don't stir the pot?' You stirred it. Everything was going smoothly before you came along. Well, before Lilly came along, actually. You both started noticing what others were oblivious to." She lifted the gun.

"Please...don't," I whispered. "You're always telling me to

keep a sense of humor. Maybe someday we can laugh about all this…"

And then—her mask slipped completely. Gone was the faux sweetness she used in the office. No more grandmotherly warmth that she wrapped herself in when making tea. She was something else. Almost feral. A lifetime of rage uncoiled behind her eyes. "There's nothing funny about being an old woman without a pension," she said. "I don't owe you an explanation, but…" She stepped closer. "I gave almost my entire adult life to the Adele Cummings Foundation." She paused. "Don't get me wrong—I've loved almost every minute of it. I believed in the mission. Adele Cummings's money is changing lives. Except mine."

Her voice cracked. "I've had two and a half decades of watching grant advisors come and go—strutting around Ravenscroft in their Chanel and Valentino. Sipping tea, booking trips to Paris and Switzerland. Buying handbags that cost more than a car… You have no idea what it's like watching women half your age earn six times your salary just for being young, attractive, well-spoken, and connected to the *Forbes* list."

As her lip curled, her grip tightened on the gun. "The advisors at Adele Cummings hardly even work. Not really. Not in any meaningful way. Applicants generally come to them. They don't have to scout. And they seldom ever write reports. They leave all that to me. Because I do it so well. Blowing smoke up my old heinie.

"There are hundreds of thousands of dollars in discretionary funds to use any way they want in order to find deserving artists to support. But they're all lazy. I've sat in black-box theaters in the East Village with forty folding chairs and no air conditioning, watching solo shows so raw and brilliant they left me shaking. But could I offer the artists a grant? No.

"I've stood shoulder to shoulder in Brooklyn basements, surrounded by noise and sweat, listening to some seventeen-year-old trans girl spit poetry that could gut a man in three sylla-bles. Have you ever been to a cabaret night at Club Aurora, Timothy? Of course you haven't. Neither have the advisors. But I have. Because sometimes the most electric performance in the city isn't on a stage at Lincoln Center—it's in a basement lit by a disco ball and rage. I even noticed you at the Quantum Gallery. You saw me there and thought it was Ms. Klotz. That's how good I am."

She spat the next words. "I was never even considered for promotion to an advisor's position. Ever. I would have been bril-liant. I know more about the foundation's programs than any of those people ever will."

She pressed a hand to her chest—furious, wounded, shak-ing. "But no. Adele Cummings insisted I was 'too valuable' running her goddamned office. She gave me a stupid title—'cor-porate concierge,' hoping that would appease me. No raise. No extra vacation time. Just a fancy label that means nothing."

She took a breath so sharp it cried through the air. "I could have filed for age discrimination or something. I could have made some noise. But I didn't. Because I didn't want to risk my job—I'm too old to go on interviews again. And I didn't want to bring a stain on the foundation's reputation."

The gun steadied in her hand. "Every day, I smiled at the advisors. I complimented their bracelets, their shoes, their new diamonds. I organized their travel schedules. I ordered their damn lunches—their 'healthy' miso-glazed salmon salads from Sweetgreen." She leaned in, her voice a venomous whisper. "All while I did the grunt work that kept the entire place func-tioning."

Her eyes blazed. "And still—I'm invisible to them. They could smell it on me, you know. That I wasn't wealthy like them. That I didn't belong in their glittering little club. Of course, they never said anything overtly. They're too well raised. They were subtle about it. They knew I could never afford a week in Aspen.

Or a Dior clutch. Or a four-hundred-dollar facial. I remember Mrs. Raymond giving *you* a gift card from Valentino. She'd never think to give one to me!"

A bitter tear slid down Mrs. Johnston's cheek. Her grip on the gun tightened. Her shoulders squared. "And do you know what happens when you spend decades being invisible? You realize people are not only not interested in the details of your life... They're not even paying attention to the details of your job."

Her voice dropped to a low, vibrating growl. "So it wasn't hard to start skimming a little from accounts. Nothing dramatic at first. A few hundred dollars here for Broadway theater tickets. A few thousand there for something at Tiffany. It was all money no one would ever miss, because no one ever looked at the petty cash ledgers that I handled. Why would they? The foundation keeps tens of thousands on hand. All I have to do is submit a request for topping up the funds to some idiot at the bank. No questions asked."

She let out a harsh, humorless laugh. "But after twenty-five years on a salary that wouldn't buy a studio apartment in Queens, I realized something. I was getting older. And retirement in New York is an impossible joke on what I make. And no one—no one—was going to provide for me. So I had to provide for myself."

She leaned in, her eyes bright and wild, the scarf glinting under the bad alley light. "I started moving money around. Building my own future out of scraps."

Her voice steadied into something frighteningly calm. "I was going to stop. I'd already decided. Lillian Trent's grant was the last one I took. I thought I could end it there. Then she threatened to go to the state's attorney general's office—NDA or not. That would have ruined everything. My retirement. My reputation."

Mrs. Johnston took a deep breath. "So I handled it." She said it simply. Like she'd mended a tear in a shirt. "I bought a good wig from Andrew DiSimone's on Lexington. A real one—human hair—in Ms. Klotz's style. And I swiped her foundation ID badge and her signature dragonfly clip. She and I are about the same size. And people see what they expect to see in a crowded nightclub with bad lighting."

My stomach twisted.

She went on almost conversationally. "Manhattan Moon was packed that night. I'd intentionally not made a reservation. And I pulled a VIP move as 'Stephanie Klotz' and got a place standing by the bar. Anyone who saw me would have remembered the pushy woman with the plain hairstyle—and her ostentatious dragonfly. Of course, everyone was focused on Lillian Trent. I watched her show, and when the audience was fully engrossed, I slipped away through the front entrance and re-entered from the alley to her dressing room.

"Immediately after the show, Lillian came back to freshen her makeup before greeting her fans. I was waiting. Surprise is the best diversion. She didn't even have time to scream. Just a choked sound. Her hands clawed at the scarf... The struggle didn't take as long as I thought it would."

My brain exploded as I pictured the grotesque scene that had occurred just moments before I found Lillian's body.

Mrs. Johnston smiled. Monstrous. Satisfied. "And then I went back to the bar. If anyone had seen me, they could say I'd been there all along. I even lost the damn hair clip on purpose. If anyone did remember whom it belonged to, they'd point their finger at that woman from the Adele Cummings Foundation who insisted on seeing the show. And that woman would be Stephanie Klotz.

"And you, Timothy..." Mrs. Johnston continued. "You're just like her. Like Lillian, I mean. You're tenacious. Couldn't leave well enough alone. I knew when Ms. Klotz tasked you with cleaning up the miscellaneous files, you'd be the perfect puppet.

It would prove that you went into the restricted files. Every file you opened. Every document you lingered over. There's a record, of course. And...you copied that thread of emails between Lillian and me..."

My stomach flipped. She knew.

"I saw you open Lillian's NDA. And those budget files you thought were misfiled? I moved them there myself. I wanted to see how far your curiosity would go." She leaned in, eyes bright with predatory satisfaction. "And you did exactly what I wanted. You poked around. You followed the trail like a little bloodhound who didn't know he was sniffing around a trap. You were easy to manipulate, Timothy. A few moved files. And you walked right into my hand."

She raised the gun to my chest. My spine pressed against the dumpster. My breath caught halfway up my throat. I shut my eyes. I didn't want the last thing I ever saw to be Eleanor Johnston's face.

"Goodbye, Timothy Trousdale," she whispered. "I'll be sure to tell SwellHire Top Temps that you were a model employee... and you type really fast."

I braced—every cell in my body screaming.

And then—

Something shifted along the far side of the dumpster. A sound. A distraction. A soft thud. Just enough that Mrs. Johnston jerked, startled. "Rats! I hate bloody rats!" she snapped, looking frantically into the shadows for vermin.

And in that single moment when she was distracted, the back door to Manhattan Moon opened. A silent silhouette entered the alley's shadows. Then a voice—calm, steady: "Mrs. Johnston? Eleanor?"

Mrs. Johnston pivoted toward the voice.

The figure stepped forward into the half-light. A silver-haired woman. Even in the dim alley, I recognized her instantly —Ms. Klotz's mother.

But before I could form another thought, Mrs. Johnston made a strangled sound. "Adele!" she gasped, voice cracking into something sharp and hysterical. The gun jerked in her hand. "Go back inside, Ms. Cummings. It's nothing. Everything's under control."

Did she say "Adele"? And "Ms. Cummings"? My thoughts raced, stitching the names together. *The* Adele Cummings? Philanthropic royalty? If this was Adele Cummings... Then who on earth was Ms. Klotz's mother? A cold, dizzy wave rolled through me so fast I thought I might go under.

Mrs. Johnston's face twisted with panic and humiliation. And suddenly, it made sense why the advisers always deferred to Ms. Klotz. Why she wielded so much power in the office when she wasn't even an official advisor. Why Mrs. Johnston was now unraveling at the seams.

Because this woman wasn't just Ms. Klotz's mother. She was the woman who owned the entire bank that Mrs. Johnston was ripping off!

Adele Cummings stepped farther into the alley.

Mrs. Johnston's breathing quickened to small, frantic bursts. "I've... I've caught a thief," she said confidently. "I was just about to call the police."

"Really?" said Ms. Cummings. But it wasn't a question. It was more "I hear you; I don't believe you."

Mrs. Johnston let out a strangled laugh. "You don't understand. He was going to steal my ring! And my Rolex, too!" She thrust her hand into the air, displaying the oversized stone I'd admired since my first day at the foundation.

Adele Cummings gave a soft, dry chuckle. "Cubic zirconia? A Rolex knock-off? Even a thief wouldn't bother."

Great. I'd admired a fake diamond ring and a watch that didn't keep the right time.

A new calculation flickered across Mrs. Johnston's face— rapid and volatile. Her panic crystallized into blazing eyes.

"Maybe this is turning out even better than I planned," she said. "I'll tell the police Mr. Trousdale attacked us both. An easy story to sell. I was trying to protect you—but I missed." Her voice dropped to a low, chilling rasp. "I can be a terrible shot... when I want." Then she raised the gun at Adele Cummings. "Now, get over here with Timothy," she hissed.

Adele Cummings did not move. Not a muscle. Not a flinch. "Not likely," said Ms. Cummings. "I'm too old and too rich to take orders from anyone."

And just then, there was another sound behind the dumpster. But this time, Mrs. Johnston didn't turn to investigate. Just another rat, probably. Her eyes jittered between the billionaire and me. Her breath came fast, shallow, unhinged. She raised the gun slightly, recalibrating, deciding whom to kill first. Timothy or Adele? Adele or Timothy? Who posed the greater immediate threat? Whose death could she more easily explain? Her mind was doing the math.

I felt her decision forming like a storm front gathering pressure. If she shot Adele first, I could lunge and overpower her. But if she shot me first, Adele Cummings probably couldn't do anything but stand by and wait for her own execution.

Mrs. Johnston realized that logic. She pivoted the gun toward me. Time dilated—slow, suffocating.

"Put the gun down, Eleanor," said Adele Cummings.

But the words only enraged her. "Don't tell me what to do!" Mrs. Johnston screamed. "For once, I'm the one with all the power! You've bossed me around for over twenty-five freakin' years! And you"—she jabbed the gun at me—"you ruined everything! Had to snoop. Had to pry!"

Her hand tightened on the grip.

A sound—small, dull—from behind the dumpster. *God. Rats. I hate rats, too.*

She flinched. Barely. Then she turned back to me. The gun lifted again.

Then it happened.

A blur exploded from behind the dumpster—

Brad!

Full-body velocity. Instinct. Fury. He slammed into her like a missile.

The gun fired. CRACK. A deafening blast. It ricocheted through the alley like a scream.

Brad and Mrs. Johnston hit the pavement in a tangled heap.

Silence. Just for a second. Sharp. Ringing. Awful.

"Brad!" I shouted, already running. Adele was beside us in an instant.

Brad pushed himself upright—eyes wild, chest heaving. "I'm okay," he gasped. "She—she didn't get me."

Mrs. Johnston lay sprawled, unconscious. Not shot—but bleeding, her head having slammed into the asphalt.

Brad swallowed. "I felt her skull hit hard. But I think... I think she's alive."

Adele knelt beside her, her face a storm of relief, pity, and heartbreak.

I stood frozen, shaking, the adrenaline crashing out of me in waves. If Brad had waited even one more heartbeat, we would have died. All three of us knew it.

Ms. Cummings looked up, eyes locked on mine. "Call 911," she said quietly.

45

The alley behind Manhattan Moon looked like the aftermath of a gang rumble—police cruisers jammed the narrow space, their blue lights pulsing against the brick walls. A crowd from the club and curious passersby milled around, filming with their phones. Officers moved briskly, police radios crackling. An ambulance idled near the mouth of the alley as paramedics tended to Mrs. Johnston, wrapped in blankets, an oxygen mask fogging faintly with each breath.

Brad, his hand in mine, stayed glued to me, anchoring us in place. We'd given our statements first to the responding officers, then again to a detective, each retelling draining what little energy I had. My body felt hollowed out, as though all my adrenaline had burned through and left nothing behind but exhaustion.

"How'd you know?" I asked, wondering how the hell Brad knew I was in trouble.

"When you didn't come back from the bathroom, I got a weird feeling," he said quietly. "I went looking for you. Mrs. Johnston was following you out back, and I knew something was wrong. So I slipped out the front, ran around through the alley, and by the time I got there…" He shook his head. "She had the gun up. I didn't even think. I just moved. Let's go home."

We'd made it halfway down the alley when a voice called out and stopped us. "Mr. Trousdale!"

I turned. Ms. Klotz stood a few feet away with her mother.

"My office. Tomorrow morning. Nine o'clock."

My response came out calm and weary: "No, thanks. Not interested." For a moment, I wondered who had spoken for me. I stood there, faintly stunned. I couldn't recall ever saying anything remotely insolent or disrespectful to someone in a position of authority. I'd built an entire life around compliance and obedience. And now, nothing cataclysmic happened to me. No lightning strike. I wasn't instantly vaporized. What startled me most wasn't the audacity of what I'd said, but the ease of it. As though the voice had been there all along, waiting for me to stop doubting its power. Maybe this wasn't a new strength at all. Maybe it was simply strength I'd finally decided to use.

And then another shocker—

Ms. Klotz said, "Please."

I was fairly certain this was the first time in recorded human history that Ms. Klotz had used that word. *Please.* She nodded toward Brad and said, "Bring him too."

I looked at Brad. He shrugged. He was game if I was.

For a fraction of another moment, Ms. Klotz's eyes scanned me—not dismissively this time, but as if recalibrating. Then she met my gaze properly. She didn't say a word, but I sensed she was seeing me differently. She turned, heels clicking sharply against the asphalt, disappearing into the night with her mother.

"Well," said Brad, "that felt ominous."

"Ominous is generous," I said. "I'm getting my ass handed to me in the morning, and you're being invited to see me fed to the lions."

∾

The next morning, we arrived at Ravenscroft, and Smudgy greeted us with a half-hearted wag of his tail. I thought he sensed that this was not an ordinary morning.

"Pretty great place to work," Brad said, looking around and admiring the old-world feel of the building. When we reached Ms. Klotz's office, she barely glanced up when I knocked on her doorframe. She lifted her coffee mug for one last sip, then rose from behind her desk. "Follow me," she said. (No good morning. No thank you for coming.)

She led us to the second-floor library. Floor-to-ceiling bookshelves. A marble fireplace. Without a word, she reached for a brass wall sconce beside the fireplace. At first glance, it looked like any antique light feature—aged metal, faintly dulled with time, exactly the sort of fixture you'd expect in a building like Ravenscroft. Then she gently tugged at its base.

Something clicked.

OMG! The bookcase opened. Think *Young Frankenstein*. There was a hidden passageway. I was astonished, but frankly, every rich person I'd met in New York (there was only one other) had a hidden room in their home.

The passageway led to an office—huge and expansive. A broad antique desk dominated the space, its leather inlay worn to a soft sheen. The only visible technology was a landline phone and an iMac. Before I had time to take it all in, Adele Cummings rose from a wingback chair set deep in an alcove at the side of the room.

"Good morning, Mr. Trousdale! Mr. Bradford. I'm happy to meet you both properly," she said with enormous warmth, and she seemed genuinely delighted to see us. "May I call you Timothy? I'm Adele. And I'm mortified that you were caught up in all that attempted-murder absurdity."

The alcove had been prepared for entertaining: a low table, graceful leather-upholstered chairs, and a silver tea service. Steam rose faintly from the pot, carrying the scent of Earl Grey.

When we were all settled and holding cups of tea, Ms. Cummings said, "Timothy, Brad, it seems I employed a monster."

D'ya think? I said to myself and offered a harsh glance at Ms. Klotz—my personal *bête noire*. But that wasn't who she meant.

"Mrs. Johnston confessed to the murder of Lillian Trent," Ms. Cummings continued. "She's been formally charged. And the security cameras in the alley behind Manhattan Moon will show her attempted murder—of us."

Ms. Cummings sipped tea, then looked directly at me. "I spoke with Mrs. Johnston at the hospital this morning. She begged me to understand her side of things. Said she wasn't 'stealing' from the foundation—only 'reallocating' funds. Apparently, she believes there's a difference. 'Deferred compensation,' she called it. She said when Lillian Trent threatened to take up the matter of her missing grant—which she'd embezzled—with the state's attorney general, she had to be silenced. And so did you."

46

M s. Cummings's gaze settled on me. "There are a few things I'd like to explain, Timothy. You've already discovered that Stephanie—Ms. Klotz—is my daughter, Helena. A few years ago, she got… I'll say 'off track,' as children of the super-rich sometimes do. My fault. She had everything money can buy—private schools, a personal jet, houses everywhere. Everything people insist should add up to a meaningful life."

She paused, as though weighing how candid to be. "I've seen children of the super wealthy drift into entitlement. I did not want my daughter to become someone who believed society's rules were optional simply because she could afford to ignore them."

Stephanie Klotz, er, *Helena Cummings* stared out the window, her expression neutral, as if she'd heard all this before and was bored by it.

"I did not want her to become someone who mistook money and power for identity," Ms. Cummings continued. "So I cut off her allowance and gave her a job. Here at the foundation. With a fake name. Our attorney, Jason Pritchert, came up with 'Klotz.'" She glanced briefly toward her daughter. "Her mission was to monitor the day-to-day activities here. It's astonishing what goes on when no one knows anyone is watching.

"Helena's a clever woman. I admire her. She's got her father's shrewdness. Right away, she caught a whiff of something rotten going on."

Helena Cummings shifted in her chair and picked up the thread of her mother's explanation. "Suspicion is useless without proof," she said. "Calling attention to Mrs. Johnston too soon could have driven her to camouflage herself deeper. I needed evidence that would survive scrutiny. It took a long time. She had to grow comfortable with me being here—even if she didn't know my true identity. Then you came along, Mr. Trousdale. You were inquisitive. Your fingerprints quickly started appearing in files where they should not have been. You complicated matters for me."

Brad, who had been listening in silence, spoke before I could stop him. "You can't blame Timothy for his curiosity," he said. "From what I understand, Timothy was given assignments that required him to go through the foundation's files."

Helena's gaze flicked to Brad, cool and appraising. "Curiosity wasn't the problem," she said. "Interference was."

Brad didn't raise his voice. He didn't need to. "With respect, Timothy was doing the job you told him to do. If that interfered with a plan you didn't share with him, that's on you." He paused just long enough for the words to settle. "You can't punish an employee for being thorough."

Helena folded her arms, unapologetic. "I was protecting an outcome," she said. "Not Timothy's feelings."

Obviously.

She didn't wait for a response. "Mrs. Johnston was setting you up to take the blame for her embezzlement," Helena said. "It started with the MacLaine Dance Company mess. She noticed your second-hand clothes. She knew you weren't like the rest of us."

I opened my mouth to explain, then closed it again.

"She assumed," Helena continued, "that being surrounded by money would do something to you. That watching people treat abundance as ordinary—casual, never having to count pennies—would leave you feeling envious. In her mind, you were someone on the outside looking in. Grateful to be here— but quietly tallying what everyone else had and you didn't. Pure projection, of course."

Helena's mouth tightened slightly. "She believed eventually you'd decide you deserved a piece of the pie. As she did."

I'd had enough of Ms. Klotz's insinuation. "That's just so wrong!" I nearly bellowed. "I'm not envious of anyone. Sure, everyone here seems to be loaded. But I don't resent them. I wear second-hand clothes now, but I won't always. And I'm certainly not envious of the foundation's money. I'm inspired by it. And by what Ms. Cummings does with all that she has."

The room went very still. Helena was reassessing me—recalculating—and said, "Mrs. Johnston also saw how quickly you doubted your own innocence when it came to those 'lost' dance company funds. She was pretty sure you'd quietly accept blame for Lillian Trent's missing money, too. That you'd be too embarrassed to push back on accusations. Also, that you'd never imagine she was stealing right under everyone's noses. She underestimated you. And so did I."

For a moment, I honestly thought I might laugh—because what she'd said felt absurd. I'd been almost a hundred percent sure Ms. Klotz was behind the missing dance company grant money.

"You blamed me for the missing funds," I said. "You accused me of 'fiddling.' You made me feel incompetent. Like a complete screw-up. Does that explain why you treated me like a contagious disease?" I asked.

"It *explains*—but it does not *excuse*—my behavior," she said.

I hadn't intended to speak bluntly, but I felt entitled to express my true feelings. "You made me stop loving this place... and my job. When I first came here, I thought it was the most amazing thing ever. And I thought Adele Cummings was the most extraordinary human being alive."

I looked at the great philanthropist. "I think what I loved most is that you did your work quietly. You gave away hundreds of millions without making much of a fuss. That seemed amazing to me. It still does. I want to be you when I grow up."

I was surprised by how much I apparently needed to say. "I took the work seriously. Maybe too seriously. I believed in what the foundation stood for. I read your original handwritten mission statement. And I believed in you."

I let out a breath and said carefully, "When I read about your husband—about Charles Brandt—and his disappearance, I felt genuinely sorry for you. You had to carry an unanswered question for decades.

"I'm sorry," I added quickly. "That was out of line. None of my business." I shook my head. "But the articles I read about that time in your life stayed with me. And I thought you were... remarkable. For getting on with your life while people speculated." I trailed off, acutely aware of how exposed I suddenly felt.

I could tell Ms. Cummings was unsettled by what I'd brought up. For a long moment, she said nothing. When she finally spoke, her voice was solemn. "Charles, my husband, didn't disappear in the way the world believes," she said. "Not in the way I allowed them to believe." She folded her hands in her lap. "We were at our villa in Italy. By then, I'd discovered his other life. The woman—and men. We talked about it. Calmly. Thoroughly. Very adult." She paused. "I was young, and at the time I didn't think I had the right to expect better.

"When you have absolutely everything else—more money than God—it's easy to convince yourself that love is the one place you should be grateful for whatever scraps you're given. That wanting more would be unseemly. Ungrateful." She lifted her eyes to mine. "I mistook being fortunate with money for being undeserving in love. Like it was a trade-off. One or the other."

She looked briefly at her daughter. Then, in a calm voice, she said, "We reached an arrangement, Charles and I. He would leave—permanently. In exchange for more than enough money for ten lifetimes. He had to vanish. Completely. No contact. No return. Ever."

A fortune in exchange for disappearing and never seeing his daughter again? For agreeing not to exist?

"The mistake," Ms. Cummings said, "was that we only told our attorney, Jason Pritchert. Not friends. Not the staff. That night, Charles went for what appeared to be an evening walk. When he didn't return—he'd taken the jet to Antigua—one of the maids took it upon herself to notify the authorities. A missing person report was filed before I had time to stop it."

The image settled into place with chilling clarity.

"A rich guy vanishes from a cliffside villa," Adele continued. "The assumptions write themselves. An accident. A suicide. Something darker. And I—his wealthy, visible wife—was suddenly at the center of it."

She exhaled slowly. "I should have told the truth then. Not because I paid him to disappear—that part would've been easy to explain." She paused. "But because I'm an exceptionally smart woman. And telling the truth would've meant admitting just how completely I'd been deceived. By a man I trusted."

Her mouth tightened, just slightly. "I didn't think it was anyone's business either. I chose what I thought was the lesser humiliation—to be suspected, even pitied, rather than to be known as a fool."

After a brief pause, Ms. Cummings said, "Now you know

more than almost anyone else on the planet. That is why you can no longer work here."

Her words landed firmly on my chest. Not with surprise, exactly. For the past week, I suspected I was on my way out.

"You know too much," Ms. Cummings said. "Not in a dangerous way. In a human one." She inclined her head slightly. "And it's not fair for me to ask you to pretend otherwise." She folded her hands together. "You were caught up in something that never should have touched you. The embezzlement. The violence." A faint, rueful smile splayed across her lips. "The foundation must remain untangled from all of this. For your sake as much as mine."

Brad's hand found mine as we both listened silently.

"Of course, this will not be framed as a dismissal," she continued. "You will leave with my full support, a narrative that protects us both—and a severance check that I think you'll find is generous. You came here in good faith. You leave with that intact.

"The public version," she went on, "is that after recent events, you chose to step away to pursue your own work. Other opportunities. Writing." She met my eyes. "I will ensure that anyone who asks understands what a loss this is for the foundation. This is not exile, Timothy," she said. "It is release. You have a whole life and career ahead of you. I hope you won't let anything stand in the way of your dreams. You deserve all the success you can imagine."

She smiled genuinely and openly. "And Timothy," she added, "I have no doubt you will do something interesting with your life. You have marvelous potential as a writer. I read the quotes you wrote for our anniversary book. They were better than anything I could ever have thought of myself. We'll credit you with the one that says, 'Philanthropy is love translated into action.' That's how I feel but could never put it into words."

EPILOGUE

Brad and I left Ravenscroft without ceremony. No final look back. No dramatic last words. I didn't even say goodbye to my office. I wasn't sure I trusted myself to do that without breaking down. (I did stop to pet Smudgy goodbye.)

We stepped into the chilly morning, and for a moment the world felt oddly flattened—as if sound and color had been muted. I was acutely aware of feeling hollow. I liked routine, and now that I was unemployed, I had no specific plan. No next step was fully formed.

We ordered an Uber and rode back to his apartment, holding hands mostly in silence. The kind of silence that settles in when something has ended and something else is standing just offstage, waiting to be presented.

When we got inside, Brad set his keys down on the entryway table, removed his coat, and immediately pulled me into his arms. He held me with a strength that made me feel grounded.

"You're destined for great things, Timothy Trousdale," he said softly. "I believe in you. In what you're about to do next." He smiled against my hair. "And I believe in us."

That was all it took. I hadn't realized how much fear and gloom I'd been stockpiling until those words dismantled me all at once. I pressed my face into his chest and let the tears come. The *oh, thank God I'm safe* kind.

"I'm allowed to be a little sad," I said, my voice muffled and wobbly.

"Of course you are," he whispered. "But you're not allowed to stay there." He pulled back just enough to look at me. "Because this—believe it or not—is a beginning. That sounds cliché, but trust me. One day soon, you'll look back and say, Ah. That's when everything finally started to go right."

Brad made tea. He always made tea when he wanted to fix something that couldn't technically be fixed. We curled up on the couch, knees touching, steam rising in our mugs, and talked about what might come next. About my writing. About the check the foundation would be sending—enough, he thought, to buy me a bit of time to maybe work on my book before heading straight into another office temp job.

Then he suggested a trip. Maybe to his mother's second home in Abbots Clover, England. Quiet mornings. Long walks. A place with no expectations, no institutions, and—he grinned —"No dead bodies."

I smiled—an unguarded, genuinely happy smile—for the first time all day.

Brad put on music—the Jane Oliver album he'd once found at a garage sale—and told me again how Lillian Trent's voice had reminded him of Jane's. He held out his hand, and we swayed together in the middle of the living room to the song "Stay the Night," my head against his strong chest, his hand warm and certain at the small of my back.

Just us.

The music faded into the background, and we drifted toward the bedroom, still holding on, as if letting go even briefly might break the spell. The world outside—all of it—receded until there was only this moment and the promise wrapped inside it.

What remained was a future not yet written.

There was no doubt at all about who I wanted the main characters in my life story to be:

Me. And Brad.

ALSO BY RICHARD TYLER JORDAN

<u>Polly Pepper Cozy Mystery Series</u>

Final Curtain

A Talent for Murder

Set Sail for Murder

Remains to be Scene

A Corpse in the Castle

Shadows at Midnight

Murder and a Missing Manuscript

Murder in Mint Condition

<u>A Timothy Trousdale Mystery</u>

Breakfast at Timothy's

Suite Charity

<u>LGBTQ+ Titles</u>

Strangers in the Night

Overnight Sensation

Gay Blades

One Night Stand

ABOUT THE AUTHOR

RICHARD TYLER JORDAN began his career in Hollywood, spending 30 years as a senior publicist at the Walt Disney Studios, where he worked on marketing campaigns for more than 500 feature films. He later turned to writing novels and is the author of the Polly Pepper cozy mystery series, including *Murder and a Missing Manuscript, Shadows at Midnight,* and *A Corpse in the Castle* and several more. He is also the author of the novels *Breakfast at Timothy's, Overnight Sensation, Strangers in the Night, Gay Blades,* and *One Night Stand,* among others. He also wrote the non-fiction book *But Darling, I'm Your Auntie Mame!* Jordan is an American expat writer living in a 500-year-old stone cottage in England. For more information about him, visit www. RichardTylerJordan.com.

A small press bound by the belief that every voice matters.

Sign up for our newsletter to learn about new releases and more.
https://oliver-heberbooks.com/subscribe/

Follow us on social media:

facebook.com/oliverheberbooks

instagram.com/oliverheberbooks

amazon.com/oliverheberbooks

youtube.com/@OliverHeberBooksPublisher